The Corporate
Chameleon

The Corporate Chameleon

Jim A. Roppa

authorHOUSE®

AuthorHouse™
1663 Liberty Drive
Bloomington, IN 47403
www.authorhouse.com
Phone: 1-800-839-8640

© *2012 by Jim A. Roppa. All rights reserved.*

No part of this book may be reproduced, stored in a retrieval system, or transmitted by any means without the written permission of the author.

This book has included some true events. However, these events have been fictionalized to fit a story line. All persons appearing in this work are fictitious. Any resemblance to organizations or real people, living or dead, are entirely coincidental.

Published by AuthorHouse   06/13/2012

ISBN: 978-1-4772-1142-7 (sc)
ISBN: 978-1-4772-1140-3 (hc)
ISBN: 978-1-4772-1141-0 (e)

Library of Congress Control Number: 2012909377

Any people depicted in stock imagery provided by Thinkstock are models, and such images are being used for illustrative purposes only.
Certain stock imagery © *Thinkstock.*

This book is printed on acid-free paper.

Because of the dynamic nature of the Internet, any web addresses or links contained in this book may have changed since publication and may no longer be valid. The views expressed in this work are solely those of the author and do not necessarily reflect the views of the publisher, and the publisher hereby disclaims any responsibility for them.

"Your clock of life is wound but once by the Divine. No mortal was given the right to know exactly when the hands of time will stop. This very moment is the only time you own. Live, love, and labor with purpose for your clock may soon be still." . . .

The Mailman

Acknowledgements

To Sheila, who was wise enough to have me document in a "Bucket List" my desire to write this novel, you are my guiding light.

To Sue and Sharon, who were honest and thorough in their critique and editing, thank you for your encouragement to continue the process.

To my family and friends, who were inspirations for the words in this novel, I am forever indebted.

Prologue

A child is *evaluated favorably* when he is viewed as healthy and active.

A child is *acknowledged positively* when he is celebrated as outward and competitive.

A child is *rewarded generously* when he is acclaimed as skilled and accomplished.

A child is *loved unconditionally* when he is personified by faith and family.

For one child, he will surpass all adult criteria, but silently suppress taboo behaviors and norms. Secretly, he will hide obsessions, paranoia, distortions, rationalizations and retributions. For this child, he will have NO LIMITS, have NO FEAR, and allow NO REMORSE.

FOR THIS CHILD, KILLING IS JUSTIFIABLE.

PART I

Chapter 1

As with the rest of the country, the 1920s were tough times in this Midwest river town called Peoria, Illinois. Peoria was a sizeable city in the heart of Illinois, midway between Chicago and St. Louis. As such, the town was a thorough-fare for all travelers coming from Chicago heading south or for those traveling from the South to Chicago. River boats and freight trains regularly stopped in Peoria as they made their journey with their cargos to satisfy bountiful markets north, south or west. As with most river towns of any size, all sorts of people migrated to and through its city limits and surrounding small towns.

Peoria's major industry started when a flour mill was constructed in the 1800s. The livestock industry followed and produced a large export businesses for some of the best meats in the nation. Other business were beginning to show promise: carriage factories, pottery makers, wholesale warehousing, casting foundries, glucose factories, ice harvesting, farm machinery manufacturers and furniture makers. The dominant manufacturing companies in Peoria were Kingman Plow Co., Acme Harvester Co., Selby, Starr & Co., and Avery Manufacturing Co. In the late 1800s, Keystone Steel & Wire developed the first wire fence and would become the nation's leading wire producing manufacturer for over a century. At the turn of the century, one of the first commercially available gasoline-powered automobiles in the U.S. was developed in Peoria. When agricultural implement production began to decline, a new industry unfolded. An earth moving and tractor equipment company was formed in 1925. The new company became known as Construction Tractor Co and would establish Peoria as its world headquarters.

There was another side to this seemingly conservative, God-fearing town. Peoria had become a home for distilleries. The ample supply of grains combined with the rich knowledge and expertise of those ancestral brew masters who settled in the region ensured alcohol was plentiful for the up state, thirsty Chicago market. At one time, Peoria had 22 distilleries and multiple breweries which came to produce the highest amount of internal revenue tax on alcohol in the entire U.S.

Nestled in a valley between high pitched banks of the Illinois River, Peoria would see a building boom of beautiful private homes, schools, parks, churches, as well as municipal buildings while the rest of the country was feeling the constraints of the approaching Great Depression. The town was populated with the new rich from these industries, trades and services. Influential and powerful landowners and farmers also had a strong voice in the region. Of course, providing the labor were those poor souls looking for the American dream. Because of the times, these journeymen were ever present given there was a large populace of job seeking labor always in transit.

This river town called Peoria seemed to be able to balance the good with bad as well as anywhere. On the north side, mansions overlooked the Illinois River from elevated bluffs. The Illinois heartland was blessed with simple folks who believed in God, country, family and hard work. The Midwest ethic for hard work was inbred from father to son. Giving your all was well understood and appreciated. Little towns had sprung up in the surrounding areas, mostly filled with farmers or tradesmen who supplied goods and services. Strip miners lived in some of these outback small towns. On the south side of the balanced scale were all the vices of Chicago, only on a smaller scale. Peoria had a well known red light district, often frequented by those God fearing men as well as Peoria's well established gentlemen. Even during Prohibition from 1920 to 1933, during which the sale, manufacture, and transportation of alcohol for consumption were banned nationally as mandated in the 18th Amendment to the US Constitution, Peoria seemed to be immune to the laws of the land. Peoria was one of the major bootlegging areas during the prohibition. In Peoria, liquor and beer flowed as waters in the Illinois River. Gambling also prospered in these early wild "Midwest" days. The roaring twenties led to a gangster era in many cities and Peoria was no exception. Control over these vice industries was not for the faint of heart.

The beautiful foliage, the nip in the air, and the harvesting of grain were God's gift to this region. The drama of the fall season in the Midwest had been in full swing but was showing the approaching signs of winter. A most unlikely course of events was about to unfold. While God was putting his final touches to his painting of another fall season, man was negating these sensual pleasures with the most painful of internal challenges. The depression had brought out the best and worst in the city. Soup kitchens were meeting the bare essentials for their constant onslaught of hopeful, God fearing lambs. The ruling class who had full stomachs was happy and content with their righteous giving of table scraps to those who served them. But, for one of Peoria's new working class, Vincencio Dominic Antonini, he would have no idea how his life was about to change. An event in which he was about to be called on to serve would launch the American dream for some and a nightmare for others.

Chapter 2

Vincencio was the eldest of three sons born to Giovanni and Dominica Antonini in Gizzeria, Italy. Gizzeria was a little town in the province of Catanzaro in the southern Calabria region of Italy. Calabria was a narrow peninsula extending into the Mediterranean, located at the toe of the "boot" between the Tyrrhenian Sea to the west and the Ionian Sea and Gulf of Taranto to the east. Many residents of Gizzeria had close family ties to the south in Sicily. Italy and Sicily were only separated by the Strait of Messina. At the narrowest point between Capo Peloro in Sicily and Punta Pezzo in Calabria, Sicily was only about five miles in the distant. Although the sea was ever present, Calabria was mainly a mountainous region.

In general, most of the lower terrain in Calabria was agricultural. The lowest slopes were rich in vineyards and citrus fruit orchards. At higher elevations, olives and chestnut trees were nurtured. At the highest elevations dense forests of oak, pine, beech and fir trees grew. The contrast between the blue of the sea, the browns of the fields and the greens of the trees, was a picture of nature that would a young boy would never forget.

Vincencio's family lived very modestly. They were the typical struggling southern Italian family who worked as tenants on shared land. They were proud people content to live off the land and their animals. The family raised sheep and tended olive trees. They existed on savory meals of pork, lamb, or goat dishes, vegetables, and fish. Pasta, as in most parts of

Italy, was a staple. With each and every meal, Giovanni Antonini ended every meal's prayer with, "May God and our Lord always know, we put forward our lives to our Faith, our Family and our Friends." This pledge to God was the thread woven into all the members of the Antonini clan and all were expected to follow this earthly commandment.

Faith to Vincencio was embodied in the person who would influence him most, Father Stephano. Father Stephano had had the privilege to be selected to perform his understudy service in the Vatican. He was pragmatic, dedicated, and had a zest for life. He cared more about the practice of religion than the politics. He was the most well spoken person Vincencio had ever come across. Little did Vincencio know Father Stephano, this devout Catholic priest, had such an astute knowledge of the Bible and command of a plethora of languages that the Catholic leaders were closely mentoring him to elevate him in the Catholic hierarchy in Rome. But, as a young priest, Father Stephano was an idealist, a dreamer who felt he could do more for God if he lived among the Italian people. In a private meeting with a Vatican archbishop he revealed his plans.

"Your Holiness, I have made a life decision. I have visited many churches throughout Italy. I know my calling is to serve God by reaching out to the Italian people, where they live. I ask that you grant a request to be assigned a parish away from Rome. After a couple of years going from Church to Church, I have a special love with southern Italy." Father Stephano's request was granted.

The small parish Catholic Church in Gizzeria became his podium for him to pass on the teaching of his Lord. He also was the head priest, scholar, and educator for the small school that was attached to the church. While at the Vatican, Father Stephano had learned and mastered five languages. English was his love and secretly he hoped to have the opportunity to travel to America.

It was no surprise that Vincencio caught the attention of his teachers and Father Stephano. Vincencio exhibited early in life that he was very bright. He excelled in the local Catholic Church school. He read everything he could get his hands on. He absorbed his world like a sponge. Vincencio was intelligent and learned quickly information was valuable and powerful. His appetite for learning seemed to border fanatical. He learned languages, studied the arts, but most of all, began to comprehend a world outside of Gizzeria. He never dreamed of actually experiencing another world.

Father Stephano was so impressed with Vincencio's ability to learn that he took Vincencio under his wing. On Sundays after Mass, the good father would push the arts, the sciences and social graces far surpassing any normal curriculum. He knew Vincencio could master languages so they practiced Spanish, Portuguese, French, Greek and his passion, English.

"Father, why do we spend so much time on English? It is such a difficult language with words spelled one way but with many meanings. I have learned the meanings of words that I am not sure when I will use them."

"My son, one day, God willing, you may be in a position where language will set you apart from others. If you are viewed in a positive light, doors will open for you to choose your future. Learning leads to knowledge, experience leads to wisdom, the ability to communicate all you know well and to be understood by your fellow man is divine."

The Father often prayed that Vincencio would one day have an opportunity to show his exceptional abilities.

Chapter 3

The early 1920s were very difficult times and were going to get worse. Southern Italy was among the poorest regions of Europe and impoverished Calabria was hit extremely hard. The inhabitants of the region had only one choice: consider immigrating. Families were being split up. Whether the pressure of political or religious persecution, overcrowding at home, or just plain poverty, much of Italy, especially southern Italy, farmers were forced to leave the land and move to the industrial centers of northern Italy, the rest of Europe, Australia and the Americas. Argentina, Brazil, Canada, and the United States would see an onslaught of Italian immigrants never before seen.

On what started out as any other day, the raw facts of life were about to hit the Antonini family. Vincencio remembered the day well. It was a bright sunny day. The farms were preparing for another planting. The trees were beginning to leaf out. The hills were changing from their winter brown and putting on their new green spring attire. A breeze was blowing in from the sea and seemed to caress Vincencio face. Even faced with the presence of hard times, he felt God's promise in his heart.

It was April 20, 1920, one day short of his 18th birthday. A high pitched whistle rang out, then a voice. "Vincencio, where are you? Please come into the house. I need you." Vincencio could hear his father's whistle or voice a mile away. When Vincencio came through the back door, his mother and father were standing in their small kitchen. The aroma of the pasta sauce cooking filled the room. His mother had been crying. Even

Jim A. Roppa

as he looked at her, the tears seemed to be trying to escape one by one from the corners of her eyes.

"What's wrong?" Vincencio asked, not wanting to hear any response.

"My son, I have been talking with my friends and local merchants. There are even tougher times coming to Gizzeria, Calabria and all of Italy. Many families are looking to travel to new countries to make their mark. In the future, it will be harder to feed and keep our family going. We have always dreamed of having our own land to house and feed our families here in Gizzeria. It will not happen. You are old enough and strong enough to be the one from our family to go to try to find work and help the family. Son, I would not ask this of you if there were any other option. You can keep half of what you make. You will send other half for the family. Vincencio, we are putting our faith in you to take the lead for the Antonini family in our quest to find a better life, a better world. I have saved enough money for passage for you to travel to America. The family will travel with you to the port south of here where you will board a ship to take you to America. My brother in Sicily has given me a name of a person in the city where you will land in America. The city is called New York. This man will find you and will show you where you can live. He will help you find some work. He has connections who will hire you. There are no limits what you can achieve in America. Vincencio, learn their language well, study their customs and ways, and then find a city where our family could come, grow and prosper. Vincencio, remember this. You will be lonely at times, you will dream of the family and our country. You will long for the love of your mother, your brothers, and hopefully of me. Shed your tears in the dark. When the light touches your face, show no fear. You are an Antonini. We are proud people. We come from people who once ruled the world. You too can make the Antonini name a name to be respected. And finally, what ever decision you make or action you are forced to take, have no remorse on the consequences of your actions." His father's voice trailed off. He walked up, gave Vincencio a long, loving hug, kissed his cheek, and walked out of the room.

Vincencio heard his father perfectly: *have NO LIMITS, have NO FEAR, and allow NO REMORSE.*

Vincencio's mother walked up to him. "This is very hard for your father and me to ask that you do this. We love you more than our lives, but this sacrifice cannot be put off. We will tell your brothers. We will leave tomorrow. Vincencio, you have the looks of your father, but you have my heart and soul. Let your mind be that of the family. I love you, my beautiful son. We will never forget this day." She kissed his cheek, brushed his black hair aside, patted his shoulder and walked out of the kitchen.

Vincencio had a feeling of helplessness in the pit of his stomach like nothing he had ever felt. His tears swelled and ran from the corners of his eyes like a stream. He looked out the window at the olive trees and the garden. He took a deep breath. His father was his hero, his mother was his saint and his brothers were his best friends. He knew what was being asked. He knew he was the one to go. He knew he had to go.

Vincencio wiped the last tear away, turned and walked out of the kitchen. He headed straight for his room and found a small bag lying on his bed put there by his mother. He put in his only pair of good pants, shoes and two shirts. He looked into the mirror and wasn't sure what he saw. Yes, there was a young boy, taller than most in his town, black hair, and a body of pure muscle from the hard work of the land. He once had a smile and confidence that could charm the most obstinate landowner or merchant. He had the looks that made every girl in the city hope to make him her husband. Yet today, all he could see was a confused, frightened boy. He wondered if his family name or the many lessons from the priest, or the century old ways of his people could be the source where his strength would have to come. He only had himself to rely on in a new land. He took another deep breath, felt the sunlight on his face, wiped the last of his tears aside and with a barely audible sound said, "No Limits, no Fear, no Remorse."

He was no longer a boy. He was ready, was America?

Chapter 4

That night the family gathered around the kitchen table. His mother and father must have made the decision months ago to save for a boat ticket and to have such a last meal spread out before them. He tried not to make the analogy that this must have been similar to the feeling Christ had when presented his last supper. Various vegetables and meats that had be packed in olive oil, Sopressa (sausages), 'Nduja (cold cuts), and cured *sardelle rosamarina* (sardines) were on plates in the center of the table. Caciocavallo (Cheese), and *Lagane e Cicciari* (a pasta dish with chickpeas) were the main course. *Cudduraci* (Fried, honey-sweetened pastries) and 'nzudda (baked biscotti-type treats) rested on a side table waiting to be served as his parting dessert.

"Let's pray. Dear God in Heaven most high. May God and our Lord always know, we put forward our lives to our Faith, our Family and our Friends. Please watch over our son, Vincencio, who leaves tomorrow for America. He is a man who has served you well, his family well. We do not ask for ourselves because so many are in the same situation as we. We pray for them, their families. Father, dear Lord, may we see our son again, may we all be together again someday. May we all look into each others eyes and see tomorrow. In the name of the Father, the Son, and Holy Ghost we pray. Amen. We will leave tomorrow early." The meal was eaten in a room of such silence that the site could have been mistaken for the most spiritual of shrines.

Morning came early, especially if one had not slept through the night. As Vincencio prepared to dress, he couldn't help but think of another day when getting dressed was a momentous part of his life. That day was the day he was to be confirmed in the church. "This day was going to be a life altering one. Vincencio, do not let your family feel the void that has come to your heart." Vincencio bowed his head, "Dear Father in heaven most high. As you gave your son, my father is giving his. While your son paid the ultimate price, this son feels that his life has ended as he knows it. Dear Father, I will pray every night to your son. He will know my pain, my longings, and my fears. He will give me strength to meet the next day. I pray in the name of Jesus Christ, my Lord, my savior." Vincencio dressed in his work clothes, put on his favorite hat, his only hat. He picked up his tattered bag, went to the door, looked at his still sleeping brothers, and closed his eyes tightly so as to burn in the vision. He turned and walked out the door to find his father waiting.

"I will have your mother get your brothers ready for our trip. I want you and me to walk up the mountain one more time, sit, and look out at the sea." As they walked up the mountain, his father put his arm on his son's shoulder. He never took it off. As they sat on a large rock nestled among the trees, his father looked at Vincencio. "My son, if only I could be the one to shoulder this heavy burden we have placed on you. From the time I saw you at your birth, I knew you were going to achieve so much more than I have for this family. You are a smart boy. My son, I cannot give you much for the trip. Here is all the money that I can provide. The greatest gift I can give you is my name. It is the most precious thing this family possesses. Take this gift and make our family proud. We all love you." When he had finished his soft, heartfelt goodbye, they walked down the mountain.

The family was ready to travel to the port. His father had obtained a horse and a large wagon. His mother was in the back with his two brothers. "You ride up front with me, my son. You take the reins. Today, you are the head of this family." As he handed the reins to Vincencio, his father turned to his mother, reached back for her hand, and gave it a squeeze. As he turned back to the horse, Vincencio flicked his wrists. The reins hit the rump of the horse and the wagon lunged forward.

Vincencio still remembers the trip to the port, the tearful goodbyes. His brothers were especially humble like he had never seen them. When Vincencio was ready to say his final goodbyes, he kissed each of his brothers on both cheeks. His oldest brother Antonio whispered in his ear, "You are my hero, my brother. When you call for me to come to America, I will come as quickly as I can. I will not forget my promise to you."

Dominic, who looked so young, returned his kiss of love and respect to each of Vincencio's cheeks, "Vincencio, I will get stronger and will work very hard to ensure father does not feel he has to take on your work. I will do my share. Don't worry. I will see you again someday. I will be a man, strong like you."

His mother came up to him, looked deep into his eyes. "I may have brought you into this world, but God will help you survive in it. Trust in Him. Know your mother is praying for you every night. Take this my Virgin Mary medallion and my necklace. Wear it around your neck. Think of me each night as you pray. I love you my son."

The fog horn on the freighter bellowed out an unforgettable sound. This creature of the sea was letting the world know that it was time to venture to the ocean. Vincencio's father stepped forward. He gave Vincencio a hug so tight that he could hardly breathe. "Vincencio, go. Conquer America. You are an Antonini. Your family loves you and will pray for you. Remember my words. There are no limits on what you can become. Have no fear. It is better to try and stumble than do nothing. You will learn from every experience. This will give you knowledge and wisdom. You will succeed more than you fail. Finally, whatever you decide to do, have no remorse." He kissed each of Vincencio's wet cheeks, turned, gathered the family and headed away toward where they had left the horse and wagon.

The fog horn sounded again. Vincencio knew this was the call of the unknown. He took a deep breath and walked toward the gang plank. A man with papers was calling out names and marking his list of passengers. When he heard his name, he yelled out, "I am Vincencio Dominic Antonini. I am traveling to America."

Chapter 5

"How many days have we been out at sea?" an old man was asking to no one in particular. "I know I have been sick for two days at least."

"It has been 4 days", a faint voice from the darkness whispered. Vincencio didn't care about counting days. He just wanted off this floating coffin. He wanted to jump overboard and swim back home. The voyage had been long, cold, and damp. Vincencio would have nightmares of this voyage long after he hit dry land. The night often brought not only violent storms, but also the streams of silent, hidden tears. The hull of the boat packed with immigrants like himself, all with nothing but lines of despair etched in their faces and wearing their worldly belongings. Yet even with the deplorable conditions they were forced to endure, without exception, these immigrants all shared a common belief. This belief was grounded on a genuine personal faith and a prayer they would have the opportunity to show their unyielding work ethic. Their dream was to establish a fountain of opportunity that would spout rewards not seen in America since the pilgrims first stepped on North America soil.

Upon hearing "Land Ho", the belly of the ship began emitting numerous languages; thunderous applause that one could only think was the result of a victorious celebration. Everyone raced to the deck. There she was, the lady of green, the Statue of Liberty. Along side was another island where the ship was to dock. Vincencio heard someone say this was the little Island where they were to be processed . . . Ellis Island. Ellis Island was to be the main entry facility for immigrants entering the United States for the next 3 decades. Vincencio ran to the rail of the ship. He shielded his eyes from the direct sunlight and saw his destiny, America, New York City. Vincencio Dominic Antonini had survived the voyage and was about to enter the United States of America.

History will report that there was a myth that surrounded those who operated Ellis Island. According to published documents, government officials on Ellis Island did not compel immigrants to take new names against their wishes. In fact, no historical records bear this out. Documents recorded many years after the first large wave of immigrants hit Ellis Island supported that immigration inspectors were under strict bureaucratic supervision and were more interested in preventing inadmissible aliens from entering the country rather than assisting them in trivial personal matters such as altering their names.

Many years later when Vincencio revisited New York and Ellis Island, he had to laugh as he read this document in the halls of the Ellis Island museum. "That is not how I remembered it." What the hell did compel mean anyway? Forced? There is no force when all you think you are to do is to follow like sheep, hope you do not get rejected or piss off an inspector because he may be having a bad day.

"Italians, Greeks in this line, French to the left, Irish and English to the right." A man in a cold blue uniform shouted as they entered a building where luggage was everywhere.

People looked like they were in a daze, confused, trying to understand what they were to do next. Vincencio was glad he had learned Basic English from Father Stephano back in Gizzeria. He only caught the first part of the instructions but he instinctively started to move quickly to the lines where the man was pointing. His father's last words of "No

Fear" rang in his ears and would be ever in his mind. He would not second guess his actions. His actions took him to the front of the line.

"Do you have any papers, birth records?" a square-headed, broad-faced, chubby cheeked clerk asked already knowing the answer. "No? OK, don't worry. You are just another Italian without papers, a WOP, I am going to ask you 29 questions like name, occupation, and do you have any money on you, things like that. You look like a strong healthy boy. Are you here by yourself? Coming over to make a name for yourself, are you? I bet you are another Italian coming to America to make it rich and send money back home. Well, good luck kid. It has been a long day so let's get you moving. We will start with an easy one. Name, what is your name? Whoa son, take a breath. I know you are scared, but let's try this again. This time try to speak your name slower, not so fast. Say it again."

"Mister, I am not scareda. I understanda and can speak English." Vincencio held his head high and his shoulders pulled back. My name is Vincencio Dominic Antonini."

"Well if you say so kid. Son, this is America, we speak different English and our words do not have vowels on the end of our words. If you want to get me to sign your paper, I wouldn't speak unless I ask you to speak. I am hearing you say your name is Vincent Dominic Anthony. Isn't that right? If so, sign your name under the line like I wrote it and you can move on to the next station." Vincencio was given a pen, showed where to sign a paper he hadn't read, but he understood if he was going to keep moving, sign the name like the one printed above. "You learn quick kid, you may make it. Great job, move along."

Vincencio knew he spoke English better than most. The smart ass clerk just wanted to make a point of authority and get him to the next person. And Vincencio did not want to get into a debate on his first day in America. So Vincencio Dominic Antonini became Vincent Dominic

Jim A. Roppa

Anthony with the stroke of a pen. He wanted to turn and tell that pea brain Neanderthal that A, E, I, O, U and sometimes Y are vowels, but his better judgment won out.

The process did not go so well for some of the people he had met on the boat. Those with visible health problems or diseases were sent home or sent to the island's hospital facilities. Generally those immigrants who were approved spent from three to five hours at Ellis Island. Later, while living in New York, Vincencio would hear that many died on Ellis Island while being held in the hospital facilities. When asked if he had any skills, Vincencio knew the right answer.

"I am a tailor; I can make clothes, shoes, or anything else you might want to wear." He was glad his priest had told him that if they asked what kind of work he did, tell them he worked in a shop which made clothes. New York did not have much interest in farmers, those who were tenders of sheep or olive growers.

Some unskilled workers and immigrants were rejected outright because they were considered "likely to become a public charge." Some of the boys from Sicily were actually denied admission to the U.S. because their names were associated with people who had committed crimes in New York. Those who did not pass through the gates of Ellis Island to America, returned to their home countries. Ellis Island became known as "The Island of Tears" or "Heartbreak Island".

To Vincencio, Ellis Island was his admission through the Pearly Gates of Heaven. Now he had to find out how to be blessed by the hand of God.

A man who spoke Italian gathered up the first batch of the Italians who had come through the line. "My fellow Italians, welcome to America. We will now get on another small boat and head to your first home in America, New York. Do not make trouble, listen, work hard and make those who hire workers want Italian workers to work for them." He guided them to a small boat. "When we reach the city, you will be assigned places you can stay in New York." Once they landed and the assignments were made, the man wished them well and vanished. Vincencio would learn that the group was taken to a section of New York called "Little Italy".

With each minute the boat approached the city, the city grew before Vincencio's eyes. The buildings were so tall, so many people. Vincencio could only hear his father's words, NO FEAR. The group was swallowed into the belly of the city. There they were taken to some tenement rooms where 4-6 men would sleep on the cots provided. In the first week, Vincencio was just making it by with little to eat, when he heard a man call out his Italian name. "Is there a Vincencio Antonini in this room?" He was the contact that his father had said would find him and hopefully would put him to work.

Vincencio walked up to the man. "Si, I am Vincencio Antonini". When Vincencio acknowledged he was the person who he was looking for, the man spoke in Italian.

"Is your father Giovanni Antonini from Gizzeria?

"Si, Giovanni is my father. Are you the person who may have some work for me?"

"Your father is a good man. If you are half the man, you can make it in America. I promised your father I would try to find something for you to do in America. I know a man and have spoken to him about you. He is honest and is looking for young Italians who are strong and can work in the coal mines of Pennsylvania. The job comes with the promise of food, shelter and decent wages. I will not lie to you. The work is hard but this is an opportunity most do not get, so I suggest you take it. Work hard and make your family proud."

"Si, of course I will take the job and go to this Pennsylvania. I am ready. When do I leave?" To Vincencio, it did not matter what kind of work was required at the mines or where Pennsylvania was located. Vincencio Dominic Antonini, or Vincent Dominic Anthony, or Vinny, was ready to face the challenges of life in America. He was always going to be the first in line to sign up. Vinny often thought about those first days.

He later would tell his sons and grandchildren, "I decided to keep the American name to ensure that, if I had to show my papers, I would not have any problems. I also thought that I could fit in better with the Americans I would work for or live around. Someone had told me that there were some Americans who did not like the idea of people coming to America and taking jobs that they could do. So, within three days, I was put on a train and ended up in a city called Pittsburg. There I worked for a year in the mines around the Pittsburg area. I never complained. I listened, watched, and learned the ways of the Americans. I worked hard, took every job offered, and, when others shied at the dangers, I stepped forward. Because I worked hard and always helped my fellow miners, they were loyal to me. I praised my fellow workers, and helped them when some struggled. I made many friends. Even with all the hard work, I worked extra hard to improve my English and was determined to lose my Italian accent. This hard work paid off. One day I was approached by my boss."

"Hey Vinny, want a better job? I have been offered an opportunity to open a new mine operation in another location. If you will go with me to Illinois, I will make you a pit boss. You will make more money and not have to put your back in it anymore". Vinny's boss never doubted for a second that he would be able to get Vinny to agree to come with him.

Another train ride, another city, another mine. Vinny and his boss ended up in a place called Decatur, Illinois. The mine was located in the south end of the city down by a large lake.

"Vinny, you should feel right at home here, there are more Italians in this mine than locals."

It did not take Vinny long to win his crew over. They quickly knew he was a fair man who cared about them. He would take all their complaints and ideas to the bosses. If someone was having a bad day, he often stepped in and took over their position until they felt better and regained their strength. When anyone was needed to push the boundaries beyond safety considerations, Vinny was always the first to volunteer to take on the task at hand. For Vinny, there were "NO LIMITS and NO FEAR".

Chapter 6

It was 1924. Four years had passed. Vinny had done what his father had asked him to do. First, he had never missed a month where he did not send some money back to his family in Italy. He had often prayed that the money would reach them. Vincent had some philosophies that he always kept in his thoughts. He would always listen, learn, earn and share. True to his mission, Vincent had made a life for himself and was ready to send for his family to join him. The first to come over were Vinny's two brothers, Antonio and Dominic. For Vinny, he thought Decatur was going to be the place where all of his family would eventually live. This was not to be.

Within a year of the brothers coming to Decatur, Vinny and the rest of the miners were told that the mine was going to close. It was determined that the mine had played itself out and the coal mine shafts would be closed. Just like that, Vinny and his brothers were out of work.

The very next morning after the announcement, Vinny's boss, who had brought him to Decatur, asked him to stop by his office. "Vinny, if you will relocate immediately, I can get you a job in Peoria. It is a bigger city, so more jobs are available for people with skills." Vinny laughed out loud at the statement. This was not the reaction his boss expected.

"I am sorry to laugh. I know this story. I have lived it before. I know what it is to have to relocate to bigger cities because there is no work. I have moved from Italy to America, from New York to Pennsylvania, from Pennsylvania to Illinois. If I have to move again, I will once again move. I can and will start all over again. It is like where I started, the same situation, just a different city, a different time. Do you have work for my brothers as well?"

"No Vinny. I could only get their commitment to hire you. They know me. I vouched for you. They hired you on what I said about you. There were not other jobs in that particular mine for anyone else. I am sorry."

"You have always been honest with me. My family will find a way to make it. Thank you for your help. Are you going to Peoria?

He hung his head, "No, I am going out west. I am not happy about it because I have to leave my family. It is a different type of mining so I have to go back a few positions to learn the business. Good Luck Vinny." So Vinny was offered to work in a new mine in a new city.

He met with his brothers to advise them on where to go to seek out new job opportunities. "Brothers, we have to set out for other cities and begin again. We each have some money to live on until we find work. Whoever has work, will help support whoever needs the help to keep going. We continue to send some money back to our parents. We cannot let them know of our situation. We must and will survive this setback. Antoninis always survive. Remember our fathers words: Antoninis have NO LIMITS, NO FEAR, and NO REMORSE, regardless the task at hand. I will travel to a city called Peoria. It is 60 miles northwest from Decatur. There are some strip mines there where I have a job, so we will have money coming in for us to share as we need it. Antonio, you go to the city called Chicago. It is 200 miles north and is a big city like New York. There is a large Italian community there. I have a name for you. A man I met in New York runs a restaurant on a street called Cicero. Go there first. Ask around and see if something develops. Dominic, you head for St. Louis. It is 200 miles south of here. It is also a big city with a large Italian community located in a place called "The Hill". I have some names of some people who may be able to point you in the direction of some work. First make sure you follow all leads in the Italian sections of these cities, work whereever you can find something. Build your contacts. We will contact each other each month to ensure we all can get by. Remember, if any of us is struggling, the others will help out. We Antoninis will prevail."

The brothers did not waste time complaining or dwelling on their situations. The very next day after they had their talk, the brothers said their goodbyes and set out for their next chapter of their America chronicle. As they prepared to go, they all embraced. "Antonio and Dominic, over the past year, your English has gotten better, but now you must work very hard to perfect it. I will not be around to help you. So listen to those around you. Interact with people every chance you can get. Pick up old papers or books that you may find and practice reading. I love you, my brothers." Like his father, his voice trailed off, he turned and walked away. He now knew, like his father, he did not want them to see the tears in his eyes.

Vinny found work in the strip mines around a little town called Canton. He knew that this job could end in a couple of years. Vinny became intrigued with the locals who had a survival culture cradled in the fields, the forests, and the waters of the rivers and surrounding lakes. Vinny learned to fish and hunt as well as those who had lived in the area for generations. He loved the vastness of the outdoors and the break from having to work in claustrophobic mines. The fish he caught, the animals he trapped and his garden kept his hunger pangs at bay. His bounty from the land was what kept him alive. Money from furs supplemented his mine pay. He squirreled as much money as he could in hopes to re-unite his family.

The cornfields had seen their harvest, and the ducks and geese were starting to their migration south. This Midwestern river town was in the fly way for these migrant fowl in their search for warmth, food and open waters. Vinny wasn't ready to give up the dream that led his father to America. He had learned a language, learned to survive. He wasn't ready to go back to the underground coal mines back east or work new ones opening out west. He wasn't ready to have his name etched on a tombstone as the only thing that was left for his family. What he was ready to do was . . . anything.

"Hey Vinny, what are you doing this Thursday? We have a job for you if you want it." It was Angelo Bartello, a friend who had come from the same region in Italy. Angelo was known as "Angel". Angelo was one of the first people he had met in Peoria. They bonded like brothers. They shared everything. Both men vowed they would survive and prosper one day. Angelo seemed to always be in the right place and was constantly making "connections". Angelo was a fisherman back in Italy. When Angelo had come to Peoria, he lived off the Illinois River and surrounding lakes to survive. He became so knowledgeable of the river, the best fishing holes, the best places to trap that he was sought after to guide or professionally fish or trap for some local companies. He and Vinny had made enough money to buy out an old trapper's land down around Havana, Illinois . . . about 30 miles south of Peoria. Together, Angel and Vinny built a cabin that had expanded over time to hold 8 hunters or fisherman. So when Angel said he had a job, Vinny thought he was going to help clean fish or harvested game.

"Angel, don't you know that I got the Rockefellers coming by for dinner Thursday? But since you are such a good friend, I will give them a call and push the dinner to next week. What have you got in store, scales or guts?" laughed Vinny.

"Vinny, my gumba, you are always so happy and never complain. I need to have you come down to Havana. I came across a guy who said he knew some guys from Chicago who were looking for a place to do some duck hunting. He told them about our cabin. A guy came to look the place over and wants the place for a weekend, plus will hire us to guide. He said they just want to get away from everything and everybody." Angel seemed to be more excitable than normal. "Are the Shelton Brothers still running booze?"

"As far as I know when they are not being shot at. Why? Are we going to need to run down some beer or whiskey?"

Angel couldn't contain himself. "We need both, the best you can find. Vinny, money is no object! AND . . . I need the best hookers from Aiken Alley. We will need them for 2 days."

Vinny was at a loss for words, which was as rare as folding cash. Vinny always was quick on his feet and had comebacks for every occasion, but unlimited money? Angel was playing a joke on him. "And I bet you are going to pay me $20 for my time."

Suddenly, Angel's eyes narrowed. His voice lowered as he approached closer. "Vinny, can you do it? We need to figure out a way to get the booze and hookers. If you can make this happen, I promise you, we will get paid more money than we have ever made. We need to impress these guys. Make them think we are players in Peoria. Vinny, this is our big chance. We have earned this. You are my only friend. We may never get another shot like this one. Are you in or not?"

"Angelo, if you say this is our shot, I have never doubted you. I will do what I can to try to get what you need. But remember Angelo, if we do get the goods and cannot pay, our shot may be literal. I will have to go see the Sheltons for the goods we need. The Sheltons are not nice guys."

Chapter 7

It was two weeks after Angel and Vinny had been together. It was a clear, glorious fall day and trees along the river were in beautiful fall colors. Vinny was a charmer but he could not envision how he could fill Angel's order. Vinny had a way with words. He was persuasive, and had a reputation, a known history of doing what he said. This time was different. This was not like past successes using his charm, words or any other con for a free chicken or building material. Not this time. He had to shake things up. He had to be armed with something special to fill Angel's order. Angel had provided him with the fire power he needed.

While the infamous Volstead Act prohibited the sale of alcohol in the United States, for the most part, there was little done to enforce the prohibition law. This especially held true in Peoria. The illegal production and distribution of liquor, or bootlegging, was rampant. The locals knew that the national government had little means or desire to try to enforce every border, lake, river, and speakeasy in America. By 1925, numerous speakeasy establishments were operating in Peoria.

Vinny had an odd job doing some home repair in the upper North Side. During these hard times, Vinny had learned the trades, could cook, waited tables, cleaned houses, did yard work, fixed and washed cars. He worked odd jobs for Robert Jackson for over 3 years. Robert was always telling his wife and kids how much he liked Vinny, how reliable he was, how hard he worked, and he could do anything. He had even taught Vinny to drive his car so he could act as a driver when Robert and his wife were to attend the parties thrown by Peoria's elite. But all Vinny knew was Robert didn't appreciate his skills enough to offer him a full time job or even pay him a decent wage. Vinny knew Robert was a man of position, not power. Robert was a man who used his position to keep others in theirs. His constant rib to Vinny was to tell him when he was working, "Vinny, if nothing else, you Italians may have weak minds, but strong backs." Vinny needed some "business" clothes before he made his trip downtown. As Vinny was taking the clothes off the line he couldn't help but think, "Robert, some day you are going to see we are the same, in body and mind." Vinny grabbed one of Robert's collared white shirt, a pair of black dress pants. "It's show time!"

It was a Monday. Vinny put on his "borrowed" shirt and pants. Cinched up his belt, slicked down his cold black hair, combed his hair straight back, and looked into the broken mirror. He put on his favorite hat that George the Greek had given him for work he had done. Finally, he put on the coat that he had stored, his father's wedding coat. He looked back into the mirror. He looked thin but he had an air. Could he pass as an owner of a business or would they take him straight to the undertaker, properly dressed? He looked around the one room shack. A smile came over his face. He spoke into the mirror with a voice so soft, so full of hope that it could have been mistaken for the young priest who lived back in his hometown of Gizzeria, Italy. "A journey starts with the first step. A miracle happens with chance or opportunity. This is the day my life turns around. I have **NO LIMITS, NO FEAR**, and **NO REMORSE**, regardless of what I encounter."

First call, take a trolley down to South Adams Street and ask the brothers Shelton to "loan" him some liquor. If he did not get thrown out, beaten or worse, he would make the second call to Aiken Alley where he would request a two night "loan" of four ladies from Madame Marge. He had heard of her beauty and explosive temper and how she had cut more johns than the local butcher had chickens. Vinny couldn't wait to meet her and make his requests.

The trolley stopped to a screeching halt at Adams and Main Streets. Vinny walked past the town hall, past the police station, down through the park to a street where he knew the Sheltons ran a little "speakeasy". Vinny wiped the sweat from his forehead. He knew the sweat was not from the walk, but from the excitement and uncertainty that lay before him. He took a deep breath and practiced his opening line. He clenched his fist, looked to the sky, said a prayer and opened the door. He was about to enter the stronghold of the Shelton brothers, Carl, Bernie and Big Earl Shelton. They were key figures in the underbelly of Peoria. The Sheltons, whose lawless activities included gambling, bribery, bootlegging and murder, were said to have Peoria under their thumbs. In this area of town, it was said that one couldn't spit on the sidewalk without permission from a Shelton.

He walked to a table in the back and without hesitation, firmly said, "My name is Vincent Anthony. I am here to see Mr. Shelton. It is important business that only Mr. Shelton can hear." The Shelton brothers started their reign in the 1920's and were well known for bribing public officials and fighting other gangs over control of the bootlegging and gambling in central and southern Illinois. The men had gained fame and money through their use of strong-arm tactics. Carl, Bernie and Earl together ran a large and powerful gang of family and other followers who enforced distribution in their territory. And here Vinny was staring face to face with Carl Shelton. He knew the other men at the table had to be his brothers.

"No shit?" A man who looked like a grizzly bear quickly stood up. "How about you tell me what is so important before I break your nose and throw your Guinea ass out." Vinny wasn't sure how this would end, but he knew he had to finish what he set out to do. He had heard the rumors that this bootlegging gang was often described as "America's Bloodiest Gang". Suddenly, Vinny was wondering if he were going to be the next notch on these big goons' guns. Vinny knew he was no match for this man and hastily looked around for something to defend himself with or an exit should he have to run for his life.

For Vinny, he knew his words were his only available defense he could muster. He had to show NO FEAR and godly confidence. "Mister that would be the biggest mistake you could make. I don't doubt for one second you could do what you say, but you should consider what my employer and client would do to you for not hearing my business proposal." Vinny was dancing like it was for his life, and it well could be. "Mr. Shelton knows my client and my bet is before my client would get to you, Mr. Shelton would have a serious talk with you about your judgement. Therefore, I will ask again, may I speak to Mr. Shelton and Mr. Shelton only?"

The bear laughed. "If nothing else paison, you said that without peeing your pants. You got balls. I will see if Mr. Shelton will talk with you." He looked around the room, and with the others laughing at some unspoken joke, walked up to Vinny and put his arm on his shoulder. He leaned down closer to Vinny's left ear, and lowered his voice that sent a chill through Vinny. "OK whoever you are and whoever your client is, you want to speak to Mr. Shelton. Well start talking. I am Shelton. If this is some attempt to get work, or some excuse from one of my clients, I will not be happy. So, who is this employer?" He walked Vinny over to a corner table and both men sat down.

"Mr. Shelton, I am here on urgent business, not to waste your time. We were contacted to accommodate a group of hunters who will be coming down from Chicago this Thursday. We were told if this weekend meets the group's expectations, we could expect many more such visits. These businessmen want a place to relax, to hunt, and to get away from everything and everybody. No one is to know they are coming. My partner and I have a hunting establishment in Havana. We are just starting our business and need to upgrade our social capabilities and amenities. That is why I am here. For these gentlemen, we need to have freely available beer and whiskey. The man who came down from Chicago to check out our place mentioned he was aware of a couple of Peoria establishments had the social amenities that are required. He provided me locations of the establishments and the names to ask for their assistance. So I am here." Vinny purposely stopped and waited for the next question. Vinny was prepared and ready for whatever would happened next.

"Well Mr. Anthony, unless you tell me right now who these businessmen are and how they know about my place and me, your time is up. Understand?"

"Mr. Shelton, the person who came down to check out the place was a Mr. Frank Nitti. I was not familiar with the gentlemen, but you may know of him. He said that things had to be perfect for his boss." Vinny knew Shelton would recognize the name so he again paused to let the name of the boss be a tidal wave when he divulged it. "Mr. Al Capone." He let the name sink in and saw the face of Big Carl Shelton pale. Shelton seemed to actually slouch a little in his chair like he had a little air let out of him. "Mr. Shelton, I do not have the money to cover the amount of liquor we should have on hand for such an illustrious client. My partner and I want to show we have a business to which he would want to return. Will you help me?" Vinny was done. He had fired all his verbal ammo. Vinny had reached decision time versus the other scenario, inflicting pain time?

Carl Shelton leaped to his feet. Vinny jumped from his chair to brace for an attack. Had he misjudged his performance? "Bernie, come here. I want you to get a truck, fill it up with 5 cases of our best whiskey and 10 barrels of beer. Have it ready for Mr. Anthony when we return. Understand?"

Shelton turned to Vinny. "Why did you say locations and names? What else are you going to need and who else are you going to see? If you need anything in this city, I can help you get it." His tone was all business. He was serious about the question he asked, and sizing up his opportunity.

"I was instructed the businessmen enjoyed company. So once I had secured the liquor, I was going to go down to Aiken Alley to see if I could hire some ladies of the evening for the weekend." Vinny now was on elevated ground. The name he came armed with brought him untold credibility. He was no longer an odd job laborer. Now he was a businessman acquiring goods, making deals with his suppliers, and finalizing a contract for his partner.

"Let's go. Ira, you drive. Mr. Anthony, I think I will accompany you to Aiken Alley. I may be able to help you with your next order." Carl Shelton was already headed for the door before Vinny could say or do anything. He jumped up, and with his back as straight as he had ever walked, sauntered past Bernie and Ira. He looked over his shoulder at Bernie, "Could you throw in a couple of extra bottles of liquor so we won't run out?" Bernie quickly looked to Carl and shook his head in confirmation. Carl already had his mind fixed on their next visit.

Vinny could not remember the last time he rode as a passenger in a car, but it sure beat his normal mode of transportation. The old Ford traveled down Adams, made a right turn, and rambled up Main until it got to Summit Street. A quick left and about a mile down the road, another left was made down a side street that had become famous, Aiken Alley. Vinny had only heard about this place. He never had the money to pay for "love". Come to think about it, he had not taken any time to consider a lasting relationship with a woman since he left Italy. It wasn't that he did not like women, on the contrary. He was a handsome man. Women seemed to want his company. When he had free time away from his many labors, he could always find a woman to spend some time with. Too many of the women he met were looking for someone to help them in these tough times and were often too eager to share their bodies to sway a prospect. Vinny hadn't been swayed but did enjoy the physical nature of the company. It would be sometime later that Vinny would meet a beautiful Italian girl by chance in another town. Women were the last thing on his mind right now. Too much was on the line.

Vinny's day dreaming was interrupted by the quick stop of the Ford. "Jesus Ira, are you ever going to learn to drive?" blurted Carl Shelton. Ira just laughed and sarcastically said, "Want me to get the door?" Carl grabbed the door handle, "Wait here asshole. We won't be long."

The two climbed the stairs of a Victorian white house that had a big porch. The door appeared to suddenly open by itself. Carl rammed his way through the door followed by a wide-eyed Vinny. Another world was suddenly opening up. Hopefully it wouldn't swallow him. A black man was holding the inner doorknob and welcomed the gentlemen. He was dressed in the whitest shirt and a black suit. He was six foot four and weighed at least 220 pounds. This man was as sturdy as a concrete pillar. One look into his eyes, Vincencio knew that even though he played a humble servant who catered to the masses who came through the door, he could instantly turn into the most violent of enforcers. He was the protector of the House and all who inhabited the place. The house was beautiful, chandeliers, lace, big chairs, a big stair case and girls. It was still too early for johns to be coming. There were a few who seemed to be left from the previous night. "Where's Marge?" Carl Shelton was now in charge, at least in his mind. Vincencio was sure that Shelton did not see the black man slowly move his right hand inside his coat. Vincencio guessed he had a weapon should Shelton be there to cause trouble.

Chapter 8

The car ride to Madam Marge's establishment took 15 minutes. Vinny couldn't believe the speed of the next course of events. Madam Marge DeJarnette was called down to the foyer. She was a stunning woman, who appeared to be in her early 40s, tall, thin, big breasts and hair as auburn as fall leaves in the forest. With her hair pulled back tightly, Vinny thought she looked like a countess. One look at her, Vinny came to the conclusion the stories that judges, lawyers, police, and high brows regularly visited this house were true.

"Why Mr. Shelton, what brings you here to my establishment? I have not seen you in over a year. How have you been? I heard you had some trouble with some of your associates. Are you alright? You still look like you could go all night."

"Marge, this is Mr. Anthony. We would love to take advantage of your hospitality, but we are here on business that requires your immediate attention." He charged Marge like a football player ready to make a tackle. The black man started to move toward Shelton. Carl Shelton grabbed her arm and led her to the side of the room. He whispered something in her ear. Vinny guessed the conversation ended with the name . . . Al Capone.

Marge wasted no time to respond. A quick look at the black man stopped him in his tracks. She clapped her hands two times. Her face was now like stone. "Benjamin, come here" The black man ran to her side. She looked at Vinny then at Carl, "This is a real honor. This could be big for my house. What is mine is yours. I will have the girls ready in an hour. Would you like for me to personally manage the activities of the night? My man servant Benjamin and I will prepare for the guests immediately." She and Benjamin were starting to move toward the parlor to get things moving.

Shelton was already racing toward the front door. "Mr. Anthony will decide who will attend. He will return within the hour. Let's go, you have work to do."

Riding back to the speakeasy was like being in a dream. Vinny actually felt a little giddy. Vincencio Dominic Antonini had acquired beer, whiskey, ladies of the evening and vehicles to move the merchandise without any upfront money. More importantly, he had convinced Shelton and Madame Marge that he was a business man, a man with very important connections. *Angel, your partner has met his end of the bargain.*

What a beautiful fall day. The day was a collection of sensual art. The leaves were a canvas of color: the burnt sienna, the gold, the red and orange of the trees were magnificent. The chill in the air was a calling card for the rapidly approaching winter. Water fowl were in constant motion in the river and surrounding flyways. Angelo had remarked that he had never seen so many in his 10 years on the river. The men stood in front of the cabin, looked at each other, smiled and walked in. They had cleaned the cabin from top to bottom. They had decorated the cabin with borrowed stuffed fish and game. Now they just needed to stock the cabin with booze, broads and clients.

Vinny was the first to hear the truck. It seemed to groan as it came down the lane to the cabin. Vinny had personally filled in all the holes in the lane to ensure his merchandise and clients were not bounced around. Two broad shouldered men got out of the back of the truck. The driver and his passenger jumped out. "You Anthony? Bernie Shelton said we were to deliver some booze to you. Got some liquor and beer for you. Carl Shelton also told us that he wants you to give these two special bottles of liquor as a gift to one of your guests. Got it? He said he would work out the payment details later." They unloaded the liquor, then brought out four large metal tubs and placed them on the side of the cabin. Next the two big boys lugged huge blocks of ice and placed them into the tubs. "We will be back each day to see that you have everything you need and bring more ice." Vinny looked at Angelo, both knew that neither had thought about having to keep ice on the beer or ice for the liquor.

"See you gentlemen tomorrow. Please tell Mr. Shelton we are in his debt." The men laughed, jumped back into the truck and were gone like servants who had just served a meal.

It was close to 2:00 in the afternoon when Vinny heard the next sound of a motor. It must be the girls. He stepped outside to see a large car enter his lane. As they approached, he could make out the driver, the black doorman, with Madame Marge next to the front passenger window. Sitting between them was a young girl. In the backseat were three more girls. When the car stopped, the black man ran around and opened the front passenger door. Out stepped Madame Marge in all her gala. She wore a gown that sparkled like a million stars. It was cut down in the front and back highlighting her breasts, her small waist and rounded derriere. "Mister Anthony, we're here. Where would you like the girls to be positioned? I assume you and I will be greeters. My man, Benjamin, will stay with the car unless you need him. Shall we go inside?"

Suddenly Vinny felt the cabin needed to be rebuilt from the ground floor. Somehow, Madame Marge and the cabin did not seem appropriate. "Madam, please excuse the accommodations. We are not accustomed to having such a refined lady as you."

"Mr. Anthony, this is a grand hotel to some of the places I have entered. You are a true gentleman and we are here to ensure you are happy with our services."

Vinny opened the door for Madam Marge, "Please come in. This is my partner, Mr. Angelo Bartello. Vinny, this is Madam Marge, proprietor of an establishment in Peoria. She has graced our presence with four ladies for our clients from Chicago"

Once Angel had picked up his jaw from the floor, and placed his eyeballs back into their sockets, he recovered well. He grabbed Madame Marge's hand which she had extended, bent forward, and kissed the top of her hand. "We are honored to have such a beautiful woman grace our establishment."

"You Italians know how to treat a woman. It is nice to meet you Angelo. Would you two please call me Marge? I would like to look around at the room and the back rooms if you do not mind." Not waiting for an answer she wandered around to check things out. The girls came through the doors like ducklings following the mother duck. They were quiet and seemed to be waiting for Marge to speak. "Girls, I want you to be seated when the guests come. We will wait for introductions, and then you will follow my lead on how the night will proceed. I suggest you freshen up. There are some pitchers of water in each room. Now go, we have little time."

Chapter 9

The stage was set, the actors were in place. Where was the audience? If the guest of honor did not show, Vinny and Angel knew that this would be their final day on earth. All the actors seemed to have opening night jitters, and until the opening scene was underway, there weren't any known remedies to cure their nerves. The discussions between the actors were trivial chit chat at best. Angel could not keep his nerves in check. He was as nervous as an expectant father. Every 10 minutes he would jump up and look out the window in anticipation of seeing his guests arrive.

"Ladies and gentlemen, it is show time." It was around 6:00 with the sun settling down on the west side of the cabin. The sound of cars coming up the lane was now pounding in everyone's ears and caused all hearts to race. Everyone jumped to their feet as if they were about to address royalty. Three cars stopped in front of the cabin. Angel and Vinny opened the door and came outside onto the front porch. When the door opened in the lead car, Angelo recognized Mr. Frank Nitti. He stepped down and walked forward. "Mr. Nitti, welcome back. I hope all went well on your trip down. No trouble finding the place I assume." He waved for Vinny. "Mr. Nitti, this is my partner, Vincent Anthony. He acquired all the provisions you requested. We hope they meet your expectations."

Frank Nitti was all business. His face had a stern look on it that caused Angelo to shiver. This man was now in charge of these surroundings and until he felt comfortable, no one else would either. "Angelo, I want to look around. Don't move. Stay right here." Nitti turned and looked at the trailing cars. Without a word, the doors opened and 4 men jumped out. They were carrying Tommy guns which were obviously not for duck hunting. They each went to the four corners of the cabin. One additional man got out of the car and walked up to Nitti. The two stepped on the porch and Nitti turned to Angelo. Both had pulled a pistol and held it at their side. "Mr. Bartello, what will I find when I open the door?

"There are five women in the cabin. We have one main room with our couches and stove and four sleeping rooms, all are vacant. Would you like for me to show you around."

Nitti gave Angel a look that conveyed his contempt for anyone suggesting he wanted or needed anyone's help. Angel froze on the spot he was told to occupy. Nitti turned, opened the door and went in with his gun. The trailing man silently followed and closed the door behind them.

It seemed like an eternity before the door to the cabin opened again. Nitti stepped out, walked to the first car and opened the back door. Out stepped a man who needed no introduction. Vinny thought the guest of honor was shorter than he imagined. The broad rim of the hat he wore partially covered the top of his forehead. It was the scar on his face that was his calling card. It drew your attention, but not your eyes. Could you believe it? The notorious Al Capone was standing in the flesh before Vinny and Angel.

"Boss all is ready. I will have the boys bring in the luggage. Your room is the first one on the right. We can start the hunt tomorrow morning. Tonight we will rest." Why was Nitti suddenly acting like a tour guide? Was he worried about what kind of reaction he was going to get from Al Capone? My god, if he was worried, suddenly Vinny and Angel were petrified. Apparently it showed.

"Everybody relax. I am here to try something new. I have heard that duck hunting would be a good time as well as a challenge. I am sure we will have both. I just hope I can hit a few of these ducks I heard so much about. As for the accommodations, this is a fine cabin for hunters for Christ sake. It is not supposed to be a royal hotel. Boys, let's get into some comfortable clothes, prepare something to eat, drink some good wine and booze. Then tomorrow, we get to kill something." He came over to Vinny and Angel, held out his hand. "For the next three days, call me Al. And relax; if I wanted", he let his voice tail off. "I have all the opportunities I can handle in Chicago. The only thing that will feel Al Capone's wrath flies. Let's check out your establishment." With that he put his arm around Vinny's neck and shoulder and they started walking toward the cabin. "Calabrese?" asked Al.

"Si, my family comes from Gizzeria." Vincencio responded in Italian.

Don Capone then communicated something in Italian that Vincencio heard but could not quite process. "Before the weekend is over, I may ask a favor of you. Do me this favor and I will be forever grateful and in your debt."

"Mr. Capone, Al, I am at your service. To have you visit our establishment is an honor. While we have never met, my brother who lives in Chicago has told me of your generosity to the people of Chicago and how you have helped the working man in Chicago. We know you have even generously given to the soup kitchens in our city. Your caring and generosity for those of us who have come to this country and work hard says you are a man of the people. I, like most working men, would do services for you without question." Vinny thought that came out well. Now the only remaining question was, what kind of favor could he ask down here in Havana? No matter, this was Al Capone. He would respond.

Vinny opened the door to the cabin for Al. Following him in, he first introduced Madame Marge, who gave Vinny such a grateful look that he dropped his eyes in a moment of shyness. He quickly gave an explanation of the cabin layout and encouraged Al and his entourage to enjoy the evening. He motioned to Angel, who knew it was time for them to exit. "We will be back around 5:00am to fix some breakfast. We should try to be at the river before the sun comes up. Hopefully, we will see lots of ducks in the fly way and be shooting by 7:00. See you tomorrow morning." With that final curtain call, Vinny and Angel left to go sleep in Angel's run down truck. Angel got the seat in the truck cab, Vinny slept in the truck bed. A tarp had been laid over the truck bed to act as a make shift tent to provide shelter from the elements. Life was good as both men fell asleep knowing they had passed the first test.

Chapter 10

It was colder than normal. Over the night, a cold front had come through. Thank God for tarps, heavy blankets and layers of clothes. Vinny couldn't wait for the morning. The surrounding river caused the air to feel like an ice mist. When Angel and Vinny got to the cabin, it was obvious the "ladies" must have performed and left for Peoria to return later that night. As Angel and Vinny were about to go in the cabin's front door they were startled by a voice. "I would stop right there." It was not a request but an order that both men knew must be obeyed. "We have to ensure you are not carrying any weapon before you meet with the boss." They were roughly patted down over all their bodies. Vinny could swear that the search was conducted rougher than needed, but Vinny knew he was being informed that he was lower on the food chain. "You're good".

Vinny and Angel went in and cooked the day's breakfast. Nothing starts the day like the aroma of coffee, with bacon and eggs frying in lard. It was all Vinny could do to keep from chowing down. This amount of food was something Angel and he could only dream of having and sampled only on rare occasions. But Carl Shelton had sent down a stockpile of food along with the booze. It was going to be a banquet for Vinny and Angel when this group was gone.

Al and his boys started to come out of their dens of hibernation. "Vinny, so you are a cook as well as proprietor, hunter and whatever else? Smells great and I am so hungry I could eat the whole pig and a chicken not just their by products." All laughed. The group was served and acknowledged their gratitude for the breakfast. Hell, these boys were polite and didn't grunt or nothing.

"Mr. Capone, Al, Angel and I are excellent cooks. Wait until you eat our pasta and meatballs we have for dinner, basic, but Old World. For lunch, we will eat in the field. We have prepared some antipasto, meats, cheeses and olives. When you are finished with breakfast, we will head for the duck blinds we have set up. We have already set out the decoys. Our two black labs in the blinds will retrieve the downed ducks. It is cold on the water. Dress warm. Did you gentlemen bring guns or will you use the guns Angel has for guests?" Angel's guns were two old shotguns that Angel and Vinny used. These antiques had seen generations of duck hunts. Suddenly Al and his crew let out belly laughs. Vinny immediately realized what he had said. With a smile, the ever eloquent statesman Vinny blurted, "Gentlemen, I did not make myself clear. I meant do you have hunting shot guns. Not Lumparas, but shotguns".

Al gave a wave of his hand. One of his boys brought out two cases which housed two of the most beautiful shotguns Angelo and Vinny had ever seen. "These are guns from an Italian count who hunted game in England, Europe and Italy. He gave me these guns as a gift. We have plenty of ammo, so I think we are ready to drop some ducks. Vinny, I will hit a duck won't I?"

"Al, I think you can do anything you set your mind to. We just need to get to the blinds to ensure that we are there when the ducks fly by." As the sound of chairs being pushed back from the table was heard, Vinny turned to Angel and whispered. "Please God, may the sun and sky be shadowed by hundreds of ducks flying past our blinds." Angel made the sign of the cross on his chest and just shook his head.

"Vinny. You worry too much. I have faith. We will get to shoot at ducks. Al Capone is going to get his limit. By the way, I will not be in the blind with you. I will set up to the blind to the left of you. Every time Al shoots, I will shoot as close as I can to when he does. No matter. When the duck falls, you know what your role is. Nice shot Al! You are a natural. We only must ensure that he does miss one or two to not be too obvious that we are kissing his butt."

When the group reached the river, Al and Nitti said they would be in the blind with Vinny. Al shouted out three crew names to go with Angel. He then looked over at one of his group and coldly said to Nitti, "Have Johnny come with us." Nitti motioned to Johnny to come over.

"Johnny, you come with Al and me." Johnny looked liked he had received a Christmas present.

The two blinds were about 50 yards apart and were now filled with a potpourri of anxious hunters. Every size, shape and hunting attire could be seen. The only two who looked like they were going to hunt and retrieve ducks were Vinny and Angel. The guns in Angel's blind were obviously loaners; the guns in Vinny's blind were obviously heirlooms. Each blind had their Labradors positioned and ready to retrieve. Now where were the ducks? No problem, as the sun began to rise, the horizon was filled with an approaching cloud of noise. Vinny had seen the flyway full of ducks before, but he had never witnessed anything like this. Angel was right. Not to worry. A blind first time hunter could point toward the noise, pull the trigger and would probably hit something. Vinny exhaled a lump of despair, "Thank you God."

Vinny and Angel started blowing their duck calls. Lead ducks put down their wings in a glide position aiming at the decoys in front of the blinds. As the ducks approached, Vinny whispered, "Gentlemen, when I touch you on the shoulder, rise, aim in front of the ducks about a foot, swing the gun to your left. Fire at will!" Vinny touched Al's and Nitti's shoulder as did Angel with the hunters in his duck blind. Shots were fired, ducks fell, and novices were already pounding each other's backs with a confidence of an expert. The day was positively perfect. Lunch came and went. Success was now visible rather than a wish. Dead ducks were lying in a huge pile in the blinds. The sun was starting to set low in the west. It was around 4:30 in the afternoon.

Al Capone put his arm around Vinny's neck and pulled him close to him. He kissed Vinny on each of his cheeks. "Vinny, this hunt was terrific. I cannot remember when I have had this much fun. I did not think I would like being out in the cold or find shooting ducks so competitive. I did not want to miss one, even though I did miss a few."

"Well we hope tomorrow brings the same." Vinny was both relieved and a little taken back by the open display of gratitude.

"We may leave tonight after dinner. We need to get back to the windy city. Business, you know how it is? So I suggest we head back to the cabin and eat an early dinner." Al looked at Nitti who suddenly stood up and left the blind leaving Al, Johnny and Vinny. Vinny watched Nitti go over to the other blind. He spoke to those in the blind. Without hesitation, the men and Angel got up and headed toward the cars.

Nitti returned and informed the group that he had sent the others back to the cabin to start dinner preparations. Al turned to Vinny and asked him what he normally did with the decoys at the end of a hunt. "Well, Angel and I wade into the water which is only about 3 to 4 feet deep. The decoys are weighted. We just throw them into this small boat next to the blind over there. Then we take them back to the cabin so they don't get lost or stolen. Since we will be back tomorrow, we will just leave them in the water until the end of the hunt. No one will bother them tonight."

Jim A. Roppa

"As I said earlier, sorry to say, we have to leave early tomorrow morning to get back to Chicago. Frank and I have an appointment that came up right before we left the city. You have been a great host so we will help you pack up the decoys right now."

"No need, Mister Capone, ah Al. Angel and I will come back later after dinner and get them. If it is too late, we will pack them up tomorrow morning."

"Vinny, I insist we pack them up now." Vinny knew he was through with this debate. "Vinny, you go over to the other blind and get the little boat and Johnny will help you get the decoys. Johnny, put on those waders over there and help Vinny gather up the decoys." Johnny did not hesitate and jumped at Al's request. He put on the brown rubber waders and started to wade out waist deep to the decoys. Vinny headed over to the other blind to get the boat.

As Vinny was walking over to the other blind, he looked back to see Johnny up to his waist in the dark backwater of the river. Vinny shouted back to Johnny, "I will get the decoys here from this blind. You grab your decoys by the weighted ropes. We will toss them in my boat." Both men started their retrievals and began to work their way to the middle where they could throw all the decoys into the little boat.

Nitti was laughing. "Hey Johnny, throw one of those decoys up in the air. Al wants to see if he can hit something without Angel around. Heave it as high as you can." Johnny took a decoy and with all his might, launched the decoy in Vinny's direction. Vinny looked at the launched decoy with the weight tied to it and saw it was only three or four feet above the water and wondered if he should hit the water. He took a quick glance at Al and Nitti. They were not pointing at him or at the duck decoy. "Johnny rats don't fly, they are only meant to die". Al's face was a red as a flare with his scar white hot as a burning fuse. Both men had their guns aimed at Johnny and, in unison, fired repeatedly until their guns were empty. Johnny's head exploded like a watermelon and was almost completely gone. His body seemed to fall in slow motion backward toward the water. As his body lay in the water, an oozing dark red hue began to spread around the headless body, the same color as the setting sun. Chunks of Johnny's skull and brain were floating on the water. Blue gills were starting to hit the brain matter like it was fish bait. Then both men turned their attention and looked at Vinny. They were no longer laughing.

"Vinny, get that bum's body into the boat with the rest of the decoys. Bring him to shore." Nitti was already moving to the point where he wanted the body to be brought.

Vinny was trembling and ready to vomit, not from the carnage before him, but from his hyper active nerves. The sudden warmth between his legs was not from river water but the urine that involuntarily had left his body. He flung Johnny's body over the side of the boat like a sack of potatoes and began to wade his way toward the shore. He was terrified of what he knew was coming next. He knew he couldn't swim to freedom so he did what he was told and brought Johnny to shore. How was he ever going to get out of this? He was not ready to die.

Nitti and Al were now standing over the body with the shotguns that had terminated Johnny. The barrels were warm from the rapid firing. With a calm, soft tone, Al turned his attention toward Vinny. Like a priest giving last rites, Al began his eulogy and sermon by the Illinois River bank. "Vinny, do not be afraid." He pointed his shotgun at Johnny. "This man sold his friends out to people who caused us harm. What you witnessed is what happens to any man who betrays me. He cost the lives of 4 of my men, my family, who were ambushed by one of my rivals. I was supposed to be in the car with them, but fate had other plans for me. I cannot stomach someone who is not loyal. Someone I gave work to, someone who ate at my table. I told you when I arrived that I may need a favor. Do you know of a place to bury this bum's body so that it will never be found? I have had you checked out. You are a good man, an honest man, a man of his word. I will give you a choice. If you cannot grant me this favor, I will respect your decision. I know that I can trust your word that you will never ever talk about what happened here. I would like for your help. I really do not want to take this piece of shit back in one of my cars. Will you take care of this for me?"

Vinny wasn't confident he had much of a choice. The way he had it figured, if he said no, both Angel and he would be the latest guests to the heavenly hotel of the deceased. He knew he could ask God to forgive him for doing what Al Capone had asked him to do. He also knew he could quickly forget the dead man with no face. Vinny had seen death before. He had not ever seen murder or the aftermath of revenge. He looked to the sky, said a quick silent prayer, crossed himself and turned his attention to Al. The next words out of his mouth could be his last. He knew he had to present one of his best performances of his life.

"Mr. Capone, I do not condone the taking of a life. I am sure you feel you had ample cause to take the action you did. I do know of a place not far from here. I will do what you ask and you have my word that no one, not even my closest friend, Angelo, will ever know what happened this night. While I do believe that you would not harm me as you said, I am not as sure of the safety of my partner who I love as a brother. I would like to hear your word that you will ensure his safety. He will never know what happened here. I do know of a place, an old abandoned mine where no one will ever find this man."

"Vinny, you are just as I was told. You did not ask any guarantees for yourself but for others. You have my word that nothing will ever happen to Angelo or you or anyone in your family. Frank and I will head back. I will send a car for you. You will not regret performing this special favor for me." Al and Nitti left, leaving Vinny with the recently departed Johnny and a heart that felt like it had pounded its way outside his chest cavity.

"Johnny, I will take you to a beautiful spot. I will give you a respectful burial. I will say a prayer over you. And Johnny, there will not be any one who will ever know where you rest." Vinny knew of an old abandoned mine shaft that was just off the river. He could take the boat with the body and would have to drag Johnny for about a half a mile. Vinny had come across the opening to the mine one day while out hunting and trapping. He thought the small opening had been dug out by an animal, but upon examination, found it to be some sort of abandoned air shaft. When Vinny reached the shaft he was a little winded. "Johnny, you have the forest, the river, and mother earth in which you will lie. God will pass judgment on you when your soul comes before him. I pray for your soul. In the name of the Father, Son and Holy Ghost, please accept Johnny into the kingdom of Heaven. Amen." After sliding Johnny into the shaft, Vinny gathered up river rock. He carried rock to the opening until he could not lift anymore. To the first time adventurer, the opening could no longer be viewed as anything but part of the landscape.

Chapter 11

It took around three hours before Vinny could dispose of the body and return to the cabin. As Al had promised, a car had been brought to the river and left for him to use. Once Vinny had disposed of the late Johnny in the mine shaft, he had jumped into the car and returned to the cabin. Angel was waiting for him. "Vinny, where in the world have you been? It is almost nine o'clock. Everyone has left. Did Mr. Capone tell you that they had to leave? Mr. Capone said to tell you he had urgent business that required he leave immediately. He said he was sorry he could not stay over until tomorrow. I have pasta and wine for us to eat and celebrate. Vinny, we did it." It was obvious that Angel did not really want to know where he had been or really cared that the hunting party had left. He probably thought Vinny had packed the decoys away, returned the dogs to their kennel and cleaned the ducks. The decoys were packed away, the dogs were in their kennel, the ducks cleaned and Johnny was in a rocked-filled hole in a dilapidated old mine. "Mr. Capone gave me this and said I should give it to you."

It was a note which said, "Vinny, for the inconvenience you have gone through for this hunt and for our having to leave so abruptly, please accept the car you are driving as a gift and my personal thank you." The note was signed, "Enjoy the car. More to Follow. A". Vinny couldn't believe he now had a car, but was a little unnerved by what could or would follow. Now that he had disposed of a body and given his word he would never discuss the matter with anyone, was he now so indebted to

"A" that he would return to hunt again or, worse yet, kill someone else for him to bury? Hell, maybe he would decide to kill him next time!

"Angel, we now have a car." Vincent could hardly speak. He only held up the note and looked at Angel. He felt exhausted.

"Vinny, that is not the half of it." Angelo opened a box he had laid on the table and pulled out the money they had been paid. "Vinny, look at how much money we were paid for a one day hunt. This is more money than we have earned in all our jobs over the past two years. Vinny, there is more. Al said he would take care of what we owed for the liquor and the girls. Can you visit both Madame Marge and the Sheltons to ensure we are off the hook? If not, we will need some of this money to pay our debt."

Despite the night's macabre events, Vinny found that he was uncharacteristically calm and surprisingly quite famished. "Angel, I will go to Peoria tomorrow to see if we are clear of our debt. This is our chance to do something with this money. This is only the beginning. As for now, let's say a prayer of thanks and eat." Vinny held up his glass of wine. "Salute. Here's to my best friend, my partner. May we live to see many more successes." Neither man could remember when wine had tasted so good.

As both men fell asleep, each said an extra heartfelt prayer of thanks. Both men knew the love each had for the other. They were more like brothers than friends. As Vinny felt the serenity of slumber falling over him, he wanted the events of this day never to be forgotten. Angelo and he had reached beyond their limits. They had proven they were willing to take risk and show no fear. Rewards were reaped but, given the events of the day, he knew he would have to deal with the consequences and say numerous prayers for the passing of the life he witnessed.

As for the hunters, they would come back for more duck hunts in following years. However, the hunts seemed solely for sport and would be uneventful to the local natives. There was always plenty of food, drink, and entertainment from the Ladies of Peoria. On these hunts, the only targets that were openly shot were migrating ducks. The only lingering question in Vinny's mind was, was there any unsavory thing crammed into those car trunks other than luggage? With each trip, did the occupants of the cars rid themselves of hidden burdens before they returned to their concrete jungle called Chicago? It was a question Vinny did not even consider pursuing.

PART II

Chapter 1

When Vinny had gone to Peoria the following day, he found out that Al Capone had indeed been true to his word. Someone in his organization had settled the outstanding debts for the liquor and entertainment. When he went to see Carl Shelton, Carl, no longer Mr. Shelton, had personally demanded he stay for a glass of wine. During the course of the next hour, Vinny was assured in no uncertain terms, if he ever needed anything, anything, he had only to ask. Vinny left with the nagging feeling that Shelton could change like a chameleon and hurt him. Vinny's sixth sense said, stay away from him and never come back. It was not to be a worry. Within the year, Carl Shelton and his brothers would be terminated. Rumors about who authorized the hit of the group were rampant. For Vinny, it meant he just stopped looking over his shoulder.

At his next stop, the surreal dream continued. As he prepared to enter the domain of the beautiful Madam Marge, the door seemed to open on its own. Vinny was greeted by a smiling Benjamin who had opened the door. Benjamin quickly led "Mr. Anthony" to Madam Marge's private quarters. Madam Marge was still a countess in Vinny's mind. "It is so good to see you again, Mr. Anthony. We hope you received excellent reports on our services. While the festivities were short lived, your clients seemed to enjoy our company. Our establishment an overly generous payment for services rendered. I wanted to personally thank you. Should you ever need our services again or if you ever need an escort for yourself, I would feel it an honor to take your arm anywhere."

"Madam, it has been my honor to meet you. I will always remember these past few days. Should I ever attend an event which require a regal lady accompany me, you will surely be the first I request. Are there any other expenses that require my attention from the past weekend?"

"Mr. Anthony, you are more than current. My establishment thanks you." Vinny chatted for a few more minutes and eloquently excused himself. Those who frequented this renowned establishment would soon learn his name. The word spread quickly through all levels of Peoria society that Al Capone had been in the area and that a man by the name of Vincent Dominic Anthony had a special relationship.

A week later while finishing laying the stone for a new walkway to the back yard garden at the Robert Jackson residence, he was startled to find Robert and another well dressed man standing behind him. "Vinny, this is Mr. Henry Hamilton who is president of the Central National Bank of Peoria. His bank handles all my business transactions. It is the only place I trust to handle my affairs. Henry contacted me because he heard that you had done some work for me. He wanted to meet you and, when he could not determine how to get in contact with you, he came to me. I will leave you two alone to talk." As Robert Jackson turned to leave, Vinny couldn't help but notice both men seemed a little nervous.

"Mr. Anthony, my bank recently was given some money to be placed into an open account which is to bear your name. We were told that the money was the result of an inheritance from a relative of yours who had passed away back in Italy. First, let me say that I am sorry for your loss. Also, as part of your deceased relative's wishes, he apparently owned a very well established company in Italy and you are to receive ongoing payments from the profits of that company as long as it is in existence. I am here to assure you that I am personally at your service should you need anything in the future. Please stop down at the bank at your convenience and we can go over your account and financials in detail."

He shook Vinny's hand and quickly left. Vinny stood there like a Roman statue with his hand stretched out. He couldn't speak. He only nodded to affirm his understanding of what was said as the banker walked away. I have my own account? What relative? How much inheritance? And what did he mean by, I was to receive ongoing payments?

Robert Jackson appeared out of nowhere. He actually seemed to stutter. "Vinny, you have been working for me doing my odd jobs long enough. I know of a full time job if you are interested. Once you have conducted your business with Mr. Hamilton, come down to the stock yards and we will talk about the job."

"Mr. Jackson, of course I am interested in something permanent. Whatever it takes or whatever the job, I will do it."

"Great. But first, meet with Mr. Hamilton. Let's stop working on this walk way. I will get one of my other workers to finish this job. We will see you Monday and we'll talk about the job."

Vinny was soon to learn that he was about to become a man of means as well as gaining an elevated reputation. Angel had been a prophet. A once in a lifetime event, for Vinny, an unspeakable event, was about to change their lives forever.

Chapter 2

Vinny couldn't sleep. Tomorrow he was going down to the Central National Bank of Peoria to find out what all this inheritance business was. Tomorrow Vinny wasn't going there to satisfy a curiosity, he was going there as a client of the bank, a customer. As Vinny dosed off to sleep, he instantly began to dream of how the meeting would take place.

The bank was one of the largest buildings in Peoria. The building was ten floors high, huge white columns lined the front door with stately white marble covering the façade. It was one of the main focal points of the city. Vinny had only been there once. One day, he was walking by and curiosity drew him to walk in to take a look. Once through the door, he saw the ceiling to floor marble columns. Vinny wondered if the marble had come from a quarry in Italy. He slowly entered the main room with a very high ceiling. Vinny's first impression was that he had entered a church. Tellers were on the right behind well polished counters. Brass cages on top had an opening for customers to exchange money with the tellers. On the left were desks filled with heads down clerks working with large ledgers. In the corner resided a plush office where everyone intuitively knew was the president of the bank. Little conversation could be overheard or, if someone did speak, it was in a hushed tone.

Vinny woke with a confidence he had never felt. He was ready for the next chapter of his new found adventure to unfold. In just a few months, he had gone from just another "WOP" to someone who had friends in some of the most unusual circles. Now, he was to meet with those who controlled the money. These were the men of power and position. They knew who controlled the city, who would develop the city, and who would prosper in the city. It was a tight-knit band of men and Vinny was about to meet one of the most influential. Vinny put on his only business clothes and set out for the bank. He still had not told Angel of this good fortune. It was still an unknown and he did not want to raise any false expectations. Angel was his friend and partner. Vinny never for a second thought of not sharing some of the fruits of this meeting. When it came to integrity, Vinny was second to none. The same could be said for Angel.

Vinny stopped in the middle of the main hall and observed what was going on in each sector of the bank. He casually walked by the tellers and heard the conversations going on between the teller and customer. He heard the interchange among the clerks going over the books. When he was ready and thought he had a good grasp of the situation, he walked over to the small desk outside the Bank President's office. "May I help you sir?" The president's secretary was in her fifties. Her hair was pulled straight back. Her dress was dark gray, which matched the tone of her voice.

"Yes you may. I am Vincent Anthony. I am here at the request of Mr. Hamilton. Would you be so kind as to inform him that I am here?"

"Certainly, Mr. Anthony. We have been expecting you. I am to take you right in." Vinny was surprised at how much her disposition had changed from the initial exchange.

Mr. Hamilton must have seen Vinny talking to his secretary. He was standing at the door and greeted Vinny as if they were old friends. "Mr. Anthony, it is good to see you again. Mr. Anthony, we are going to be seeing each other regularly. I think we can call each other by our first names. Call me Henry, may I call you Vincent?"

"Of course, Henry". What is going on? Vinny's head was spinning and his heart was pounding, even hurting, but Vinny knew he had to keep up his business façade. After all, he was asked to come here. Whatever was going to happen, he couldn't be in any worse shape, or could he? Something was up and it involved him. He had to be ready for any turn of events.

"Vincent, I will come straight to the point. You have had $25,000 deposited in your account. We certainly can agree that $25,000 is a substantial amount of money. We also were informed that you would be receiving an additional $1000 per month for an indefinite period of time. This bank is a well known, respected caretaker of this city's wealth. We know how to protect your money and to help it grow. We are offering you our services. We will help you manage and make the best decisions when it comes to your best interests. We are also in the know on how to help you with your investments in the future. Peoria is a growing town. We have potential to be one of the most influential cities south of Chicago."

Vinny was in a daze. He heard $25,000 dollars, $1000 per month and not much more.

"Vincent, are you with me on this? Do you grasp the importance of having our bank help you?"

Vinny took a deep breadth, not sure what was going to come out of his mouth. He knew that his next few words could be some of the most important of his life. "Henry, as I am sure you know, I am a most modest man. I have had to work hard just to survive. I am most appreciative of your offer, but there are a few questions I hope you would permit me to ask and provide some straight answers. First, I need to be educated on how the banking system would use my money, but, just as important, how I would be able to use my money, now and in the future. And second, how could I benefit from having this bank versus another protecting my money?"

"Vincent, you are quite right. I do apologize for being so presumptuous. I jumped to the bottom line and, frankly, am impressed with your response and questions. I have checked you out. You are known all over town and have a good reputation. You are honest, hard working and, probably your most notable trait, a quick study. Let's begin. You have a solid asset and ongoing working capital coming in. You have a benefactor that by default is a low risk guarantee for future opportunities. And finally, you have skills that may be useful in future endeavors the city may have opportunity to utilize. Questions so far? Hearing none, I will address your specific questions. Let me answer the second question first. The depression will not last forever. Signs of recovery are already being seen. The government is going to put people back to work all over the United States. Prohibition will not last forever. When it is abolished, Peoria wants to go into the liquor business. We are not going to compete with the beer providers because they are entrenched in the northern cities where the brew masters have come to reside. We want to go into the liquor business, whiskey. We have two huge markets, Chicago and St. Louis. Currently, we get quality products from the south. We also know of some European masters who would come to Peoria. We think this business would be able to ship via the river, truck or rail both north and south. As the rail develops and branches out, so would our ability to move our product to a broader market. It so happens a person who shall not be named wants to have an interest in the company when liquor becomes legalized. He could guarantee mass distribution. Your assets would fund the development of the business. Your name came up as someone who could over see the creation of the company and then manage the workers. However, since we do not know when the development could begin, your job at the stock yard will help you with your management skills. There, you will earn a good wage to keep your income at a level you have not had. If, for any reason, you would need additional monies, then you would come directly to me. Now, have I answered you questions to your liking?"

"Henry, you have put a lot on the table. I am not sure I quite grasp the magnitude of what you are saying, but rest assured, I am a man, who, when I do have a grasp, will perform better than one could imagine. As to the future, I will leave the negotiations for the liquor company to you. As for my situation right now, I will take the stockyard job and work hard at becoming a business man. If I can only be perceived as half as competent as you are, I will have achieved much. I can handle people and know who I can trust and who I must assist. I respect those who have achieved success. Sometimes I may appear that I am reluctant to challenge those who hold power, but, should I be faced where power is being abused, I can be most notable. However, there is one matter where I could use your knowledge of the city. I will also need some money. I have a partner. We are developing plans to open an Italian restaurant on the edge of town. He would run the place. Do you know of any establishments for sale that could be purchased for a reasonable price?" Vinny had not forgotten Angel and thought, why not go for the brass ring. They had not talked about any such venture, but hearing the potential of open booze, the new group of clients he would come into contact with, plus the bank behind him, how could they lose?

A slight smile came across Henry's face as he gazed out the office windows into the main hall of the bank. "Vincent, you are a quick study. You are going to go places. Let me see what I can find out about the establishments in our city and see if anyone is open to selling to your partner and you. I will get in touch with you should something come up. If there isn't anything else, here is a thousand dollars to get you through until your first pay at the stockyards. Vincent, you have been given the opportunity of a lifetime. I do not ask questions as to how or why. I do want you to know that you can learn from me. However, I too am a business man who can be as you say, notable." I look forward to years of a successful relationship." With that speech, Henry Hamilton stood and extended his hand.

Vincent rose and with the stateliest, strongest voice he could muster, he said, "Henry, we will have a successful relationship for years. As my partner and I, and one day my family, become part of the America dream, I will always remember and owe those and their families the respect and support of my family. Thank you for taking the time to explain the possibilities for that dream. Good day Henry." As Vincent turned to the door, he prayed he could walk without falling. The America dream was no longer something to come; Vincent was knee deep in it. As he reached the street and the cold air hit him in the face, he stopped, looked up and down the street, smiled and began to run in the direction where he knew he would find his partner Angel trying to come up with another scheme to keep food on their table. Vinny knew the two of them would no longer ever have to worry about the staples of life. From now on they would be concerned with building their families' circle of life.

Chapter 3

As Vinny entered the room in his business attire, walking with a renewed confidence that caused others to stop and move aside, he saw Angel sitting alone at a back table. His head was down and he seemed oblivious to anything but the paper he was reading. Vinny approached and stood like a statue until Angel finally felt the presence of someone standing over him. At first, he did not recognize Vinny with his new persona. "Yes sir, may I help you?" His eyes started at the mid section and ran upward until he met Vinny's solemn face. "Christ, is that you Vinny? You sure look like you are ready for the undertaker with your fine clothes. Why are you dressed like this? Where did you even get clothes like this? Is there something wrong?" He looked into Vinny's eyes expecting some tale of woe only to suddenly see a twinkle, a widening of the eyes and a smile come across Vinny's face that he had never seen. "What is it?"

Vinny stood in front of his best friend, raised his arms and held out both of his hands palms up. Angel had questions but reached out to his friend. Vinny grabbed his hands and squeezed them with a tenderness Angel knew was a touch of the love they shared for one another. Vinny pulled Angel close to him and gave him an old country hug and kiss on each cheek. "Angel, you have always been there for me since I came to this city. You have always shared equally with me, your food, your shelter, your ideas, and your work. It is now time for me to repay you." Angel was about to speak, but Vinny quickly cut him off. "There are not enough words for me to tell you how much I owe you and how I love you as my brother. Our lives are about to change. You are a smart man, a loyal friend. I am going to have a permanent job down at the stock yards. With the money from the yard and money we will make at our odd jobs, we are going to open that restaurant we always talked about it. Angel, my dearest friend, you will run the restaurant. Today, something happened. I have someone looking for a place to open the restaurant. You need to start thinking about what we will need." Angel fell back down in his chair and silence engulfed both men. Vinny sat down. It seemed like hours passed even though it was seconds. Then the corners of Vinny's mouth started to creep upward. Both men let out laughter causing everyone in the place to look toward them. Vinny and Angel could have been on an island. There were no other people in the world at that moment but them.

"Vinny, I am not going to ask you one question. I believe you. I will start my thinking on how we can have the best restaurant in Peoria. You will tell me this unbelievable story one day when you feel it is the right time. You are my brother. Nothing will ever come between us. Anyone who tries will answer and wish to God that they had never been born." Angel's thoughts and feelings had gone from maniacal to cerebral as each word came out of his mouth. A tear trickled down his face. His eyes left Vinny and looked down at his trembling hands. Vinny reached up and gently wiped it away. He wrapped both of his hands around Angel's right hand.

"Angel, you and I will have no fear. We are Italians, no, Italian Americans. This is our country now. This city is where we will build our most treasured possession, our families. You gave us the first building block of our future when we pulled off the hunt with Alphonso Capone. Since then, everything has been going our way. Now we must acquire more cement, more blocks. The restaurant will be our first step on our journey to the future. Angel, we must make a small list of men who share our dream and values. We will surround ourselves with those who we know understand loyalty. And as you did with me, we will share our rewards. This will be our silent family."

Chapter 4

It seemed like ages since Vinny had left Gizzeria. While he longed for his family, his old haunts, the land and sea, so much had happened to him. He had gained credibility for his family name, he had money coming in, he had purchased a house that the bank had on their books and wanted to sell. Vinny had learned the stockyard business and was the lead handler. He had a car and had worked hard with Angel to get the restaurant up and running. Vinny had even developed a social life and was getting serious about a beautiful young girl he had met. Everything seemed to be going perfectly. It seemed so simple. Vinny had never dreamed he would ever see Al Capone again but fate once again stepped in and dealt him an interesting hand.

Vinny had received word that his brother, Antonio, was having some tough times in Chicago. Vinny decided to visit him. He had never been to Chicago and was a little curious as to the stories he had heard. He thought he might need some cash to help Antonio, so he visited his friendly banker, Mr. Hamilton and requested an advance. "What brings you to our bank Vinny?" While Mr. Hamilton always personally handled Vinny's request, he was always brief and to the point.

"I plan to visit my brother in Chicago and I would like to ensure I have enough spending money for the big city and whatever may unfold." Vinny also wanted to be brief. He did not want non family knowing anything family related.

"Do you plan to seek out any other old friends while in Chicago?" This question did not even register with Vinny. Vinny must have worn his confusion on his face. "To the point, Vinny, do you have plans to meet with Mr. Capone? It might be a courteous gesture to at least let him know you are coming to town."

"You know Mr. Hamilton, I am not sure of my schedule or how much time I will spend in Chicago. I am quite sure that Mr. Capone is much too busy to take time to meet with me. It is not readily known how to get in touch with Mr. Capone even if I did have the opportunity. Of course, it would be a pleasure to see him again and to say how much we appreciated his past business." Vinny had tried unsuccessfully to erase the name of Capone from his memory. He sure as hell did not want to meet him in Chicago. He hated using the analogy to let dead dogs lie.

The Friday that Vinny was to leave for Chicago, he heard a knock at his door at his home on Adams Street. He opened the door to be confronted by a very large man, six feet two. His head was topped with a hat drooped to one side. His face was etched in lines, no smile. His eyes were steel gray and lifeless. His head looked as hard as a bowling ball made of marble and rested on mile wide shoulders and a chest that looked inflated. His arms were iron pipes leading to sledgehammer fists. Legs were oak tree trunks seemingly attached to feet set in concrete. His appearance was disheveled, nothing neat or tidy about him. His suit was wrinkled, his hair uncombed. Vinny could tell immediately he was a craftsman in his secret profession. This man was a man who could endure pain beyond human tolerances. He was born to do one thing, intimidate and if called upon, to take intimidation to reality.

"May I help you?" Vinny asked.

"My name is Marcello Rubio. I have the honor of going with you to Chicago. I will present you to Mr. Capone. I understand you are ready to leave today." Vinny fell silent. He felt this could be the final installment from Al Capone. He knew he had no choice. He was going to have a passenger to Chicago. The trip was long and silent. Marcello Rubio stared ahead at the road for five hours. Vinny was not going to try to crack this vault with small talk. Friday night, as they approached Chicago, the lights on the horizon had the glow of a sunset. Vinny wondered if he would see the next sunrise. He ventured a question to Marcello. "Do you work for Mr. Capone?"

"No." The answer was short without any further clarification as to why he was going to Chicago with Vinny. "I was told how to get to where we are going. I will direct you. Keep driving and follow my directions." After weaving through the streets of Chicago, Vinny was told to stop at a restaurant on a street called Cicero Street. The big sign over the front window of the restaurant looked like Italy's flag. The name of the restaurant was stenciled over, *La Familia*. The two got out of the car. Vinny retrieved a package in the trunk and both men entered. The smells of Old Italy caused Vinny to think he had traveled back to his homeland. Italian was spoken by everyone in the restaurant. Everyone in the restaurant looked at the two men then went back to their meals. At the back of the restaurant with his back to the back wall sat Al Capone, Frank Nitti and two other men whom Vinny assumed were body guards.

Vinny approached, but was suddenly stopped by the two hulks at the table. They patted him down, looked in the package, and then looked to Al. "He's clean."

"Vinny, I told them you did not carry, but we do not make mistakes." Vinny suddenly realized that Marcello was not behind him. He must have left when he walked to meet Al. Al held out his hand and, without hesitation, Vinny kissed the top of his hand. "Vinny, I am so glad to see you again. We had been talking about you, weren't we Frank?" Not waiting for a response, Al continued, "Before we conduct business, you must be hungry. They have the best salami, bread, pasta, and wine. Mario, bring me a plate for my friend." Like a well oiled machine, the plate was in front of Vinny before the last part of the request was completed. Vinny began to eat. After a few bites, he wiped his mouth to signal his appreciation for the meal and to acknowledge he knew that dinner was not what he was here to do. Vinny wanted to know the real reason.

"Mr. Capone, Al, it is an honor to join you at your table. I am quite sure this meeting was not a coincidence since only a few people knew I was coming to Chicago. Whatever the reason, please allow me to present a gift from Angel and me. It was Angel who came up with the idea. There is a man in our area who is sought after for his life-like duck decoys. Both his carvings and paintings are excellent. We want you to have this one." He reached into the package and brought out a mallard duck decoy that easily could have been mistaken for a real duck. Al seemed to be entranced by the gift. He rolled it over and over in his hands, and then set it down in front of him as gently as if the decoy were made of crystal.

"Vincencio, please accept my gratitude to Angel and you. I cannot tell you how much your gift means to me. It is truly a piece of art and I know it comes from the heart. I will give it a place of honor in my home for all to see. As for you, it seems duck decoys continue to bond us together." With that remark, Frank Nitti let out a laugh. Al shot Nitti a look that suggested the statement was only for Vincencio and him and was not being shared with him. Frank quickly returned to his rock-hard stoic expression. "I understand that your brother lives in Chicago and you have come to see him. I believe he lives in this neighborhood, correct? How is he doing?" Vinny suddenly felt very uneasy. How and why did Al want to know about his brother?

"Yes, my oldest brother, Antonio, does indeed live in this neighborhood. I was quite surprised Marcello stopped at a restaurant in this area. To be honest, I was not very confident I could find his residence without asking once I got to Chicago. But to answer your question, my brother has fallen on some hard times. I am here to see if I can help him."

"You could have come to me. I would have seen what I could do." Al interrupted.

"Mr. Capone, Al, with all due respect, this is a family problem that one should not burden such as important man as you." Vinny put on his diplomat persona and hoped it would suffice.

"What are you going to do? Give him some money? Ask him to come to Peoria to live with you? Or do you think he could be of service to stay in Chicago and work here? Vinny, I told you earlier that Frank and I had been discussing you. It just so happens that we are going to ask you for a favor. By granting us this favor, we can help you with your brother." One thing Vinny learned in America, if you do the simplest of favors, legal or otherwise, requestors now have you on the hook to repeat. Vinny knew he could not say no to what may be asked. He only hoped that someone's life would not end in exchange for his brother being granted a new one.

"Al, what is it you wish for me to do?" Vinny asked still committed to take action.

"We want to buy your hunting cabin. With all the dealings Angel and you have going, I am sure you are not finding as much time to have hunting parties. We would appreciate you discussing this with Angel. Should you agree to selling, we would like to handle the transaction as discretely as possible. We also have heard of a job for your brother in the construction business. Could you give us an idea on what direction your answer could take?" Vinny knew Al Capone expected an immediate positive answer. The two conditions were actually two gifts one could not turn down. Angel was working every day and night at the restaurant and never mentioned any intention to seek out hunters. As for his brother, anything that Al Capone could offer would be a gift from the heavens, if it was a legitimate job.

"I am sure that Angel and I would be willing to sell the cabin and would agree with your price. You have always been most generous. As for my brother, I think I could speak for him and extend his most gracious appreciation for any job that he could assume." Vinny did not ask any questions on why they wanted the cabin because he did not want to know the answers. He would rationalize in his mind that this meeting was strictly a business deal where both parties had something of value the other was willing to part with at a fair price. This was a quid pro quo deal, not anything illegal. Vinny would never know that this seemingly straightforward cabin sale was going to be the payment to his silent passenger, Marcello, for a future job Marcello would perform for the Capone organization.

Vinny left the restaurant on Cicero Street then drove alone to the residence of his brother, Antonio. The residence was a basic flat on the fifth floor of a run down seven floor brick building. Antonio was so happy to see Vinny. When he opened the door, he gave Vinny an embrace and a kiss on each cheek. Vinny detected a tear which soon evaporated as Antonio quickly gained his composure. Vinny smiled and could almost hear his father, "NO LIMITS".

"Antonio, how have you been? I have missed getting your letters. Our father and mother keep sending letters asking about how we all are doing. When I haven't heard from you in a month, I thought I would come for a visit. We have a lot to talk about. I am still at the stock yard, Angel is working hard at the restaurant, and Dominic is working the river in St. Louis. He says he is getting strong as a bull lifting grain sacks. How are you doing?" Vinny knew the answer, but he wanted to let

Antonio have the opportunity to get things off his chest, clear his mind, and see what direction he wanted to go.

"Brother, I am not doing as well as Dominic and you. I may be letting the family down. I cannot seem to find a job which will lead anywhere. I am only making enough to eat and sometimes I work to eat. I am sorry to have to sit here and tell you such a story. I did not write because I was ashamed and thought if I told you what was going on that you would want me to come back to Peoria. I have to make it on my own. I may be the youngest son, but I am grown up enough to make it on my own." Antonio was a proud Antonini. Like his brothers, he took on the last name of Anthony when he came to America. Vinny could see the pain in his brother's eyes. He had to be delicate with him and he knew he had to help. Once his brother got a job where he could show his dedication, Vinny knew he would be fine.

"Antonio, I am here with some great news. I hope you will think so as well. It just happened someone I had done some business with was moving to Chicago. I mentioned I had a brother who lived in Chicago. I told him what an intelligent, hard worker you were and that you were looking to move to another job. He was happy with the business we had and said he owed me a favor. He said he would ask around to see if his people knew of any job openings. He sent me a letter and said when I came to visit you in Chicago, come see him. I met with him before I came to see you. He had a job opening with the Santucci Construction Company. They are in the road and rail business. He said they would like to have you work for them. They want you to come down to State Street on Monday and will assign you to a work crew. Antonio, this is a great opportunity. I know times are tough. Until you get paid on this job, please accept this money from me. You can pay me back later." He put the money on a table nearby which signaled to Antonio the deal was final. Vinny stood. Antonio stood. They embraced each other so hard neither could breathe. They talked and drank Chianti well into the night.

The next morning, Vinny prepared to return to Peoria. "Antonio, I truly believe our family name will one day be known by many. Dominic, you and I are in the first few chapters of our family novel in America. We are brothers. If you ever again have any problems, you contact me immediately. Only together can we reach our dreams." Vinny again embraced Antonio. "Antonio, you will have success I am sure. You have no limits on what you will do to succeed. You are fearless and take full responsibility for what each day unfolds. You are my brother and I love you. Our family is so proud".

In the next few years, Vinny would see his associations with known gangsters come to an end. When it did, Vinny was well established with a sizeable cash reserve.

Chapter 5

It was 1929. The Great Depression was spreading to a worldwide economic disaster. The impact on humanity at large was as close to hell as one could imagine. It was the largest and most severe economic depression in modern history. Historians would report that the Great Depression originated with the United States stock market crash on October 29, 1929, known as Black Tuesday. The poor, middle class and even the wealthy were panicking at the thought of losing their land, homes and fortunes.

Peoria seemed to be an exception. Yes, Peoria had its share of down trodden, but this city in the heart of the United States continued to prosper and grow. An elegant 14-story hotel, the Pere Marquette Hotel was built and featured 288 beautiful guest rooms. Charles Lindbergh made a "first" air route, Contract Air Mail route #2, which began running mail from Chicago to Peoria to Springfield to St. Louis and back. It was rumored Lindbergh offered Peoria the chance to sponsor his trans-Atlantic flight but Peoria leaders refused. The plane would have been called the "Spirit of Peoria". Peoria's underbelly had also not missed opportunities to continue to prosper during these years.

Peoria was well known as the wildest city between Chicago and St. Louis. Chicago had its own gangs led by Alphonse Gabriel "Al" Capone, nicknamed *Scarface*. Capone was "the" gangster who led the Midwest crime syndicate dedicated to smuggling and bootlegging of liquor and other illegal activities during Prohibition. Of course his captains of his inner circle kept a close eye on Peoria activities and, as such, had some soldiers of his syndicate try to take over Peoria's vice rackets. These men were not taken seriously and were seen only as a front by the local power. They knew these goons did not have the "real" backing of Capone. That did not stop the locals from trying to partake in the lucrative booze business.

A man named Clyde Garrison who was a local gambler had Peoria politicos in his pocket. He wanted to branch out into the bootlegging profit. He had invited the Shelton brothers to be his partners. This tandem soon launched a power play to drive out any competition in Peoria. These men ran Peoria. Garrison handled the politicians; the Sheltons provided firepower. The Sheltons seemed to be at war with the entire state. They eventually gained control of gambling and liquor distribution in downstate Illinois to St. Louis. When prohibition went into effect, other gangsters attempted to take over the Sheltons' bootlegging operation to no avail. They only achieved an early grave.

When Capone started to blatantly ignore Prohibition laws and basically thumb his nose at US law, politicians in Washington D.C knew they had to deal with this gangster. Capone had now gained the attention of the Federal Bureau of Investigation and was placed on the Chicago Crime Commission's "public enemies" list. Capone's criminal career was under very close scrutiny and would end in 1931, when he was indicted and convicted by the federal government for income-tax evasion. This distraction allowed the Sheltons to have a monopoly on downstate Illinois.

Carl and Bernie Shelton were murdered. Earl seemed to evaporate. No one ever claimed credit. However, the grapevine had said the hit was the result of the Carl crossing Capone. It was only known 20 years later a man who lived in a hunting cabin close to Havana, Illinois would confess on his deathbed he was part of the hit squad that helped kill the

Sheltons. The local papers dispelled the claim and said Marcello Rubio, the man who had accompanied Vinny to Chicago, was a loner who lived in the woods and was just trying to gain notoriety on his death bed to compensate for his miserable hermit life.

When Peoria's elite were scurrying to make any deal to save their investments, Vinny felt he needed to meet with Harry Hamilton. "Vinny, you are not impacted by these recent financial events. Let me personally assure you, your money is safe. As you know, when each deposit from your "good fortune" was received, we took the cash into our bank. Again, when your monthly deposits were received, they were in cash. Vinny you have accumulated large sums of cash which are held in our banks largest safety deposit box in the bank." Vinny interrupted.

"Harry, I am reading people are jumping out of buildings in New York, mostly bankers who do not have money for their so called investors. I have trusted you completely, but it may be time for me to count the money we have compiled over the years."

When Vinny had asked about the safety of his money, Harry could say with total confidence, nothing could touch Vinny's money except Vinny. It was a matter of life or death, Harry's life. He knew the consequences from the first meeting with Frank Nitti, Vinny was to be protected, period. Harry took Vinny to the vault to count his deposits, or his cash stash as Harry thought of it. However, Harry already knew the amount of the deposits since he kept a separate ledger of Vinny's transactions. In these hard times, Vinny now was part of the elite, he just didn't know it. But Harry did. Neither Vinny nor he was going to be a statistic of the Depression. Harry also knew if he did take care of Vinny's interest, he was not going to be a statistic. Harry was still a man who looked out for his own interests when presented opportunity, so he knew exactly what his next opportunistic recommendation would be to Vinny. Vinny's cash and Harry's contacts were going to make both men set for life.

Chapter 6

"Is it always so windy and cold in Chicago? Lake Michigan is beautiful in the summer, but it is really a coin flip whether March will go out like a lion or lamb. I hear you are looking for possible locations to build a distillery for fine liquor? My name is Harry Hamilton from Peoria. I believe we may have the perfect location for your venture." Harry looked the man across the table directly in the eye and with his most assuring, confident manner, continued his business proposal.

"Peoria has had past business dealings with Mr. Hiram Walker. You may not have known this, but Peoria first became acquainted with Mr. Walker when he delved into the cattle breeder business. Many of his cattle graced our stock yards and were transported to St. Louis, Kansas City and elsewhere. Through mutual acquaintances, we also were very familiar with his whiskey products. Mr. Hiram Walker actually brought in Illinois lawyers to assist with the famous contracts case known as "The Pregnant-Cow Case" which proved to be a legal precedent for buying and selling breeding cattle though the case seemed petty. Mr. Walker had agreed with a banker, to sell him a cow of distinguished ancestry known as "Rose 2d of Aberlone" for $80, and both parties believed Rose to be sterile. When Mr. Walker discovered that she was pregnant and worth between $750 and $1,000, he refused to deliver her. The banker sued and prevailed in the trial court, but lost on appeal based on the legal expertise brought from Peoria on contract law rules of rescission of contract by mutual mistake. Because both parties believed they were contracting for a sterile cow, there was a mutual mistake of fact, and therefore ground for rescission."

"I take the time to articulate this case to again make the case that Peoria and Mr. Walker did have successful business relations, that Peoria has a wealth of solid businessmen and business professionals, and, lastly, to set the stage that Peoria is renowned for the many distilling companies that believe Peoria is well suited for the processing and distribution of their products." Harry was not going to let this business venture slip through his bank's fingers. He was ready to take some liberty with facts. The next words out of his mouth could be a deal breaker if interpreted as a threat, a threat he and he alone was conjuring up.

"I also want to demonstrate our commitment to making your business a success. One of our investors, who has history with our Peoria Bank, has a past history with the Walker family. This investor's family knew Mr. Walker as an American grocer and distiller, and the name sake of the famous distillery in Windsor, Ontario, Canada. They had business connections and capital which was used when he lived in Detroit. They helped him purchase land across the river in Canada, and helped establish a distillery on the banks of the Detroit River. As we all know, this was the genesis of Mr. Walker selling his whiskey as Hiram Walker's Club Whiskey. These investors also came to Mr. Walkers' aid when his Canadian whiskey became very popular and American distillers became angry, and forced the US Government to pass a law requiring that all foreign whiskeys state their country of origin on the label. With our investors' family ties, this move backfired and Hiram Walker's Canadian Club Whiskey became more popular. All parties benefited and both company and investors' financial positions improved many times over. As I alluded in my opening of this commitment, my bank has an investor from the family of original investors of the Hiram Walker Company. He is eager to continue this long standing relationship." Harry took a pause to let his last selling point sink in. He could only hope that the man sitting across the table did not know exactly the full impact of the family he was illegitimately representing.

"Mr. Hatch, this concludes my presentation. I firmly believe that Peoria has all that a company like yours is looking for and is willing to commit. We can make your company successful, profitable, and notable."

The Hiram Walker & Sons Distillery remained in the Walker Family until 1926 when it was sold to Mr. Harry C. Hatch. Harold Clifford "Harry" Hatch was a self-made millionaire industrialist who made his fortune in top of the line whisky. His most notable products were now Canadian Club whisky and Ballantine's Scotch whisky.

Mr. Harold Hatch was a smallish man. His moustache covered his mouth to the point that when he spoke, his lower lip was seldom seen to move. His eyes however revealed the type of business man he represented. The eyes were piercing, his pupils were the size of a pinpoint, and a stern glare was always present. "Mr. Hamilton, let's get right to the point. I can only guess who your investor family may be. I am not interested in knowing anything other whether you can deliver. Let's be candid here, you know I own the rights to Hiram Walker products. I have been one of a number of Canadian distillers who prospered by shipping our products into the United States during these prohibition times. Prohibition will not last. Americans love their beer and liquor. The political winds know how to survive from election to election. The American people will demand this law be overturned and we want to be ready with a legitimate distillery here in the United States. I will review your site plans, will assess your labor force, and will definitely look at the financial aspects being offered by your bank. We will have an answer for you by the end of the month. Thank you for your interest. AND my company will only abide by contractual agreements, not investor expectations. We will be a law abiding company with an American flag in front of our office. Do you understand my conditions and if so, will you represent them to all investors? We will only do business through reputable financial institutions."

Mr. Hatch had let Harry know he understood his last sales point, but even though Hatch was probably dealing with some family to get his liquor distributed in the U. S., there was to be no links to his company or him. Harry was more than relieved that his ploy would go no further. "Mr. Hatch, the only financial interactions would be through my bank and my personal hands-on approach to providing any and all services you could require in Peoria. I am well connected and a respected citizen. We look forward to your answer."

As Harry drove back to Peoria, all he could think of was whether he had sold Peoria as the next site for a Hiram Walker Plant. This would elevate him in the social circles as a leader for the future, as well as bring new dollars into his bank and personal billfold. He smiled, "I know exactly the capital it will take for this distillery and where to get it. Mr. Vincent Anthony, if fate is with us, you are going to be a very wealthy man."

Chapter 7

Life had become good for Vinny. He had money in the bank, a full time job at the stock yards, supplemental money coming in from the restaurant he owned with Angelo. His brothers were getting established in St. Louis and Chicago. He and his brothers had been sending money back to his parents and had asked them if they were ready to come to America. Yet something was missing in his life. That missing piece was soon to be revealed.

Marianno Travato was one of the best butchers in the stock yard. When Vinny was placed in charge of hiring and supervising for the business, Angelo had told him of Marianno and asked, as a favor, would he hire him. Marianno was a hard worker, never missed a day of work, never complained. He was always ready to do whatever was asked. He was a butcher by trade. He had arms like iron pipe and thick hands. He could lift an entire side of beef and put it on hooks without help. He was always smiling. His family had come to the states from the Tuscany region of Italy. He was always bringing Vinny homemade "Dago Red" that his family made. Marianno reminded him of his younger brother.

"Hey Vinny, what are you doing this Saturday night? It is my father's 80th birthday and we are going to throw him a party. It will be great. There will be plenty of great Italian food, wine, bocce ball, and music. My family lives in Toluca. It is about an hour drive. We will stay overnight because I know we will drink too much. What do you say? Come meet my family and enjoy our table." It was obvious from Marianno's voice that he was pleading for Vinny to accept. It would be an honor for Marianno to bring his "boss" to a family dinner.

Vinny weekend routine was always the same; close up the yard, visit Angelo at the restaurant, drink too much wine, go home, sleep, wake up and go to church at Saint Philomena. It was time to break the cycle. "Marianno, I will go. Thank you for inviting me. Give me directions and time and I will be there." Marianno grabbed Vincent like a side of beef and spun him around with his feet six inches off the ground. Vincent felt sorry for the side of beef given the pressure he felt on his ribs and back.

"Vincent, thank you, thank you. I will write down the directions and time. See you Saturday." With that thought Marianno set Vincent down gently and went back to his station at the yard. Vincent smiled and took a deep recovery breath. "Marianno has a good heart as well as a being as strong a bull."

Vincent did not know much about Toluca so he asked around. He learned that it was a small community, mostly Italians who had worked in strip mines, trades, and services. He was looking forward to spending the day with Marianno's family. It would be good to hear his Mother tongue, taste the food and drink the wine. He knew it would make him yearn to see his parents. He had only been back to Italy once and still felt like it was only yesterday when he had left.

The directions to Toluca were straight forward. Travel up the river north, head up though a number of little towns on Route 17. Spring was around the corner. You could almost smell the spring vegetation with each rain. It was a sunny cool day when Vincent hit the main street of Toluca. The main street was lined with little houses on each side with the locals sitting outside eyeing him as he passed. He found the street that Marianno's family lived on and turned into a gravel entrance way. As he made his way toward the two story white house, Marianno came running out to meet him. It was obvious that half the town was here to celebrate.

"Vincent, you made it. Thank you for coming. My father will be so honored to meet you. Come in side." Vincent was hoping Marianno would curb his excitement and not carry him in the house.
"Marianno let me get something out of my car that I brought as a gift for your father. I have a brother in Chicago and he was able to get me two of the finest liquors, Tuaca and Grappa from Italy. I want to give them to your father. I also have this box of chocolates and bottle of the purest Italian olive oil for your mother. Please help me carry them in." Marianno grabbed the two bottles of liquor. Vincent carried the gifts for his mother. As the two approached the front door, it opened.

"Please come in Mr. Anthony. My brother has told us so much about you. It is a pleasure to put the face to the name. My name is Carmella Travato. Let me introduce you to our mother and father. Do not worry about all the other people. My father has a number of brothers and sisters and friends. You will meet them throughout the day."

Vincent could not believe his eyes. "It is a pleasure to meet you." While the words came out of his mouth, he felt he needed to clear his throat, take a deep breath and hang on to something. Standing before him was a vision. Vincent had studied works of art, but never had he felt such an attraction from what his eyes were scrutinizing. He wanted to stare, to etch Carmella's face in his mind. Her long black hair that draped her shoulder and back was as dark as any coal he ever mined, with a shine that seemed to highlight her face. Her smile revealed the whitest teeth and full lips. As she turned to lead him to her parents, Vincent couldn't help but notice the curvature of her body. His mind went back to a magnificent marble statue he had seen on a family visit to Rome. "Vincent, are you coming? My parents are in the next room."

Vincent felt a nudge from behind from Marianno. "Go on. Neither my parents nor my sister will bite."

Vincent entered the adjourning room. It was set up for the party with the guest of honor, Mr. Travato, sitting in a big chair in the corner by the window. Standing at his side was his wife. As Vincent approached, he fought back tears as they reminded him so much of what he left back in Italy. The pair were icons of senior Italians. "Mr. and Mrs. Travato, my name is Vincent Anthony. My family name is Antonini from Gizzeria, Calabria. You have done me a great honor by allowing me to come and celebrate your milestone day of birth. You should take pride in your son. He does your family proud as he goes about his work. We are friends. I have just met your daughter and she has the beauty of her mother. Please accept these gifts which I hope you will enjoy." Vincent handed the chocolates and olive oil to Mrs. Travato. Marianno handed Vincent the Tuaca and Grappa for him to give to his father.

Mr. and Mrs. Travato accepted the gifts, both with a genuine smile and a truly gracious "Gracie". Mr. Travato spoke in Italian, "My son has told us about you. He says you are a man of integrity, a man of heart. Welcome to my home. Marianno, Carmella, please make Mr. Anthony feel at home. Fix him something to eat and pour him a glass of wine to drink. Your gifts will warm my wife's and my mind, heart and soul. May I live another day to enjoy them."

Carmella gently touched Vincent's elbow, "Let's go into the kitchen. I think you will enjoy the food that has been prepared. As for the wine, well, Marianno is the expert on which bottle will satisfy the most discriminating of palates." Carmella's touch had sent a shiver through Vincent. He had been with women. He was no choir boy. What was so special about this woman? He did not know. But one thing he did know, he wanted to see her again and again. He now knew what was missing in his life: someone to stand by him, someone to be his wife, someone to bear his children.

Vinny spent the entire day going through the motions of being interested in people's family lineage and their conversations. All the while, Vinny kept track of Carmella and with every opportunity, tried to capture her attention. During the family dinner, he sat across from her lost in thought. *"I look into your eyes, we talk without words. Have I found the missing part of my soul? As we talk, it is if we know what each is thinking and feeling. We seem to like the same things, laugh at the same things. Carmella, may I see you again? Do I dare speak to Marianno about my feelings toward you? Tomorrow I return to my orchestrated life. How do I begin to include you? This is possibly the most important thing I have done since leaving my homeland."* Vinny's mind raced only interrupted by the social matters at the table.

"I will definitely ask Carmella if I can see her again before I leave. I want to talk privately with her father. It is only honorable to tell him of my intentions. No Limits, no Fear, no Remorse!"

That night, as Vinny prepared for bed in Marianno's room, he said a prayer to his patron saint, Saint Assisi. "I call upon you, blessed Assisi. Look into my heart. Know that I, as you lived, am of humble beginnings. I have always tried to put others before myself. Tonight, I am praying to you in the name of my Lord to ask forgiveness for I am only thinking of myself and the desires I have for a woman, Carmella Travato. If it is God's will, I plan to ask permission to court her. I ask in your name for her father to know that I would be a good man to her, care for her, and would make their name proud. In the name of the Father, the Son, and the Holy Spirit, Amen."

Chapter 8

Vinny woke early. He dressed and went to the bathroom to prepare himself for the task before him. He could smell breakfast being prepared in the kitchen, so he followed the scent like a dog to his bowl. There, cooking, were Carmella and her mother. Carmella turned and, almost in a shy manner, said, "Good morning. Did you sleep well? We hope you are hungry. Mother is preparing some bacon from hogs we have raised to go along with biscuits and eggs. She has a batter of pancake mix if you really want to fill your stomach for the entire day."

"I will pass on the pancakes. Mrs. Travato, it smells wonderful in here. Even after all the food from yesterday, I cannot say no to this breakfast. Is there anything I can help you with? Put dishes on the table?".

It was easy to see where Carmella got her looks and smile. "Young man, you are our guest and all we need from you is to enjoy the food and our company. It is not often we have such a handsome young man for breakfast."

Was this a sign that Carmella did not have any suitors calling on her? Vinny felt a surge of courage. No limits, No fear, No Remorse! "Carmella, may I have a word with you?" She nodded yes with a confused frown on her face. The two went into the parlor. "Carmella, I do not really know how to begin. When we first met, something inside me told me that you were someone special, someone I would truly enjoy being around. I must admit that I could not take my eyes off you all day yesterday. While

I understand you do not know much about me, I would ask you directly, may I see you again? I am not a man who acts spontaneously, but if you would do me the honor of seeing me again, I would hope that you would know the kind of person that I am and would continue to see me. In respect for your family, if you say that you would see me again, I would ask your permission to speak to your father to tell him of my intentions. What do you say? May I call on you again?" Vinny stopped, his body felt as weak as if he had worked a whole week at the stock yards. His heart was racing as he held his breath for Carmella to respond.

"Vincent, I too felt that you were special and that I would like to see more of you. Quite honestly, I did not know how you would feel knowing that Marianno was my brother and that he worked for you. I am only 19 years old. My father and mother have been very protective, so your thought of talking with my father is a good one. But know this Vincent, I am a woman and I can make up my own mind. We will see each other again."

Vinny reached out for her hand. Both were more than nervous.

"I will talk with your father. As for Marianno, we are friends first, co-workers second." Vinny couldn't wait to approach Mr. Travato.

After breakfast, as Vinny was preparing to leave, he told Marianno that before he left, he wanted to thank his parents once more for the wonderful day and wished them well in the coming years. Marianno told Vinny that his father was sitting in the parlor and that he would wait by the car. Vinny re-entered the house and walked by Carmella who was standing in the door way. As Vinny entered the parlor, Mr. Travato looked up from an old chair he obviously had claimed as his over the years. Sunlight coming in through the windows bounded off his balding head. He smiled and made a gesture for Vinny to come in and sit. "Vincent, are you ready to leave?"

"Yes sir, Mr. Travato. But before I leave, I wanted to wish you health and say, if I am as healthy as you when I am your age, truly God has blessed me. I also am humbled by the hospitality that was shown to me in this house and town. You treated me as family, which I miss." Vincent spoke in Italian, "Senore Travato. I stand a humble man before you. I am 23 years of age, I have a good job, a house, a car and believe people would describe me as God fearing, honest, and caring. When I came to your home, the last thing on my mind was that I would find something that I did not know was missing from my life. The very first time I saw your daughter, a feeling poured from my heart like I have never known. I sit here before you to ask if you would give me permission to see your daughter again. My intentions are to try to win her favor, for her to want to be with me. If it is your custom to have a chaperone for a given period, I will follow your wishes. Senore Travato, would you give me your blessing to see your daughter again?"

Senore Travato's Italian response was slow and direct. "Vincent, I will give you my blessing. But know one thing, should you hurt my daughter or the name of my family, a vengeance will fall upon you that would make hell seem like heaven. We cherish our daughter. Marianno is the protector of his sister. You seem like a fine young man and your charm is as captivating as the taste of fine wine. It is obvious from you coming to me that you were raised in a fine family. I congratulate your father and mother. I will not ask that you be chaperoned for I know my daughter. She is strong, intelligent and can make her own decisions as a woman. All I ask is each time you call on my daughter, you do not forget her mother. Have a safe travel back to Peoria." The conversation was over.

Vinny stood, leaned forward and grabbed Senore Travato's hand with both of his. "I will do your daughter and this family proud. On the name of my family, you will not regret your decision. I can now only pray that I can prove myself to Carmella."

Vinny retreated and headed back to the door. As he passed Carmella in the doorway, he touched her arm, "If you would so grace me, I would like to call on you. I will send word back to you to see when we can again be together for a dinner, a drive, or whatever you would want to do. I need only for you to say yes that you would see me again."

Carmella dropped her eyes, "Yes I would like to see you again. I cannot wait until we do see each other again, Vincent. Until then, have a safe trip back to Peoria."

"Marianno, I am ready. Thank you again for inviting me to your home. You have no idea of how happy this visit has made me. I am forever in your debt." Vinny shook Marianno's hand, jumped into his car. As he drove out of Toluca heading back to Peoria, his mind was on everything but the drive. As he pulled into his house, he could not even recall the drive. The only thing he did remember was the beautiful Carmella. He could not wait to tell Angelo that he met his future wife. The Vincent Anthony family tree had just taken root.

Chapter 9

The restaurant had been named "*Cucino Italiano*" and had become the best restaurant in Peoria. Angelo was a terrific proprietor. He catered to and charmed the clientele. He cared about his staff. He gave personal attention to food preparation, and mostly, he felt he had brought a little part of his homeland to this place. When Vinny walked in, as he always did, Angelo raced to embrace him and kiss him on both cheeks. He would turn to all his patrons and proudly announce, "Ladies and Gentlemen, may I introduce you to my partner and best friend, Vincent Anthony."

"Angelo, come sit with me. I want to talk with you." Vinny had a special request of Angelo.

Vinny had been seeing Carmella for three months. He had been working hard at the stock yards and was doing well. He had been meeting more and more prominent Peoria people and was being offered the chance to become a silent partner in a new Peoria brewery once prohibition was over. Angelo would not know of this partnership. It wasn't he wanted to withhold this information. Vinny didn't want to have to explain how he could have accumulated such a sizeable sum of money for such an investment. With all that was going on, Vinny knew he still felt he was not complete with his life dreams. Vinny had already contacted his two brothers and told them of his plans. Their reaction was one of family approval. Vinny wanted to share his plan with the person who knew him best, Angelo.

The two men went to the back of the restaurant to a table that was always held for the most important patrons. "Angelo, you know we have been together for almost two years. You have helped me, educated me, and backed me. What I have I owe to you. I want to get married to Carmella Travato. It would honor me for you to be my best man and the godfather of our first child Carmella will most certainly bear. As my wedding gift to you, I want you to be the sole owner of this restaurant. You and you alone make this business a success. You and you alone should reap the rewards of your hard work. I want to get married in three months on October 1st. I have sent word to both my brothers and my parents. I have asked my parents to come to America. It has six years since I left them in Gizzeria. They are getting up in age and I want them close to me so I can care for them and see that the last days of their lives are days of faith, family and friends. I am working with the bank to find a house that I can buy for them. I can only pray that I can find a place where they will be happy in the Midwest. What will they do without the smell of the sea, the hills of Italy? Pray for me Angelo. Tonight, I intend to ask Carmella to marry me." As the tears crept into his eyes, he looked at Angelo for him to take up the conversation.

"Vincent Anthony, you are truly an amazing man. I knew it the first time we met. You are a man of integrity, a man of heart. You do me such a great honor to be your friend, an honor to be your best man, and a brother at heart. I will always be there for your family and you. I will not argue with you regarding the restaurant because I know, once you make up your mind, it is senseless to try to change it. I thank you. Vincent, congratulations, Carmella will make you a wonderful wife. Now we must celebrate!" Angelo stood and yelled to one of the waiters, "Bring me a bottle of our best wine for my friend. He is getting married in October. Put a bottle of wine on every table so that all here tonight will help me celebrate this joyous occasion." The entire restaurant began clapping. Vinny stood with the grace of a crowned prince ready to claim his princess. He extended his right arm to the tables at the far left of the restaurant, slowly bent at the waist, and with the gesture of appreciation, took a slow quarter circle bow until his arm reached the right side of the restaurant.

Vinny had three glasses of wine with Angelo. Why is it that when one drinks, the one thing people always do is reminisce? Angelo and Vinny laughed at some of the stories. They cried at how far they had come and the memories of their past. They sat in silence and let their lives pass through their veins and settle in their hearts. Vinny stood. "Wish me luck, my friend. I know I could not go on without this woman. She makes my life whole. I look forward to the future knowing she will be a part of it." The two embraced and kissed each other on each cheek and smiled. A goodbye was not necessary or appropriate. They both knew that each would be there for each other until they passed on to another world. Vinny walked to the door of the restaurant and approached his parked car.

As Vinny opened the door to his car, he looked back and knew he would see Angelo in the doorway of the restaurant. "Bravo, Bravo."

Vinny waved, got in his car and headed for Toluca.

It took Vinny an hour to get to the Travato home. He didn't feel at all nervous. Vinny could only feel the anticipation of seeing Carmella. He knocked on the door. Mrs. Travato answered. She looked at Vinny, reached for his hand and led him into the parlor. No words were spoken. Mr. Travato looked up, nodded his head and swept his hand toward the kitchen. Vinny walked into the kitchen to find Carmella sitting at the table. She had pulled her hair back tied in a white ribbon. She wore a simple straight linen white dress. As her eyes met Vinny's, she stood and walked toward him. Hand in hand they walked out the back door and stood in the yard. The sky was filled with stars, not a cloud in sight. The moon was bright with a faint hue. It was Vinny who spoke first,

"Carmella, you are the most beautiful person I have ever met. Your beauty is not just visible beauty, but the beauty inside your body, the tenderness of your heart, the humble nature of your soul; it has left me where I worship you. I cannot live without you. I love you. I need you as much as the air I breathe. I am here to ask you to marry me, to be my wife, to bear my children. I will make you proud. Carmella, will you marry me?" He brought her hands to his lips and gently kissed them.

Carmella let her senses capture the moment from the warmth of his lips on her hand to the warmth that was sent through her body like electricity through a wire. "Vincent, I love you too. I will marry you. You captured my heart the first time I saw you. With each time we went out, you treated me like I was special and were always a gentleman. When we first kissed, you were gentle. You did not rush our relationship. I must admit to you, I cannot wait for our wedding night to show you how much I love you." She put her hand on the Vinny's neck and pulled him toward her. She kissed him. They held each other tightly. "Let's go into the house and let my parents know of our plans."

Vinny had many more glasses of wine that night. So much that Mr. Travato asked that he stay over night. A couch had never felt so good. While he drifted off to a sound slumber knowing his head would cry out in the morning, for the moment, he wanted to remember this night for ever.

"No amount of wine will ever erase the memory of my beautiful Carmella's full lips saying I will marry you. Before I sleep, Heavenly Father, in your name I pray. May God and our Lord always know, Carmella and I put forward our lives to our Faith, our Family and our Friends. Amen".

Chapter 10

October 1, 1930 was a night to remember, the night the prophecy was fulfilled for the Antonini family. "Dearly beloved, we are gathered in this house of God, to marry Carmella Rosa Travato to Vincent Dominic Anthony . . . for the Travato family to join with the Antonini family. Saint Patrick's Church is so blessed to have these wonderful people be a part of this church and to hold their most solemn ceremony in its midst. From the turnout, it is obvious that you both are loved by your family and friends."

Vinny did not hear much of the following words. As he looked out at the faces in the church, he could see his Italian and American history. Angelo, his brothers and Marianno stood at his side. In the front row sat his mother and father. Both had aged but they still looked like they had the strength to climb the hills of Italy. Their skin was still a light mocha from the sun, and their smiles were in fact the sun to him. He looked at his mother, so saintly in his eyes. "I love you." He mouthed and blew her a kiss. He glanced at his father who still looked like he could wrestle the toughest ram. No words had to be spoken between them. Both nodded with pride and smiled at each other, *No Limits, no Fear, no Remorse.*

Vincent was happy that his parents were willing to come to America and leave their friends and ancestry behind. They truly seemed to love the house he had bought for them high on the Peoria bluffs overlooking the river. His mother thought he must be rich to be able to buy such a house. His banker got this place for next to nothing. Vincent had put in a garden for them and some vegetables were actually harvested. Behind them sat the many people who he had cultivated from his working and personal relationships over the past two years. Vinny's mind seemed to wander all over the place. *Where could one go in Peoria and see such a diverse group, from stock yard handlers, fisherman, hunters, and men of questionable business interests, bankers, politicians, friends and family. I know that I have accomplished more than one could wish. I pray dear Lord that I have not disappointed you in what I am. I do wish to thank you for my family, my beautiful Carmella and my family and friends.* Before he could finish his thoughts, the wedding march sounded and Carmella and her father stood at the back of the church. For a fleeting second, Vincent thought, *The Lord is ready to take me to heaven. My knees are ready to give way, and there entering the back of the church is the angel who is to take me to heaven. Take a deep breath, close your eyes.* He reopened his eyes and had a smile as wide as the Golden Gate bridge as his angel assumed her position by his side.

Carmella was standing beside him. Her father gave her away. Candles were lit, songs were sung and the vows were shared. It was a traditional but special Catholic wedding. At the cake cutting ceremony, the newly weds made sure to visit briefly with each guest. "Angelo, you were the "best" best man to ever stand next to a groom. But you cried more than the parents of the bride." Carmella's brother, Marianno, stood beside Angelo during the ceremony. Vinny could not hide his amusement, "Marianno my new brother. Never have I seen a man who stood so straight, looked so solemn in such a perfectly pressed suit. If I did not know better, Mr. Hobbs the mortician must have mistaken you for his next corpse and embalmed you instead. My friend, the wedding is over. Drink some wine, eat some food, and dance the night away. We can now have fun." It was obvious. Marianno had bought the suit for the wedding and had probably never had to wear a tie this long.

"My son, you have made this family proud. When you left Italy, your mother and I went to see Father Stephano every day to pray for your safety, good health and good fortune. Our dream for the family to be reunited has come true. Now you can be the first to make the family grow. I want to give you my pocket watch. It was my father's. Pass it on to your son." The watch was beautiful. Vincent had never seen the watch. It had the family name engraved on the ornate gold watch cover.

"Thank you father. It is an honor to carry such a treasure. It will be kept in a safe place and only displayed at the most prestigious of occasions."

Antonio and Dominic had stood beside Marianno. Now both were competing to see who could drink the most wine. "You two have always been trouble. Mind your manners or I will have our father teach you some." They all laughed, hugged, and looked admiringly, reverently at their father and mother. "But when you dance with my Carmella, you make sure you tell her what a great brother you have and how lucky she is to have me for a husband."

"Brother, it is better we just keep our mouths shut. We know how many Italian girls you chased and how many of them wanted you for their husband. We will just stick to how wonderful your brothers are and how we made you successful." Again laughter and hugs all around were enjoyed by all.

"Vincent, your wedding was beautiful. Your family is what I expected, truly wonderful and full of charm and humility. I know this is your wedding day, but I have a gift from a past friend. Please accept it from me. He could not be here but wanted you to know that he thinks of you often and thanks you for always keeping your word. I also want you to know that we are proceeding with the building of the distillery. If you could come by the bank next week, we need to sign some papers with myself and the other partners in this venture so that we will be positioned to open once the liquor laws are repealed. I promised that you would have an investment that would serve your family for years to come. Together, may our good fortunes continue." With that brief exchange, Mr. Hamilton handed Vinny an envelope and returned to a group of men Vinny did not know. Vinny took the envelope and placed it in a pocket inside his suit. He would look at the contents later.

"Vincent, you have ignored me enough. Come with me, I want to introduce you to my mother's sister and other members of my family who you have not met. They are all excited to meet this man who captured my heart. Be brave, my prince. I will keep you humble as you try to charm them. Have I told you today how handsome you look and how much I look forward to tonight?" With a twinkle in her eye and mischief in her heart, Vinny wanted to grab her and kiss her right then. How could a man worship a woman as he did her? She could ask him to do anything and he would do it twice just to make sure he made her happy and met with satisfaction.

"Carmella, we have only been married for an hour and already I am at your mercy, being tugged around like one of the cattle at the stockyard. Please tell me there will be no pain to this exorcism I am about to have performed on me." He tried to show his displeasure but could not hide how he really felt as he cradled her hand and followed her.

"You are such a baby, Mr. Anthony." Carmella could always tease him and bring a smile.

"You are such a temptress, Mrs. Anthony."

"Then let's get through this night so we can be on our way to Chicago for our honeymoon."

Chapter 11

When Vincent had told Mr. Hamilton he was going to spend his honeymoon in Chicago during one of his visits to the bank, Mr. Hamilton demanded Vincent let him make the arrangements. He would not take no for an answer no matter how much Vincent stated he did not want to impose on him. It came to pass by the graces of Mr. Hamilton the Anthonys were going to spend their honeymoon at the Drake Hotel in Chicago. He had arranged for a suite the size of past houses Vinny had lived. Mr. Hamilton also informed a past acquaintance of Vinny's intentions.

The drive took four hours and most of the evening but the newlyweds did not seem to notice the time or the miles. They just sat quietly anticipating the night, their first passionate night as husband and wife. Somewhere between Peoria and Chicago, they did stop to get gas and something to drink. Vinny could swear everyone in the little country store gas stop was staring at Carmella and thinking how beautiful she was. Of course Vinny knew they must be thinking how important he must be to have such a wife. "How can I be humble when I am with Carmella?"

They arrived around 10:00 pm at the Drake. A bellman met them at the side of the road and helped them out of the car. "You must be Mr. and Mrs. Anthony. Welcome to the Drake. We will park your car and take your bags to your room. There will be no need to stop at the front desk. Here is your room key. Enjoy your stay sir."

Vinny was at a loss. How did they know who he was? "Excuse me. Here is something for your service. But we have never met and have never stayed at this hotel, how did you know who we were?" Vinny tried to give the man a $5 bill.

"Sir, that is most gracious. But I cannot take your money. All employees here in the hotel were given a picture of your wife and you. We are to be at your disposal. I cannot take your money." But before he could get away and park the car, Vinny grabbed his arm.

"Young man, I must insist that you accept my offer. You are performing a service for me and I always reward quality service, especially from someone who seems happy performing it. I once did such services where often I was taken for granted. I want you to know I appreciate your service and have enjoyed our brief encounter. So again, I insist that you accept my offer." Vinny placed the $5 dollar bill in the man's hand, and shook his hand tightly. "Thank you again." Vinny turned and with Carmella proceeded to their room. He was afraid who might be watching him. A picture of Carmella and him had been taken and circulated without their knowledge. Only one person wielded that kind of power that he knew. Vinny then remembered the envelope in his inside pocket.

"Vinny, I had no idea that you went so out of your way to make this evening so special. I am so impressed. Do we have this kind of money for such luxuries? Don't answer until we are going back to Peoria. I do not want anything to disrupt the fairy tale I am living right at this moment. Let's get to our room. I am really tired from the wedding and drive. Let's make the most of the rest of the time we have before we go to sleep." Her tease was enough to make Vinny want to climb the side of the building in hopes of getting to his suite faster.

"My Lord in Heaven, Vinny, this room is like entering into paradise." The room was spectacular with a balcony overlooking Michigan Avenue.

"Vinny, this room has a living room so spacious we could house a whole family in here." The room had a luxurious couch, two huge chairs for reading, high ceilings with crown molding and colorful art on the walls. "Vinny, come here. Have you ever seen such a bathroom in your life?"

As for the bathroom, Vinny could only remember being in one other such an ornate bathroom. That one was in Madam Marge's establishment. When he had gone back to her establishment to again thank her for helping him, he needed to use her facilities before returning. He still remembered the exchange. "Madame, here is something for you to share as you like with your ladies for the services the other night. I know that you probably received some compensation from others, but because of my partners and my good fortune, we felt we should share some with you. I will not accept no for an answer. I would however require directions to the men's bathroom." When he came back, Madame Marge had looked inside the envelope he had given her before visiting the bathroom.

"Mr. Anthony, you are truly a gentleman of honor. I will share this with my ladies. You truly understand people. We were honored to help you out. We will always be indebted to you. All you have to do is ask."

Carmella interrupted his daydreaming with a cry that one couldn't differentiate as coming from fright or total awe. "Vinny, come see this bedroom. Hurry! Oh Vincent my darling, this is the most romantic room anyone could have ever imagined for a wedding night. "To say this room was the master bedroom was an understatement. The room was as spacious as the living room. Vinny had never seen such a big bed. Four large wood bedposts rose from the floor to the ceiling like columns he had once seen in Rome. Chiffon had been draped from all four posts. Pillows were everywhere. The walls seem to be covered in maroon velvet. Pictures of statues, fountains and flowers were on the walls. Fresh flowers were on the tables and the candles that were lit around the room provided a warm faint glow like a shrine. Carmella grabbed Vinny and kissed him so hard that he actually heard his back crack. "Vinny, everything is perfect. Thank you, thank you."

"This is just for you, Carmella on our special night. I love you." What else could he say? Whoever reserved this particular hotel and room deserved a special thank you. Was it Hamilton or . . . Capone? It did not matter. Nothing was going to spoil this night. It was special. Carmella was a special lady. Their wedding was a special time in their lives. This hotel was a special place for their wedding night. And this bedroom was soon to be a special room for their love making.

As Vinny waited patiently for Carmella to finish her preparation in the bathroom for their love tryst that would last for hours, Vinny could not know just how special this night would be. Their love making was like everything else about the two. They did not need a sex manual to figure out what to do to satisfy each other. They entwined their bodies so tightly, they became as one. They did not rush. The two made love in the glow of the room with their bodies tingling with each touch of the hand or lips long into the night.

As Carmella drifted off to sleep, Vinny got out of bed and went to the closet where the envelope was in his suit pocket. He retrieved the envelope and opened it.

> *To The Lovely Carmella and My friend Vincent,*
>
> *Please accept the wedding gift that I have given to Mr. Hamilton. He will handle the transaction as he has always done. It is my honor to have you stay in my city for your wedding night. I hope you enjoy Chicago and this hotel. I have taken the liberty and arranged for a private Lake Michigan cruise and dinner tomorrow night. The musicians and singer are some of my favorites in the city. If you have*

> time after the cruise, maybe you can visit one of my establishments for a champagne toast to your first day as a married couple. A driver and car will be at your disposal for the entire evening. A.

Uneasiness crept over Vincent's entire body. He knew he could not turn down the gift or evening that had been presented. Yet he did not want Carmella to know about his relationship with a gangster. He decided not to show her the note or tell her about the "transaction" that was conveyed in the note. He would deal with Mr. Hamilton and the transaction later.

The car was ready when Carmella and Vincent walked out of the Drake. He did not tell her what was planned for the evening because he did not really know the details, only the grand scheme. "Sir, my name is Ermanno. I am at your disposal for the evening. All you have to do is ask and I will make it happen. If you are ready, we will head to the lake for your dining experience." With the passengers loaded into the car, Ermanno drove the couple to the Chicago Pier where a large boat sat in the harbor with lights from head to tail. It seemed the entire gangplank was lined with men standing at attention in white waist coats and gloves. Carmella looked at Vincent. "Vincent, this is beautiful and quite the surprise. I had no idea we would have our first dinner on the water. You truly are a man of surprises."

"My first dream of a new life in America was experienced on a boat. Having my true love with me is my dream come true. This too should come true on a boat." Vincent did not know what else to say. This was going to be a surprise night for him as well.

The evening was perfect. The stars were out in full. The moon hung bright over the lakes horizon and seemed to light up all of Lake Michigan. The air was just cool enough that when they stood by the rail, being in each others arms seemed to take the chill off. They were the only two passengers that night. A full orchestra played while the boat silently motored parallel to the shoreline of Lake Michigan and they ate. The meal was more than superb. It was a combination of delicacies from America, and Italy. The desserts must have been prepared by a French Master Chef. "Vincent, women dream about such a night. I love you, my husband. I will tell our children of the romantic night you prepared for me." As she wiped a lone tear from her face with her napkin, Vincent rose from his chair.

"My beautiful Carmella, would you like to dance with the man who will love you until the day he dies. May our children know the love we share for each other and the happiness we receive from each other. Come dance with me so that I can squeeze you tight, kiss your neck and whisper in your ear. I can only hope prying eyes will not be too envious of us." This brought a smile to her lips.

There was still one more question that had to be answered. Was he going to see A tonight? If he did, how would Carmella react? How was this night going to end?

Chapter 12

The boat had docked and the gangplanks were laid to provide the honeymoon guests exit to the mainland. The cruise had come to an end. As Carmella and Vincent departed, Vincent could see his driver and car at the ready. He checked his watch, 10:30. Carmella saw him check his watch. "Vincent, are you checking the time? Darling, it is early. I promise not to keep you out to late, but we are in Chicago. The night is young. Let's have our driver drive along the lake then we can go back to the hotel and to our boudoir. OK?"

"I will take my queen anywhere she so desires. My love, your chariot waits." As they approached the car, the driver opened the door and extended his hand to Carmella. As any royalty would do, she took his hand and gracefully glided into the backseat.

"Sir, where would you like for me to take you?"

Vincent responded per his new bride's wishes, "Ermanno, may we take a drive along the lakeshore. My wife and I have never seen the city at night. Are there other points of interest we should see before we head to our hotel?"

With the polish of an experienced ambassador, Ermanno made his suggestion. For Vincent, he could only silently pray that this tour of Chicago landmarks would continue to positively please his new wife. "Sir, the drive is an excellent thought. The lake is calm, the moon is bright and the city lights will reflect quite well. May I suggest we take Lake Shore Drive up to the north end, and then return to the city for an evening toast at one of Chicago's finest nightclubs? Many of Chicago's finest often go there."

"OH VINCENT, CAN WE?"

"Ermanno, won't we have a problem getting into such a frequented nightclub?" You could almost hear the wishful response that Vincent wanted to hear in his voice. Vincent knew that Ermanno would have no problem getting them into the nightclub.

"Mr. Anthony, as you know, I have connections with the manager of the club. I think you are teasing Mrs. Anthony. I am sure Mrs. Anthony and you will be able to gain entry." Ermanno turned and looked at Carmella. "Mrs. Anthony, I am glad that you want to experience this nightclub. It has the best entertainment in Chicago. Mr. Anthony is being quite the joker. Mr. Anthony has arranged for a bottle of Champagne and a table for a toast to the longevity of your marriage. Mr. Anthony, shall I proceed with the lakeshore drive?"

"Ermanno, I had no idea you could so eloquently convey my plans for the night. Now my wife expects a most exciting night. Let's go." The car engine roared and Ermanno headed the car north along Lake Shore Drive.

"Vincent, this night is so beautiful. You said you could see the sea from your home in Italy. I am dreaming we are driving along the sea coast in Italy. I want you to have loved me in Italy as you do here in America."

As the car turned to head back into the city, Vincent could only wish Carmella and he were in Italy. Vincent was so anxious of what could unfold in the nightclub. He could hear his father. "Things may happen which you cannot control. Think with your head, act with your heart. NO FEAR."

The car stopped at the front of an unassuming building. Two large men stood by the door. Obviously, they were to ensure those who entered the building were invitees. As Ermanno opened the car door and the couple climbed out, the two men approached. "Mr. and Mrs. Anthony, welcome to the Big Easy Nightclub. We have your table ready." One of the men knocked on the door.

A man with a tuxedo opened the door. "Ah, Mr. and Mrs. Anthony, my name is Benito. May I take you to your table?" Benito held out his arm for Carmella to take. As they entered the building, Vincent was amazed how large and luxurious the room was. As Benito led them across the room to a table which had been roped off, everyone in the nightclub seemed to be straining to see which important person had entered. The table had the whitest table cloth with crystal water glasses. In the center of their table was a tall white candle in a sterling silver candle holder. On one of the chairs were a dozen roses. A bottle of Champagne was placed next to the other chair. As Benito and Carmella reached the table, Benito led Carmella to the chair with the roses. He picked up the roses and pulled it back for Carmella to sit. He placed the roses in her arms and said, "Congratulations Mrs. Anthony." He quickly moved to pull the chair out for Vincent. "Mr. Anthony, may I pour the Champagne?"

The Champagne was poured and a silent signal was made to the orchestra. The piano player began to play some melodic tune very softly. An announcer walked to the center of the stage and spoke into a microphone. "Ladies and gentlemen, we have a special guest here tonight who wishes you join him in a toast." The room darkened and a spot light focused on Carmella's and Vincent's table. Another spotlight suddenly focused on a table on the other side of the room. This table had curtains and gave the appearance of an atmosphere for seclusion. This table was for the very elite. A man at the table rose. At his table were men and women dressed in the finest of apparel. The room went silent. He had no microphone but when he spoke, all could hear his voice.

"I want to make a toast to a couple who have come to my favorite club to celebrate their wedding." Carmella was completely speechless as she realized the gentleman was talking about them. She reached over and squeezed Vincent's hand to let him know how special he was making her feel. "I know this man as honorable. He is a man of faith and family. His marriage to such a beautiful woman also tells me he has an eye for the finer things in life. So please raise your glasses to Mr. and Mrs. Anthony. May Mr. Anthony be not so busy making a living he forgets to make a life. Salute" He raised his glass and slightly moved it toward Vincent. Vincent raised his Champagne glass and gestured back. Then Vincent turned and touched glasses with Carmella. Both took a sip of Champagne.

"Vincent wasn't it nice of the owner to give us a toast. Do you know his name? He seems to know you?" With the darkening of room, and even though there was a spotlight, the gentlemen was on the other side of the room. Carmella did not recognize him or notice the scar on the side of his face.

"Carmella, he is the owner of this place. As Ermanno said, arrangements had been made for this night. You are right. It was nice for him to give a toast. He probably does it for every special event. It is part of the entertainment and keeps people coming back. I believe his first name is Al." Vincent was spared more conversation because the band started playing and a singer started her set at the microphone. Carmella was totally entranced in the performance. When the singer encouraged the audience to get up and dance, Vincent took Carmella's hand and led her to the dance floor. At around 12:00, Vincent suggested they return to the hotel. On the way out, he led Carmella over to the owners table to introduce her and to thank his host. As he approached, he did not see his host. "Excuse me, my wife and I would liked to thank our host for the toast and the wonderful table and champagne. Has he left?"

Vincent was relieved when he heard the response, "Yes, something came up that required his personal attention."

"Would you be so kind to inform him my wife and I came by to extend our appreciation for the night?

One of the men rose and extended his hand to Carmella. "Mrs. Anthony, I will ensure your gratitude will be passed along. I am sure he would have liked to meet you. Have a great stay in Chicago and a wonderful marriage."

Ermanno and the car were waiting at the front door when they came out. "Let's go to the hotel Ermanno. This has been some tiring night for us."

When they reached their hotel room, Carmella led Vincent straight to the bedroom. "Vincent, you gave me an evening that I will never forget. Now I want to love you in such a way that you will never forget." As Carmella took off her evening clothes, Vincent could not help but notice Carmella had an incredible body. Her voluptuous breasts seemed to defy the laws of gravity. Her stomach was flat and led down to her rounded hips. Her legs were long and lean that would make any nightclub dancer envious. As for her butt, you could serve tea off that perfectly rounded butt.

Little did Vincent know as they reached climax together after a slow passionate sexual encounter and exchanges of "I love you now and forever" the seeds of their passion had reached their destination of purpose. Nine months later, Carmella would bear a son. It would take only five weeks for Vinny to learn Carmella was not only the most beautiful women he had ever met and one of the most amorous lovers one could ever want, but also, one of the most fertile women he could have ever married.

Chapter 13

It had been a cold winter thus far in Peoria. Carmella was pregnant and due around Christmas. Vincent and Carmella's families were so excited about the upcoming birth that they contacted them daily to see how Carmella was feeling. Christmas in the year of 1930 came and went without a new arrival. Vincent had joked with Angel one night regarding a Christmas birth, "I bet in the month of December, God receives more prayers from Carmella's and my family for a Christmas birth that will be only second to the prayers for the birth of baby Jesus."

But on New Year's Eve, Carmella went into labor and delivered an 8 pound 8 ounce baby boy, Francis Samuel Anthony, at 2:00am January 1, 1931. The new parents had named their son after St. Francis of Assisi and planned to call him Frankie. He was a beautiful baby. His head was covered with cold black curly hair. His eyes were dark as the night. Round chubby cherub cheeks called out to be kissed. A sister, Thomasine, would join her brother a year and a half later.

When the parents of Carmella and Vincent came to see the baby at the hospital, Vincent knew their respective mothers would shed tears of joy. Little did they expect their fathers to be so emotional. "He looks like you did when you were born. Vincent, you have truly done our family proud. You have the first Antonini or Anthony born in America. You have made a life for our entire family here in America. You have grown to be a fine man, husband and now a father. I cannot tell you how much your mother and I love you. We are so proud to be your parents." This was only the second time Vincent had ever seen tears in his father's eyes.

Carmella's father was just as sentimental. He kissed his daughter's forehead, stroked her head as she lay on the hospital pillow. He leaned over and whispered in his daughter's ear. Vincent did not have to ask her what her father had said. The look Carmella gave her father, the love he knew they shared and the soft smile that came when she said, "Thank you father. I know." She turned to look at her mother. "Mother, when you get home, will you tell Marianno that my baby is so much more handsome than he was when he was born?" They both laughed. Vincent loved his wife's sense of humor. She could always make the moment so much better by being in the room.

"Carmella, you are a devil to want to tease your brother. But I will tell him. You know he will want to come and look for himself and he will say that Francis looks just like him. He will try to get Vincent into the argument you know. Vincent, Marianno will tell you Francis looks more like a Travato than an Anthony."

"I know Marianno. I will tell him our son has the brains of his mother and the heart of his father. Whoever he may look like will have to be a burden he has to carry because it is what it is. It won't matter because he will have no fear." With that comeback, Vincent glanced at his father. He had heard those last words before he left Italy and he wanted his father to know his son would carry them forward in whatever journey he was to follow.

Vincent went over to a small bag he had brought to the hospital. He reached in and produced two bottles of wine and opened them. "Vincent, can you bring wine into a hospital?" Carmella asked, fearing a nurse may soon enter her room.

"I brought this wine and these glasses so we I can make a toast to my perfect wife who gave me a most wonderful son, and also to have this blessed event shared by our two families as a moment for which we must give our thanks and celebrate. Everyone, please hold your glasses most high. To Carmella the love of my life; she graced my life by becoming my wife. She enriched my life by giving me a family. Now I toast the rest of you for making this family what it is today." Vincent had never been so happy. By marrying Carmella, he had inherited another family he loved as deeply as his own.

Carmella's family had a hunger for life that one could not escape. They viewed each day as a blessing from God. They never complained and could always find something to bring a smile or laughter. Vincent's parents got along so well with them. The two families would get together at least once a month to talk about the old country and reminisce. Of course, they would always talk about their grandchild and his many movements or sounds that predicted his future fame and fortune. "Francis is going to be famous in this town. I see him being possibly a cardinal, an owner of many properties, a banker, or maybe even a doctor. It is good we agree he is not going to be a farmer or raise farm animals." This seemed to be a foregone conclusion expressed by the grandfathers and a nurturing process that Vincent was to pursue. Of course, Vincent would always try to have the last word.

"It is nice that Carmella and I have been given your choices on how we are to raise our son. We can only hope to meet your expectations and that Frankie will enjoy the profession you have selected." Vincent would always sound tough but would then shake his head and laugh. "You all know that the men in our families really have no choice in this matter. The mothers always make the man in case you have forgotten. They only let us think we have input into their already made decisions."

Chapter 14

Much has been written about the circle of life. Vincent was to experience it in 1931. The birth of his son started the year off with emotional highs that left him in wonderment. He had reaffirmed he would always remember his roots, his trials and tribulations, and would never compromise his values or integrity or put his family at risk. He was about to experience the emotional highs and lows over the next 18 years that would again test his inner strength like never before.

Under the guidance of Henry Hamilton, Vincent had become a prominent person in Peoria. "Vincent, there is not a public figure or prominent leader in this city who doesn't respect you. You truly have won over the most cynical with your charm and eloquence. When we first met, I knew we would be friends and could both become very prosperous. Vincent, you have become a rich man. You remain humble and a man of modest means. I am the only person who knows that you are probably in the top ten richest men in Peoria." Henry Hamilton had invested Vincent's money wisely. The enthusiasm in his voice as he spoke was accompanied by a beaming smile. One could easily see he was proud of Vincent's success. After all, Vincent was his star pupil. Vincent would always listen to his proposals, then ask wonderful insightful probing questions. Henry would always take the time to ensure Vincent understood the pros and cons of every business deal. With Vincent's conservatism, Henry actually felt he personally had become more analytical and made better decisions.

"Vincent, together we have purchased surrounding land when valuable property had became available. We have invested in the stock market and had a run of extraordinary good fortune with the boom in the economy. We have the rewards to show why people call this period the so-called roaring twenties. What I am about to propose may seem counter productive to actions we have taken to date. And to be honest, my recommendation comes from being around you for these past years. Vincent, I want to propose to you that we take a very conservative position and cash out of most of your stocks in preparation for getting into the brewery business."

"Why Henry, did you say we should take a conservative position?" Vincent actually laughed out loud. "This is a first. You are always pushing me to go further. I remember you telling me to look to the clouds. That is where the future is when Charles Lindbergh made his first mail route from Chicago to Peoria to Springfield to St. Louis and back. I also remember how upset you were at local leaders who rejected Lindbergh's offer for Peoria to sponsor his trans-Atlantic flight. The plane would have been called the "Spirit of Peoria". I had my brother Dominic join with those investors in St. Louis. He did alright. But, if you say we need to look locally to invest our money, I will take your advice. I am assuming we will sell my stock portfolio you acquired: Radio Corporation of America, General Motors, aviation, and telephone stocks?"

"Yes, Vincent, I am suggesting the entire portfolio. I feel this is the right call. If I am reading the tea leaves correctly, here we are in June and the economy seems to be slowing and even in some cases contracting. We have had a great run in the stock market. I really think the stock market could go through a series of unsettling price declines."

Vincent followed Henry's recommendation and exited the stock market. When Vincent next met with Henry it was to go over final numbers from the sale of the stock. "Vincent, I received the final cash from the sale of your stock. It is now safely in the belly of my most protective vault. Here is the ledger with all the transactions and the final amount you have in my bank. I think you will find the amount to be most gratifying." Henry pushed the ledger over to Vincent for his review.

"My God, Henry. Is this for real? I knew we were doing well and that stocks had continued to rise over the years. But never in my wildest dreams could I have foretold these total dollars. I am in total disbelief."

What started out as a payoff for the one indiscretion he would hide to his dying day had multiplied ten fold into a fortune. Vincent had completed his transactions by July of 1929. Little did Vincent know that the stock market would hit its high in September of that year and would not regain this level for another twenty five years. By October, these declines caused investor anxiety and events to come to a historical head. The stock market crash of 1929 caused the most powerful to become most humble.

Others in Peoria had not been as fortunate. Vincent had heard that one of the most prominent landowner who had made his fortune in the mining business did not fare as well. Here was a man whose family ancestry went back to early settlers of the area. He was now bankrupt. Vincent had read of men killing themselves because of the losses they had encountered. Vincent could only shake his head and wonder. "I have had setbacks, but never to the point to kill myself. How could I do that to my family, my God? What would it say about me: I had such a dependence on money that I could not start again? I can never forget where I came from, how I got to where I am now, and what I need to teach my children so they never find themselves in such despair. They must learn to have no fear!"

Chapter 15

Prohibition had become increasingly unpopular during the 1920s. Peoria had gone through the 1920s as if "Repeal" of this unpopular law was just around the corner. Beer and alcohol was never in short supply. Vincent had told Henry that he would invest in a brewery when it was officially legal to brew. Henry understood but when the winds were shifting in Congress for action, he began in earnest to bring a major brewery to Peoria. On March 23, 1933, President Franklin Roosevelt signed the amendment to the Volstead Act known as the Cullen-Harrison Act, allowing the manufacture and sale of beer, alcohol and light wines. "Vincent, by the end of this year, we should see the ratification of the Twenty-first Amendment which makes it legal for a brewery in Peoria. We are positioned to be a partner in this new venture. I also did not have to commit your entire fortune to get this partnership. Congratulations Mister Brewmiester. You are in the alcohol manufacturing business."

It was in 1935, Vincent first noticed his long time friend Angel was having more and more health problems. "Vincent, you worry too much. It is only a cold. I will go to the doctor and get some medicine. I will be alright. I have to get back to my restaurant." That was always Angel's answer to "how are you feeling?" or "what have you been doing to yourself?" or "are you working too hard?"

But one morning, October 3, 1936, Vincent got a call from Angel. "Vincent, are you busy?" A cough interrupted his question.

"No, what is wrong? Is something wrong? You never call me."

"I seem to have a little problem (cough) that has come along. I need your help. Can you please come over to the restaurant? (Cough) I am sorry to have to ask you this, but can you please hurry?" (Cough)

"Angel, I am on my way. Keep calm. No Fear. I will be there in 10 minutes". There was no response. Vincent yelled to Carmella, "Something is wrong with Angel. I have to go to his restaurant. I will call when I know what is wrong." Carmella could tell by the panic in Vincent's voice that he felt this was an emergency. She did not have time to respond before she heard the door slam and Vincent's car start. The sound of gravel thrown by the tires caused her concern about Vincent's safety.

"Angel, where are you?" Vincent screamed as he entered the restaurant. At 9:00 in the morning, Vincent had never seen the restaurant so empty and quiet. An eerie feeling crept over him and he continued walking through the restaurant.

"Vincent, I am back by the telephone." Angel's answer was weak almost a whisper with an ever-present cough. Vincent ran to the sound of his voice.

Angel was sitting on the floor with the wall phone still in his hand. A large amount of blood was present on the front of his white shirt. He looked up at Vincent with hallowed, apologetic eyes. "My cold seems to have gotten the best of me. Can you take me to the hospital? I think I am very ill. I am sorry, Vincent. I had no one else to call."

"Shut up my friend. You know that I am always on call for you. I just wait around with bated breath for you to call so that I can hear what is going on in your life. Angel, can you walk?" Angel attempted a smile at his friend's attempt at sarcasm only to be interrupted by another cough and to spew more blood.

"I don't think I have the strength to walk, Vincent." Vincent did not hesitate. Action was needed and needed now. He bent down and, with an unearthly strength picked up Angel as if he was a young boy. He hustled through the restaurant to his car. He placed Angel in the passenger seat and rushed him to the hospital. Vincent had never had doubts about his life, but for the first time, he had an unsettled feeling that he wanted to dismiss, fear that his friend was in a life or death situation.

Vincent slid his car into the entrance of St. Francis Hospital. He leaped out of the car, swung open the passenger's car door, grabbed Angel and made his way into the hospital entrance. "We need help, get a doctor over here." A nurse and an attendant in their sterile white uniforms and shoes rushed to the two men with a gurney. Vincent and the attendant placed Angel on the gurney.

"Vincent, you are my brother, my family. You have always been my strength, my life and for this I love you. Take care of my restaurant. It is our legacy as friends. Please say a prayer for me." Angel closed his eyes and stopped breathing. Angelo Bartello had died. And on that night, a piece of Vincent also died. Only as he left the hospital that night could his body feel the exhaustion of the events that had occurred.

Vincent learned later that Angel had numerous health problems that had gone untreated. He had black lung, pneumonia, and cancer of the lungs. Only God knew where else the cancer had spread.

On a sunny day in the autumn of 1936, Vincent gave the eulogy for his best friend, Angel. "As I look out over this gathering who have come to remember my friend Angel, I see faces laden with sadness. I too first had moments of despair and questions of why my friend had to leave us so soon. Angel was not your ordinary man. He was a special man. He gave when he himself was in need. He shared regardless of the request. He befriended those who were lost. He loved man, he loved nature and, most of all, he loved his God. To those of us here in this celestial, holy setting, weep not for Angel. He is with his God, our God. AND our God is all knowing and loving. Angel is in the place he called his final reward. Angel, my friend, I will keep you alive in all I do. You will be remembered by your friends and me until we can join you. Angelo Joseph Bartello, we will miss you. My friend, we now say a prayer that has been one my family has said for many years. I hope it serves you well and meets with your approval. Let us pray. Dear God in Heaven most high. May God and our Lord always know, Angelo Joseph Bartello put forward his life for his Faith, his Family and his Friends. Please watch over our friend, Angel, who left us to enter into the kingdom of heaven. He is a man who has served well. Amen."

Chapter 16

Vincent's father had started to show his age as he sat at the Sunday dinner that had become an Antonini family ritual after Angel's death. Vincent did not want a week to pass that he did not have personal contact with those he loved most. "Vincent, I have been hearing good and bad things from our friends and family back in Italy. As you know, after you left, a man named Benito Mussolini became Prime Minister of Italy. He has done some good things for Italy. He had a public works program that employed many people and helped with the water and sewer problems of Italy. He created many new jobs and helped with the public transportation of our country. But he is power hungry. He now calls himself Il Duce and has self proclaimed himself, "*His Excellency Benito Mussolini, Head of Government, Duce of Fascism, and Founder of the Empire*". I am hearing that he is becoming very close with Germany and that Germany is looking to expel Jews from their country. Germany is said to want to create a master race. What is this world coming to? Do you think Germany is heading for a war? Could they draw Italy into it? Where would America stand?"

"I have been reading that one of our Ambassadors, Mr. Joseph Kennedy, is saying that Germany is only trying to address issues in their country and America should stay out of their political issues. I am not so sure what is going to happen, but if something does happen, we are now Americans. This country took us in and our family has prospered. If a situation arises where America is threatened, we would have to take an American stance as our gesture to give back."

The Corporate Chameleon

Two weeks later on September 1, 1939, Germany declared war and invaded Poland. It would be only a matter of time before subsequent declarations of war on Germany were taken by most of the countries in the British Commonwealth and France. World War II had started. As with most families in America, the war was about to have an impact the Anthony family.

Well into 1941, a large majority of the American public continued to oppose any direct military intervention into the conflict. This war was viewed as a European issue and America should stay away from taking sides. However, Germany and the United States were engaged in naval warfare in the North Atlantic as early as October 1941. While these conflicts were actually occurring, the United States remained undeclared and continued to officially remain in a neutral political position. By 1940, it was a foregone conclusion that the United States was going to be brought into the war. Frankie Anthony decided he must answer the call. He would represent the family and enlisted in the United States Army.

Frankie did not consult with his father. At one of the family Sunday dinners, he asked for everyone's attention. "This family knows that this European war is going to demand America get involved. Fighting is taking place all over the globe. If we are to protect our family here in the heart of America, I felt an Anthony was obligated to do his part for the American way. I am that Anthony. Last week, I enlisted in the Army. I believe the time will come when America will send troops to Europe and is quite near. When the day comes that soldiers are needed to fight, I will be there. Father, Mother, I know I am young, but you have brought me up and have always told me to stand up for what I believe. Father I am a man and ready to do my part. You came to America when you were my age. I will return to Europe. I will do my part, show No Fear, and return." The room was silent as he sat down.

Jim A. Roppa

"Son, you have made your decision. This family will respect it and can only pray for your safety. We are proud of you." Vincent spoke with authority, but his heart was filled with concern and apprehensions.

As fate would have it, Frankie ended up in the invasion campaign of Italy as an infantry foot soldier in the U.S. Fifth Army. On September 9, 1943, ground forces of the U.S. 5th Army landed at Salerno, Italy against heavy German resistance. Over the course of the days that followed, no campaign in western Europe cost more in terms of wounded or loss of life suffered by infantry forces. The German 10th Army came close to repelling the Salerno landing. While Frankie did not lose his life in the war, he did lose his lifes' purpose and way. Three events would unfold in this campaign which would shape the rest of Frankie's adult life.

Chapter 17

"Frankie, you scared?" It was Mike Kelly, a Peoria friend who had enlisted with Frankie. Mike was a typical youthful looking 18 year old Irish kid with bright red hair. Mike was the jokester of the outfit. But there was no hint of frivolity in his voice as they sat shoulder to shoulder in a landing craft.

Frankie wasn't sure anything could come out of his mouth. He took a huge deep breath and yelled back. "Hell yes Mike. Listen, that noise you are hearing is the enemy. We can have no compassion for the enemy. We have got to kill those bastards if we ever want to see home again. When we hit the beach, don't run straight, run in a zigzag pattern. Shoot at anything that moves ahead of you. And if I hit the ground, you hit the ground. I will cover your ass, you cover mine. Have No Fear. We can do this. Sound like a plan?" The door to the landing craft opened before Mike could answer.

The two literally had to jump from their landing craft into knee high surf. Water splashed up over their boots but neither felt anything. Both could have pissed themselves and not known it. There was only one thing on their mind. Find some cover on the beach and live to see tomorrow.

"Frankie, we made it. We are alive. I can hardly breathe. I need to catch my breath." Mike and Frankie had run, dodged, and miraculously made it to a little mound of turf which gave them some cover from gun fire.

"Mikey, we have got to get off this sand and run to those trees over there and dig in. Then we can see where the hell we need to go with the rest of our company." Frankie took off and dove behind a large clump of scraggly trees. His entire body was saturated with sweat or sea water. Who could tell the difference? Both were salty. He turned to see if Mikey was coming. Mikey was 50 yards behind him, face down. "Mikey, Mikey, are you all right?" No response. Mikey did not move. Frankie put down his gun and ran back to Mikey. He grabbed Mikey's shirt and back pack and pulled him with every ounce of his God given strength back to where he left his gun and some semblance of protection. "Mikey" He turned Mikey over. Mikey had no face. Whatever had hit him had hit him in the nose and seemed to explode out the back of his head. Brain matter was everywhere in his helmet. Frankie's mouth opened and he screamed but no sound was heard.

"Soldier, unless you get your ass moving, you will be dead too." Frankie looked up to see a sergeant crouching behind an adjoining tree. "Don't you ever leave your gun again! Hear me?" The sergeant took off. Frankie grabbed his gun and headed off in the same direction. For the rest of his life, no matter how much alcohol Frankie would drink, he would forever see Mikey's bloody face each night in his nightmares. It was always the same dream. Mikey would be telling a joke with his eyes sparkling, his freckled cheeks grinning, then a loud bang. Mikey's bright red hair would start to ooze blood. His hair would become matted and a darker wet red. Mikey's face would be severely disfigured with a huge hole with brain matter exposed. Frankie would just sit there staring at the hole and wonder if he was like the Dutch boy who stuck his finger in the dyke to stop the ocean from coming in, could he stop the blood? From the eventful day forward, Frankie slept very little.

The 5th Army took Sicily and began to move north. Little did Frankie know that the German army felt that the defense of Italy was to be a fight to the death. To lose Italy was to open the door to Germany itself. Therefore, the Germans were to make the most of the natural defensive geography of Central Italy.

Orders were given by the highest German command to prepare a series of defensive lines across Italy south of Rome. Two lines were to delay the Allied advance to buy time to prepare the most formidable defensive position on the west of the Apennine Mountains.

"Damn it. Are we ever going to move from this position? We have been stalled for months. I want to get to Rome. Then we can meet some of these beautiful Italian women I been hearing so much about. I think we have earned a night of hot passionate sex, don't you Anthony. Hell, I may just screw one of your long lost cousins." Jerry Craig was a muscular tall farm boy from Iowa who loved to tease Frankie. The two had spun up a friendship fighting side by side for the past six months. Frankie liked Jerry but was a little sensitive to the constant Italian jokes and references. But hell, in six months, Jerry had become Frankie's best friend and had gained Frankie's trust and loyalty.

"Aren't you going to find the girls a little out of your league? I thought your pick up line was baaaaa. If they won't put on a wool sweater, you won't be able to get your dick hard."

"Fuck you Frankie. We will see who fucks the prettiest girl. I got five bucks says my dick will drill the prettiest Dago in Italy. You in?"

Suddenly, the two were interrupted by their sergeant. "Hey, we got some guys cut off from our lines up about 10 miles from here. We need some volunteers to go get them. Any of you heroes here want to volunteer to go with me?" Sergeant Williams asked.

"I will." Frankie was always first in line just like his father. He also liked battle because he did not have to think, only kill men with funny shaped helmets.

"Damn it Frankie, you need a checkup from the head up. Why do you always have to be the first to volunteer?" Jerry Craig blurted, then mumbled something to the sergeant about he would go if Frankie goes. Something about he had to protect Frankie because Frankie was going to owe him five bucks.

Frankie could hear the gunfire and mortar explosions as they approached the mountainous terrain. The volunteer group of 10 men had been walking for over an hour. "Here is the plan. Anthony, Craig and I will circle around to the left, the rest of you men, when you hear us engage, come up over the ridge and give us some cover. Shoot at any flash or anything that moves. We will go in and lead our guys back here. When we get here, we will all high tail it back to our company. Got it?" Sergeant Williams was a brave leader. He always had a plan and never hesitated to take action. He never asked his men to do anything he did not do first. Frankie liked that about him.

Frankie, Craig, and the sergeant set off. The three made their way to a hill about two miles from the place they were to rendezvous once they retrieve their fellow soldiers. Once they got to the top of the hill, they surveyed what was before them and found themselves looking down on a firefight. It was almost surreal, like sitting in the balcony of a movie theater. Only this time, the story was real. They could see six American soldiers dug in and firing their weapons from behind a wall. On the other side around a small farm were 10 to 20 German soldiers trying to pick them off one by one. Frankie could see one machine gun set up with four German soldiers firing from a small enclosure. "Anthony, did you bring your mortar and shells? Set up. Fire a round or two and take out the machine gun. We will then run to the wall, cover the guys, and get them moving. If any of us gets hit, whoever is standing is to get the rest out of here and back to our company. Ready? Anthony, hit those bastards with your first shells or none of us may get back."

Frankie set up the mortar and set the angle he felt would hit the target. He loaded the shell and it fired almost as quickly as he let the shell fall into the cylinder. The shell exploded three feet from the machine gun. Frankie saw where the shell hit, quickly adjusted, reloaded and sent another round in a matter of seconds. It hit the target dead center. "Great adjustment Anthony. Four Germans down, now let's go get our guys and then hightail our asses out of here." The three men began to run as the Germans started to advance and began firing at their position.

As the three men got to the pinned down soldiers, the Germans decided to rush their positions. As the Germans began to advance, Williams yelled out to Craig to start leading the men out. At that moment, the sergeant was hit in the shoulder and dropped to the ground. Frankie was quick to return fire. "Jerry, go! I will provide cover and will take care of Sarg. You guys follow my buddy. Fire and fallback." The pinned down men were ready to move and started to shoot over their shoulders when Frankie yelled. "Go now!" Frankie leveled his rifle and started shooting at the advancing Germans. He hit a couple but more were getting close.

"Sarg, you ready to move?" About that time, one German soldier had reached their position. Frankie jumped to one side as a round barely missed him. Frankie fired and the German soldier let out a scream but did not fall. Frankie without hesitation charged the hit soldier and brought him down. He pulled out a knife he always carried and stabbed the soldier repeatedly in his neck to the point he almost severed his head. Frankie jumped back and looked at the soldier whose eyes stared back at him seemingly wondering what had just happened to him. "Come on Sarg, we are getting out of here." He helped the Sergeant stand, flung one of the Sergeant's arms around his neck, grabbed his rifle and headed out shooting blindly over his shoulder. The two ran as fast as they could toward a clump of trees. They reached their safe haven and began the long trek back to their company.

When they reached their company and the medics were coming for his sergeant, Williams stopped them and called for Frankie. "You saved my life. You single handed saved the lives of the other men by staying behind and providing cover. I am going to recommend you for a medal. You are a hero." Frankie was given a bravery medal and the account of the heroics was actually wired back to the Peoria newspaper by the U.S. Army to be published. While his family was rejoicing at his heroic actions and the fact he was still alive, Frankie took little consolation from being presented a medal. Frankie only felt an inherent responsibility and duty to show No Fear. Saving his life or worrying about the possibility of death never entered his head. Life and death were never consequences for Frankie's actions.

Frankie had his demons. Each night, Frankie was visited and haunted by the mutilated bodies and casualties of war. One of those casualties was his best friend, Jerry. Jerry, later in the war, had stepped on a landmine while Frankie and he were "point" soldiers in Northern Italy to fight retreating German and Italian soldiers. One minute Jerry was calling out, "Hey Dago, you still alive over there? Careful now, we do not want any Germans jumping out of the bushes and scaring you." Frankie could only shake his head at the laughter he heard coming from Jerry. In an instant, Frankie heard an explosion coming from the vicinity of Jerry's position. Suddenly, it was raining Jerry's body parts. Frankie screamed out for Jerry. In his nightmares, Frankie swore he heard Jerry call his name. "Frankie, fuck!"

It took four major offensives before the 5th Army eventually broke through German lines to capture and take possession of Rome in June of 1944. Frankie had the good fortune of spending a month in Rome primarily the result of him being promoted to Sergeant and being reassigned to another unit. It was at this time, Frankie concluded his trilogy of mind and soul adjustments. It was while Frankie was in Rome that he met Gianna Bella Biacci selling handcrafted goods on the street. Gianna was a kind, soft-spoken woman who had a smile that made you feel that you had known her all your life. Every chance he got, Frankie would find where Gianna was selling her goods. He wanted to be near her, talk to her. He would always buy something that he would give away later to fellow soldiers or town passersby's. Gianna loved for Frankie to stop by. She would practice her broken English. Frankie would practice his rusty Italian. He finally asked her if she would go out with him to get something to eat. Gianna took him to a little place the locals went. Over the next three weeks, Frankie saw a lot of Gianna. She gave him a picture of herself which he always carried in his shirt pocket.

"Gianna, you know that I will be leaving soon. Meeting you was a gift from God. You have been so wonderful. I have enjoyed the time we have spent together. I know that I am infatuated with you and relish the kisses, the walks holding hands, and sleeping with you. I want this to last forever." Frankie's heart was heavy this night. He was to return to the fighting in the next few days. He actually felt he was in love with her.

"Francis, you are a beautiful man. You treated me with respect. You were gentle with me and never rushed me to be with you. I too wish for this to last. You will go soon and have to fight the Germans some more. I do not think war will last too much longer. When you are done, you come back? Yes?"

"I will. I will write you when I can to show you that I am still alive. I will carry your picture forever."

That was the last time Frankie would ever see Gianna even though he did write to her for over two years after the war. He would carry her picture in his wallet until the day he died. However, no letters were ever returned. Those who read his letters never told him what actually happened to Gianna. He got bits and pieces of information from local officials to whom he had sent inquiries. He was told from one that she was killed by a bomb, from another that she was raped by an American soldier and went to live somewhere else in Italy where she got married. While he always knew the chance of them being able to re-unite was little more than a desire or dream, he was having a hard time coming to terms the probability it was one chance in a million of them seeing each other again. For Frankie, Gianna was love at first sight. The romantic night they had together, the passion they shared, and having been blessed with their chance meeting, was heaven sent, was engraved in his mind and permanently sealed in his heart.

By the end of the summer of 1944, the Allies had moved from Rome through Florence and were part of the invasion of Southern France. Frankie and his company were told that they were going home the spring of 1945.

Chapter 18

Frankie first saw her in the morning light aboard the US Army transport bringing an entire company of soldiers home. There she was, The Statue of Liberty. Freedom was worth fighting for and, in many cases, dying for. Frankie's mind flashed back to his father. He could almost hear his father telling the stories of coming to America and passing through this very sound headed toward Ellis Island. He felt a sense of deja vu combined with the longing to see his family. He wondered how he would face his fears of the future and purge the haunting of the past three years.

"Welcome home son, your mother and I are so happy to see you back safe and sound." Vincent tried to speak the words with pride, but the shakiness of his voice and the tears in his eyes couldn't mask the relief and love he was feeling. The strength that rose within him when he gave Frankie a hug actually caused Frankie to grunt. Everyone laughed. The kisses on Frankie's cheeks were like past days of his youth. Carmella couldn't wait for her turn with Frankie.

"Vincent, you are cutting his air off. Let go, I want to see my son. Frankie, give mama a kiss." Frankie missed his family. His parents were just the same. The house was the same. The smells of the kitchen the same, Peoria was the same. "Frankie, the entire family is waiting for you inside. Come in, let's celebrate, have some wine, then we eat. You have lost weight eating that Army food. I have cooked your favorite meal. Welcome home son, we love you." Inside the house were all the branches of his mother and father's family tree. When you added past friendships, it seemed that the whole town had somehow squeezed itself into every room of the house. The homecoming was overwhelming. For Frankie, he only wanted to forget the war and fantasize about his lost love, Gianna.

Frankie was given a job in the distillery where each night he became quite familiar with the distillery's many products. Frankie was more than a sampler of the products. The alcohol dulled his senses and in his mind He needed his nightly drinking to help him fight the constant nightmares about the brutalities of war, the maiming and the loss of life. However, the alcohol could not erase the emptiness, the loneliness, or the longing for Gianna. Frankie was alone and adrift in a sea filled with life.

One Saturday night Frankie was asked by a fellow worker if he would like to attend a benefit supper at the Itoo Hall in Peoria. The Itoo Hall was a gathering place where the Peoria Lebanese community often congregated for various events. This particular benefit was for a fallen Lebanese-American soldier who had lost his life in the war. Proceeds were to help his wife and child. Since coming home, it seemed there was always some type of social function with a war theme. It was either some celebration for a safe return, remembrances for fallen soldiers, fundraisers for injured soldiers, or just some politician just wanting to keep his name recognition alive. Frankie wasn't excited about attending such an event but agreed to go. The club was a white block building on the west side of Peoria with rows of tables. Patrons were always fed and alcohol always available. A priest was routinely present to ensure those in attendance that God acknowledged their generosity. The benefit turned out to be quite a surprise. There were wonderful Lebanese dishes, a small band, and plenty of alcohol. Sitting at a table crowded with strangers and having a full stomach of food was somewhat alien to his system. Maybe it was the constant intake of alcohol that allowed him for a brief moment to imagine he was having a good time.

As he sat there and smiled at the appropriate times, he looked up and could have sworn he saw Gianna walk into the hall. Life is all about moments and this was one of Frankie's. Frankie thought his heart had suddenly started beating in his throat and he actually thought he could faint. He had to swallow hard to keep from choking on his drink. He jumped up to get a closer look. This moment was going to be savored. As he approached his imagined vision, the woman was not Gianna. But her features, her black hair, her captivating beauty, caused Frankie to stare and for the first time since returning from the war, see a person for who they were. A feeling of contentment swept over him like a wave of warm sunlight. The beauty glanced over in his direction only to wrinkle up her forehead as if to say, "Do I know you?" Once she had eaten and settled in at a nearby table, Frankie couldn't resist the urge to walk up to her and introduce himself. He was driven like a moth to a flame.

"Excuse me for the intrusion. My name is Frank Anthony. My friends call me Frankie. I am here with a friend who knows the family. Are you a member of the family? If so, you have my sincerest condolences. I was a soldier and felt honored to come to this benefit." He paused hoping for an opening.

She seemed to be studying Frankie, extended her hand and then spoke. "Mr. Anthony, Frank. I am Greta Shanine. No, I am not a family member. I too came here with a friend who is one of the departed soldiers family. We go to the same church, Saint Sharbel's Catholic Church. So on behalf of my friend, we do thank you for coming. I have heard of the Anthony family. Would you like to join us?" The rest became history. The two dated for 6 months, Frankie proposed, and a wedding took place at Saint Sharbel. On the bride's side of the ceremony sat the hierarchy of the Shanine family and elite of the Peoria Lebanese community. On the other side of the aisle sat the Anthony and Travato families and the elite of Peoria's Italian community. This marriage was not just about two people but also the marrying of some of the key decision makers within business, political, judicial and law enforcement in all of central Illinois.

One of the non family invitees whispered to his wife, "My God, all these people look alike. Look at all this black hair, dark eyes and white teeth. This looks like one big family instead of two. Are we sure the love birds up there aren't cousins?"

"Shut up you fool? We do not want these people mad at us. I do not think they would find your observation very funny."

Everything seemed perfect, except the one secret he vowed must never be disclosed. Frankie Anthony continued to fight his demons from the war. The constant nightly vision of his best friends getting torn to pieces, body fragments landing on him, blood painted into his being, had Frankie yearning for a reality escape. Frankie had become a closet alcoholic, capable of creating drinking oasis in a number of places. He was a master illusionist and a master at keeping his secret hidden from family and co workers. To an Italian, the family name is as sacred as the Pope. Frankie knew he had to preserve and protect the honor of his family name. He was certain that he could keep his "extra" drinking in check, managed, and well hidden. After all, his drinking was only done to help him sleep. Frankie knew he could keep Greta from thinking he drank too much. He wanted to make sure to keep his new Lebanese connections strong and in no way be compromised or destroyed.

The world was getting back to a level of normalcy. Babies were being born like never before. This generation was called "Baby Boomers" for good reason. Frankie and Greta were no exception. In 1947, within their first year of marriage, Greta became pregnant and gave birth. Greta had a very difficult time during her delivery. She was totally exhausted and wasn't sure exactly what the doctor was saying as the birth was transpiring. Had she heard the doctor declare there was another baby coming? Had she delivered more than one child? Her state of confusion continued since the nurses had taken the baby or babies immediately to an adjoining room. Greta was told to rest and that she would see her children once they had been thoroughly checked over by the attending medical staff. "Children, you said children, not child. I want to see my husband and I want to see him now!" Frankie was brought into the delivery room which was normally not allowed. "Frankie, I don't know what is going on! Where is my baby, is something wrong?"

"Mr. Anthony, the doctor is in the adjoining room making sure all is ok. Your wife is fine, just tired and confused from a difficult delivery. I will go get the doctor. Please remain calm. I am sure all is ok." Frankie looked into his wife's hollowed eyes. She looked absolutely exhausted but was the Madonna in his eyes.

"Greta, you are so beautiful. I am sure our baby is fine. They are just checking whether all the toes and fingers are in place." Greta was about to speak when the doctor came in through the side doors.

"Mr. and Mrs. Anthony, I am happy to inform you that you are the proud parents of monozygotic twin boys. Your twin sons' physical appearances are identical to say the least. Truly identical twins are a rarity around here so we wanted to make sure both boys were healthy. And judging from their lungs and their energetic arm and leg movements, I'd say you are going to have your hands full. Congratulations. Mrs. Anthony, I know the delivery was very difficult. Your body will need time to recover from this ordeal. I am going to admit you for a stay in the hospital with instructions that you will remain in bed for at least a week. Mr. Anthony, Greta will be fine, she just needs to rest and time to regain her strength. I have seen twins before, but never in my experience have I seen two babies look so much alike. The only thing that I can factually state that is different is their fingerprints."

Frankie was still in a state of shock, "Twins? Why didn't we have some idea? My God, this is wonderful. Greta, you are truly a blessing and have produced two miracles for me. I love you so much." He reached down and gave his wife a strong, heartfelt kiss. Greta could see the pride in her husband's eyes and could feel the love in his gentle stroking of her hair. She was spent. All she could do was smile lovingly at him and squeeze his hand. She was much too tired to reach out to him to embrace. She closed her eyes and fell off to sleep. She now had two children, two identical children.

"Mr. Anthony. Mr. Anthony, we need to have the names of your sons for the birth certificate. We like to get the names as soon as possible. So, if you have some names you can provide, we . . ." As the nurse's words trailed off in the distance, Frankie could only stare at the woman who had given birth to twin sons. His family tree had taken root.

Chapter 19

"Greta, are you ready to hold your sons?" The nurse was beside herself with excitement as she handed the babies to Greta. To Greta, they seemed like loaves of bread, all bundled up in tight blue blankets. Their heads were covered in knitted hats.

"Can we unbundle them? I want to see their little hands and toes." Greta wasn't about to wait for an answer. She unwrapped one, then the other. She studied each one from top to bottom. "My dear God, you have allowed me to give birth to identical twins. How in the world do I tell them apart?"

The nurse was listening and quickly responded, "Greta, I used an old trick you could use. I painted the little pinky toe of your first born with red fingernail polish so that when you named them, you would know which one came first and be positive on the name. Just leave the fingernail polish on until you can tell them apart. See, this one has the polish. He was your first born."

"What a good idea." Greta was almost giddy holding her new arrivals. "We want our sons to be close, to look after each other. Frankie uses the phrase that he wants his boys to always know that the other has his back. We want to raise them to always know that family comes first and, if God is in their corner when the bell rings, they should have no fear. Frankie and I have come to agreement on their names. I want to wait for Frankie to tell you officially."

Jim A. Roppa

As if on cue, Frankie came into the sterile hospital room as the women were talking. "Frankie, it is time to give our sons their names. Would you please provide the names we have chosen to give to our sons? Nurse Betty has been patient. But she needs the names to complete the birth certificates and some other official papers so we can take the boys home." Frankie could see Greta could not keep the names bottled up inside her any longer.

The nurse wanted to get the process started. She asked the obvious first question, "So how did you come up with the names?"

"Well my wife is very religious so she wasn't about to have a name that wasn't biblical in nature. As for me, well, since the twins will have my last name Anthony, I felt Greta should be the one who got to choose their first and middle names. After all, by the grace of God, she did all the wonderful work, so she should have the honor. For our first born son, he will be named after the apostle Thomas, the one called 'Didymus'. Thomas means 'twin' in Aramaic, as does 'Didymus' in Greek. I think he would like to be called Thomas over Didymus don't you think? Unfortunately, the scholars do not know actually who his twin was or we would have named our other son after him. Some of the ancient scholars believed Thomas was actually the twin of Jesus. We would never burden our second son with the Father's Son's name. So we chose a New Testament name, Mathew. In the New Testament, Matthew 1:3, there are references to twins. Their manner of birth suggests the older was to serve the younger much like it was to apply to Esau and Jacob. As for a middle name, we felt they should have a name or initial to remind the twins they were born together. I suggested we select the letter S which is the first letter of my wife's maiden name. Our twins will have uniqueness in their first name, unity in their middle name, and the linage of Shanine and Anthony always in their blood. So please assign the names of Thomas S. Anthony and Mathew S. Anthony on the appropriate birth certificates."

The boys physical appearances were carbon copies. As the boys aged, grew and matured, they developed their own distinctive personalities. Thomas or Tommie would be the talkative brother who tended to show interest in intellectual matters, spoke fluently and, as an adult, would openly display his high degree of intelligence. Mathew or Mattie was also very talkative, but rather than visibly exhibit his intellect, often used his brawn as well as his brain to control situations when he wanted to take a lead role. While Mattie wanted to be in command, Tommie was highly adaptable and behaved cheerfully. Mattie was more positioned. He saw things from a perspective of outcomes which could impact his family or himself. He guarded his emotions and feelings like diamonds in a safe. Tommie thought things out. Before he would act, he always thought through his action and subsequent consequences. He was a detailed planner. Every move was as orchestrated as a precision dance recital. Mattie was more on the fiery, impulsive side. He displayed a wide range of interests. When he had made up his mind on a course of action, he was inclined to speak loudly, take charge and act. He was overly confident and never doubted his next move to take over a situation. His motto was *Take action now. Doing something, even if it is wrong, is better than doing nothing. Even if I am wrong, there is always another move to rectify and make it right.* Later in life, Mattie maintained his own dual standard, one for him and one for others, but when it came to his actions, he used his superior intellect to ensure his actions met with favorable results.

The boys would come to know their strengths and weaknesses at a very young age. Each helped the other and, where one may falter, the other was always there to pick him up. Personality would be their key to the future. They had the right biological makeup to be whatever they aspired to be. Future events would be instrumental in influencing and embedding their adult behaviors, decisions and actions.

PART III

Chapter 1

"Pop, are you all right? Pop, can you hear me? Wake up!" For a 10 year old boy, who happened to be walking home from a friends by the way of a shortcut through the cemetery, to find his father slumped over the steering wheel of his truck was like a four year old finding out there was no Santa Claus. Even when the charade was finally exposed, you did not want to believe it. To suddenly find your hero, your father, incapacitated and not moving was terrifying. How can a boy comprehend such a situation? What was his father doing in the cemetery? Was he dead? The door to the truck was locked. But Mathew Anthony, Mattie, was in a state of panic. He pulled and pushed on the door handle until the truck was rocking as if it were buffeted by tsunami waves on the high seas. Suddenly through the driver side window, Mattie saw his father's body move. His father seemed to be in a stupor, but was able to sit up. His head bounced off the back window of the truck.

Francis Anthony, wasted from whiskey, had been discovered. He peered out the window trying to focus on objects that were a thousand miles away, totally out of focus. The rocking of his truck only confused the moment. As his cloudy eyes rolled around in their sockets without reason to stop, Frankie tried to gain control of his senses. He looked down from his truck and saw his son, Mathew. He could see his lips moving but his hearing sense was not processing up to speed. He reached for the door handle, opened the door and stumbled out. An empty bottle of scotch whiskey lay on the seat beside him.

His father bent down and hugged his son tightly. As he spoke, it was an outpouring from his heart. "Mattie", he seemed to be pleading with his voice barely above a whisper and such saddened, broken eyes, "promise me you will remember me all your life, both the good things and the bad. You now have seen me at my worst moment, but know all men have weaknesses, and today, you will become stronger knowing mine." In years to come, Mattie would remember his father as he was at this moment. As a young man, those memories had faded a bit, but he never quite absolved himself of his father's early death.

His father was an accomplished closet drunk. When he did drink, he was not loud or belligerent nor did he wish to be around others. One thing he knew, once he swallowed one drink, he could always rationalize another. Mattie always remembered the desperation in his father's voice that day in the cemetery when he said to him, "Son for me, one drink is one too many, one more is never enough." His father's "social tolerance" capacity was up to five drinks. After seven drinks, he was drunk. Mattie's discovery in the day in the cemetery was because his father had crossed over the "drunk" line and had finally discovered the "alcoholic's lush" line.

Cold showers, aspirin, eye wash and strong coffee were staples required for survival and lasting another day without being discovered, fired from his job or chastised by his family. But his mind controlled his drinking. His memories reinforced the degree of his drinking. He just couldn't ever forget the trials and tribulations of war, the smell of death, the ocean of blood. Drinking did not dilute the nagging memories. Drinking brought an escape through forced unconsciousness he preferred to call sleep. The hangovers were a sort of refuge in themselves. The lingering pain took his mind to the levels of reality that he had to confront while awake. Every day was just another day. No matter what joys or personal pride that he received through his family, they could not erase his past demons and haunts.

That day in the dreary cemetery, something strange came over Mattie. As he heard his father's words and felt his arms around his shoulders, Mattie realized he was no longer in a panic. He suddenly was thinking about the first time his father had taken his brother, Tommie, and him, hunting ducks. When it was his turn to shoot, his father reminded him to focus on the ducks and not to think about the noise of the gun, the recoil from the shot or passion for the duck. Mattie thought to himself, *"Anthonys know the drill. No limits, No Fear, No Remorse. There isn't anything in this world I cannot achieve. I have no fear of anything nor do I feel any remorse. Killing these ducks is fun.* When Tommie had let out a grunt when he fired the gun and then rubbed his shoulder, Mattie had shown no reaction the first time he shot his father's 12 gauge shot gun and the recoil kick sent a sharp pain through his shoulder. He was tough and he felt the excitement he had shot and killed a duck.

Mattie had grown to accept his father's drinking, but he couldn't recall the day he became ashamed of him. Even though he loved his father deeply, he absolutely despised him for his inability to conquer liquor. To Mattie, this weakness allowed others to take advantage of him, to ridicule him, to look down on him. His mother had felt his father's pain when he finally told her of his drinking problem. She would stay with him because she truly loved him and knew his inner soul. She wanted to keep the family together for the sake of the children. As the problem became common knowledge among her side of the family, they began to distance themselves and only tolerated him when in forced company or conversations. With each passing day, the family name had more tarnish. In his high school years, Mattie tried to totally avoid being around his father. He often wished he would disappear.

Once Frankie could no longer make it through the work day without taking a drink, his father gave him a job managing some rental properties he had acquired over the years. He paid his son well enough to keep a roof over his family's head and food on the table. As principal owner of the distillery, he supplied his son with the necessary bottles of contentment knowing full well the end it would bring. Frankie knew he had failed his father and family. With each day, he tried to work hard watching over the rentals. But each day, his body demanded more stimuli from the bottle to go on. Frankie found that he had very little appetite and ate only when he had dinner with his family.

Other than his wife, the only other people who remained unconditionally devoted to Frank Anthony were his parents. Mathew and Thomas Anthony could not help but admire their grandparents as they stood by their son as his invisible protection shield. Mathew grew exceptionally close to his grandfather, Vincent.

It was the summer of the twins' senior year in high school when another incident transpired that began to solidify the twin's personalities. "Boys, I am happy you came with me today to help me fix up one of the houses we rent. It will teach you some skills with tools and you are much stronger than I, so you will be a big help with the lifting we will have to do as we fix the roof." Neither boy was happy to be there. When the group arrived at the rental house, their first task was to unload the roofing material from the bed of their father's truck. The boys had each grabbed a bundle of roofing shingles and were walking toward the house. As their father grabbed a bundle, he let out a yell.

"Christ, what is this?" The boys turned to see their father had dropped the shingles he had selected and was holding his nose. It seemed his nose had become a hose and blood was gushing out of the nozzle. As the boys reached their father, he had sat down and had his head bent back. "One of you pinch my nose." Mattie grabbed his nose. "Damn it, son, your pinch is like a vise. Ease up a bit." Both laughed. Then the trio just sat motionless and silent for about ten minutes. The bleeding wouldn't stop. The elder Anthony knew he had to take charge.

"Tommie, you drive. I know enough about wounds to know when they are not going to stop bleeding and know when there is a need for some medical help. We need to go to the hospital. Mattie, help me up. I can hold my nose but am awful weak from the loss of blood. I need to lean on you. If I pass out, Mattie, you pinch and keep pressure on my nose until we get to the hospital."

Two weeks later, Frankie called Mattie to him. "Son, today I am supposed to have the gauze taken out of my nose from when they packed it at the hospital. When I was in the back with the doctor who got the hemorrhage in my nose stopped, he told me I needed to check myself into the hospital for some tests. I think if I go back, they may force me to stay in the hospital for a couple of days. I cannot do that. So, I want you to take the gauze out. Will you do that for me?" Mattie knew his father was afraid the hospital would check him in and his constant fix of alcohol would be interrupted.

"Pop, I am no doctor. What if you start bleeding again?"

"If it starts bleeding again, we go to the hospital. You do not have to be a doctor to pull out the gauze. Just take your time and gently pull it out. Here, I have some tweezers for you."

Pop, if you can take it, then I can do it. No problem, thought Mattie. For some reason, Mattie actually was thrilled to perform his father's field surgery request. Mattie expected to see blood spewing out of his father's nose with each pull of the gauze. The gauze was about a quarter of an inch wide and was packed in his nose like an accordion. Without hesitation, Mattie pushed his father's head backward so that he could see inside the nose better. Mattie started to laugh.

"What is so funny?" His father asked rather puzzled.

"Pop, I have been pulling and pulling. Are you sure they did not go up into your brain with this packing or is your schnozz really that big to hold all this stuff?" They both laughed but his father still winced with each tug of the gauze. After about four feet of gauze, the end saw the light of day. Mattie's father gave a sigh of relief. No blood came gushing out or even a trickle.

"Great job son, you are now a medic with your first success story. Hope that you will not have to perform any more operations."

"Hey Tommie, where you been? You will never guess what I just did. I took the gauze out of Dad's nose. Man was that fun. You should have seen him. I know by the end of the ordeal, he needed a drink. You have to say one thing about him. He is still one tough son of a bitch."

CHAPTER 2

It was only six months after the nose bleeding episode Tommie and Mattie were again called to help their father. On a bright hot summer afternoon, the boys were outside. Their mother had come out on the back porch and called. "Boys, I need for you to come into the house for a minute." As the boys came through the back door, still rough housing, pushing and shoving each other, to their surprise, their grandfather was in the kitchen with their mother. "Boys, as you know, the last couple of days your father has not been feeling well. He wants to see you in our bedroom." Actually, their father had been in his room for about a week. The boys had only briefly seen him as they said good morning or good night and went about their daily activities. Being young and boys will be boys, they really did not pay much attention as to how long their father had been laid up in his room. He sounded ok and always responded when they spoke to him either leaving or going to their rooms.

When the twins walked into the bedroom they were taken back. Their father's face resembled a grapefruit, round and a dull yellow color. At first they thought it was from the lighting in the room but quickly realized the light coming through the window was not tinting their father's face, but accentuating the reality of the situation. Their father also had a bulge under the covers on his stomach. Was it a pillow? "Boys, I am doing very well. I have not gone to the bathroom for two days." He pulled the covers back to reveal swelling in his stomach that rivaled a woman's girth who was about to give birth. "Boys, I am not the father that I first set out to be when you were born. We all know why and I am so ashamed. I want you to know how much I love your mother and you. If anything happens, please do not spend any time dwelling on the past. Be a phoenix. Become stronger than I ever was and be the person who I could never be. Make your mother, your family proud. Follow your grandfather's example. Be two men who rise from the ashes and become pillars of the community. Become men who are respected and sought out. Make this town forget the Anthony the drunk. Let them marvel at the Anthonys the successful."

Tommie had analyzed the severity of the situation and interrupted. "Pop, you have got to get to the hospital!"

"Tommie, I will go in a week if I do not get better. I am not in any pain. I think if I can just go to the bathroom, my stomach will go down and I might look a little better."

"Pop, you could die in a week!" Tommie yelled through his tears. It did not take a doctor to know their father's body was beyond normal healing processes. He needed medical attention along with heavenly intervention.

Mattie looked at his father, his mother, and then his grandfather. He suddenly had a strange feeling pass through his body like a low voltage shock. Everyone in the room knew that his father was going to die. He was not going to get better. *Why am I not close to crying or becoming hysterical like Tommie?* Mattie just wanted to ask questions regarding how his father was going to die and when. His mother had her head down as if she were praying. He was ashamed of his father but loved him unconditionally. His father was his father and no one would speak ill of him. Whenever he talked about his father, it was usually a fabricated story about a mythical father. Suddenly, Mattie knew what he needed to do for his father. "Pop, do you need for me to get you a drink?" he asked.

His mother quickly looked up and straight into his eyes seemingly asking him silent questions. His grandfather stood very straight and stoic, but Mattie thought he actually gave him a slight nod. His father smiled, and Tommie screamed his shock and disappointment, "Mattie, are you crazy? What is wrong with you? Pop is sick. If he doesn't go to the hospital, he is going to die. Do you want him to die?"

Mattie was quite calm, "No, Tommie, I do not want Pop to die. I want more than anything for him to live for Mom, grandfather, you and me. This is not our decision. We are not doctors, a medic maybe." He paused, looked at his father and the two shared their intimate moment. "I think our mother and father need to determine what is best. Should Pop go to the hospital or should a doctor come here? If Pop wants a week to decide his fate, then Mom and Pop should have their week." His mother slowly lowered her head again and then spoke with authority and a sense of peace.

"Boys, we have spoken to the doctor. Your father is not well and will not get better. He and I have discussed the situation. If my love, your father, is to leave us, both he and I want all the time left to be together. We want our family to be together to the end, together. Understand?" With the end of her sermon, she silently cried. There was no fear, no remorse in her words, only acceptance of the inevitable.

"My wonderful sons. We have called you in here to learn of our situation and our decision. Even though I am not in pain, there could be pain as my illness progresses. I want your word that you will help your mother through this and be there for her, for me, at the time she will need it most. I have not told you enough how much I love you and how proud of you I have always been. I know we can count on you to be strong going forward." Their father's voice trailed off. He was exhausted and the twins knew it was time for them to leave the bedroom.

"Father, you can count on us to do whatever is necessary. We will pray for you and mother." Mattie's words were firm and strong. He was speaking for both his brother and him. Tommie had calmed to the notion that "the illness" not being called by its medical name was now running its course. His father was not going to get better regardless of the treating facility. The only medical help that was available would come from their doctor. The medicine would provide temporary comfort the last few days of their father's existence.

Mattie and Tommie had learned the name of the potential illness that could befall their father, not from their mother, but from their grandfather. After the nosebleed incident, one day when their grandfather had come by the house, he had taken Mattie aside and prophesized the coming of a terminal illness called "cirrhosis of the liver". Mattie had researched in great detail about the illness. "Mathew, your father told me of the time you found out he was an alcoholic and was very drunk. He told me how you helped him take the packing out of his nose. You kept the incident to yourself to protect your father. You showed courage. Most boys, and I would say most men I know, would have absolved themselves of the responsibility you took on your shoulders. Your decision was for the family, not yourself. Mathew, you are the strong one, the fighter. I can see it in your eyes. I need to talk quite candidly with you. Your father has been a very troubled man for a long time stemming from the war. Things happened which tormented him every day of this life. War causes a man to do things he must. But some men cannot forgive themselves or forget the past. When your father came back, he was not the same man who left to fight for his country. He chose alcohol as a way to ease his troubled mind. Make no mistake, never was your father not loved by his family and never did your father not give his total love to his family.

"Alcoholic cirrhosis is caused by alcohol abuse and can only be treated by abstaining from alcohol. Your mother and I hoped and prayed he could control his drinking. He couldn't. Your father became an alcoholic. All knew, if he did not control his drinking, he could develop cirrhosis in his liver. Cirrhosis is generally irreversible, and treatment usually focuses on preventing progression and complications. What will happen is that your father will become jaundiced. That means his skin will take on a yellow color. His blood normally carried from his intestines and spleen will flow more slowly and the pressure increase. This will lead to fluid leaks into his abdominal cavity. Insufficient blood supply will happen to the kidneys causing them to fail. Finally, all the collateral blood flow through vessels in the stomach and esophagus will become enlarged and likely to burst. Your father will then die. I know this is hard to comprehend, but you need to prepare yourself. You must be strong for your mother, your father and your brother. Show no fear for her and your father. I, myself, am not destined for this world for many more years. You and your brother must continue to bring honor to our family name."

The next chapter of their family heritage novel was about to be written. Their grandfather made sure it was properly presented and digested. Mattie was anointed to ensure his brother and he continued the family legacy.

As his grandfather had outlined the phases the cirrhosis would pursue, it did. His father did not cry out or beg for death. When the pain passed through his body, it caused him to spasm. Every inch of his body, every muscle; he felt the jolt of pain as if he was being executed from the shock volts of an electric chair. Only this pain was recurring and came every two to five minutes. When the pain hit, his father would look at his grandfather and smile. His last words were, "To my God, I am ready to enter your kingdom. To my wife, you are the love of my life. I was blessed to have you by my side. To my father, I did have limitations, but have no fear of my demise. My only remorse is for any dishonor or embarrassment I may have caused my family. I accept all consequences from my actions. To my sons, you are my miracle of birth and a part of me is in you. I will live on through you." He looked at

Mattie. "I will take that drink now." He actually laughed, shut his eyes and ceased to be.

The family gathered, held each other. Vincent Anthony was the first to speak. "My son, Francis Anthony, is gone. No parent should live so long as to see any of his children pass on before they do. Francis may have had his faults, but we his family honor his name, relished his love, and admired his finer moments. Greta, you and the boys will always be well taken care of. Boys, one day I will call on you for a favor, please honor me." As he prepared to leave, he asked Mattie to help him carry a box to his car. "Mattie, when you first saw your father sick and learned he was in his final days, why did you offer him a drink?"

Mattie wasn't worried about his answer because, if he had it to do all over again, he would still ask his father the question again. "Grandfather, I asked Pop if he wanted a drink because I was hoping he would want one and that it would be his last. I hoped the drink would put him to sleep as it has done so many times in the past. I wanted Pop to have immediate sleep that would take away his pain and he would drift away peacefully. I did not want to see him suffer or see mother cry anymore. Whatever world Pop sought out or would go to when he was drunk, he must have thought it was better than when he was not drunk. I just wanted to help him get to his world faster."

Mattie would always remember the day his father died. Why didn't he cry like Tommie?

Chapter 3

After their father passed away, the twins' grandfather assumed the father figure role in their lives. He would come over for dinner each night and stay until the boys would go to bed. He was always telling them stories of the old wide open days in Peoria. He was adamant that they learn to be able to protect themselves, so he enrolled them their first boxing lessons, then a karate school. He stressed the boys must appreciate both the physical and mental requirements and philosophies of self defense. Always the eloquent orator, when their grandfather spoke, the boys were captivated by his words. "Boys, I hope you never play the role of the bully or the person who thinks he is to be treated special. There are going to be times when someone will challenge you. Some will want to hurt you. If you ever feel that you are going to have a confrontation with someone, then you must have your mind go into an attack, not defensive, mode. Your brain is your best weapon. The person who will confront you generally uses intimidation tactics to scare you. In a meeting it could be a raised voice, cuss words, or personal innuendos. If they mean to hurt you, they will come with their fists balled to do battle. Some will be too afraid to come at you directly and will look for a cheap shot to take you out. For today, let's talk about the one who wants to fight. He will come at you with his hands down by his side and his chin stuck out showing facial anger and intent. Why? To intimidate. He wants you to run or be so afraid that you just stand there and take his punishment. Let him come toward you. When he is almost to you, that is the moment when you attack. Hit him directly in the nose. His eyes will water and he will be temporarily startled. He will most generally bring his hands up to his nose. Then you hit him in the stomach hard. This will knock the breath out of him. From there, you had better finish him and not let him get his bearings."

Tommie listened and hoped he would never have to do battle. It seemed to him there should be another way than risk getting hurt. Mattie, on the other hand, couldn't wait to see if the words were true. Boys will be boys and brothers are always wrestling. Each night, the boys honed their self defense skills on each other. It did not take long to test the theory in the real world.

One lazy summer afternoon, the daily pickup baseball game was being played in the empty lot in the boys' neighborhood. A play had occurred that caused the two sides to try to interpret the rule. Tommie was probably the only one in their neighborhood who ever read a baseball rule book. "For an overthrow, you only get to go one base, you cannot keep running."

"Bullshit Tommie! Or should I say Tom Ass the Wise Ass? You are always the one who thinks he knows all the answers. Not this time, the run scores. Discussion closed." Johnny Magoulias, the resident Greek in the neighborhood, was the oldest of the group. He was always bossing everyone around and generally, the group did what he said. This time, for some reason, Tommie wanted to debate the rule.

"Come on Johnny, you are wrong. I can go get the rule book and show you." On this day, Johnny was not going to have his authority challenged. "How about the run scores or I kick your ass?"

Tommie was about to say the rule was not worth fighting about when Mattie spoke up. "Johnny, if my brother says the rule book says the runner can only advance one base when the ball goes out of the playing field, then it is one base. The runner goes back to third base."

"Oh, so now you are the expert. How about I kick your butt all the way back to your WOP house then your brother's?" He came at Mattie. Mattie felt a rapid beating in his chest, heat surge in his neck, and waited until Johnny was about three feet from him. Johnny's hands were balled and white knuckled, and down at his sides. Mattie could hear his grandfather's voice, "strike first." Johnny's chin was stuck out with his mouth spouting all kind of tough trash. Mattie took one step toward Johnny and with his full weight behind his fist, hit Johnny square on the nose with his right hand and followed with the left to the side of Johnny's head. Johnny had a look in his eyes of disbelief, then immediately let out a cry from the pain he now felt. When Johnny grabbed his nose, Mattie punched him hard in the gut. Johnny let out another sound like air escaping from a balloon. Down he went. Mattie hit him at least four more times. Blood had dripped from Johnny's nose and dotted Johnny's blue t-shirt. It was only when Tommie grabbed him and told him to stop, did Mattie come back to reality. He was breathing hard. He wasn't done with Johnny.

"Johnny, if you get up, I swear I will beat the living hell out of you. And if you ever try to pick a fight with my brother or me again, you will have to deal with both of us. If there is a next time, we will not stop. We will hurt you bad. Do you understand?" Johnny did not move or make any attempt to speak. He knew how playground justice worked. Johnny Magoulias was no longer going to call the shots for this group. He also knew he would never, ever anger an Anthony again.

"Mattie, you really beat Johnny up. You hurt him. I think we could have gotten out of that without a fight. What do we say to mom or grandfather? Will Johnny tell his parents?" Tommie had never seen his brother so angry or, for that matter, so tough.

Mattie turned to his brother and smiled. "That felt good. Johnny is a big mouth. I wanted to do that for a long time. Tommie, no one is going to talk down to our family. We do not have to fear anyone. If a fight is called for and you do not want to be a part of it, I will fight for you with anyone. Understand. People cannot tell us apart. So we can use each other for anything that might arise. Brother, with your brains and my who knows what, we are a force to be reckoned with." Mattie put his arm around his brothers shoulders, gave him a hug and they both laughed and wrestled with each other all the way home. "I think we should tell grandfather about what happened today"

Tommie loved his brother and would do anything for him. But Tommie saw something that day that scared him. As Mattie was pounding Johnny into submission, Tommie never forgot the look in Mattie's eyes. It wasn't anger, it went beyond anger. He seemed possessed. Even when he was pulled off Johnny, he reacted like a wild animal fighting to keep his coveted prey. There was only one word for Mattie's action: vicious, killer vicious.

Chapter 4

THE BOYS HAD grown up to be extremely handsome young men who stood out in any type of crowd, highbrow and lowbrow. By their senior year in high school, they both had molded their bodies into truly athletic specimens. Their weightlifting had sprouted broad shoulders. Their running had narrowed their waists and shaped lean, muscular legs. Following in their parents' most predominant growth genes, the boys stood six feet two inches tall. Over the years, through many social and religious functions, and daily "mind your manner" sessions instructed by their mother, the boys had become confident, purposeful, commanding, yet without the hint of any arrogance or entitlement. Their facial features were as appealing as any male model on the cover of Gentleman's Quarterly. They had a crop of coal black wavy hair as thick as any briar patch. Their eyes matched their hair. When you talked with them, you immediately felt you knew them. They always seemed interested in what you were saying and listened to every word that was being spoken to them. Each boy sported a Roman nose of prominence and distinction which highlighted their European heritage. The final touch was their sturdy chin resting on a strong neck that pronounced bodies that were well muscled, chiseled and athletic.

Thomas, or Tommie, as Mattie would forever call him, had taken on the role as the irreverent "big brother", always dispensing advice on every topic, whether personal, social, physical, academic or later, professional and political. Mattie idolized his big brother, even though big meant older and older was by less than two minutes. Thomas was the deeper thinker, Mattie the carefree one, often called feisty by his grandfather. As he grew up, feisty became spirited, then insubordinate, then rebellious, then the type who did what he wanted and not what he was told. Both had the uncanny knack to play the role of the other with perfection. They each loved to take on the other's identity and fool others. It was their secret game to see who could achieve the other's identity the longest without detection.

The twin brothers were loyal to each other beyond comprehension. They had pledged to each other to always support and be there for one another. They shared the same dreams, the same goals. Like their grandfather, they intended to protect and elevate the name Anthony to an even higher position of respect, honor, and achievement. Tommie had come to know his brother had different views, different ways of doing things and could react totally different to situations than what he would do. He sensed his brother's inner turmoil and had viewed his darker side on various occasions. Tommie always felt that Mattie's mind and feeling had been permanently altered as a result of how he felt about their father. Both brothers had experienced the embarrassment of their father's drinking problem. In his later years before he died, his appearance, his speech and his physical demeanor left no doubt he had a major drinking problem. The boys' schoolmates had quietly talked about Mr. Anthony being a drunk, but kept their comments to themselves, especially after Mattie had beaten a fellow student into submission when he had made a passing comment, "Anthony, talked with your old man today over at Sheridan Plaza. He almost knocked me over. What does he drink, 100 proof? I hope he doesn't smoke. If he does, when he puts the match up to his mouth, he may . . ." Before another word came out of his mouth, Mattie broke his nose and loosened his front teeth.

Tommie felt it was his calling, his duty to keep his brother out of trouble, and should trouble arise, be there for him. As the "older" brother, he had to address any indiscretions or dirty laundry that could jeopardize the family name.

Chapter 5

It was just another Monday morning school day. Tommie and Mattie were standing in their driveway waiting for one of their friends who lived down the street. The three had walked to school together since grade school. His name was George McClellan. George, or Georgie, was a shy kid, on the chunky side. Georgie was always the small kid growing up with smooth girlish facial features. When he spoke, which was on rare occasions, he had a thick-tongued speech impediment that caused neighborhood kids to kid and taunt him. Children can be cruel at times. They often told Georgie he talked like he had Downs Syndrome. Now, even at 17 years old, he stood only five foot six. He always walked with his head down, shoulders hunched. Georgie rarely laughed. When Georgie was young, his family had been rather prominent, but when his dad died, his family fell on tough times. Maybe the boy's close bond with Georgie was that he had lost his father like they had or maybe they just liked watching out for him, no matter, there was a bond. Everyone knew, pick on Georgie, you get the Anthonys. Today, Georgie was late. This irritated Mattie. He didn't like waiting and he hated it when other people were in the driver's seat. Mattie made everything personal without hesitation or boundaries. It was how he motivated himself. It was how he got by in this judgmental world. Mattie selected who he would allow a relationship to form, to bond, or be best friends. "Where the hell is Georgie? He is never late. When he gets here, I am going to let him know I am pissed. I hate to wait."

"Relax, Exlax. Old Georgie is probably just moving a little slow. We got plenty of time to get to school. What are you going to do when we get there? You never want to talk with anyone. You think they are all a bunch of phonies. Christ, Mattie, you are a relationship dropout. You find people boring. We are going to wait for Georgie. Look there, here he comes now." Sure enough, just as Tommie predicted, Georgie came walking around the corner. Head down, collar on his shirt turned up, moving slower that usual. "Hurry up, Georgie, else old Mattie here may run you all the way to school." Tommie laughed and punched Mattie on the arm.

Georgie walked by Tommie and Tommie gave him a swat on the butt. "Georgie, let's get this body of yours moving!" joked Tommie.

Georgie swirled, dropped the two books he was carrying, raised his fists all balled up, and was ready to take a swing at Tommie. "Don't you ever touch me there again or I will kill you."

Mattie grabbed Georgie from behind and wrapped his arms around him. "Jesus, Georgie, what has gotten into you? All Tommie did was slap you on your ass." Both Mattie and Tommie were completely surprised by Georgie's actions. They had grown up with Georgie. In the many years they had known him, never once had he shown any aggressive tendencies. Something had happened and they could see it in Georgie's teary eyes.

"Georgie, what is wrong?" Tommie's voice took on the compassion and serenity of a professional psychologist. He put his arm around Georgie. Georgie started to pull away, but Tommie hung on. "Georgie, you know we are your friends. We have been your best friends forever. Tell us what is going on. Come on. Let's walk into our garage so no one can see you crying." Tommie pulled out a handkerchief he had in his back pocket of his blue jeans and pushed it toward Georgie.

The Corporate Chameleon

When they got to the garage, Mattie went in first and turned on the light. He pulled up an old wicker chair that was stored in the garage. Tommie continued his probing questions. "Did something happen at home? Are you sick?" Whatever it was must have been on Georgie's mind forever because when Tommie asked him once more, "We are your friends we are here to listen and to help. Georgie, what is it?"

Georgie started to cry so uncontrollably into the handkerchief that he could hardly catch his breath. Then, as if the water faucet had been twisted and turned off, Georgie stood up as straight as any soldier. He looked directly at Tommie, then Mattie, with a peaceful expression which was another first. "I considered hanging myself last night. I would have too but I stopped when I thought what it would do to my mom. She would have no one. I couldn't have her spending her remaining years asking herself what she had done to make her son want to leave her that way. I couldn't have her wondering, crying every night for the rest of her life like I have done for the last eight years."

What had happened that could cause Georgie to think about killing himself? What? "Georgie, what's happened? Mattie and I will help you. God damn it, tell us." Tommie had lost his passive nature and was bordering on losing his control. Mattie could see Georgie's talk of hanging himself was pushing Tommie to his reasoning limits. Tommie was about to hyperventilate.

Mattie felt only a sense of intrigue. His only thought was to take control of the situation. "Georgie, tell us what is eating at you which could cause you to consider taking such a drastic action. You cannot shoulder whatever it is by yourself. If there is one thing you can count on, it is that neither Tommie nor me will ever tell anyone about it or what you have just told us."

Georgie looked away as if he was leaving his world behind. "If I tell you, you will no longer want me to come around. You guys are my best friends. You have always been there for me and included me. If I had had a brother, I would have wanted him to be just like you guys. You are more than my friends, you are what I want to be when I grow up."

Mattie still had the floor. "Georgie, if there is one thing that our grandfather keeps reminding us is that friendship and loyalty are worth their weight in gold. Once you have it, you keep it. By you telling us your secret, you are telling us you trust us completely. We would respect that and you will have our everlasting loyalty. We will not cast a stone or judge you. You are Georgie, our friend, and will always be Georgie, our friend. Now what has caused you so much pain?"

Georgie took a deep breath. "Father Patrick. It started back when we all went to Spalding Academy. I was 10. You remember how he was always yelling at me to be more athletic, to lose weight? One day he brought me into his office. He had me touch him to show that I wasn't afraid of anything, that I could be a man. Then he touched me. He did things to me and made me do things to him. This went on for a couple of years. This became our little secret. When I finally grew up and knew it was wrong, I told him to stop, to leave me alone. He laughed and told me he would tell my mother I was spreading tall tales. He said he would tell the other priests that he caught me with another boy. It stopped only when I went to high school. But yesterday, after Mass, he came up to me and whispered that he would like to start seeing me again. He said he loved me. I didn't know what to do. So I went home and thought about killing myself. What am I going to do? He will never leave me alone. I am so ashamed."

"Georgie, you are going to stay away from Father Patrick. We have heard stories about him. Let Tommie and me think about this. We will go talk with the Father. Don't worry. Come on. We need to get to school. If we are late, the old head Nun will be waiting at the door." Mattie looked at Tommie. Mattie's teeth were clenched so hard his jaw muscles bulged liked he had boulders in his mouth. Tommie had seen that look before. Father Patrick was definitely about to have a "come to Jesus" experience. Tommie was sure of that. He needed to make sure he kept Mattie in check.

Chapter 6

Monday after school, Tommie and Mattie had talked it over about going to see Father Patrick the next evening. Tommie, being the problem solver and the deep thinker of the twins, had found out that on Tuesdays and Thursdays, Father Patrick always went to the gym weight room to lift after school hours. "Mattie, no one is ever in the weight room after school. This would be a perfect time for us to approach the Father for a quiet chat. Mattie, I am not sure what we are going to say, but let me take the lead." Mattie did not respond, he just wanted to kick Father Patrick's ass. Tommie and Mattie Anthony decided they needed to pay Father Patrick a visit, the sooner the better. A Tuesday encounter was set.

The weight room was adjacent to the basketball gymnasium. It was like all weight rooms, stagnate air, the smell of stale sweat and balm. Free weights lined the one wall with weight bars and benches positioned around the room. "Hey, Father Patrick, we didn't know you were going to be in here. Mattie and I decided to workout a little tonight after school. Do you mind?" asked Tommie, ever the charmer.

Father Patrick was in his late forties and took pride in his youthful athletic appearance. Ever since the boys had first met him, they knew the Father liked them. He was always massaging their shoulders in one of his classes or patting them on the back in the hallways. He liked to hang around the locker room after their football or basketball games. They had heard the rumors and agreed that the Father enjoyed watching the boys come out of the shower room. But since the father had never made any move on them, they did what most did, ignored him. Father Patrick stood almost six feet tall. His face was almost square which sat on a thick neck. His hair was receding, but still dark black with a sprinkling of gray at the temples. He liked to wear his hair short. The good Father was the type who, when challenged, always went on the offense. His mouth was lined and rigid like you would see in a military drill sergeant. This man was a machine, totally in charge. He would raise his voice, square his wide shoulders and stick out his barrel chest. His face was stern with brown eyes that seemed to penetrate your very soul. He was a master at intimidation. He was a strong confident man. This was his parish. After all, he spoke for God.

"Well boys, good to see you. Why don't you get into your gym clothes and we will work out together." *Maybe even shower together*, thought the father. "Before you go get dressed, could you help me out and spot me. I want to go for the gold tonight and set a new record for the bench press. Put on 300 for me, will you?" As he lay down on the bench, the boys began to put on the weight on the bar. It was obvious that the Father wanted to show the boys his strength. Mattie looked at Tommie and both spoke to each other without words. *This is perfect.*

"How many reps do you want to do Father P?" Mattie asked as he and Tommie stood on each end of the bar and lifted the weights over the head of the Father to his two waiting hands poised adjacent to his chest.

"I usually do 10 without a spotter. With you guys as my spotters, I don't have to worry about the weight dropping on my chest, so tonight I will try for 20, an Olympic gold medal for me. I will show you boys what this man can do and then you can show me how much you can do."

As Father P began his push for the gold, Mattie began counting the reps out loud. As the father started to really struggle with pressing the weight upward off his chest around 15, Tommie knelt down by the good father and softly spoke in his ear, "Father P, you need to let Georgie McClellan be. He is our friend and, if you keep bothering him, I swear, I will cut your dick off. If I hear that you bother any other boy, I will cut your dick off. Do you understand?" When he finished he stood and pushed the bar with weight straight down hard on the good father's chest. "Do you understand?"

The father grunted when the bar hit his chest. The weight of the bar restricted the father's breathing, but his anger spewed heated words out of his mouth like an active volcano. "Why you little son of a bitch. That hurt like Hell. Get this fucking bar off me. I cannot breath. When I get up, I am going to teach you boys a lesson. No one and I mean no one, talks to me like that. I do what I want when I want and with whomever I want. I do not care who your grandfather is or how much money he donates to this school, I will take you down. You will cut my dick off? You could end up sucking my dick. Don't make threats you can't back up. Do you understand?

Mattie was unusually quiet without any hint of concern over Tommie's actions. "Father, how many boys did you molest like Georgie? One, ten, or a hundred since you have been at this parish? You took advantage of young boys who trusted you. We trusted you, father."

"Fuck you, Mathew. Before this is over, you will want me to fuck you. You boys have crossed the line. Get this bar off me, I can't budge it. It is crushing my chest. Hurry up."

Tommie continued, "You are an evil man, father. You scarred our friend Georgie for life. You called me and my brother a son of a bitch. You have defamed and offended my brother and mother. You have belittled my grandfather. You have sodomized our friend as well as others. You want to fuck us. When does it stop? Father, if you can do three more presses, Mattie and I will grab the weight and set it down, if not we will leave you to get the weight off by yourself. Mattie, let's help the father with the first one." Mattie couldn't believe what his brother had just said. So this was what Tommie was like when he actually got terribly upset. He got even. Mattie turned to look at Tommie, with surprise and a hint of admiration actually registering on his face. Tommie was known for his quiet demeanor. If the words had come from anyone else, Mattie would have had a strong reaction to someone taking the lead and not following his order, but coming from Tommie on such a distasteful subject, Mattie was actually intrigued and wondered what would next come out of his gentle brother's mouth. He was proud of his brother and liked what he saw. Together, Mattie and Tommie helped the father begin his final three lifts.

The boys could see the hate in the father's eyes. *I will show these boys my strength and resilience, and then when I get off this bench, I will show them the bowels of hell.* On his second of three lifts, the good father's arms trembled but he managed to get the bar up.

"One more father and we can all go home."

To prepare for the last lift, the father took in as much air in his lungs as he could hold and let out a prolonged grunt. As he hit the mid point, he could not lift the bar any higher. The bar seemed to shiver and suspend in mid air. Then the bar and all the weight dropped hard on the father's chest. "Father, you are not the man you thought you were. Did you pass out, can you hear me? Well, so much for you going for the gold.

Tomorrow you are only going to feel pain and see a black and blue chest, you pious hypocrite?"

Tommie spoke nothing but truth. Tommie's sermon heightened the pent-up anger in Mattie. His thoughts focused on the father not being allowed to wake up tomorrow from this temporary slumber.

"Tommie, Father P is evil. He will make trouble for us. I imagine he cracked some ribs or worse. If we take the bar off him, then he will tell who knows what kind of story. Tommie, we cannot let him ruin anymore lives. We are going to leave the bar on him. It is between God and him on how he gains the strength to get the bar off. I am sure he will get the bar off. If not, someone will find him. They will think he accidentally dropped the bar because he had too much weight. Father P will have a hard time making up any other story. Go see if there is anyone in the hallway. If clear, we should leave."

When Tommie left to check the hallways, Mattie put an additional 25 pound weight on each end of the bar and two others by the bench. As Tommie, ran to the other end of the gym to see if the coast was clear, Mattie rolled the bar off the father's chest onto his neck. He had made sure the Father's head was looking straight up. When the bar had rolled onto the neck, the crunching sound of the larynx giving way to the massive weight could be heard. To make sure that the father chances of seeing tomorrow were significantly diminished, Mattie spread his arms to shoulder width and press hard down on the bar for at least a minute.

From the back of the weight room, Tommie called to Mattie, "Mattie, the hallway is all clear. Let's go." As Mattie left the weight room he looked back and remembered one of his grandfather sayings, "Expect nothing, anticipate something, and appreciate everything". *What did I expect would come out of talking to Father Patrick? Nothing. What did I anticipate? Threatening the good father. What do I appreciate? Everything from Tommie taking charge to the very demise of a wicked man. And as the good father had often said, "nobody mourns the wicked.*

Mattie had willfully taken a human life. It mattered not that this was his first and ultimate disconnect from normalcy and humanity. He felt no remorse. His actions had moved him on the outside of human normalcy. From this day forward, he would have to look in and adjust while in their company.

As Georgie, Tommie and Mattie approached their high school the next morning, they encountered a parking lot filled with police cars and an ambulance. The entrance to the school was abuzz with fellow students milling about talking. "What's going on?" Tommie asked totally oblivious that the scene could be related to their previous night's action.

"We're hearing there was some kind of accident that happened in the gym. One of the teachers overheard a policeman saying that it looked like a priest hurt himself. We think it may have been Father Patrick." Georgie, upon hearing the name, looked directly at the newfound student reporter, gave glancing looks at both brothers, looked to the heavens and smiled like a cat that had just eaten the canary. When news of the accidental death of Father Patrick was actually made public, Georgie wasn't the only boy who said a special prayer, thankful for the end to their private nightmares.

Tommie privately prayed each night for forgiveness and wondered, if they had taken the bar off the father's chest, would he have lived. He would never speak of that night to anyone including Mattie. He would never know Father P would have lived except for the punishment inflicted in secret by his brother.

Mattie felt justified, no remorse, no regret. He only wished he could have ended the reign of pain much sooner for Father Patrick.

Georgie now slept as sound as a newborn baby without a care in the world. His life would take on new meaning. One thing Georgie knew for sure was that his friends had spoken to Father Patrick.

Chapter 7

"To my family, I want you to know my life has been the American dream. I love you all. I was born to a family of faith, and love. My parents were role models for value and integrity. I came to America, found employment, met wonderful people and made lasting friends. Good fortune smiled on me. I was blessed with a family and, through hard work and good fortune, made a good living. My parents, my brother, my son, many close friends have gone before me to make a place for me in heaven. I love my Lord and am at peace. Dear God in Heaven most high, may God and our Lord always know, we put forward our lives to our Faith, our Family and our Friends. Heavenly Father, please watch over my family." After his barely audible voice trailed off, Vincent Anthony had uttered his last words, "I had no limits to what was possible, I had no fear of the unknown and I can lie here and be at peace because I have no remorse. Heavenly Father, My dear Lord, your will be done." Vincent Anthony closed his eyes and died. His generous heart had finally run its course.

The priest ceremoniously performed the last rites to finalize closure. The family members listened, made the sign of the cross, kissed Vincent on the forehead, and departed the Saint Francis Hospital room. At age 86, Vincent had lived and died like most souls would want. There was only one who did not shed a tear that day. Mattie was very sad and yet, disappointed. After losing his grandfather, he was crestfallen. The only person who truly knew and understood what was inside him was gone.

Mattie was never again going to ever feel the kind of feeling he had inside at his grandfather's passing.

"Ladies and gentlemen, as executor and lawyer to Vincent, shall we begin the reading of his last will and testament? After the reading of the will, it will be executed accordingly. Let's begin. I, Vincencio Dominic Antonini, alias, Vincent Dominic Anthony, being of sound mind authorize my executor upon my death to follow my instructions as follows. To the remaining member of the Antonini family, my brother Antonio, I bequeath ownership of the distillery. To my beloved and most beautiful wife, Carmella, I bequeath all my worldly possessions; property, assets, insurance policy and other business interests. I have left a private letter for Carmella to read regarding some of the pledges I have made to the remaining family members. It will be her responsibility to perform these pledges. As we all know, Vincent was articulate and to the point. These were his wishes. As for the specifics for execution, there are pages and pages of detail. He meticulously made a list of all his possessions a month prior to his death. I will perform the necessary legal duties in order to comply with transfers and other inheritance legalities."

Two weeks later after the reading of Grandfather Vincent Anthony's will, Greta and her twin sons were asked to come over for dinner at Grandmother Carmella's house. The night was a warm musty night in Peoria. As was commonly the case in July, the humidity was high and sticky. All the windows were open at the grand house Vincent had built ten years earlier on Grandview drive. Ceiling fans gently turned in every room. As the trio walked up the winding sidewalk to the front door, they were met by a stately dressed Grandmother Carmella. Even though she had medical problems on this night, she stood tall, dressed in a plain black dress with her favorite strand of pearls that had been given to her by Grandfather Vincent in Chicago so the story went. "Hello everyone, I am so glad you came. Boys, I hope that you didn't have other plans. Greta, how do you keep looking so young? Come in, I have some lemonade for us. How are you doing?"

"We are all fine. But more importantly, how are you doing? This is such a big house for one person. Why don't you come and stay with us for a while?" Greta had been worried about Grandmother Carmella since the funeral. Greta knew she was not a well woman, but tonight, Greta wished she could look as glamorous as Grandmother Carmella at her age. Tonight, Grandmother Carmella looked like royalty, so poised, so elegant.

The little party drank their lemonade in the living room and made small talk. The boys were trying to show respect but wished they could get on with the dinner and head back home. Dinner was a culinary surprise. Grandmother Carmella had personally prepared a traditional Italian dinner. She had to have spent hours in the kitchen. "Wow, Grandmother, this meal was fantastic. I am coming to eat here everyday." Tommie loved to compliment and tease his grandmother. She was special and he wanted her to know it.

"Why thank you Mister Thomas. What a wonderful compliment and you can come here anytime you want. Let's go back into the living room for our dessert. I need to talk with you before you leave. I have something that I need to get. You all go in the living room." She left the group and returned with a tray of Italian sweets and coffees. She also had some envelopes on the tray.

"I have three envelopes, one for each of you. Grandfather Vincent and I had many talks about you. Greta, our son Frankie loved you completely. Even in his darkest times, he often told us of his love and openly wept as he tormented himself over his failure to be the husband you deserved. We always were appreciative of how you took care of him and stood by him. Here is an envelope we hope will show you how much we love you." She handed the envelope to Greta who looked at it as if it were a treasured heirloom being passed from one generation to another.

"Boys, I have an envelope for each of you. I do not know what is inside them. Your Grandfather left me a note instructing me to ask each of you to read the letter and then destroy it. He asked that you not discuss your letter with anyone. He knows how you two are. You share everything. He said after you have read the letter, you would know why you are not to share the contents with each other." The boys accepted the unopened envelopes and thanked their Grandmother. The rest of the evening was small talk about the past, upcoming events and other pleasantries. No one spoke about the envelopes. Even on their return trip to their house, conversation was centered on the wonderful dinner and how well Grandmother Carmella looked. Once they got to their house, they went to their separate rooms to open their envelopes.

Greta opened her envelope. Inside was a short letter which read,

> To My Dearest Greta: You are a God fearing, good woman. You loved and watched over a good man. You do this family an honor by carrying our name. You have raised a wonderful family. For as long as you live, you will receive a monthly amount from a trust that has been set up for you at the Central National Bank of Peoria. Go meet with a banker by the name of Mr. Caudel Montgomery. He is an honest man. We have spoken many times about what was needed to ensure you are well taken care of. He will handle your affairs and work to ensure your account is well managed. Your account number where you will receive the money is CNB2021. Also, I pray that you will encourage the boys to go to college. They would be the first Anthony to attend college. They both have the academic achievements to be accepted in any university that they may choose.

I have provided Mr. Montgomery names of contacts to help them get into any university in the United States. Money has been set aside for their education. We love you Greta and the boys. May God bless you. Vincent Dominic Anthony

Tommie couldn't wait to open his envelope. He ripped it open like it was a Christmas present from his Grandfather. Why couldn't he share the contents? He silently read the contents.

To My Most Insightful Thomas S. Anthony: I have watched you grow into an intelligent, analytical young man. You think before you speak. You consider the consequences of your actions, especially if the family could be impacted. You and I have had many talks about the business world. You have a gift for business. I would take it as a personal favor if you would consider going to college. Northwestern University in Chicago is an excellent business school. Thomas, you are the one member of this family to continue the Anthony legacy. I believe you have the leadership characteristics to take the Anthony name to the highest level of recognition. I do not request such recognition for glory or prominence, but for respect. Respect should be for our God, our heritage, our loyalty to America and our fellow man. Thomas, I ask you to take on the responsibility of watching over your grandmother, your mother and your brother. They will need someone to be there for them. You are that person. You do not ever have to worry about having the financial means to carry out family business. A Mr. Caudel Montgomery will contact you at the proper time to go over any financial procedures you may require. Focus on your future, your true loves, and the family. Keep your mother happy through your achievements. Keep your brother on the straight and narrow by being there for him, to offer him counsel and to offer him another perspective.

You are not only the oldest brother but the wisest.

Lead without control! There are no Limits on what you can achieve. Have No Fear and aggressively pursue them. Grandfather Vincent Dominic Anthony.

Mattie did a nose dive into his bed. He threw his envelope on his night stand. His head and his heart were playing tug of war. *Why Grandfather? I need you here, not in heaven. What is in the envelope? Are you sending me a final plea to try to change me? We have talked and talked about how I feel about things. I do love you, but I cannot change. Your written words will not make me change.* He got up, grabbed the envelope and angrily tore it open.

To My Independent Matthew S. Anthony: I have watched you grow into a strong willed, confident young man. You always put the family first as I did for my father. I would do whatever was asked. I know that you were ashamed of your father and carry that shame where ever you go. But how can you be so judgmental of a man when you did not walk in his shoes? I said one day I would ask you for a favor. This favor is as hard for me to ask as it was when my father asked me to leave Italy and come to America. I believe Thomas will go to college in the fall after graduating from high school. He is an idealist and will try to rationalize as the oldest Anthony brother that he should be first to join the armed forces and go to Viet Nam to prove his family loyalty and courage to his country. He is not strong enough to survive such an ordeal. My request to you is for you to step forward and join the armed forces, the Marines, like your father. Only then will you know your father completely. Only then will you find the person you will become. You are a warrior, a survivor. Make Thomas promise not to join with you. He should be the one to watch over the family from here.

When you return, I pray you will go to college. Graduating from a top university would become your most prized medal you could earn for the family. You do not ever have to worry about having the financial means to carry out my request. A Mr. Caudel Montgomery will contact you at the proper time to go over any financial procedures you may require. Focus on your future, your true loves, and the family.

You are not only the strongest brother but the only one who could survive such an ordeal.

Command without compromise! There are no limits to your capabilities. Have No Fear about what tomorrow will bring and have no remorse on the road you will travel. Grandfather Vincent Dominic Anthony.

Per their grandfather's wish and their grandmother's instruction, both boys went to sleep that night knowing what was to be written in the next chapter of their life. All that remained of their grandfather's private requests were tiny bits of paper which would be thrown in the trash. Mentally, the letters would forever be embedded in the Anthonys very DNA.

Chapter 8

"Mattie, we only have a couple of weeks before we graduate from Spalding High. We have got to start thinking about what we are going to do. Have you thought about college? You know we have to go to college if we are going to get good jobs. I know that Grandfather had trust funds set up for us when we reach 21, but I do not think we should rely on his money. We do not even know the details of the trust. We need to earn and pay our own ways. I think I might stay close to home and go to Northwestern University. It is close to Chicago and I really want to see what it is like to live in such a big city. What do you think about going with me?" Tommie was feeling Mattie out.

Both boys had taken college entrance examinations and had their IQ tested as well. Both boys had IQs numbers close to those associated with genius intellect. Little did anyone realize that both boys possessed eidetic or photographic memory. The boys possessed an ability to recall images, sounds and objects from memory with extraordinarily detailed vivid recall with extreme accuracy and with an abundant volume. One of the boy's first insights into their gift was after they took an aptitude test in primary school. In the test, they were to study an image for 30 seconds and, after a period of time, they were to attempt to recall the image to their tester. The boys laughed that night as they told their experience to each other. "Tommie, you should have seen the lady when I told her what I saw. I did not even tell her all I saw because I wanted to get back to my class. She said I was excellent at maintaining memory for a short time. I can still see the picture as if it were standing right there in front of me."

"Me too! Mattie, was your picture of a pasture with farm animals, a big red barn with a rooster on top, and corn growing?"

"No, mine was a picture of a zoo with a lot of animals, a lion eating some meat, a monkey with three bananas, some zoo keeper with a bucket of fish and goofy glasses."

Learning came easy, but it was their personal drive that brought notice. They both were not content unless they had excelled at what ever they took on. Both were Valedictorians of their high school class and expected to achieve top honors when they went to college.

Mattie had no intention to go with Tommie. He had already approached Peoria's local Marine recruiting office and asked for some information. "Tommie, you know how I hate all that rah rah stuff. I know I should go to college, but I need some time to think about where I would want to go and what I would like to do. You know what you want, so I say go after that dream. Mother would be so proud and would visit often I know. She still talks of her wedding night in Chicago like it was yesterday. She loves Chicago. You have Uncle Tony living up there so you could always call on him if you needed anything. I really am thinking about joining the Marines and see the world."

"Are you nuts? See the world? Right now, every soldier heads for Viet Nam. Mattie, if you go sign up for the Marines, then I am going with you."

"Be real, Tommie. First, they would never take twin brothers and put them in battle together. One would go. The other would go to Germany or be kept state side. Mom would be alone. She would worry about both of us. She does not need that. You have to stay and provide her with constant re-assurance that all will be ok. You hear me. You are not going to join the Marines, under no circumstances. Swear on our family name that you will not join the Marines and will go to some university. Tommie, do you swear?"

Tommie knew he had promised to go college so reluctantly, he knew what his response must be. "I swear, Mattie. But before you join up, will you give this some serious thought? Please consider going with me. Just think of all the fun we could have together. When you have a final decision, we will tell Mother of our plans. OK?"

That May, 1961, Greta and Grandmother Carmella attended the high school graduation of Thomas and Mathew Anthony. The pride of the Anthony and Shanine families were never as evident as when the boys were announced to the audience as co-Valedictorians. Creative, clever thinking was an inbred characteristic both boys shared. They agreed to both give a speech on the same topic, The American Dream. They thought that this topic would have made their grandfather very proud. Thomas' speech focused on the pursuit of the American Dream and that achievement was within every graduate's reach. Good fortune always resulted in achieving one's goals when one set his sights high and planned accordingly. Mathew's speech took on a different tone. The American Dream started with oneself. When barriers came, and they were sure to come, one had to be strong, confident in one's capabilities to knock down those barriers. Do not shortchange your limitations. Conquer barriers with no fear. Do not let anyone tell you that you could not do something.

In July, 1961, Tommie received his acceptance papers from Northwestern University. One week later, Mattie got his official orders to report to St. Louis, Missouri, for hearing, visual and physical evaluation. Unless you were really impaired, it was a foregone conclusion you would pass. The stage was set for the boys to go their separate ways for the first time in their lives. While each possessed a unique personality, to the outsider, they were identical in everyway.

On August 12, 1961, Mathew S. Anthony boarded a train in Peoria bound for St. Louis along with 5 other young men. When Mattie reached his assigned seat, he looked out the window and waved to his mother and his brother. He quickly suppressed loneliness for the first time in his life. This was his destiny. No Fear! His support structure was no longer going to be there for him. He was going to have to make loneliness an art form. His grandfather had said no fear in whatever you were to undertake. Size up the challenge, and then meet the challenge head on. Mattie philosophized about his future. *For what is about to unfold, I am a mystery even to myself. I wonder not from self pity, only from a frustration of not knowing of the subject which I must be all knowing. I will learn how to be the best that I can be. No limits, No Fear, No Remorse.*

The St. Louis armed services induction center was similar to the stock yards Mattie had worked one summer. Instead of cows, pigs or sheep being herded into corrals, it was people. Whether the person had enlisted or been drafted, the empty look in their eyes spoke volumes of their confusion on the future. During the eye examination, unbeknownst to Mattie, a Drill Instructor had walked up behind him. The DI slapped Mattie on the butt hard. "Congratulations boy, you are one fine physical specimen who is going to become one hell of a marine. Take this card and get in line over there. When you complete the rest of your evaluations, son, you are one of the fortunate sons that are going to Parris Island, in beautiful Beaufort, South Carolina." It was everything that Mattie could do to not retaliate from the piercing sting coming from his butt slap. Mattie would spend thirteen weeks cut off from the civilian world adapting to the Marine Corps lifestyle. During his training, he was exposed to a variety of subjects including personal hygiene under all circumstances, close order drills, and, his favorites, weapons and the Marine Corps Martial Arts Program. Mattie received the maximum score in the standard physical fitness test, excelled at combat-oriented swimming qualifications, and qualified as an expert in rifle marksmanship. Mattie was recognized as the top recruit of his company.

"Private Anthony, the company commander wants you to report to HQ on the double."

"Sir, you wish to speak to me?"

"Anthony, you are a special recruit. You have both the physical and mental attributes to make a superior Marine. I have put you in for Marine Officer Candidates School. We usually look for college graduates, but after reviewing your high school credentials and the aptitude test we gave you, you scored off the charts. You would have no trouble becoming a graduate lieutenant. You will be heading to our Marine Corps Base in Quantico, Virginia. Good luck son. We need officers like you to lead our brave men to victory in Viet Nam. Don't let your country down." Mattie reported as ordered, and did graduate with honors as a First Lieutenant. While there, he also had the opportunity to meet some recruits going through some of the same training. But they were headed for assignments with the Federal Bureau of Investigation. As it so happened, the FBI Academy as well as the Drug Enforcement Agency principal research and training facilities were located on the same base.

Mattie had liked his basic training immediately. He knew he was in the right place when his basic training drill sergeant, a recent graduate from the killing fields of Viet Nam, told him that he wanted them to remember two things. "Gentlemen, you will be going to Viet Nam. The enemy is motivated to defeat you, to kill you. Your motivation is simple. You eliminate those who are your enemy. When in combat with the enemy, when in doubt, empty your magazine. After the fighting has stopped, the only thing you should feel when you kill is the recoil pain from your rifle. Do as I say, for you will witness first hand that growing old is much better than the alternative—dying young."

Chapter 9

Vietnam 1965: Mattie was in the final days of his second Viet Nam tour. He had learned the ways of the jungle well. He had studied and, better yet, tortured his enemy to learn their ways on how to stay alive. "Gentlemen, nothing can run away with your innocence and taint your blessed Holy Water like Viet Nam. Here you set your own rules and truly play your own game. You can rationalize that you are neither a man nor monster, but creator, judge, and exterminator. You will become like me, a man without a conscience. No Fear, No Remorse." He had accomplished what his grandfather had asked he set out to do, to understand what caused his father's internal struggles. War caused his father to seek out alcohol to erase his demons. Mattie went down another avenue. Mattie had become oblivious to pain, relationships, and caring. He had become disillusioned and cynical about his fellow man. When you reach a place where you do not believe in anything, you do not worry about heaven or hell.

Mattie looked at his platoon of mercenaries. "Gentlemen, the world is not what we want it to be. It's not what I want or you want. What matters is what our country wants. We are normal people placed in abnormal circumstances. I have searched for meaning. I have walked in the belly of the beast. Welcome to my world." Mattie now knew what his grandfather had meant when he asked him not to judge his father until he understood where his father came from. The killing, maiming, drugs, alcohol, and sex were all staples of war. He had dipped his toe in the water and chose not to let it destroy him like it did his father. Mattie was not big on concepts, but if there was a Hell, then he understood he must be in it. Viet Nam was Hell on earth.

"I would rather burn than get burned. I want to pass through the flames of death and rise from the ashes of rejuvenation like a Phoenix." Mattie once shouted at the top of his lungs during his first fire fight. He was a man intent on taking out his inhibitions on his enemy. Kill or be killed. He was a man possessed. That day he single handedly killed 12 VC. He took extreme pleasure on two kills. He had stalked as if they were prey and terminated them with his serrated knife. His adrenaline was pumping through his veins so feverishly that he almost decapitated his two conquests. He still fondly remembered his first mission and one of his sergeants saying, "Soldier, you like this shit. I have never seen anyone so eager to engage with the enemy to get his ass blown away. Son, you are a born killer. I do not know how long you will be with us, but boy, you deliver death like a mailman. Nothing stops you." Over the next two years, word had spread among the American and VC troops about some Special Forces guy they called the Mailman who was ruthless, cold-blooded, merciless and suicidal fearless. His exploits, covert missions and body count were topics of many a camp,s nightly conversation. The mailman's real name seemed to evaporate in the heat of Viet Nam.

Mattie's second tour of duty was coming to an end. He knew the mission he was about to take on could be his last mission. Prior to leading his men out into the Viet Nam bush, he was told to report to Colonel Scott Johnson upon his return. Mattie was sure that he would be given his orders to return to stateside where he would resume his "normal" life.

Mattie's mind had erected all the defense mechanisms for re-entering normal society. *Marines, sailors and airmen give their lives in the line of duty that is often trivialized under the rationalization and expectation of war. Overlooked are thousands more who come home on stretchers, horribly wounded,* mangled to face months or years in military hospitals. Then are those who are, like my father and now me, disfigured in the least understood annuls of medicine, the brain. Unless we seek help or go off some deep end and display erratic behavior, we are left to find our own peace or cures. We are left to our "normal" lives. What the hell is normal? My abnormality is my normality.

The normal cannot understand abnormal thinking or behaviors. Therefore the theorem must then be, abnormal does not have to understand or accept the normal. Or being in the normal character mode is very uncomfortable to the abnormal. How do one disguise abnormality? Everyone has their ghosts. What is a normal life? Any minute could be an event to cause my last breath.

I like being alone. Isolation, being completely alone takes away the need to be normal. When alone, I can truly hide the person who I want to set free. When I am alone, there is no pretending, no hiding. Being what I am, I also know that there is no time to relax. My most pressing need is to find a way of life where I can find a safe refuge. My biased opinions would be considered forbidden by society thus must be hidden from the most discriminating eyes and ears. Hell, the Big Bad Wolf lives inside all of us. We just don't want others to see it. So we control it, hide it and 99% of the time never let the wolf howl at the moon. Not me!

Lt. Matthew Anthony and his men were ready. They had traveled deep into enemy territory and had reached their destination coordinates undetected. As they lay camouflaged in the jungle, the group watched their target, a small little community of Duong Chi Lai. According to reliable informants, this community housed some of the local leaders of the Viet Cong and was a central logistics site for guns and ammunition. This community was nothing more than a clearing within the dense jungle vegetation. The nine houses were little more than huts built to keep rain and sun off the village inhabitants. Their animals, chickens and pigs, were allowed to roam at will in unkempt surroundings.

To a man, Mattie's team was tired. From the point where their helicopter had dropped them off, the team had covered 25 miles through dense jungle to get to their destination by early morning light. Mattie and his men ate rations and drank stale water out of their plastic canteens. When this group of men traveled, they traveled light. Their mission was always the same; hunt, destroy, and get back alive as quickly as they had arrived. Mattie felt an adrenalin surge in his body giving him his last reserve of energy as he took one more look around to ensure his men were in position. Above his head, the jungle canopy was coming to life. Birds began to squawk and flew about. The sun was rising. Movement in the village drew everyone's attention. All the Marines were now on alert. From out of the central hut came a small man dressed in the uniform of the VC, straw hat, black shirt, black cut off pants and sandals. It was the man that Mattie had seen in photographs. This was one their main targets.

Mattie had three points he always reminded his men before heading out on a mission. No one gets left behind, no one is to die on his team, and when the order was given, his men were to kill anything that moved. He wasn't going to let even a child escape the wrath. In this world, children were soldiers too. He had witnessed a child calmly walk over to a soldier and lay down an explosive, then ran. The grenade exploded and took the life of an American soldier on his team. This was war. There was to be no compassion in war. If you live with the enemy, you die with the enemy. When nothing moved, the men were to burn the remains and get out. He would leave no time for conscience to get an upper hand. Only this time, Mattie needed to extract some information from his target. He had instructed his sniper that when they engaged their target and had a clear shot, he was to shoot him in his knee cap, if possible, both. Mattie signaled to his sniper that the man who had just come out of the hut was indeed their target.

Killing was not for the faint of heart. Too often people turn soft after witnessing a downed body or the savageness of the deed. Killing was a nasty business and it was easy to lose your nerve if you didn't operate under tight constraints. He had hand picked his team from listening to nightly camp stories he had heard while he had been in the bush. Put a bullet in the head, dispose of the body, and move on. Don't look over you shoulder. This was war, no fear, justified.

The morning heat was climbing. The area was quite calm. In Viet Nam, the heat engulfs you like a sauna even though it was only daybreak. Steam rose about the village clearing as if the village was being cooked on some earthly stove. Mattie felt the beads of sweat beginning to run down his face and back. Mattie signaled for his men to get ready. They all readied for the assault. Mortars were positioned and at the ready, grenades ready to be launched, and every M-16 has been shouldered and a target sighted. Mattie held up his right hand so that all could see he had two fingers pointed at the sky. In two minutes, a rain of death would commence. Mattie relished the adrenaline rush just before the assault. From the very first time he fired his rifle in basic training, Mattie loved the sound of the shells being ejected from his M-16. The heat from the barrel of his rifle confirmed he was truly engaged in his quest to annihilate the enemy.

Mattie gave the signal and, with the precision of a surgeon, the sniper fired the first shot. The target seemed to look dazed and sought to understand what had just happened. In a split second, his shattered knee gave way and he began to fall, simultaneously as a bullet found his other knee. His scream had brought others running out of their shelters into the deathly rain of bullets, mortars and grenades. Mattie's men had taken their conductor's signal and in unison, brought the very bowels of hell to this village. The people who had run out of the structures fell within six feet of their exit points. Some of the villagers had guns, others did not. No matter, they were enemy, they would die. After only five minutes, the conductor of this orchestra cut the music. For the next five minutes, silence. No one moved from either the orchestra pit or their fallen audience.

Another signal and the team cautiously moved out of their camouflaged positions toward the hut structures. Each hut was carefully searched and anyone left in the huts were brought out and sat by the downed target. A soldier with a flame thrower was brought up and waited for orders for when the huts were to be torched. The rest of the team had positioned themselves and waited. They knew if any other people had managed to hide in the huts, when they tried to flee to escape the flames, they would meet the same fate as those who had exited earlier. Within 30 minutes, all of the villages' inhabitants, 26 in all, would be dead. To those who cared to count, 14 men, six teenage boys and six women would no longer be among the living. In Mattie's emotionless mind, the enemy was wicked and nobody should mourn the wicked.

The only thing that truly drove Mattie during his entire tour in Viet Nam was to live for another day. Nothing else mattered. There were no rules, no conscience, and no beliefs to cause him to hesitate or cloud his motives for even a micro second. Mattie did not believe in anything so he did not worry about his actions sending him to heaven or hell. Mattie stressed to his men that it was better to kill than to be killed.

Mattie sat up the downed target who had lost a tremendous amount of blood. His shattered legs dangled like they were puppets on a string. "You speak English?" Mattie shook the man to ensure he had regained some amount of consciousness. The VC did not respond. "Yong Ho, ask him where are the weapons? Are they hidden in an underground tunnel system around here?" The VC still did not respond. "Shit, you are going to make this uncivilized by not answering." Mattie took his large knife and cut open the VCs black shirt. Yong Ho, ask him again and tell him if he does not answer, I will begin to cut him like one of his chickens or pigs. I will slowly strip the skin back all over his body. Tell him he will not die, he will only feel pain. Tell him." Yong Ho translated the English to Vietnamese. The VC leader replied. Yong Ho smiled. "What did he say?"

"Basically, fuck you. I cleaned it up so you would not get your feelings hurt." The men laughed. Mattie pushed the leader onto his back. Mattie motioned for two of his men to hold his arms. Like a hunter gutting a downed deer, Mattie sliced the man's stomach as precisely as if he were going to perform heart surgery. Instead of cutting deeply, he cut another slice parallel to the first cut. He then basically took the knife and began to slowly strip the skin between the two incisions. The process reminded Mattie of how he took out bacon from a package one strip at a time. The VC leader's piercing scream could unnerve any human moral fiber, but not Mattie's or his men.

"Ask him again. Only tell him this time I will strip much more slowly." Mattie knew that stripping the skin causes significantly more pain than a deeper cut. He knew he would get his answer this time. And he did. One of Mattie's men went to a spot 100 meters from the hut where the leader said they could find the entrance to the tunnel. The soldier came back and acknowledged the tunnel in the underbrush. Mattie turned to the leader and the few other prisoners who had survived the initial onslaught and, without emotion, said, "You are about to be a casualty of war. May your higher power accept you into his arms." He picked up his M-16 and shot them all. Mattie sent one of his "mole" men down into the tunnel. They encountered only one young boy who was to guard the stockpile. He was quickly killed with close range pistol fire. Charges were set in the dirt cavern room with all the weapons and detonated when his men were clear. The entire village was set afire.

The last VC who felt his knife had a low pain tolerance, and told him more than he expected. His interrogation on identification of supply trails, troop movements, etc. also yielded accurate information on this place. "Destruction of this site should disrupt the VC supply chain for at least a month. Hopefully in that month, we will kill more VC than they kill of us." *This was a great day,* thought Mattie. "Let's make for the barn, boys." The order was given and the men, like slithering snakes in the underbrush, set out for their base camp.

Mattie took in a deep breathe and exhaled loudly through his mouth. His mind was at ease. *Ah, just another day at the office. Good over evil. Under all this pressure, it is easy to see what I can do, am capable of doing. Viet Nam have given me a clearer picture of who I am. The requirements of this war has convinced me the only way to survive is to be the bigger monster. Since war has made us all monsters, my conscience won't let me take any blame for whatever happens. I can live with this. Therefore, the only remaining question really is, am I evil's enemy or his handyman?"*

Upon their return to base camp, Mattie held a debriefing with his CO to go over the events and actions. Mattie detailed, as much as he felt needed to be told, to his CO who congratulated him on his successful mission. Then his CO told Mattie to report to Colonel Johnson. When asked, "About what?" The CO just shrugged his shoulders and said, "get moving."

Chapter 10

"Colonel, you wanted to see me?" Mattie had never met Colonel Scott Johnson. He had heard through the grapevine that this colonel was not just a career soldier, but also tied to the CIA. Mattie always suspected the CIA was in their midst given some the covert ops he was sent on. One mission into Cambodia, one in Thailand and once even to a spot he swore was in China, were beyond the eyes of the media and most stateside politicians. Whoever wrote the book on "be all you can be" definitely had the colonel in mind. The colonel was around six foot one. His marine haircut, ridged forehead, square jaw and cold dead eyes would cause most to look away. He filled out his fatigues with a body that only came from disciplined workouts. Mattie could tell from his thick hands that he was a martial arts expert. On a table before him was a folder with the name Mathew S. Anthony across the top.

"Welcome back, soldier. Word is that your team was able to neutralize and destroy a critical link in the enemies' supply chain. Were you able to interrogate their leader and get any useful intelligence? Silly question, from what I hear and read, you always get what you set out to do. You have received just about every medal one could earn here in Viet Nam. Yet, again from what I hear, you refuse to even wear your rank with your platoon. Apparently you have become sort of a ghost legend by US and VC troops fighting in this country. Are you the man that people fear and refer to as the Mailman?" The colonel paused to allow this man with dirty fatigue pants, cut off t-shirt, and a bandana around his head to speak.

"Colonel, I am an American soldier. I was someone who at a point in my life wrote a blank check payable to the United States of America for an amount of "up to, and including my life". In my mind, the fact I am still alive after two tours of duty is my only gauge as to my deeds and my honor to my country. Every soldier here in Viet Nam has a nickname. I am sure there are all kind of names which I am called, starting with Mr. Asshole, Doctor Dick and who knows what. I do not pay any attention to what is used or who is doing the talking. I lead my men the best I can, perform to the best of my abilities, and try not to rationalize what the fuck we are doing here." Mattie was already bored and wanted nothing more than to go back to his private solitude and go to sleep. Sleep, what a concept for the mind. Sleep, escape for some, nightmare for others. "If the colonel has nothing else for me, I would like to get back to my platoon."

The colonel picked up and opened the folder. He pulled out a sheet of paper. "You have received a promotion to major. You only have two months before you are to return to the states. You are somewhat of a novelty. Coming up from the enlisted ranks, making it all the way to the rank of major, and decorated to the hilt, the brass back in Washington does not want you to become some VC trophy. So we are sending you back to the states tomorrow. Pack up your things, get drunk with your platoon tonight and be ready to board a helicopter at 0600 hours tomorrow. The helicopter will take you to Da Nang where you will catch a series of planes until you land stateside. Understand?"

Mattie stood. "Colonel, I want to complete my . . ." Mattie was interrupted.

"Son, you do not understand. You are no longer a warrior. You are going to be transformed back into civilian human mode at 0600 hours tomorrow. There is no discussion. However, there is one other matter I would like to discuss. Please retake your seat and listen to what I have to say. I too am leaving tomorrow for a new assignment. In the coming years, there will be different types of wars to be fought than the type here in the jungles of Viet Nam. The wars will not be with guns so much as ideology, technology, politics and wealth. There are forces being birthed that may well try to undermine the very foundation that our forefathers sought to preserve in their writing of the Declaration of Independence. Major Anthony, you are a man who comes from a God fearing family of flag wavers with humble beginnings. These new forces wish to take that away from America, to weaken America any way they can. Russia, Cuba, Central and South America, all should be on our radar screen for future actions. There are terrorists in our very midst. Corrective actions will be required. These corrective actions one would not call a war because war ends. These will be special interest actions that could continue for years. My new assignment is to put together a company of employees who will have solid military background and experience along with others who will have strong business acumen. I would like to enlist you into this company. Would you consider joining our little company? When we get back to the US, would you take a few days and come with me to Washington to hear about our company and how you might be of value and benefit?"

"Colonel, I will meet with you, but I want you to know upfront. My next mission is to complete college. I made a vow to complete a request from someone I admired more than anything. Once I complete college, I am free to pursue any thing I deem meets with my aspirations. So why don't I save us both a little time. I assume your company will offer various services around the world to thwart your so called actions. You say that your company will be in the business for years, so if you think I could be a valuable asset to your company, contact me after I graduate. I may be interested. So sir, if you will excuse me, I am going to get drunk with the most honorable and bravest men I will ever know."

Jim A. Roppa

As Mattie prepared to be dismissed, the colonel gave him his last order, "If you are so aggressive, win at all cost kind of a guy, honor your vow by applying at an Ivy League school. See if you can keep up with the royalty of intelligence and society."

"I may just do that." Mattie said his goodbyes to Viet Nam with those he respected most. Some he would never forget and some he would forever keep on his "specialty" list.

Chapter 11

Four years had passed since Mattie had received his honorable discharge papers from the United States Marine Corps. Standing at this honored lectern, Mattie's mind flashed back to a more somber time. There he was standing at attention, his back as straight as his line of sight to his commanding officer to whom he offered his departing salute. He did not want to leave. There was still work to be done in this hell hole called Viet Nam. This chapter of his life was over. He boarded the helicopter and, as it flew him out of the bush, he could not help but wonder how he could ever go back to his normal, new life, the next phase of his adult journey.

The reunion with his mother and brother was a special moment. The relief he saw in his mother's eyes as she kissed him and held him tight etched into his heart. She ranked up there with the Virgin Mary in his mind. His mother and brother had written him religiously telling him of their daily lives, keeping him current with local news and achievements. In return, Mattie had only written a handful of letters while stationed in Viet Nam. How could he write about the current events he was orchestrating? His letters were short and sweet with little reality of his feelings or activities. The letters were almost carbon copies of one another filled with the same few words, "Dear Mother and Tommie, I am alive and doing well. I love reading your letters. Glad all is well with you. You do not have to worry so much about me. I am fine. I will send you another letter when I come out of the bush. Your loving Son and Better Looking Brother, Mattie."

Upon his return to the U.S., Mattie set out to complete the last leg of the quest ordained by his grandfather, to get a college education. Mattie immediately began to apply to a number of the best universities in the US. Tommie tried to persuade Mattie to attend Northwestern University in Evanston where he had graduated with honors. "Mattie, Northwestern is one of the top rated business universities in the country. You need to re-acclimate yourself with the business world. I know the professors, the courses, and together, you will be the next Anthony to graduate Magna Cum Laude." Tommie couldn't help but take a few jabs at his brother. Oh how he had missed him and prayed every night for his safe return.

"Tommie, if I went to Northwestern U, got better grades, dated more women or the professors liked me better, you would be pissed for life. I cannot be responsible for any insecurities you harbor. Besides, I prefer a top university, not some second rate "wanna be top" university. I think I am more Ivy League material. What do you think about that?" Mattie had only spent a month in Peoria when he received notice that he was accepted to Harvard University. His family was elated. The entire city of Peoria, the Italian American Club and the Lebanese Itoo Club were abuzz about the news of Mattie's military honors and his acceptance into Harvard University. Tommie was so proud of his brother's admission into Harvard that he couldn't wait to tell everyone he worked with about the next chapter of his brother's saga. Mattie said his goodbyes and set out for Harvard, the oldest institution of higher learning in the United States and, a little known fact, the first and oldest corporation in the United States. Tommie, a newly educated scholar of industry, had actually provided this factoid.

The transition of this stage of his life went as smoothly as if the event were preordained. With the name of a realtor given to him by his mother, Mattie took only two days to find a place to live in Cambridge,

Massachusetts. It was at this time that Mattie really became aware of how far his family name and his grandfather's contacts could reach out. Between his grandfather's far reaching networks of business associates, his close personal Peoria friends and connected politicians throughout Illinois, and the letters of recommendation sent from a variety of Washington military dignitaries, getting admittance to such a prestigious institution was a minor formality compared to the normal process. Apparently, a couple of months prior to his admission, the Dean of the Harvard business school had received a number of calls from very important people and past graduates from around the country on his behalf. He remembered the looks he got walking across the campus that first year. Students couldn't quite figure Mattie out. Was he a grad student, a professor, or what? He was older, seemed to be so much more mature, confident and definitely totally focused. From his rigid daily 5am workouts in the student physical fitness center to the endless hours he spent in the library on his class work, Mattie displayed the unyielding will to be stronger and smarter than anyone at Harvard. Little did these students know that this ex Special Forces Marine was on a mission; get his degree, get a prominent job, and then who knew what.

In his senior year, the Viet Nam campaign was showing signs of failure and imminent retreat from Viet Nam. Anti war rallies and protests were seen nightly on television. Politicians were feathering their political careers on denouncing the senseless loss of life. The original reason for stopping the communists in Southeast Asia were no longer considered rational. Debates on Viet Nam were common place in every corner of the Harvard campus or in every coffee shop. Stories of corporate profiteering from high priced weapons to toilet seats showed how those who stayed back were benefiting from the war. One day sitting in one of his elective psychology courses, looking every bit the Ivy Leaguer, all handsome and dressed in his favorite casual sweater, Mattie became very agitated with his professor, Dr. Eugene Siebenstein.

Dr. Siebenstein was considered a genius, an intellectual's intellectual. His published papers and numerous books were heralded as "must read" in his field. He looked like a rumbled pile of clothes with a head. His hair was dirty white and wiry. His hair looked like a firecracker had gone off sending each strand of hair in different directions. Dr. Siebenstein was a bit of a recluse and had informed his students that he would never, and he meant never, be available for after class discussions. He also loved to pontificate and talk down to his students every chance he got on his superior intellectual status by saying, "should you graduate and feel one day that we could socialize as peers, think again. I have no peers." The man was an icon in his own mind. To him, "thought pioneers" who plowed the plains of the mind like Freud were so far beneath his utterances, it made him wince. Siebenstein loved to show the flaws in the theories of other leaders in the field of psychology.

Siebenstein had written numerous books on neurophysiology which involved the study of both healthy individuals and patients. He specialized in the study of cognitive neuropsychiatry in an attempt to infer theories of normal mind and brain functions by looking for differences in patterns of remaining ability (known as 'functional disassociations') which can give clues as to whether abilities are composed of smaller functions, or are controlled by a single cognitive mechanism. In his quest to understand the human psyche, he became incensed at times in his lectures and would attack phantoms who kept him from being universally admired for his writings. He was a chain smoker who smoked incessantly throughout the duration of his lectures. His fingers were so stained that they were repulsive.

On one particular day, Dr. Siebenstein wanted to express his thoughts on returning Viet Nam veterans, especially those loyal to their cause and fellow soldiers. "Today, class, let's deviate from our assigned material and discuss current events. I saw on the news today a disheveled man with his army coat, beret, and beard and carrying the American Flag. The man probably had no education, was a drug addict, and joined the army because he couldn't get a job. While drug induced, he most certainly killed indiscriminately under the belief he was making America safe." Dr. Siebenstein went on for 45 minutes on how immoral the American soldier had become. How the American soldier had no redeeming value after being brainwashed. How his mind would forever be warped about an unjust, corrupt war against people who meant no harm. The good Dr. couldn't seem to find any good in such a human being after participating in the war.

Mattie couldn't contain his resentment. He knew Dr. Siebenstein hated to be interrupted when he was espousing gems of the universal. But Mattie could take no more. "Excuse me, Dr. Siebenstein. I hate to interrupt such a well thought out hypothesis, but aren't you over reacting a little bit, or, to say the least, generalizing a wee bit? Surely you are not condemning all those brave men who died in Viet Nam. Most of the soldiers were drafted and fought for a cause that America once felt just."

The professor interrupted. He was not about to let a student take over his class and debate in an open forum. "Excuse me, sir. Who are you again and how dare you speak on matters above your intellectual grasp?" After five minutes of ridicule and other indignations to Mattie, he dismissed Mattie's question and returned to his tirade of the American soldier and their warped brains and souls.

This man had gone too far. He wanted to bring shame to American soldiers, to blame them, to cast them as future dregs of society. Mattie decided to pay Dr. Eugene Siebenstein a house call that night. He took along some trinkets he had picked up over the years at the chemistry and physics lab to share with the good Doctor. He had stood outside the Doctor's house for a good hour to determine if anyone else could possibly be inside. He knew from the Doctor's own mouth that he never had any guests ever in his home. He wasn't married and was so old that live-in parents were out of the question. He put on medical gloves and knocked on the door. When Dr. Siebenstein turned the doorknob to open the door, Mattie pushed the door hard back inside quickly, knocking Dr. Siebenstein to the floor.

With Dr. Siebenstein sitting like a Buddha statue in the center of his hallway, eyes and mouth wide open, Mattie began his lecture. "Dr. Siebenstein. There are only two recognized forces that have ever offered to die for your freedom . . . Jesus Christ and the American soldier. You better believe that I am not Jesus Christ, but by God, I am an American soldier who fought for you in Viet Nam and am about to deliver you from evil. Either you believe in me or you die. You can make the choice. I bet there is no way you can get your genius around the twisted justice that is before you. Tomorrow in class, I want you to apologize to all American soldiers and me. Will you do that? By the way, you asked who I am in class but didn't allow me the privilege to inform you that I am Mathew S. Anthony."

As he strained to regain an upright position, Dr. Siebenstein defiantly responded. "Mr. Anthony, get out of my house. I would never apologize for my comments or positions I profess. You on the other hand are about to find out what they do to college boys in jail." Dr. Siebenstein had regained his self professed human superiority and immense over-inflated self-esteem.

"I thought so." Mattie hit Dr. Siebenstein square on the jaw. Dr. Siebenstein dropped unconscious. Mattie picked up the 170 pounds of dead weight like a sack of potatoes and placed Dr. Siebenstein on his couch. He looked around and found a bottle of scotch and a glass and placed them on the end table adjacent to the couch. From the bag he carried, Mattie took out some white phosphorous and magnesium and sprinkled the chemicals on the floor next to the couch and around the room. He knew what these chemicals would do when ignited from the numerous times he used them in Viet Nam. The white phosphorus was a useful way to dislodge the Viet Cong from their tunnels or other enclosed spaces as the burning white phosphorus absorbed oxygen, causing the victims to suffocate or suffer serious burns. There was going to be a hot fire in here tonight. He found an ash tray full of cigarette butts and placed them on the floor next to the draped hand of Dr. Siebenstein. He lit a cigarette and placed it in the middle of the chemicals. In a few seconds, the lit cigarette ignited the chemicals. There was a flash and suddenly a hot fire engulfed the sofa and Dr. Siebenstein. Mattie calmly gathered up his bag and left through the front door. The street was quiet with no one out. He walked down the block. He glanced over his shoulder to see smoke beginning to seep its way out of the house. Then flames appeared. Mattie knew that Dr. Siebenstein would not be showing up to class. Mattie knew the good Dr. would never retract or be civil to any cause. Mattie calmly walked away, no remorse.

Those who investigated the fire were quick to conclude that the resident had been smoking and drinking when he probably fell asleep. The origin of the fire was around the sofa most probably caused by a dropped cigarette. The only cause for question was that the fire was so hot that the body was almost completely incinerated, burned beyond recognition. Neither the fire chief nor head police magistrate spent an inordinate amount of time or even felt compelled to determine if any unusual accelerant had been used. Sofas burn hot. Case closed.

Mattie graduated in the top 10 percent of his class. He had earned a Harvard degree in business economics and marketing. As for his psychology class, he was especially amused at receiving an A grade. Another professor had stepped in and, without the background of past performances since Dr. Siebenstein kept all his records at his incinerated home, everyone in the class had received an A. He had completed his grandfather's last wishes. He was now free to pursue his own ambitions.

Chapter 12

Mattie was relishing his past month being with his mother, traveling on weekends between Peoria and Chicago to see Thomas, and considering what he wanted to do next. Tommie was doing extremely well with AndrewPolk. The last meeting between brothers caught Mattie off guard. He should have known something was up because, just prior to heading off to Chicago, his mother gave him a camera. "Mattie, I do not have any pictures of Tommie and you together for a couple of years now. While you are there, will you have someone take pictures of the two of you together?" Mattie's mother wanted this meeting to be documented.

Mattie arrived at Tommie's Lake Shore Drive high rise apartment building around 6:00pm. He knew there was no reason to get there any earlier because Tommie always worked late. Mattie had his own key so it was 50/50 whether Tommie would be there. His apartment suite was on the 21st floor overlooking Lake Michigan. Mattie loved visiting his brother. His suite was 2800 square feet; open with minimal walls. The decorations were what Mattie loved, Mediterranean with lots of art work and statues. One wall was completely glass, opening to a balcony overlooking the lake. Mattie was about to put his key in the door of suite 2121 when the door opened.

"Mattie, you're here. It is so good to see you." Tommie gave his brother a kiss on each cheek and a hearty hug. Tommie stepped aside to reveal a woman who was coming out of the kitchen with a plate of hor d'oeurves. "Tonight, we are going to have company join us for dinner. Mattie, for the last two months, I have been seeing someone and she captured my heart. Mattie, this is Sienna Angelika Marshall, the woman I have been seeing. This is the woman I am going to marry if she will have me. So far, she doesn't have the time to bother with such things. She is totally absorbed in her medical practice. Sienna, this is my brother Mathew who I told you about. Isn't he one of the most handsome men that you have ever met?"

Mattie was aware that Thomas was speaking, but seeing this vision of a Roman Goddess standing before him left him in some sort of a trance. Mattie could not believe his eyes. She was like a *nubile* young starlet, so incredibly sexually attractive. He could not remember a time when he was so drawn to a person. Her hair was wispy, soft and quiet. He eyes sparkled like the highest priced diamonds only they held you in a mysterious trance. Her perfume was ever so delicate. Mattie knew he was staring.

What the hell are you? Some moon struck teenager. Look away. Mattie averted his gaze, smiled and nodded like he was acknowledging someone in the distance.

Mattie had to settle down and regain his wits. His mind needed to regain its composure and return to the role he had assumed. Never had he ever experienced such a feeling. This renaissance of feelings moved his inner senses to levels he was unable to control or understand. Mattie's senses were on steroids. He felt he could see her very soul, see her inner beauty as well as physical wonder. He could smell her perfume as if he standing in the middle of a meadow of wild flowers with a gentle breeze blowing. He could hear her very heart beating. He wanted to reach out and touch her arm, to feel her soft, silky, smooth hazel skin. His mouth filled with saliva to the point he had to swallow in order to speak. Her very presence left Mattie speechless. Finally he held out his hand for proper introductions. "Sienna, it is my pleasure to finally meet someone who has been able to gain my brother's favor that doesn't have something to do with his work. She had put down the tray of hor dourves on a coffee table in the center of the room and walked up to Mattie.

"Handshakes are for strangers. To me, you are apart of Tommie's inner world where I hope to be one day. At least, if I can hypnotize him into waiting at least six months while I finish stabilizing my medical practice." She walked up closer to Mattie and kissed him on the right cheek ever so lightly. As she put her hands on Mattie's shoulders and rose to kiss his cheek, her right breast brushed his right arm. Matte felt as if he had come into contact with a live electrical wire. A shock went through his entire body. He knew then that he would do anything in his power for this woman. Should anyone cause her pain or grief, they would be immediately placed on the top of his delivery list.

"So Mathew, are you ready to share your brother? We are considering a wedding date next year in May. It is a given that you will be the best man. So mark the month of May on your calendar. There can be no excuses for you not being at the wedding. Let's go to dinner now. I want to find out more about you. Are you seeing anyone? You can also tell me all of the things Thomas has kept from me. Shall we go?"

Mattie was no stranger to encounters with women. He had enjoyed the physical exchange of fluids with women on numerous occasions around the world. It calmed him, but had he just met a woman bright enough, beautiful enough, and strong enough to consider a union? He had never considered this element of love in his master plan. Love is a weakness the enemy can exploit. Mattie loved the sexual aspects of being with a woman and contentment after a sexual encounter. He never allowed himself to feel anything but the physical pleasures.

However, he knew he had to find the ultimate disguise if he were to be a corporate player. He needed a wife. Not just eye candy, but a woman with a brain, confidence that she belonged with other corporate wives, yet selfish enough to want her husband to be successful. She had to believe she was also a key element climbing the corporate ladder along side her husband.

"Tommie, I am guessing mother knew about your intentions to marry and the two of you kept it a secret from me until tonight when I could meet Sienna. She gave me a camera, so Sienna, I must apologize, we will be taking pictures or getting our pictures taken all night. Mom says take pictures, we take pictures. I hope you understand. So before we head off to dinner, you two stand together and smile like you really are happy." Mattie snapped off three pictures, then Sienna snapped a couple of the twins, and finally Tommie insisted on two with Sienna and Mattie.

"Sienna, I am famished. Let's head out to Domenica's. Unless you two have something else set up. And no, I currently am not seeing anyone. I am not sure what Tommie has said about me, but I am not going to be someone who grows old alone. I would love to find someone as charming and beautiful as you. Tommie was always the fortunate one of the family. I will yield to him being the trailblazer when it comes to marriage."

As the three entered a taxi headed down toward Cicero Avenue, Mattie came to the realization, that he had other priorities before he added the title of husband to his resume. For now, human bonds, especially marriage, could lead to complications. Complications could lead to mistakes. Mistakes lead to his capture or possible demise. Marriage could wait. Tonight was Tommie's night.

Driving back to Peoria was different this time. His brother was going to have someone enter his life who could possible have an altering impact.

For the next 200 miles, Mattie analyzed the impact it could have on his master plan. Would Tommie be reluctant to help him?

As Mattie entered his downtown apartment, the telephone rang. *Yes mother, we had a great time. I met Sienna. Yes, she is a wonderful woman perfect for Tommie and yes, I took lots of pictures. I will get them to you as soon as they are developed.* Mattie picked up the receiver, "Hello Mother."

"May I speak to Mathew S. Anthony?" It was not his mother. A man's voice was on the other end of the telephone.

"Speaking."

"Mathew, this is Scott Johnson, retired Marine colonel. I told you I wouldn't forget to call you when you graduated from college. As you were about to depart from Nam, remember we had a conversation about a new company? Now that you have graduated from Harvard, could I interest you in meeting me for dinner so we could have that little chat you couldn't make four years ago?" Scott Johnson came across as if they had just seen each other yesterday.

How did he know I graduated from Harvard? wondered Mattie. "Mr. Johnson, your timing is uncanny. I am in the process of determining my next move regarding employment. I would be happy to meet with you to hear about your company. When and where would you like to meet?"

"I was hoping to catch you in Chicago, but it did not work out. It just so happens that I have business in Peoria. I will be coming to Peoria next week. How about we meet at the Hotel Pere Marquette this Saturday for a drink, say around six o'clock. After cocktails, let's take a taxi out to the Boar's Head for steaks. Are you available?"

He knew I was in Chicago. I must ask mother if someone called and she told them I was in Chicago. "Saturday is fine. I will see you around six o'clock in the Pere Marquette's bar." *Has he visited Peoria before and stayed at the Pere? He knows about the best steak house in Peoria.* "Thank you for calling." Mattie returned the telephone to its cradle.

Something tells me he knows a lot about what I have been doing.

Chapter 13

Just hours before the telephone call to Mathew Anthony, a meeting was being conducted in Washington D. C. "Gentlemen, we have the heads of the hydra knocking at our backdoor. The Caribbean, Central and South America are powder kegs. Socialism and Communism are making some inroads. Too many radical political leaders have been elected who are not at all sympathetic to America's causes. There are too many countries that once relied on the US who are seeking other supporters, namely Cuba and Russia. We cannot have another Russian missile crisis or Bay of Pigs incident ever again. It is time to initiate project "Phoenix". We need for one of our most trusted insiders in the CIA to execute the project plan since the project may call for a select team to assassinate or capture a number of extremist leaders in Central and South America. Call Scott Johnson and have him come to my office."

At a private briefing, Scott Johnson listened to the proposal. He informed the group that he would be honored to head such an effort. "This type of action should not be a part of the agency. It should be through a black-ops group. I know the perfect man to take on such a challenge and who could form a top notch team. This man is a well-connected operative known to the agency only as the *Mailman*. The Mailman earned his nickname because of the number of special deliveries, or kills, he made with the utmost efficiency." Scott built interest by telling the group of the inside joke. "This man takes pride that he can hit anyone, anywhere, anytime. Like a mailman, nothing can keep this guy from his appointed rounds. He is considered an apparition. Gentlemen, all the agency has is a telephone number. We tried to trace the number to find the Mailman's location and his identity. What we found was that the telephone call went through so many network hubs, it was impossible to trace. As for payments, for services rendered, the Mailman accepts only electronic payments which are usually sent to Switzerland's largest bank. This bank prides itself on keeping the identities of their customers strictly confidential. We suspect the funds do not stay in Switzerland but continue on through an intertwined banking transfer process. Again, these transactions would be impossible to trace."

Back in his office, Scott Johnson sat back in his black leather swivel chair and looked out his window at the Washington Monument. "Well, well. I think it is time for me to contact my newest creation and entice him to head up this new program. Did I sell the Mailman identity or what? Those bastards swallowed the bait so completely that the hook didn't need to be set. If I do this right, I can get my promotion and position myself for a nice early retirement present. A project like this will be funded so secretly that no one will be able to determine how much money is being spent or have any trails to track the money. I could make millions on this one." With a smile on his face, he shut his eyes and let his mind wander. Given the nature of the covert actions that would be required, Scott knew that both the Mailman and he could secretly become very rich men. Scott relished the idea of him being the covert handler and sole intermediary of the Mailman. The past four years had been boring for Scott. This project got him back in the field, hands on. No more pushing paper around and glad handing. He knew he was going to have to work with a maverick, a loose cannon. In his role of handler, he would need a little time to bring the Mailman up to speed on the latest explosives, poisons, technology and political structures. If he guessed right, his star pupil would absorb the information in record time and would chomp at the bit to get into the race. This man was something special. He was born to cause havoc. He just didn't know it yet. Once trained, the Mailman would offer an array of services for his new company. Scott had already heard of a number of lucrative government "security" work and silent contacts for hot spots around the world.

Little did Scott Johnson know that early in his manhood, the Mailman, one Mathew Anthony, had developed an ingenious plan to right the world. After his exploits in Viet Nam and his intellectual and social networks he had nurtured and matured while at Harvard, he had engrained an invisible cynicism about his fellow man's greed and quest for power at the expense of the common man and America. Mattie's mistrust of his fellow man had silently grown to the point of delusion. He had come to believe that man was a putrid creature rarely able to govern his emotions, his desires, and his greed. Most of the people around him seemed only interested in opportunities to acquire wealth, power, and status. *Where were the manners, values, patriotism, the concern for the country, family, and the "down and out?* Mattie had decided he would use their greed and their wanton lust to dominate others against them in his desire to turn things around, one victory at a time.

In Mattie's mind, he had established his benchmark for any trust alliance. *I have never worried about men who come from humble beginnings, who have worked with their hands and strong back to make a living because they wouldn't care who put bread on their tables as long as the meatloaf was good and the pie homemade. It is all the well educated "God's gifts" who concern me. Today, there is a continuous fresh baked batch of mouthy college kids just out of their Ivy League oven or MBAs who feel that they are entitled, and deserve fast track promotions, ahead of those who have 10 and 15 years experience on the job. There are the yuppie snobs who secretly polish their silverware with their napkins for fear of catching some dreaded "truck stop" germ. But the ones who push me over the edge are the white-shirted businessmen on expense accounts who think every waitress can't wait to cast off their morals and lowly lives to be flirted with and be swept off their feet. I would love to have the opportunity to provide them special deliveries that don't kill, but yield lifelong pain. I won't even try to rationalize what has happened to religion. These greedy hyena evangelists were cleaning the bones of believers, taking their money, living in a private orgy of pleasure and glut. I would love to hang a few of these hypocrite bastards on an old rugged cross.*

Mattie had thought through his plan like a surgeon preparing for a complicated transplant. *To inflict this type of broad justice and pain, I will need to develop the perfect cover. I will become one of them. I will be the establishment in all the power circles. I must do this as quickly as possible. I will become more entrenched, more hidden with each passing day. Over the next few years, I will become invisible. I will become a highly successful business man armed with the most advanced global information network able to access the most highly sensitive data that has been accumulated and stored. I will also need to build a group of* "*uniquely trained professionals who could quickly be called upon with the skills they could deliver around the world.*

Mattie knew where to find many of these individuals he could recruit from his unpublished list of Vietnam specialists he had kept in contact over the past four years. This was a private list of men whose names he personally collected during his Vietnam tours. These men were legends. Their names were scribed from the rumors, stories and reported records of their heroism, their skills with weapons and, most importantly, their ability to follow orders and kill without mercy.

Mattie had start up money. After all, his grandfather had left him $1 million dollars in a trust fund which had grown considerably during his tour in Viet Nam and his stint at Harvard.

Chapter 14

Mattie was always one who, when given a time, felt he needed to be there ahead of time to check things out, to see if there were vantage points or concerns that he should consider should anything unexpected happen. He arrived at the Hotel Pere Marquette bar around 5:30. The actual bar was a 40 feet oval which was located on the north end of the room. Tables occupied the center and booths the south end. The lounge was rather on the dark, with the mahogany wood and mood lighting. With the maroon and green décor, and the brass and leather furnishings, the room was very elegant and a perfect place for businessmen to come to relax after a hard day. Mattie thought a booth would be more conducive to talking with some privacy. He made his way toward the most secluded booth in the bar only to encounter a face from the past already seated.

"Well Mr. Anthony. Early are we? It is good to see that you found me with no trouble." Scott Johnson was already evaluating his pupil. "I am so glad we could meet." Scott stood, extended his hand. The two men shook with vice-grip hands.

Mattie slid into the booth opposite Scott. A lone drink meant for him sat before him. "I took the liberty to order a cocktail for you. I believe your favorite was Jack and Coke, correct?" Given the state of the ice cubes, the drink couldn't have been ordered but a few minutes before he arrived. Had he been watched? Mattie smiled and thought it amusing to be having his first recruitment or interview with a member of the CIA, the company. The man who was to conduct his interview was exactly what Mattie had expected. The colonel had let his hair grow, but kept his blonde hair clean cut. Scott still appeared to have no sense of humor and still had the mannerisms of an ex-military man, ex-athlete. He obviously frequented some physical fitness center regularly considering his broad shoulders, thick neck and tapered body. "Please be seated Mr. Anthony. May I call you by your first name?"

"How about you call me Mattie and I call you Scott. Is this conversation being recorded? It seems appropriate that we cut out the formalities given our past association." Mattie wanted to get to the reason for the meeting.

"I can assure you the only ears that can hear our voices are you and I. I like your directness. I have gone over your resume and have read the material we compiled from your youth and military record. You seem to have a propensity to excel, generally with non conventional means. Mattie, to be direct, I am here to decide whether you are a good fit for our company. I am sure you already know our company is more of an Agency."

As far as Mattie was concerned, all government agencies, including the DEA, FBI, and CIA, were nothing but a bunch of self serving, "the end justifies the means" machines. And, like all machines, they have moving parts that will break, generally due to their ill gotten information, their timing or poorly executed plans. These breakdowns are usually not the fault of those in the field, but because of the political aligned influences and agendas. Most of the directions they followed were not from legitimate desires to remedy the societal ills of the world or to better mankind, but motivations of the leaders at the time. Mattie had done his homework as well. He had done some research on the history of espionage, not the "charter" of the agency, but from the chronicles of various campaigns that had been compromised. What were the circumstances that caused an operative or a campaign to come under scrutiny or to be compromised?

There were numerous sources including newspapers, political critics of the CIA, and books by those who need no sources, just words. All Mattie had to do was to follow the clues in the areas of communication breaches, financial enticements, loyalty reversals, sexual exploits or the breakdown of personal or political relationship influences.

"Scott, let's not waste time. I came to this interview prepared to answer direct and to the point questions. I hope you will answer in the same manner. I trust that meets with your approval." Mattie intended for his answers to be short and succinct with an element of vagueness so as not to be pinned down. "One other point before we start that I would like to get on the table. Your response could prompt a quicker decision on my suitability for the agency. Am I to assume agency equates to CIA? The point is, I do not have any interest in becoming an office employee. I realize there is always training, etc. which warrant desk time. I cannot envision myself as a desk sleuth. I want nothing short of being a front line operative. I will go through the necessary steps to qualify, but I will terminate my employment if I see that the field is not in the cards."

"Well aren't we a demanding shit! I was prepared for you, Mr. Anthony, Mattie. You seem to have connections in high places, yet seem to despise most politicians and power brokers. I believed you have openly referred to some prominent individuals as court jesters with no backbone. You have kept up your contact skills, are a recognized expert in the martial arts, and a black belt in jujitsu. You were "a loose cannon" in Viet Nam, yet you silently accomplished more than most decorated war heroes. In Nam you openly criticized the U.S. Commander in Chief for making war decisions based on economic and political considerations versus winning a war. You were very vocal in those times that you wanted to bomb everything to oblivion all the way to China. I especially enjoyed your statement that you would gun down all the hand wringing politicians and bleeding heart protesters as if they were rabid dogs. We now hear that you want to become part of the business world. How can you consider following in your grandfather's footsteps in business yet demand to be a field agent?" He paused for his question to soak in.

"What if you could have both?" Scott stopped talking and was eager to listen. He was confident on what was about to come out of Mattie's mouth. Mattie was perfect for how Scott Johnson envisioned their future partnership, a partnership that could make them both highly successful.

"You have thought of a position where I could pursue business aspirations while still having a field role? Let's say you have my attention. I would like to hear your proposal." Mattie had spoken the truth. He did want to hear his option because it seemed to be a perfect match for his private plan.

"Believe it or not, Mattie, you live in a city where a company resides that could offer you the perfect job to meet both of our needs, Construction Tractor Co. Construction Tractor is a global company. They send company representatives all over the world to support their dealer network. Dealerships are privately owned, usually by some of the most influential business leaders in their respective countries. Construction Tractor reps deal directly with the dealers. The dealers deal directly with the customers. But, these reps are fully engrained in the decisions supporting these dealerships. Construction Tractor and their dealers really work hand and glove with the customers for financing, supply chain management for parts and technical support. Their working relationships really are like a marriage. And believe me, Construction Tractor controls the financing and supply chain, so you can guess which one is the wife in this marriage. My proposal is that you go to work for Construction Tractor in the Marketing, and Sales area. They have a training program and, in eighteen months, you will be assigned to the field to call on Construction Tractor dealers in regions like Central or South America, Europe, Asia or US. As you get promotions, you could actually manage entire marketing regions, like the US, Europe, Asia, or all of Latin America. The angle is that, while you are being paid by Construction Tractor, we, the agency, or CIA if you prefer, would also pay you as an employee for field assignments in your marketing region. It would be up to you and your creative talents to determine how to keep Construction Tractor from knowing of your extracurricular activities. You would also be given the opportunity to develop a team you could use to help you with any assignment we would give you. But you would be responsible for seeing that these assignments, I believe you used to call them deliveries, are carried out successfully. Well, are you interested?"

Scott had laid the cards on the table. Did Mattie want to play his game? Scott could see the creative scenarios already playing out in Mattie's head. "Mattie, so you have full disclosure of this offer, should anything happen while you or your team is carrying out a delivery, there will be no record which would connect you to the agency. You will be on your own. As such, the financial opportunities for such work will be lucrative beyond your wildest imagination. You are either in or out. I need to know your answer now. Do we take this conversation to the next step or do we each walk away never to cross paths again?"

Mattie did not need time to think about this conversation. He had dreamed about such dual challenges and this scenario met his plans perfectly. "I am in. What is the next step? I feel that I will need some time with your experts for training and sharpening skills, time to get through Construction Tractor's training, time to put together a team. It could be one to two years before the stars align depending on complexities of actions required. Simple actions that I feel could be done could be earlier. Would this be within your timetable? One of the first priorities that I would want established is to develop non traceable communication links for ongoing dialogue."

"Agreed" With one word the meeting was over. Scott Johnson slid out of the booth and placed an envelope in front of Mattie. "Read, memorize, and destroy. I do not have to tell you why. We will be in touch. Enjoy your Jack and Coke." Scott Johnson left. There was no hand shake, no goodbye, and no emotion. This was an arrangement that Mattie thought would serve him well. Mattie signaled to the waitress for another round.

Chapter 15

Scott Johnson left the Hotel Pere Marquette through their front door, turned left and walked a block up Main Street to a waiting car. He climbed in to the passenger front seat and the car headed for the Peoria Airport. The driver in the drab suit and wearing sunglasses asked, "Sir was the meeting productive?"

"No Ronnie, this man did not meet our requirements for employment consideration. I really wonder how he passed our first cut of new recruit resumes. This was completely a waste of time. Please ensure all wiretaps, bugs, tails and files on this person are destroyed. I do not want some liberal politician some day finding out how we go about background checks on potential new employees. I want no reference to this guy anywhere. I want his slate wiped completely clean. Understand?" Scott Johnson would check next week to ensure Mattie was no longer in the system. Let the fun begin and the money flow.

In times of war, or financial or political crisis, the government is a cash cow that mints and throws money to anyone who has viable "solutions" and is able to open his arms wide enough. Scott Johnson knew the political winds were blowing just right for his arms to be spread wide with the right sails to catch the optimum wind.

"Gentlemen, I was able to get word to the Mailman that we wished to enlist his services. He contacted me and we discussed project "Phoenix". The good news is that he let it be known he could put people on the ground around the world to provide surveillance and support. His professionals would speak native languages, understand the cultures, and follow orders without question. I am convinced that the essence of this group could achieve invisible operations in lawless regions and countries where the CIA has restricted working relationships with those governments."

Scott Johnson was eager to put the terms of this operation before the elite of the CIA. "The not so good news is that the Mailman has three conditions in order for him to accept our assignment. He is demanding 5 million dollars start up, an additional 1 million dollars for each job. The only contact with him would be through me. He would supply me account information to act as a drop site for the money to be delivered per his instructions. He would be the only person who would know the names of his team. He would also be the only one to know when and how the delivery would be made. One point that he says is nonnegotiable is timing of the delivery. The precise time for the delivery is his call. It would be within a 6 to 9 month window after we supply a desired timeframe. This should be fine with us since we could claim under oath we had no knowledge of the individuals who performed actions which could surface and cause embarrassment to our country."

Of course the CIA brains who approved this program have no plans to inform the legislative or executive branch of the country. This was top secret for the good of the United States of America. The program was unquestionably the right thing to do. So the CIA's use of a private contractor as part of its plan to dispatch death squads was no longer to be discussed. When the "powers that be" require a delivery, only Scott Johnson would be anonymously contacted. Even he would not know who supplied the target or where the money would come from.

Years later, a senior CIA official would say he had doubted whether the Mailman and his recruits could pull off such high-stakes operations. But the Mailman proved to be a man of his promises. The Mailman was an apparition who kept the CIA in the dark about his actions. The CIA never had an inkling of the blurred lines of duty by using a private contractor for such a highly classified and dangerous project. The Mailman won the government's confidence by handling security and training operations. The only concern by the CIA elite was their decision to entrust one man with such sensitive overseas operations. When asked why the need for the Mailman, the answer was as transparent as glass, "for what he did you wouldn't want to leave any official American fingerprints."

PART IV

Chapter 1

Here it was June already and Scott Johnson was like a bull rider waiting for someone to open the gate so that he could take the ride of his life. Knowing the background of the champion bull he was about to ride, Scott Johnson decided to implement his own private training program for Mattie. It would be a crash course. His goal was to provide all the necessary background information and foundation tools for Mattie to build on. Scott had a vision that he would develop one of the best private sector assassins the US has ever turned out. He also had no doubt that Mattie would form an elite contingent to make use of his craft.

"Mattie, this is Scott Johnson. You have been approved for our companys' training program. You will be totally immersed in our training's four key components. The first phase is physical training which focuses on body conditioning and martial arts. The second phase will address weaponry training from knives, guns, explosives to drowning, poisons and suffocation techniques. This phase also will deal with physical appearances and how to hide in plain sight. Phase three would encompass disguise, development of new identifications and safe houses as well as an in-depth instruction on how to develop and implement undetected telecommunications capability. The final phase is more cerebral in nature and will necessitate the gathering of intelligence over time. This final stage was in-depth schooling, understanding and exposure to the most advanced technologies being used in the intelligence community, the banking community and industry. Your success is dependent on your ability to totally absorb and retain everything about the business of clandestine work."

Mattie was a sponge, not a drop would be left behind. His mind was already thinking of ways to utilize and improve on the training and information he would receive. "I have been waiting for this call. The sooner the better we get started. When do we start?" Mattie knew about learning, but knew his success would be judged on his delivery execution.

"You will have plane tickets delivered today to your residence. A list will be provided to aid you in what you should pack. A car will pick you up at the airport when you arrive. Can you make yourself available for training and report this coming Monday?"

Mattie knew he did not have any choice if he was to travel down this road. He was ready. "I eagerly await the opportunity to begin my tenure with your company." What else was there to say? "I assume we will meet on Monday for training indoctrination?" The phone went dead. Mattie didn't have an opportunity to ask how long he would be in training or to inform Johnson that he had interviewed with Construction Tractor Company just days prior to this call. Mattie bet Johnson already knew about his interview and potential start date. Mattie would know for certain if the training session lasted 6 months and fit conveniently between now and the time he would begin working for Construction Tractor.

Chapter 2

The Construction Tractor Co. manager who acted as Mattie's host met him at 0800 on a Monday morning for breakfast prior to his scheduled interview. Ironically, the letter he had received inviting him for the interview informed him that the icebreaker breakfast would be held in the Pere Marquette Hotel, the same hotel he would meet Scott Johnson. He was told a Construction Tractor manager by the name of Jean Bearnard Diaisomont would meet him in the hotel's breakfast room. He would be wearing a Construction Tractor name tag. He was easy to spot. Wearing a corporate uniform, dark blue suit, pressed white shirt, name tag on his left pocket, striped tie. Mattie weaved his way to his table, held out his hand, looked him directly in the eye and confidently declared, "Mr. Diaisomont, do not get up. I am Mathew Anthony, the person you are to meet for breakfast. May I sit down?"

"Mr. Anthony, may I call you Mathew? Indeed, please sit down. As the name tag suggests, I am J.B Diaisomont. It is a pleasure to make your acquaintance." Mr. Diaisomont had an accent, European, probably Belgium or Swiss-German. "This breakfast is a little different from those I have arranged in the past. I do not have to give you my pitch on the intricacies of the city where we have built our world headquarters. Since you grew up in Peoria, we can dispense with this portion of my welcome to our city speech. Let's order breakfast, get to know each other a little better, then we will walk the two blocks to our headquarter building. Sound ok so far? As you probably detected from my accent, I am not from Texas or New York. I am from Geneva, Switzerland. I am here on a three year training assignment. That is one of the wonderful credits to Construction Tractor foresight. If you are hired, you have many opportunities within Construction Tractor, not only to pursue multiple business careers like finance, accounting, and sales but also have the opportunity to apply those careers in international assignments."

"Please, call me Matthew or Mattie, whichever you wish. I do look forward to today. Construction Tractor is the recognized world leader in the manufacturing of earthmoving equipment. I have done my homework and believe there are a number of opportunities within the company to build a most gratifying career." Mattie knew more about Construction Tractor, its products, facilities and culture than this talking head. He was already bored and couldn't wait for this day to conclude. The two ate breakfast and conducted structured small talk then headed for the interview in Construction Tractor's corporate offices called the Construction Tractor Administration Building.

The interview consisted of three one-hour interviews with a ten minute break in between for the prospective candidate to relax, take a biological break or whatever. It also allowed time for the interviewer to clean up his or her respective notes from the specific questions they were to ask. Each interviewer then was to fill out a summary sheet with their candid comments on any observations or conclusions and make a recommendation to hire or reject the candidate. At 1230 the candidate was again to meet with his host to reflect on the interview process, next steps and goodbyes. J.B. Diaisomont met Mattie as he exited his final interview room. As they headed down to the main lobby, both men were ready to terminate their obligatory roles.

"Mathew, the interview process is completed. The next step in the process is that, after the three managers who interviewed you have met and compared interview notes, they basically vote to determine if you will be hired or rejected. If you are rejected, it means that the managers determined that our Company may not be a good fit for your interests. If you are accepted and hired, you will enter the Construction Tractor College Training Program starting in September of this year. There are a number of training programs for every facet of our business. The official word of the hiring decision will come from a personal telephone call by a manager in our Human Resources Department. You will also receive a formal letter which will document the call and the decision to extend or reject employment. Again this letter will be official notice from our Human Resources Department. You should receive the call in three days and the letter by next week. Should you be hired, you will be asked to come in and fill out various forms, receive a physical and will be told at that time, how you were evaluated and which training program Construction Tractor felt best matched your evaluation. It was great meeting you. May I say, from our conversations we had during breakfast and during the tour of our administration building here, you seem like a perfect candidate for Construction Tractor to hire. Good luck and I hope to see you again. Maybe we will work together in the future." The host then walked Mattie to the front door of the Peoria Construction Tractor Administration Building, Construction Tractor's Corporate Headquarters.

Mattie had no doubts he would be hired. He easily handled the softball questions regarding his background. The psychological questions to see if you would divulge your inner most secrets or issues were so obvious that simpletons would know what not to say. The interviewers were obviously low level managers who wanted to be liked and feel important. They were so focused on their own agendas that it was easy to provide answers that they would readily accept. The interview was a walk in the park. With his Harvard degree and class ranking, he knew very few graduates of his caliber would seek employment with this company. Mattie's secret plan was beginning to evolve from his mind to reality. He was heading to the Agency to learn what would be required to make the world right, and he was about to be hired into a company that could provide the perfect cover for what he was born to do.

Chapter 3

Mattie went to his mailbox the next morning and found a sealed manila envelope with no markings. He opened the envelope to find airplane tickets in his name departing Peoria traveling to Washington DC National Airport that very evening. He was instructed to not bring anything with him. Mattie arrived at the Washington National airport around 10:00pm. As he exited his gate into the general public waiting area, a man came up beside him, "Sir, you are to come with me. Your transportation is waiting for you outside."

Mattie, without any verbal response, motioned with his hand for the man to walk ahead. He followed him outside where they got into a taxi. This particular taxi had been modified so that the partition between the driver and passenger section was non-transparent black glass. Mattie assumed it was to protect the identity of both passenger and driver. The taxi set out on Route 1 and drove about 15 miles away from the airport and city then exited. They drove through the country, came to a road, turned left, went a mile and came to an old farm house where a black Suburban sat. The taxi stopped and Mattie got out. He could see the left rear door to the Suburban was open. He walked over and got in. The Suburban had been sectioned off like the taxi. Only this time, a man dressed in black fatigues was also sitting in the backseat. He was about the same size as Mattie, six two or maybe four. He was ex-military. Jarhead haircut with a square face with protruding jaw muscles. Mattie swore the GI Joe doll must have been modeled after this character. GI Joe spoke in a very, very soft voice. "First, I do not know who you are and you will not know who I am. I could not care less about your opinions, rights, or feelings. To those who will provide training, you call them Instructor. Instructors will call you Student. I am to run roughshod over you for the next few months. It could be as short as 4 months or as long as 6 months depending how badly you fuck up. Read this, then change into these." There it was, Johnson knew about his upcoming job with Construction Tractor.

As Mattie reached for the documents and clothes, the man threw a punch with his free right hand. Mattie instinctively leaned into the man and tried to block the punch with the left. He was able to deflect a direct hit but still felt the man's fist as he hit his forearm. Mattie continued moving forward by turning and tried to get on top. The left rear car door swung open and Mattie felt the sting of an electrified cattle prod. Suddenly hands had grabbed him and were pulling him out of the car all the while he tried everything he could think of to maneuver to safety. "Student, relax," instructed his attacker. "We are done. No one is going to hurt you. We wanted to see if you still had the martial arts survival instincts and skills. We will hone them over the few weeks." Where the other two men came from, Mattie didn't know, but they had him in their clutches like he was wrapped in chains. Hearing the words, he let his body relax. "Student, if you are ready, we will head out to your destination. We will be putting a hood on you for the next few hours. Try to get some sleep."

The drive seemed to go on forever. Mattie laid his head back and pretended to sleep. He tried to gauge where they were taking him by taking in any sounds, braking and acceleration of the engine, turns, highway speed versus city. After what seemed to be about five hours in the Suburban, the vehicle turned off the paved surface they had been traveling onto a gravel, then dirt, road. After another 30 minutes, the vehicle stopped. "Student, you can take off the hood." Mattie looked around. The only light came from the stars, the Suburban headlights and the lights of the framed lodge that was before him. Whereever they were, they were deep in a forest. "Inside there is some food if you are hungry. Tomorrow we start training at 0600."

As he entered his living quarters, he was met with a sign over his apparent bedroom. *"When dealing with trained operatives, know they are as good as you at what they do ... which means ... you cannot be just on your best game, you must be on your perfect game. One mistake can get you killed or caught."* Mattie loved the implications. He was back in his true element.

Over the next four months, Mattie couldn't get enough. He gorged himself on the physical aspect of training and in the gestation of the knowledge he was skillfully exposed to. His appetite would not be fulfilled until he had changed his training rehearsal to a live theater. Once again his body responded and he pushed his Physical Training and Martial Arts instructors to their expert limits. He listened and experimented with the latest weaponry and their killing potential. His mind was already plotting innovative ways to improve on applications for the poisons and explosives. Mattie felt he killed more animals in his training than he did people in Viet Nam. He had to laugh when one of his instructors took a shot at environmentalists when he said, "No animals were hurt in this production you are about to partake. They don't hurt because they will die before the pain starts."

"Student, this training is for you to be able to transform yourself instinctively given the situation or environment that you may find yourself in ... friendly or foe. You have proven that you excel with the transformation when something, such as a tool or weapon is placed in your hands. If the situation warrants, whatever you can get your hands on, make no mistake, and be ready to use it." Mattie also knew quite well that he had to have the same skill of expertise to wield or influence people's thinking and actions as he had artfully demonstrated with deadly weapons, explosives, and poisons. The next training sessions were as important to his cause.

The training sessions that were of particular interest to Mattie were the sessions on Disguise, how to hide in plain sight and Technology—how to know more about targets than they know about themselves. For a chameleon, camouflage is nature's slight of hand trick for basic survival. Mattie understood this basic survival requirement and was about to learn the secrets to changing his identity and couldn't wait to incorporate it into his bag of tools. He was going to be the ultimate chameleon of pretense, charade, make believe, and deceit. Given his vision of his opportunities within Construction Tractor, Mattie took to heart his instructor's prophecy. "In the real world, a chameleon can always spot another chameleon. Survival is based on who can spot the other the quickest and take action."

Chapter 4

"Once you take on a new identity, you must remember all aspects of that identity for the rest of your life. In your chosen profession, you may have to repeat it to save your life. Let's begin. Student, if you want to hide in plain sight, you have to be able to change appearances. Every day becomes Halloween and, whatever the mask must be, you must become a master of disguise. Student, the key to a new identity starts with the main features of the face. Everyone thinks you cannot change the eyes. Start with the eye transformation if you want to craft a new identity. A simple change of color with a lens, different eyebrows, lines in the forehead all impact what your viewer can recall. An easy distraction is to remember to "Smile for the camera". The smile is the easiest con tool to put a mark's mind on a specific evaluation course. It will be the most acceptable mask for most of your purposes. Also take the advantage when you encounter someone who is also wearing a mask. Everyone hides a secret identity at some time in their life. This is a human nature reality which can be of benefit especially if that person buries themselves so deeply that he can rationalize that his new identity is truly who he is. This mask then becomes more of a potential exposure than an asset because he forgets about the cause of deception. He will be easy to spot and can be a source for your agenda if need be. People remember bullies, braggerts, bull shitters, the rich, and the powerful. The same is true for the meek, the weak, and the physically handicapped or deprived. The objective then must be to determine if you want to stand out or blend in."

"Instructor, I am sure you know that my memory capacity is excellent. I retain visual images in my brain forever. Show me everything known in this field because I intend to push this wonderful art to become truly alternate living beings that could dupe even you. I feel that is the challenge I must set for myself if I am to play and excel in this game."

"Student, you have set an ambitious goal indeed. Succeed in that quest and you would truly be the master of disguise. Next lesson. To truly be a master of disguise, student, you must be able to use prosthetics. Having the latest in glues, porcelains, and plastics is mandatory. Different noses, ears, and teeth are the basic tools for dramatic changes. Once in place, only special solvents can be used to remove the pretense you created."

Mattie was given tips on how to modify his walk. Each night he worked on his walk. He could alter his stride; at times long, short, fast, ornd slow. He wanted to perfect this craft in order to always be observed as just another "Joe" in the crowd. Through his training, he had learned an individual's walk was as recognizable as his fingerprints.

For two months, Mattie evolved to his alter egos and identities. Like everything he set out to do, Mattie was obsessed to become the consummate disguise artist. He was a perfectionist. His mind could envision the desired look down to facial blemishes. His voice could take on accents, drawls, and lisps. He could listen to someone speak and instantaneously mimic them so that even their closest friends and family members could not differentiate the imposter from the real. Mattie personalized the golden rule of disguise. *Convince the mind, and you can deceive the senses.* Mattie was ready to take on his Instructors.

One night after a training session, he took out a disguise he had managed to steal piece by piece from past training sessions. He made sure his thefts would not be easy to discover. He felt the excitement of the challenge of this night growing in anticipation of the trial he was about to impose on himself. He hadn't felt this excited since he was a child coming down for the first time to see if Santa Clause had come to his house with presents. He looked into the mirror one last time. He had changed his hair color and eye brows to a platinum white. He had glued individual strands of his hair to create wiry white eyebrows. He overlaid his ears with two larger ears that had strands of hair showing in the ear canal. His final touch was to glue on a bulbous nose. He put on a pair of maintenance overalls he had commandeered from the laundry room and combat boots he took from an instructor's locker that very night. He was ready. Walking with stooped shoulders and hunched back, he dragged his right leg ever so slightly. He no longer looked like Mathew Anthony, but instead a small 70 year old maintenance man. He walked to the eating area where a few select civilians provided the meals and cleaned the dwellings. These hand-picked civilians were to leave the grounds by 2200 hours each night.

As he approached the facility, as luck would have it, an instructor was exiting the building. The man approaching him was none other than his disguise instructor. Perfect.

"About time to wrap it up, isn't it? I bet you are ready to go home for the evening?" his instructor asked. Mattie kept walking toward him with his head slightly tilted to the ground.

In a tired aged voice, Mattie played his part to perfection. "Yes, sir. It has been a long day. At my age, every day is long. I just need to empty the garbage and I will be ready to close up. Is there anything you need for me to do before I leave?"

"I do not recall seeing you here before. You new?" Mattie was now within an arms length of the instructor. Mattie quickly grabbed him. With the grace of a ballerina and the strength of a weight lifter, Mattie spun the instructor and had him in a choke hold to cut off the instructor's air supply. Immediately the instructor began to lose consciousness from lack of air. Mattie only wanted to incapacitate, not kill his instructor. He dragged the instructor to an adjacent building, tied him up, put a hood over his face and waited a short time for the instructor to regain his wits. "Is anyone here?" The revived instructor asked.

"Indeed there is. Cry out and I will break your neck. Just listen." Mattie had again modified his speech, this time to a Frenchman trying to speak English. This should truly confuse his hooded instructor. "You are not a very observant man for me to get the drop on you so easily. I could have killed you but that is not my mission. I am here for information. You obviously did not anticipate someone wanting to know more about this place. I must go." Mattie's voice trailed off as he left as if he were a whisper in the wind.

As he prepared to return to his quarters, his mind replayed one of his many instructors' words, "Never go directly to your destination, whether you walk or drive. Think about misdirection tactics in case someone sees you or is following you. Constantly check for tails in anything that can reflect, such as, mirrors, car windows, and shop windows. Look for the slightest hint of something being out of place or someone being too ordinary. When you think you are sure that you are safe, think again. There are long range recording devices, sensors that can be planted and other types of technologies solely to keep track of you. Never think you have lost someone. Bore those who may want to know your patterns to death until they get tired of the repetition and become sloppy in their duties. You only need to really lose a "tail" when you are in the midst of initial preparations for an upcoming delivery. "But on this night, there would be no one to see the events that took place, or anyone could even envision such an act taking place. This camp had grown too complacent and self assured of their capabilities. When Mattie was sure he would not be detected, he re-entered his temporary camp quarters and, with the precision of a carwash, used his cleansers to return to his original appearance and then waited with no one the wiser.

He knew the instructor he had restrained would be able to free himself in a relatively short period of time. That was his plan. He couldn't wait to see what would happen next. Just as he predicted, the instructor freed himself and set off an alarm. The entire area was locked down and instructors with guns were going from building to building looking for some intruder whose agenda was a mystery. When the door to his room was opened, Mattie was in bed feigning being awakened from a peaceful slumber.

"What's up? No one told me we would be having training tonight."

"Nothing, we just need to look around. You hear or see anything unusual?"

"Nope." And just as quickly as they entered, they left. The next day, Mattie put on his naïve inquisitive student costume and asked around about what was behind all the ruckus the night before. All the instructors were visibly edgy, especially his disguise instructor. Mattie had fooled him. He would keep his secret and remember the disguise details should he ever want to visit the camp again. He had learned the art of camouflage as well as any top make up artist in Hollywood. He could assume any identity when called upon. He now knew more ways to kill a human being than there were flights out of Chicago's O'Hare Airport in a single day. Mattie was ready to unleash his master plan.

Chapter 5

Technology training was especially innovative and interesting and, quite frankly, Mattie knew the training would be instrumental in future dealings from discussions he had had on many occasions with his brother. Tommie was a fanatic about technology and the power that information held. Mattie hoped to impress his brother with the things he had learned the next time they talked. He missed his brother.

Americans' first lines of defense and subsequent offensive maneuvers have always utilized technology sources from listening devices to devices which could track electronic transactions between companies or individuals. Having the knowledge about technology capabilities and having access to technology capabilities were two different things. The latter is where Mattie thought his brother could play an essential role.

Mattie's first lesson was on computer hacking. "Student, the challenge to gaining entry into company or personal files and records is to determine entry alternatives into those so called hack-proof computers. Hack proof only means that security methodologies were put into place to deter 90 percent of hackers. Every computer can be accessed. Most companies only truly worry about external hackers trying to access information from outside their company walls. They also put measures in place to deter the amateur employee hacker." His instructor looked more like a pimply faced college student than some counter intelligence CIA operative.

Mattie's challenge, if he was to survive in this new field, was to ensure he knew more about his targets' personal lives, professions, security, and any potential skeletons in their closets. This training session was to enlighten Mattie about all potential avenues in which he could gain access to a target's information prior to making any overt move.

"Student, you could get information from the outside, but the best source is an ability to get the information from the inside. The key to success is how one goes about recruiting or personally obtaining someone's tightly held personal information. The easiest information to acquire is information a person keeps within his home, next is his place of business. Home security is easy to override and most information in a home is kept in one spot, a safe, an office desk, or a drawer in the bedroom. Most of the truly highly confidential medical or financial records reside in some business mainframe. Mainframes are generally secured by deterrents at entry points, requiring access codes, finger print detection, or eye retina scanning, monitoring personnel in multiple locations; within the respective business. Real sophistication comes with linking and sharing information with other agencies around the country or even world. Cameras are ever present. All business mainframes have identified and protected their most highly confidential files and records with top security software programs. The easiest way to acquire a top security access code is when the codes are first introduced with their respective application software. Because those who require such codes are generally so impatient to use the information, their IT departments always put generic codes for them to change the first time they desire to use the particular information application. The more you can get close to those operatives who have these codes, the more opportunity you will have gain an access avenue to valuable, personnel, financial, customer, and product information."

In Mattie's master plan, he had envisioned from time to time a requirement for a few extracurricular personal exploits that would be conducted below the radar screen of both the CIA and Construction Tractor. Mattie was knee deep in the technology learning. His brother was neck deep in having access to technology capabilities. Mattie loved his brother and would never do anything that could compromise his safety, his respected community standing or his professional career. He was torn but his inner self couldn't help but ponder the possibilities. *Tommie has a side to him that, if I could protect him, could he possibly find my master plan intriguing? Should I consider enlisting my brother in my covert operations? Could he actually be a primary source to building my technology information network?*

Mattie needed to retain an ability to freelance and make private deliveries should the situation arise which called for such action. He inherently knew his personal deliveries would provide a greater degree of satisfaction and personal high. But he wasn't blind to the fact he would have to be extra careful because personal vendettas come with higher risk of getting caught and greater potential for accidentally involving "extras" who were in the wrong place at the wrong time. Tommie could in no way be connected to, or be implicated in such deeds.

Chapter 6

Almost five years earlier to the month when Mattie started his agency training, Tommie had sat before his recruiter. He had prepared well. He sat with his back rigid and straight. He had purchased the week before a new, custom tailored suit. His grandfather had taken him to his favorite tailor in Chicago. The suit was dark blue with a darker blue thread about every inch giving the illusion of a very faint stripe running from head to toe. He had had his cold black hair razor cut, cropped short. His hair seemed to have a natural sheen to it. Most women would have paid any amount of money to have such hair color and shine. Tommie was the definition for handsome. At 6 foot 2, silky smooth olive skin, and Cary Grant charm, eyes followed him wherever he went. Men took notice as well and silently wished for such genes. When Tommie shook hands during the introductory part of the interview, Tommie ensured his grip was very firm without being crushing. His eyes were transfixed on the interviewer's as he did with anyone he first met to make them feel a little uneasy. It gave Tommie the upper hand to be more comfortable than those around him.

"Good morning, sir. My name is Thomas S. Anthony. It is truly a pleasure to have this opportunity to interview with such a reputable company." Tommie's grace and manners were as genuine as a southern gentleman. "Sir, I would like to thank you for taking the time away from your busy schedule to meet with me. Again, it is an honor to be here interviewing for a position with AndrewPolk. Tommie flashed a smile that went off like a camera flash. His teeth were white and perfect. His smile and charisma could charm a junk yard dog to give up his only bone. Tommie had learned the art of business acumen and interpersonal skills required to succeed from studying his grandfather.

"Tommie, you must look and sound the part. Your vocabulary must be flawless, words succinct and with substance. Don't ever try to bull shit your way out of a situation or question when you do not know. Business sharks know when you are not prepared and will look for the first sign of blood in the water. They will circle and take you down. Have the confidence that you know as much as they do, have the wealth behind you that you do not have to have the job they may offer, yet show them your value if they hire you." His grandfather was a master and was more than respected in the Peoria business community. He was respected for his business skills, business purchases, and the wealth he had accumulated. He was revered for his charm and his generosity. He was the leading philanthropist in the state of Illinois.

Tommie wanted to be like his grandfather who was especially good at getting things done behind the scenes. While his brother over the years had dealt with situations in often unpleasant and violent ways, Tommie liked working in the shadows, through others. But Tommie knew that, inside, he was just as capable of being ruthless if diplomacy, tact, or sound reasoning was overlooked and thrown back in his face. Tommy was as obsessed as Mattie in his pursuit of his goals. Knowing that another way to gain leverage is to say a person's name in his presence as often as one could without sounding like he was patronizing his listener, "I see from my advance material that you are Mr. Robert Hofler. The material indicated that this interview is to last two hours. Would you prefer I call you Mr. Hofler, Robert or Bob during the next two hours? I am eager to start the interview when you are, Mr. Hofler."

Jim A. Roppa

Tommie watched as his interviewer seemed to grow a couple of inches with his reply, "If I can call you Thomas, you can call me Robert. We do have a number of questions in this interview and we will probably take the whole two hours. Your academic achievement from Northwestern University Kellogg Business School is excellent and your references are truly noteworthy. Did you know our founder also graduated from Northwestern? I am sure you were recruited by a number of companies. Why did you choose AndrewPolk as one of the companies that you wished to interview?" Robert leaned back in his big leather chair behind his large mahogany desk. He interlaced his fingers, gave a forced smile, and made a little joke as he fished for other companies Tommie might be considering. No matter. Tommie had already assessed the situation before any question was asked. This guy wanted him for their company and he wasn't going to take no for an answer.

"Robert, I have interviewed at two other Big Five Accounting Firms. I came to AndrewPolk because of their global reputation, their global clientele and the diversity of services that are offered. I feel that I can show my knowledge of international finance along with an ability to interact, persuade and lead people. I know I will start at an entry level, but it is my vision to become a partner if hired." Tommie had no doubt he would be hired. If hired, he wouldn't be worrying about some vision. He would construct the final steps of his career plan. From the day he set his academic and athletic goals in high school he began setting his sights on success. What were the hurdles he had to cross? He created a career plan; high school valedictorian at 18, college magna cum laude at 23, partner at a major accounting firm by 30, senior partner at 35 to 40. Ultimate success was gauged by being appointed to a CEO position at 46.

He was ready for the interview questions and could only dream of his potential in this company. His inner thoughts reinforced his confidence. *I love the big city life. I was meant to be in this game. Damn, I know I will excel in the corporate business game. I cannot wait to see what lies ahead.*

Hofler did bring out something in the interview that Tommie needed to keep his eye on and track in this company. Reflecting back, Tommie thought Hofler wanted to show that he was more than some HR host, that he was a valued employee within his company and knew strategic directions of the company. "I am going to give you an insider tip should you decide to join our little family. The real profitability, power and wealth for this company and its employees will not come from our present accounting practice, auditing other companies or being in the tax business. Forget about their revenue potential. The real capital of tomorrow for this company is consulting on "Information and Access Capital". What catapulted IBM to huge profits was their ability to provide computers to capture and process data better than anyone else in their industry. A whole new business venture is unfolding which will call for companies to be able to provide foundation software programmers, then analysts to interpret, then networks to share information. Having talented business minded people to consult and assist development of their information strategies will be required by every company in the world. Having talented resources to provide this direction will yield, possibly greater than IBM, profits for delivering Information and Access Capital. Having reliable, accurate, and accessible information will be mandatory to compete. Computers will enable companies to better manage their inventories, manage accounts receivable, manage their sales force, and assist in the building of better quality in their products. I am sure you scrutinized many business cases at Northwestern. Improve any one of these areas I just mentioned, you know it would impact the bottom line of the smallest to the largest company. Profitability! He who has access and the ability to utilize timely information will dictate their respective marketplaces. They will govern the business decisions of the next generation. The more information you can access, the more power and wealth one can access."

Tommie left the interview and walked the streets of Chicago basking in the knowledge he was going to work for AndrewPolk. If Hofler's

Jim A. Roppa

prognosis was anywhere close to prophesizing the direction of this company, Tommie knew he must perform extensive research into this particular business unit's potential. Tommie was good at sizing people up. His knew his future would depend on it. From across the room, Tommie could tell a lot about a man or woman by the cut of their clothes, their manicure, their shoes, their jewelry and the way they mingled. If you had rank, the room came to you or a spot was reserved. If you were a "want to be", you were like a hummingbird, gathering nectar from every flower, with your wings going at the speed of sound so as not to miss one opportunity. He could tell the people of interest. He could quickly assess the person's intelligence and substance. He was also astute enough to figure if a person had earned their station or inherited it. These were valuable facts in climbing the corporate ladder.

Tommie received his official employment acceptance letter from AndrewPolk only one week after his interview. He accepted the offer the same day. He couldn't wait to begin, to initiate his career plan to rise to the top of this company.

The one trait that his brother and he shared was their ability to be at their very best when they encountered situations in chaos and calamity. This trait would serve them well in their respective endeavors. Both brothers had prepared themselves mentally and physically to ensure a state of panic could not ever enter their mind or body. Their grandfather had trained them well to use their brains first, their charm second, and their strength third. "Boys, never react or panic without at least a couple minutes of thinking about the situation at hand, alternatives or possible effect of the next couple of minutes. Always put your emotions on the backburner and your brain on the forefront on high speed. Size up the challenge or opponent like a high jumper would for his next jump. Visualize the matter at hand. Then you can call on all of your resources to clear the bar. Panic causes errors. Remember no fear can win the day."

The second trait that they both shared was that they hated to be defeated or come in second place.

Hofler was right about his prognosis of the opportunities and direction of the AndrewPolk Company. Within a month after being hired by AndrewPolk, Tommie had found out through research, lunch table discussions, and so called mentors spilling their career philosophies that the information side of this company was the future. He also quickly realized that the old guard was resisting, but there were those who felt that the company had to make the move. Tommie knew he had to win these partners over as to his value. Tommie had to gain access to them through inclusion on various projects. When it came to technology, most of corporate America executives wanted no part of learning some technology solutions different from their "time proven" manual processes. They were comfortable with the current processes. After all, wasn't their current way of doing business their cash cow? They had people who could learn the new technology tools and provide them the information they needed to make decisions. These corporate leaders wanted someone else to do it, would come to take it for granted and expect it, and in the long run, not have to take responsibility on the outcomes. They would reap the success, but could disavow any failures.

Tommie thought it was a perfect scenario for someone bright enough, not afraid to take the risk for implementation, yet with the political savvy to allow his leaders to espouse the value of it. Tommie was the man. He rose to the prestigious position of partner in the company faster than any one could recall. Tommie's agenda was not to be partner, but to be CEO.

Chapter 7

Within the next five years, Tommie was put in charge of the primary business unit that would provide consulting information services to global companies. Tommie was ready to move up the corporate ladder. Tommie knew what he needed to be successful. His first step was to put together a business unit made up of the brightest, most articulate, information sales consultants who were to call upon the business companies of the world. These consultants promoted and touted the cost savings of the latest information technologies. Like prophets and fortunetellers, this band of gypsies gained access to the inner sanctums of corporate elite through their projections of improved profit performance and manufacturing productivity benefits that would be realized. They taunted these company leaders with the carrot that, for their very survival, mechanization of accounting systems, sales systems and manufacturing processes were a must to meet the demands of the next industrial boom. Tommie knew he had to stick with themes that were engrained in these corporate cultures. But he knew the information age would provide a global economy and those who embraced technologies would be market leaders.

Tommie was pleasantly surprised to find that, once his business unit had contracted with a company, an ongoing trust and dependency inherently was developed. These global corporations were quick to relinquish responsibilities and opened their internal business to his teams with only a signature on a confidentiality agreement. These corporations rarely did any auditing or review of their work. If they delivered what was promised, the crown jewels were Thomas' team. With such trusting relationships, Thomas would be able to create an information portal to the world's most guarded information. Data had been recorded and was being stored in companies on every business venue around the world. Governments had been contracted to help them build their systems that could store and analyze data, and communicate with their vast organizations or to keep track of others. As the global corporate and governmental clientele contracted with AndrewPolk to consult and build their application software, Tommie's organization had access to all of their information for testing and validation that the application software actually worked. Once the application software was working and AndrewPolk's credibility established, AndrewPolk was given access to information Holy Grail, telecommunication networks.

Corporations and governments wanted the latest technologies to move and process their information around the world. AndrewPolk was contacted to create networks with sophisticated integrated tools which could track, analyze, predict and offer solutions to prevent or protect. His organization had written software to track personnel information, credit information, and sensing software; developed algorithms for encrypting information for transmission safeguards against hackers; had provided engineering software for assistance in developing the next weapon, airplane or tank. Whatever was happening in the world, his organization had access to databases years before the ordinary man knew what was going on. Technology developers ensured AndrewPolk was privy to the next new product to keep their products on the forefront for prospective new projects.

After a year on the job, Tommie had met and become friends with a man named Larry Barnes. "Larry, what are you doing later tonight? Want to join me for dinner, my treat?"

"Why? Anthony, I do not want people to think we are gay. It could keep me from being promoted." Larry laughed uncomfortably at his attempt at a joke. Tommie knew the comment went deeper.

"I will take you to one of my personal favorite Italian restaurants down on Cicero. I got a project I would like your take on its viability. The owner is a friend. No one from work knows about this place so I would like to keep it that way. This restaurant is called Domenica's Cucina, my personal safe haven when I want to get away from it all. Domenica, the owner, is 80 and has kind of adopted me over the years. Understand?"

"Sounds good. Your hideaway is safe with me. I have some loose ends I have to complete today. If you can come by my office any time after six, we can head out. You drive. I take the subway to and from work. Should I be packing?" Larry liked his Italian mob reference and laughed more genuinely.

Larry was a lifelong Chicagoan and an educated accountant by trade. He loved to let people know that his mother was Sicilian which accounted for his good looks. He was stout, compact and built like a small refrigerator. He had a Roman senator's nose and pale blue eyes. He was clean cut about the same age as Tommie. Larry seemed meek, non-threatening. After a year with AndrewPolk, he requested a Sabbatical to explore the latest technologies under the guise of applying the technologies to business application and utilization. Larry excelled and became a technology researcher/expert. He was sought out by every developer of any project that was going on within AndrewPolk. IBM, Digital Corporation and Honeywell often called him in to analyze their new creations in hopes that AndrewPolk would promote their products in their dealings with top companies around the world. AndrewPolk analysts and managers alike never questioned Larry's presence in any discussion. They welcomed it. He was not much for small talk, always direct to the point. He was considered by company elite that he was a technology brain, who did not have the interpersonal skills to work with clients. He was awarded a private office which was commonly referred to as the "Think Tank", and associates joked that this office only had a door knob on the outside to keep Larry in the room thinking. As a result, Larry had little chance to make partner or even any significant opportunities for promotion when promotions were tied to client revenue goals and objectives. As a result, Larry was often passed over for jobs because of his unassuming nature and technical traits.

But Tommie recognized early that, when Larry did speak, it was obvious that this man was not only brilliant, but had thought of every possible aspect of the subject being debated or devised. Tommie really liked him. He thought of him as his Superman; mild, meek personality that was a superhero at his trade. "It ain't bragging if you can do it." Larry would often say when someone challenged his abilities or technology recommendations.

Larry could always deliver if he said he could. Larry had no fear.

"Domenica, we will have your special with my favorite Chianti. Love your new apron. Larry, this is the proprietor of this fine establishment. She is not only beautiful. She serves the best Italian food in all of Chicago. She is my girl so mind your manners. Domenica, this is Larry my friend from work." Tommie felt safe in this place. He was on a mission.

"Larry, it is nice to meet a friend of my Tommie. You must be special. He has never brought anyone here, only my Mattie. You will not leave here hungry. I will go prepare your dinner myself." Domenica was happy to see Tommie and wanted to let his guest know how special Tommie was to her. A waiter brought two glasses and Tommie's favorite Chianti from the country of his ancestors.

Jim A. Roppa

"OK Thomas, what is so pressing that you brought me here?" Larry was direct and ready to listen. Who was this Mattie Domenica had mentioned?

"Larry, what would one have to do to build a database or databases of selective information from all the clients AndrewPolk has around the world? I guess one would call this AndrewPolk's master data bank, as safe, confidential and secretive as a Swiss Bank or the Pentagon. The information would have to be compiled without the clients knowing, which means one would have to devise a way which would go undetected by resident data processing organizations of those entities. In my head, I see mainframes around the world with embedded software that could trigger itself to send designated encrypted information to computers that either stored or transmitted the information to various locations then to a central location. Larry, you know our client list. We do work for governments, including ours, the largest financial institutions, Wall Street, industrialists, scientists, religious factions, non profit agencies and so forth. We have helped develop software and other technologies to protect this information. You and I know there is going to be an information explosion with more opportunities through technology to access and share information around the world. Telecommunication capabilities will be expanding like we have never seen before. The need for our services will expand to new heights. The information revolution is approaching rapidly. Companies are going to have to be global and share information on-demand to keep ahead of their competitors. Governments will share more, financial institutions will share more. Personal information will be more accessible. What I am about to ask may seem to be monumental. Do you think a small team could put together such a telecommunication network, an information access and retrieval capability to store in a central repository as I envision?"

"Yep. I noticed you did not put any legal hurdles in the scenario. You only need to answer the key trilogy questions; Scope, who do we include, Resources, how much can we spend, and Time, when do we need the information available. Provide me the requirements for the questions, I will review them, and present a solution to you." Larry had responded as if Tommie's request was like any other challenge. "Every problem once solved is simple. Your problem has a few more variables and risks to consider. Is this an official project with the entire associated request for authorizations, funding and the rest of the bullshit?"

"No. Larry, this will be our creation, yours and mine. We will call the project Einstein. We will keep our surrogate overseers in the dark. When the solution you propose does give birth to Einstein, only you and I will know how to raise the level of intellect of our creation as we see fit. The rewards for having access to this information will be unfathomable. If we are found out, we will be terminated from our jobs, or worse, legal actions and possible incarceration. So if you want to let this one pass, I totally understand."

"What about yep did you not understand? Thomas, you are one bright bulb. Not as bright as me, but bright enough to know where you want to go and bright enough to know I am the only one in AndrewPolk who could possibly help you get there. I am not going to ask why you want this information or what you will do with it. But note, I do take you as a man of his word. All I ask in return is that when the project is complete and see the value of the work and the man, show me the respect that is warranted. Do you totally understand?"

"Yep" Both men laughed. Tommie was elated. *Hell, once I have access to the data bank and the power it will wield, Larry, you will have any world at my command.* Tommie knew exactly how he would show Larry respect. He held out his hand to Larry, "Larry, you have my loyalty. Next to my brother, you are now the most important person in my life. We will become as brothers. Anything you need, just ask."

They shook hands. Along with their host, Domenica, the "would be" Roman conquerors ate a most authentic Italian dinner, drank the most delicious nectar and talked as family would do late into the evening. With visions of information dominance dancing in their minds, they departed. Neither spoke as Tommie drove Larry to the subway. Both were dreaming of how to network and capture the worlds most sought after and protected asset, information. Larry knew how to capture data from client files via embed micro code AndrewPolk installed in everyone of AndrewPolk's client's computers. Confidentiality agreements had been signed by AndrewPolk which permitted the software to reside in clients computers. The premise was rational. Should the client have problems, this micro code ran to debug and troubleshoot. The author and keeper of the micro was none other than Mr. Larry Barnes.

Six months later, Tommie never forgot the first time Larry came into his office and asked, "How would you like to access medical records of the top 10 hospitals in the United States, or financial records of two of the worlds most private banks, or arrest records within the US, or the top land holders of Central America, or the top importers of South America or tax records of US Congressmen? I have many, many more selections from the US, Europe, Mexico, Central and South America. We now have the capability to tap into any business, government, financial institution, or private businesses AndrewPolk has ever done business with. Not bad huh? I have set up data bases around the world secretly located in the bowels of the largest computer centers. I would bet my life that they will never be discovered by the local operators of the systems. I have put code into their operations that should data bases grow too rapidly. The data would go to another center. Center storage capacities will be expanded fractions of percentages when ever centers buy additional storage. I also have set up collectors for overflow in our company data centers. I have these devices camouflaged as research devices. Since you control the budget for research, you can decide what we want to collect and how much. Now that we have the capability, we only need to start the refinement of what we collect. So where do we go from here?"

Chapter 8

Mattie had a mental list of the desired members for his elite delivery squad.

His first recruit was to ensure money, weapons, safe houses, contact lists, etc were in place within the boundaries of Canada and the United States. His second recruit was to perform the same tasks in Mexico, Central and South America. The third recruit was targeted for Europe. The fourth recruit, which Mattie was in no hurry to find, would focus on Asia and Africa. Mattie had five names for each region he planned to visit by one of Mattie's unique identities and presented the conditions of employment.

There was to be no mistake as to who would be in control and have sole knowledgeable of the intricacies of an operation. It would be the veiled Mailman. Mattie knew he could not go overboard when he considered his own security. Mattie was well aware that the fewer people who truly knew his real persona, the better. With this cadre of delivery members, his behavior, social networks, travel patterns must be constantly changed and be continually on the forefront of his brain. How many times had their grandfathered preached, *The number of confidants that you boys must nurture, must be kept at a minimum. Keep friends close, your enemies closer. Loyalty is a gift. If you find it cherish it but keep it away from the jungle if you are to protect it. To the world, everything and everyone is expendable. Know and reward the faithful. Detect and devour the jackals. Dance like no one is watching. Sing like no one is listening. Work like you do not need the money. Love like no one* has *ever hurt you and live life like you were dying.* Have no Limits, Have no Fear, and Have no Remorse."

Mattie never interviewed his perspective candidates, the Mailman did. With each visit, the Mailman's appearance was a different. If he felt his discussions went well, the recruits name made it to his "Top 10" consideration list. Those who did not meet the rigid requirements for consideration or failed to have any unique skills, the recruit would never see the Mailman again. On a few occasions, the Mailman did return.

"Mr. Sydney, I heard you made a few telephone calls inquiring about subjects I specifically asked to be kept confidential when we last met. I thought we agreed that our conversation would be kept in the strictest of confidence. You assured me that our conversation would only be between you and I. Apparently, you felt compelled to seek additional information. Did I not adequately explained was there something that did not meet your liking? I stated I did not want unknown persons knowing about my business intentions for fear that those unknown persons could possibly jeopardize or compromise my mission. I mentioned to you that our missions put us in harms way, requires us to address undesirables, or threats to our very way of life. Because of your inquiries, because you broke my confidence, unfortunately, you will not be selected for our elite team. I am here not just to inform you of that decision, but to perform the act of executioner to those who commit treason: treason against me and my country." Those were the last words the failed recruit heard.

Over the next 6 months, 5 bodies were discovered in 3 states with single gun shots through the forehead. The Mailman used untraceable, different caliber weapons on each victim. Each weapon was personally dismantled and disposed of weapon piece by piece. Each case ended the same way: lack of evidence, no persons of interest, corpses with less than reputable pasts, minimal outside pressures to solve the case, and generally overloaded detectives. Each case eventually ended up in police departments Cold Case unsolved files. The only person who ever knew why these traitors were killed was the Mailman.

From his "Top 10" list, the Mailman carefully researched records from agency databases. To begin his operations as quickly as possible, he independently contacted his top three individuals to join his secret society death squad. The Mailman chose recruits who had a passion for country and skills for killing. To ensure the recruits felt the country loyalty tie, the recruits were told they were secretly working for the CIA. Mattie had orchestrated everything with the precision of a vascular surgeon. He had trained himself and his three core team members independently so tirelessly, so selflessly over the past 6 months, that his team actually had become more like family to Mattie. He truly trusted these men and felt they shared his views on life. His team was to be elusive, secretive and utterly ferocious. They were professional in their crafts through and through. These three would be the foundation for the recruits who would follow.

Mattie called Scott Johnson on his private number for a meeting. "Mr. Johnson, could we meet at the site you chose for an interview tomorrow at 4:30? I have some mail to deliver which may be of interest to you."

As Scott Johnson approached the Main Street entrance of the Pere Marquette, someone had walked up behind him. He heard a voice over his right shoulder. "I have slipped car keys in your coat. Walk through the lobby. Take the down escalator to the parking garage. You will see a white Chevy Impala in the 15 minute guest slot right outside the exit door. Get in it and drive to the hotel written on the envelope on the seat. A key to a room is in the envelope. I will ensure you are not followed." Scott without looking over his shoulder proceeded to walk through the lobby, approached the escalator and proceeded to the garage exit.

As he exited the hotel into the garage, he saw the Impala parked to his right. Scott opened the door and read the name of the hotel he was to drive to, Jumer's Castle Lodge, suite 220. He smiled and thought, *"Mathew you son of a bitch, so you knew where I stayed for our first meet. Did you know before where I was staying or did you follow me? Either way, I did not detect the tail. Very good work. Very good work indeed."*

Scott opened the door to suite 220 to find Mattie sitting in a chair by the window. "Mr. Scott Johnson. Can I assume that only the two of us can hear our conversations?" Not waiting for an answer, Mattie continued. "I believe we should have the same understanding on the status of my charter. I currently have a select group of men who I personally trained and have a list of others who can be in place and ready for their assignment in six months. Are you ready to request mail delivery or other services now or within the next six months?"

"My, my, aren't we the trained professional? OK, I will play along until we have a trust. Mail is very welcomed. I appreciate notification. All recipients have been informed and assured me that they too appreciate your hard work. I will contact them to determine current needs or needs that are brewing. They also agreed to provide a minimum of 10 million dollars over the next six years in support of future delivery requirements."

"Scott, let's be frank. We both know that this program will be able to acquire whatever monies it will take. We also know that whatever we spend will never be reviewed or evaluated. Given the nature of the requests being made, there will never be an official agency's classified budget. There will be gratuities and contingencies that I do not want to have to justify. I assume that you will be able to handle any financial request that I will bring forward to accomplish assigned missions."

"Mathew, one fact does present itself. You are correct. There will not be any serious questions regarding The Mailman or his carriers as long as one demonstrates the ability to conduct clandestine surveillance or deliveries by being masters of disguise to maintain fictitious identities as assigned. Success is the only barometer. One mistake means the end."

"I have made contact and established my team under various disguises of the Mailman. You are the only person who knows my true identity. My most trusted members now are living in key cities around the world. Together we've established safe houses under various identities and have a stockpile of weapons. We will need cash immediately and global bank accounts as assignments dictate to acquire in-country operating capital in various currencies. Scott, we are ready for our first assignment."

Chapter 9

The Mailman's first few recruit interviews had been frustrating. He had not been impressed. *Why do guys from Chicago, LA, Miami or New York want every one to believe that in their youth they were connected with the mob? They want everyone to think they were from the wrong side of the tracks and had to be tough to survive in their neighborhoods. They still walk as if they were walking in tough alley ways or streets of the Windy City or Brooklyn. They act as if they are in the witness protection program and always afraid someone would recognize them, while really wanting everyone to notice them. What bullshit.* The Mailman did find what he was looking for.

Bill Drogemiller was a the real deal. He was true Chicago Southside tough. He stood 6 feet 5 inches. He had a neck that was thicker than it was long. His jaw was wide and strong, and his chin looked as if it were made of marble. He kept his hair cut very short like a marine who had just enlisted. He hated to think he had to look a certain way to impress. He just did not give a shit or put up any kind of front other than who he was. He was well respected in the business world as a gentle giant with brains, but one who would not hesitate to make his point of view known. The Mailman knew that, down deep, he would love for someone to get physical so he could for a moment revert to his old street fighting days. His face was that of a hockey player, stern, with fierce silver dollar sized eyes. The directness of his stare often froze, and most likely intimidated, whoever he addressed. One trait the Mailman loved about this man was that he was reliable. He could be counted on if he aligned with you.

Bill was just a kid from the Midwest without any pedigree or illusions of grandeur. He was from a family of six children. He had lost a brother in the streets of Chicago and another in battle in Nam. His father was an abusive drunk to his mother and his children. Bill had decided early in his life to get away before he hurt his father. He had joined the Marines right out of high school to escape his life, not in support of some higher cause. According to the confidential background check Mattie had prepared, Bill's father died a month after Bill returned home. According to the police report, his father basically drank himself to death and choked on his own vomit. An autopsy was not performed, but Mattie thought it was not a coincidence that the police report found bruising on the body. Mattie knew Bill had taken his revenge. Like Mattie, when Bill was done with his tour, he decided to see if the GI Bill could provide him an education. He took night classes and was accepted to Northwestern University in Chicago. He was a natural at finance and business. His instructors took to him and provided all the necessary support to acclimate him into the university. He quickly learned that red tape is easily cut if you are aligned with the right people. These people always seemed to hold the scissors and could apply the right amount of pressure to cut anything regardless of how thick. Bill kept an old saying as his life's mantra. One of his professors was the first to quote Spike Milligan, "Money may not be able to buy you happiness. But it does bring you a more pleasant form of misery". Bill felt he had earned this happiness. Bill Drogemiller had never depended on anyone, until he got hooked up with the Mailman.

The Mailman's search for the second region recruit was filled after visiting the first name on the list. Mattie couldn't help but draw comparisons between his first two selections. Where Drogemiller was a tower with legs and arms, the man across the table was five foot ten and would come to Droge's shoulders. He was Hispanic by the name of Juan Ramirez or JR. He was tall for a Hispanic with broad shoulders. A blind man could see that this man was ripped with muscle. In his basic training, JR had won every event, running, hand to hand combat, shooting, whatever. In battle, he was fearless and as vicious as a pit bull in the ring. He earned a bronze medal. He epitomized a survivor in a world filled with turmoil and war. His only blemish was his nose. It was a little off center from a gang fight back in LA where he grew up. He had moved to Miami after his third Viet Nam tour, and made strong inroads and allies in the Cuban community. He had a small business in Miami's Little Havana district. JR also had made a name for himself in the Mexican hierarchy where he grew up. Once he had made his name and enough money, he had moved his parents out of LA thinking it was safer in Miami. His hair was cut short on the side but long on top with obvious gel to keep the waves in his hair somewhat straight. This young man was handsome and could charm women with just a look or one of his smiles.

"JR, join my team. You can live in this Miami barrio as your cover. But I want to ensure we have all the assets we need in South America and Mexico. Should we need anything in Central America, I already have contacts that can supply us with whatever we may need. I assure you, you will have the opportunity to use the skills you developed in Viet Nam, and receive compensation enough to take your whole family out of the barrio to a life you can only imagine." The Mailman knew he had the right man for his assignments in Central and South America. His eyes screamed for a fight. He was waiting to hear the bell to release the repression bottled up inside him. As the Mailman put various future scenarios on the table, he couldn't help but see that JR looked like he couldn't wait to hurt someone. It didn't take long for JR to show what kind of violence he could carry out when provoked or needed.

To say the group's operatives were deep undercover was an understatement. No one in the group actually knew any other member except for the Mailman. Each operative had only one contact, the person who recruited him, trained him and ensured all skills were exceptionally developed.

Every operative knew that, if they were ever caught they were on their own. They only were provided details that supported their mission, and if caught and tortured, could only provide that information. So death was a given if caught. All members of the group spoke numerous languages and, of course, had false identities and the documents to support their alter ego identities.

The third recruit was unique to say the least. His name was Urs Frey. He was very unassuming. Urs looked more like a banker or a professor. While only 29, he was balding, a mere five foot seven, athletic but a slight build. Urs was Swiss, a cross between a German shepherd and a Doberman pinscher, void of a sense of humor. When he did find something funny, it usually was in a social setting where he had had enough alcohol to let his ultra conservative, detail oriented demeanor down a smidgeon.

The Swiss believe their intellect is superior to the rest of the world. In Urs' case, he was in fact brilliant and justly had earned his credibility in the banking fraternity in Switzerland and around the world. When it came to confidentiality, secrets were abundant and well kept in this neutral nation. It was no wonder that every country conducted some of their most intricate business or political deals in Switzerland. The Intercontinental Hotel in Geneva, Switzerland held more clandestine meetings that resolved more world issues in hotel rooms than the U. N. Swiss are the most structured people in the world. They follow orders to the letter, rules to the ultimate, process to the insane. No other country's businesses oversee their client's requests to such an extreme. The Swiss are polite, unlike the Germans. They are precise to the letter. Mattie, as a Construction Tractor representative, loved living in Switzerland. He mingled with the Swiss, hated the arrogance of the French, and resented the abruptness of the Germans. As for the Italians, he knew them well as carefree, warm and gregarious people, although, only family were taken seriously.

Mattie had actually met Urs in Geneva while on his first overseas business trip two years after he accepted his job at Construction Tractor. Geneva was the location of Construction Tractor's European Marketing office. One evening, Mattie ventured out for a walk and to see the city. The streets were alive this evening with window shoppers, lovers arm in arm or people just like him wanting to clear their heads with the night air. He came upon a quaint restaurant and decided to have a quiet dinner. The waiter who seated him was obviously nervous. Something was not right. The place was deserted except for a group of businessmen who were huddled in the rear of the restaurant. As one of the men stood up to prepare to leave, which turned out to be Urs, a large barreled-chest man jumped up and shouted, "You will stay. We are not through with our business." Mattie couldn't believe his eyes. This little man with the precision of a ballerina did a pirouette, ducked, and, with lightning speed, dropped the big guy. The giant didn't move. As he started to exit with his back to the door and still facing the group, two other men rose from adjoining tables, obviously intent on stopping Urs. Without any hesitation, Mattie jumped up from his table and clothes-lined one of the big lugs. His head jerked and he fell straight on his back, surprised and dazed. Mattie hit him again and he didn't move. Urs had narrowly dodged the other man's swing at him with an old fashioned blackjack. Once again, Urs with precision ninja like moves incapacitated his foe with relative ease.

"I think we should both leave immediately before any more help comes or the police." Mattie motioned to the door like he was making a matador's pass with his cape. Urs seemed to be analyzing his unknown helper.

"Sir, I agree, we should leave."

"I suggest you follow me?" Urs passed by Mattie and the two exited quickly. The two briskly walked down a narrow side street lined with compact cars half parked on the sidewalk, half on the street. After two other turns, Urs pointed to a car and told Mattie to get in. Urs drove around the city, constantly checking his rear view mirror. Convinced they were no longer in someone's crosshairs, Urs drove Mattie to an upscale bar called the Butte Clan. To gain entry, you had to be a member and have a key to open a solid wood door, reminiscent of a castle draw bridge. The two men were led to a private room. "Marseilles, we will have two of your rarest imported steaks with the trimmings, a bottle of your best Brunello, and crème Brulee with your best Cognacs for dessert." The man disappeared. "So, Mister whatever your name is. Thank you for helping me out. Why did you? Did you think that I could not handle the situation by myself? You are very good with your hands. You are an American, right? My name is Urs Frey. And you are?"

"I am Mathew Anthony. I am here on business. I work for Construction Tractor. Do you know of our company? As for why I helped, it was not because I felt you could not handle the situation. You are an obvious expert in martial arts. I just thought I needed some exercise. Business trips do not leave much time for exercise." Urs laughed. The gentlemen had an enjoyable evening. The dinner was perfection, the conversation intriguing. After two months of background checking, The Mailman went to visit Urs and made him an offer. Urs was dealing in illicit arms. He loved intrigue and had definite biases against certain religious factions. He was a perfect addition to the team: unassuming, smart, with contacts, and could take care of himself and others.

The core team was in place. It would be their responsibility to recruit and train their support team. Mattie was eager to test their capabilities. He had decided to wait to add his Asian member until he knew whether to attract a Korean, Japanese or Chinese member. He would discuss this with Scott but only after he had evaluated his current resources, established financial channels, checked the communication networks operational performance, and tested whether the supporting documentation that had been prepared was effective and ready for use as well as the false identities and safe houses that were available in numerous countries around the world.

The team was operational. A number of relatively simple deliveries were assigned and deliveries were made with positive results, no collateral damage or backlashes. Results exceeded official expectations. Leaders had fallen from grace, politicians disgraced, ambitions squelched, and some secondary lives terminated. The Mailman had convinced his team recruits one by one they would be, both monetarily and morally, successful. His recruitment speech was to the point. "The moral compass of the world is broken. There is no longer a true north. Whether the compass is being held by politicians, world leaders, financial moguls, or religious icons, the people we will go after are so corrupt, they couldn't find true north unless it was their place of power. If you join my team, rock-solid cover stories will be provided. You are being offered to be a part of this team because you have a damn good reason to be here. You love your country. You have demonstrated your ability to put your life on the line for your country or your fellow soldier. A whole new bunch of bad guys are out there that our countrymen must be protected from. We may be called upon to disgrace these low-life, we may have to extort, kidnap, rough them up or, when they are extreme threats, terminate them. You will be well informed of the total picture of our actions so that you understand our end do justify the means. The big difference from your past exploits is that you will be well paid for your services to your country."

To each man, the Mailman was direct, honest, and respectful of their capability and past service to their country. All he expected was to have the same in return. Over time, loyalties would sprout deep roots. The Mailman was true to his promise to reward his men well. After each assignment, the Mailman, with an identity unique to each man, would visit and provide him with praise worthy of any Nobel laureate and an envelope with an off shore bank account number for services rendered.

The Mailman's close circle of new friends, "his group", was unique. His group was more than a secret agency. It was more like a secret society loyal to the death. Only the Mailman knew that the group's backing and financial support came from the US Department of Defense. Their mission charter was simple. Perform and complete the blackest of black operations. The group had no checks or balances, and as such, the group was fanatical at completing their tasks once they agreed to the assignment. No one in the government wanted to know about this group. While silently applauding their achievements, they would publicly voice their outrage at such acts and the extent of the damage inflicted. True to their biased values, these officials were quick to offer their politically aligned statements.

Mattie's group consisted of professional operatives who could insert themselves in any country, culture, or to events where it was deemed essential for US security, protection and preservation. Missions ranged from manipulation of political processes, to blackmailing, to extortion, to election rigging. Of course, assassinations were always a consideration. His three top choices were loyal. He was proud of them and actually trusted them.

Chapter 10

Mattie entered the Construction Tractor Co. general offices 6th floor wing where he would begin his first Construction Tractor job. The wing was encircled with glass offices for the ruling class, the overseers, and the intellectually superior managers. The interior of the wing was filled with cubicles for souls of the citizens of the asylum assigned with the burden to make the glass menagerie successful. Mattie was shown his place of residency and introduced to his surrounding cohorts. His tour director couldn't help but notice that the entire wing seemed to be surveying this new recruit. *There is definitely something about this man. He is like a magnet, a natural. It won't take him long to win over his superiors and colleagues.*

Mattie sat in his cubicle and smiled as he surveyed his eight by six confine. His mind began to put into perspective the challenge before him. *This is perfect. A spy, a hired killer, a terrorist or anyone skirting the law or wanting to remain hidden is trained to use every resource he or she has at hand. Optimum resources can be made available with the perfect cover. I have that cover, a business executive from a well respected Fortune 500 company. I will use this job as an avenue to open the doors for my type of mail deliveries. I will be the most successful businessman by day, mailman by night. I will become a chameleon. In my case, I will be a corporate chameleon. Perfect. I bet that job title isn't in any of Human Resource's job descriptions.* Mattie thought and inwardly laughed at his newly coined professional job title.

The Construction Tractor marketing training program was made up of recent college graduates. Most of the trainees were selected based upon an interview to evaluate their interpersonal skills and academic achievement. Mattie was 4 years senior of anyone in the program and the same age as the supervisor monitoring the program. It was easy to excel in this program. Learn the product, learn the dealer organization structure, and develop powers of persuasion. Mattie immediately began to learn about the company's hierarchy of decision makers and career influencers. Mattie knew that, for at least a year, he would be assigned entry positions to acclimate him to both product line and corporate culture. One thing Mattie knew for sure, he needed to appear exactly like Tommie, the businessman, and not reveal his true self. *First, I will openly exhibit my loyalty to the company and praise the professional merits of my superiors. I will display humility and praise to those around me. Finally, I will exude a confidence in expressing my thoughts and decisions because I will be significantly more prepared than the corporate self centered drones who always fall short because of their entitlement positions or those who are such trusting lambs they trust others to take the first step in order for them to gauge their positions.*

Every year, Construction Tractor's Human Resources department held a meeting with each department within the company to go over all personnel in those departments who were considered future managers or who could rise even higher to become officers of the company. "Welcome ladies and gentlemen. You all have gone over your respective areas of responsibility and have provided your lists of personnel we should discuss. Keep in mind that we are to view these individuals from a global perspective. We need objective reviews of the individual, their potential and career assignments. These individuals are considered the elite individuals which are to be anointed for mentoring at the highest level of our company. We are to orchestrate their careers and monitor their individual development." Everyone in the room had heard this opening spiel from Ron Colburn for the past 10 years.

"Ron, let's get on with it. We have 100 names to discuss. I definitely want sufficient time to discuss the openings in each of our four marketing regions. We need to sort out where we should send our top prospects. Will they require new or different assignments here in the States or be re-located to assume a foreign assignment?" Always impatient to show he was in charge of the destinies of his marketing flock, Gerry Couri, VP of Marketing, cut Ron's 15 minutes of fame short. "Let's start with our new employees in our training program."

Before Ron Colburn could start the discussion in alphabetical order, the department manager, Harold Haney, responsible for the marketing training program interrupted. "Gerry, we have a thoroughbred in this year's training program. His name is Mathew Anthony. We need to get him to the field as soon as possible and carefully manage his career or we will lose him. I am not exaggerating when I say he will have my job some day and will compete for yours. He is a Harvard graduate. I find myself asking how Construction Tractor landed a man of his caliber. His family roots are actually here in Peoria so I guess he wanted to come back home to find a job. Gerry, Mathew exhibits confidence and marketing skills that others in the class can only envy. He goes beyond intelligent, he is intuitive. I have staff who have been in the field with 15 years of experience that couldn't hold a candle to him. When he attends meetings with marketing staff and marketing management and even when an officer has come for company orientation get acquainted discussions, this guy draws attention that is uncanny. He obviously is well read, well spoken. He uses his range of knowledge to impress people in every encounter and conversation. If he has one visible characteristic that his most ardent admirer or even his most envious competitor would note, it would be his sense of purpose. He is tenacious when it comes to his goals. He has self-confidence, without being arrogant, such that a Vegas odds maker would not bet against him. He knows who he is and what he wants. He has such immense charm. Hell, Gerry, you know me,

I am critical of everyone, except you of course. Yet this guy interacts with you with a twinkle in his eye so that you want him to like you, to include you in his plans. People will follow this guy anywhere. While his voice speaks softly, his words are commanding. When he presents at our Edwards Proving Grounds product demos to dealers and customers, I have never seen anyone connect and be able to penetrate the toughest of audiences like he can. Dealer people actually have come up to him and offered him a job, and routinely have asked our top managers to pull some strings so that he could be assigned to their territory. When he is challenged by the most combative opponent, he listens and smiles, immediately collects himself, then produces responses which steer the conversation back to where he wishes it to go. Gerry, this guy will one day hold a top management position and quite possibly compete for yours."

"Well, Harold, that was the most glowing report on an high potential employee that I have ever heard since I started attending these sessions. I want you to bring this young man to my office so I can meet him. If he is as good as you say, we need to personally manage his career. Let's forget about all the introductory six month jobs and get him into the meat of our business so he can get his trial by fire. We will know quickly if this is the next messiah that you say he is." For the rest of the personnel meeting, Gerry Couri only thought about Harold's evaluation. He was eager to meet this potential rising star. He sounded just like him. Anthony, Anthony that name sounds familiar. There was an Italian by the name of Anthony that had married a Lebanese girl. Could that be the same family? Gerry, being Lebanese, could find out by attending the next big event the Lebanese community would hold at the Itoo Club. Some member of every Lebanese family in Peoria usually turned out.

The next week after the Marketing Department personnel meeting, Harold Haney called Mattie to his office. "Mathew, you have been doing a superb job preparing for your assignment here at Construction

Tractor. I would like for you to meet the Vice President of Marketing, Gerry Couri. I am sure you have studied all the corporate org charts by now and know that I report to Gerry. This is an important meeting. You probably know via the rumor mill that Gerry likes to personally manage individuals who he thinks can be high achievers in marketing. Mathew, I am one of your sponsors and want you to know that you can call on me to act as a mentor for whatever may arise. Play your cards right and deliver the goods, Gerry may consent to becoming a mentor to you. And, should that happen, your career here at Construction Tractor will be a glorious one. Let's go meet my boss, shall we? Ready?"

Don't you just love the choice of words? Could I deliver? Oh I deliver, but I do not think Harold here would want to be the recipient. Mattie thought. He had heard all the rumors as to Gerry Couri acting more as a Godfather figure than a mentor to his selected favorites. He loved collecting talent. They made him look good. Word was that if you cross Gerry, your career was over. "Of course I am ready. Harold, it would be an honor to meet Mr. Couri." Mattie's excitement and sincerity in his voice was the perfect audible, just like Tommie would do, he thought. The two men set out for the 7th Floor, home of the Construction Tractor Officers and legal staff. Mattie wondered if it would be out of line if he hummed *Stair Way to Heaven* by Led Zeppelin as the two men entered the upward escalator. Mattie would, Tommie wouldn't ever consider such disrespect.

As someone who would lead a double life, Mattie knew that he had to develop dual personalities. One would house his instinctive, psychopath true self, the other a gregarious confident self-absorbed corporate leader. Both personalities needed to develop a network of people who would gather intelligence and who believed in his causes. He had to have an ability to benefit them. He knew he had to convey his feelings that he cared for their survival or their future. He needed a network of people for both personalities who had three key qualities; blind obedience, willing for self-sacrifice if asked, and total lack of empathy for their enemy or competition.

Mattie was on his way and, within five short years, Mattie would elevate himself to sales manager with a network of devout, career obsessed followers. He also worked silently to assemble his network of devout, country obsessed patriots.

Chapter 11

Mattie's telephone rang from an untraceable source, "Meet me on the steps next to the Lincoln Monument. It is only fitting our first delivery be initiated from such a historic site. I will see you bright and early Thursday morning as you walk to your morning meeting. There will be a package we would like for you to deliver." Scott Johnson was eager to try out his new team. The Mailman was to be in Washington D.C. for a conference. It was the perfect time to take advantage of his cover and see how Mattie would react.

"I look forward to meeting you. I assume this will be the last call to my office number. I will have a more secure number for you when we meet. Until then." Mattie hung up his phone in his office. Every conversation with the Mailman was to last less than three minutes. Should anyone ever want to trace the call, the inquirer would find the call had actually gone through more than five network hubs. Tracking this call to its origin was impossible. The voice was also technologically garbled and could only be understood though the technology Mattie had installed in his receiver. "The son of a bitch knows my every move. To know I had a meeting in Washington, he either has someone within Construction Tractor keeping track of me or eyes around Peoria. From this point on, he will only know what I want him to know regarding my whereabouts."

Mattie woke up in his hotel room, showered, and dressed. He wore the corporate dress of the day, blue blazer, tan slacks, and loafers. *Striped tie of course*. As he got off the elevator and prepared to leave the hotel, he stopped by the desk. "I like to walk in the morning. Coming from Illinois, I think I will walk by the Lincoln Monument and say hello to old Abe. Now which way is the Lincoln Monument from here and how much time will it take to get there and back here? I need to manage my time so that I make it back here for my meeting in the Thomas Jefferson conference room." The deception was for anyone who might be interested in keeping track of his whereabouts. His ruse was set.

The direct path to the monument was to go out the hotel turnstile to Orchard Street, turn right and walk 10 blocks. Upon leaving the hotel, Mattie turned left on Orchard walked two blocks checking periodically to see if he was being followed. Upon seeing he was not, Mattie turned right for a block and turned right again walking parallel to Orchard back toward the monument.

Walking up the steps, he caught a glimpse of Scott Johnson walking among the pillars. He walked up and stood at the massive Lincoln statue. *Old Abe seems to be staring back at me. I bet he is wondering what kind of historic mission I will be getting and what impact on the country it will have. Abe, I can only hope that this good old boy from Illinois will have a smidgeon of the impact on this country as you did. God Bless America.*

Scott had come up on his right and nonchalantly slipped a manila envelope into Mattie's open attaché. The two men began to walk away from good old Abe, "The information you need is in the envelope. We do not want this man terminated. We want him embarrassed to the point he is disgraced. Should you require additional information or resources, use the normal channels of communication. "As quickly as Scott had appeared, he was gone.

"Well, good morning to you too." Mattie said to no one. Mattie was like a kid receiving a present. His excitement cried for him to sit right down on a nearby bench in view of these hallowed grounds and rip open the envelope to reveal the target of his first delivery. He turned and, appearing as any other tourist, Mattie surveyed the historic site around him then casually headed back to his conference. Only after the conference and in the confines of his hotel room did he open and read the contents of his prized possession.

"To know your target . . . is to defeat your target." Mattie's mind began to conceive his fault tree of questions and analysis that needed to be answered. "When I focus and begin the analysis of any assignment, we have to address the key ingredients to success: identify expectations, identify power players, establish needs, over plan, then ruthlessly execute." Mattie began to read the material provided by Scott. Not surprisingly, being in Washington DC, his first delivery was to be a self appointed humanitarian politician. Nothing irritated Mattie more than dealing with politics of any kind. Even in the most casual of situations, one could feel the frustration when he had to deal with people who operated or made decisions influenced by politics. Politics were engrained in business, but nowhere were they greater deterrents to progress than in Washington DC. Will Rogers once said, "We could certainly slow the aging process down if it had to work its way through Congress".

"I would love to slow the aging process down for these fools, permanently." Mattie could feel the surge of excitement of a task away from the doldrums of corporate life. The mark identified in this first delivery was a powerful Chicago city councilman who used his connections to become an influential Washington lobbyist and activist for causes that could line his pockets or improve his media exposures. This man had more Teflon coating than a non stick frying pan. He was a powerful African American who actually lived in Illinois, but operated out of Washington D.C. He was feared by most politicians, not from his logical persuasive skills, but from his use of threats to use the race card when he did not get his way. His name was William James Jefferson, but he went by James or JJ. Behind closed doors, everyone referred to him as Slick

Willy. He had an exhaustive vocabulary. His delivery was as smooth and intoxicating as 40 year old scotch. He never discriminated when it came to his manipulative nature with either the media or his constituents. He was on a self fulfilling prophecy to be richer and more powerful with each passing day. He had been caught in many shady dealings, but routinely the matters were trivialized and dismissed.

One of Mattie's first formal engagements as a representative for Construction Tractor was held in Springfield, Illinois. The state had just passed a major highway bill and Construction Tractor, as well as, the various construction companies within the state were invited. It was at this formal black tie affair that he first heard of William James Jefferson. "Well Mr. Jefferson, you have come a long way since I first heard your name. Apparently those contractors I over heard bitching about you had reason. While attending a cocktail party hosted by the Lieutenant Governor of Illinois, these contractors indicated you had pressured the Lieutenant Governor to hire some companies from Chicago irrespective of any formal bidding process. According to your dossier from secretive wiretaps on your phone, you did have enough power to get the Lieutenant Governor to funnel jobs to these companies. You received a number of handsome kickbacks from those who got the bid for the highway work. Says here you received quite the pro bono for your influence over the years. Boy did those contractors who lost the work want to personally meet you one on one. They really wanted to send a message to you and all the other supporting asshole politicians that the gravy train was about to leave the station and they would no longer be on it. The contractors could only bitch because they just didn't have the means to disrupt the practices. I guess now they do. Me."

From a telephone booth at an adjacent motel, Mattie placed a call through his untraceable network. "Droges, we got our first delivery. You drew the ace. It is in your backyard. You being from Chicago, how much do you know about William James Jefferson? He is shaking down honest hard working men. In the next two weeks, he is going to extort, frame, then expose a very important person. This could send the banking community in disarray. We need to trump his move. Find out what you can as to his behaviors, his weaknesses. What does he do when he comes to Chicago? This guy is a wart on the butt of the State of Illinois and of his race. We want him to know that the race card has reached its credit limit. He doesn't fight for the people or against racism. When it comes to this guy, the true offender is his greed and his control. He feels that he alone, not those who are truly downtrodden, should benefit. He sucks the life of not only those who he attacks, but also those he is supposed to nurture. His middle name should be entitlement. We need to nullify this guy as a power broker. We need to find or create something so news worthy that, once it hits the general public for consideration, it would put this man out of politics for good. He is going to be in Chicago next week. I will call you back." The telephone went dead.

Chapter 12

"Whatcha got?" Drogemiller did not have to guess who was on the other line.

"The man is pure slime. He has a whole host of women he regularly visits and, for two ladies, provides support money because he has knocked them up. He basically extorts money from local businesses that helped him get elected. He uses street gangs, Black Power shit, to collect if he has problems. I haven't been able to validate it yet, but he may also snort from time to time. Apparently, he loves to show his street cred by partaking or passing some junk to his entourage of despicable cronies. This guy is a true punk. He basically is using his government position to get what he wants. The cops even look the other way for this ass hole." One could hear the contempt in Droge's voice.

"Can we get this guy with his pants down, or possessing drugs? It would be great to expose him and discredit him as a normal family man, then leak out some pictures of him with reported gang figures, snorting or getting payoffs. Let me know what you need. Remember, we need to do this in the next week. Think we can do this in that time frame? If not, we need another plan, fast." Mattie knew his proposed plan was obvious, but he needed to hear Drogemiller's response. After all, this was the first test.

"Hell, I already have put the first of your plan in motion. I know the perfect way to get one of his ladies to have him over for a fuck and snort.

Cameras will catch it all. Getting the pictures is not a problem. All I need from you is 10 grand, and the names of individuals you want to receive the tapes, video and pictures."

"Check your account, more than an ample amount of money is already there. As for the names, they will be supplied today. You will receive two keys by special delivery. At the drop we set up, one key will open the box with the names you requested, the other key will have some special instructions from me. I would like for you to do a favor for me." Mattie smiled. He was told to not make a final delivery, but Mattie wanted to send a special message to this flamboyant charade of a public demigod.

Drogemiller received the keys by special delivery as promised. He went to a post office across town where post office boxes had been set up in bogus names. He opened the first box, extracted the envelope, placed the key in the box and closed it. He repeated the same process at the second box. When he returned to his apartment, he opened the two envelopes. He was to send copies of the tapes and video to three individuals. One was an aggressive investigative reporter for the Chicago Daily News, Sal Lucciano. Few readers would ever know that the reason he was such a great reporter was that he was from old money and his family was well connected in every sense of the word. The second mailing was to Mayor of Chicago, Mayor Daily. Mayor Daily had gone through the riots of the 1968 Democratic Convention and the trials of the Hippy Seven, and he would not want another mess caused by William James Jefferson. He was tired of this peacock. There was only one boss in Chicago and it was him. The third was sent to the Democratic boss of Illinois, Aryn Buffet. He held the Democratic purse strings and wielded significant influence on which prominent candidates would be selected to occupy key state positions. Chicago politics basically ran the state of Illinois. Forget about all those elected pawns downstate who resided in the state capital in Springfield, Illinois. Chicago was really the Capital of Illinois.

Three days after Drogemiller received his instructions, buried at the end of Sal Lucciano's column was, "PROMINENT POLITICIAN UNDER INVESTIGATION. Information will be forth coming which will expose the misdeeds of one of Illinois' most visible politicians." Unbeknown to the occupant, two days after Drogemiller had received his instructions, audio and video equipment had been set up in Marilyn Manson's apartment for a drug and sex show that the players would forever regret. That night, JJ and his lady performed some of the kinkiest acts with various sex toys after snorting powder at intermittent points of the night. A bonus was JJ bragging about how he was going to destroy a major political rival in the coming week. Through the power and prestige he has gained over the years, vengeance was soon to be his. On day four, Sal Lucciano received audio and video of the encounter with a note that read, "The persons on this tape and video are Marilyn Manson and William James Jefferson. The activities occurred last night in Miss Manson's apartment, 20 Michigan Avenue, Twin Towers. If you wish to follow up on other stories, Mr. Jefferson has other liaisons he keeps. Some include children he has fathered. A list of their names and addresses has been included."

Sal almost fell out of his chair upon reading the note. He immediately called William James Jefferson. "Mr. Jefferson, this is Sal Lucciano. Would you like to comment on activities between you and Marilyn Manson last night? Sir, we have a tape and video of you partaking in illegal activities as well as sexual behavior. Any comment?"

Silence, then a burst of language unbecoming to a prominent politician spewed out like disgusting projectile vomit. What Sal did catch and capture was a threat, "You Guinea bastard, you print any of this and your career is done. I know people in high places who own your paper. I will bury you if you print this shit. Do you know who you are messing with? I am coming down to get those tapes and audio. Have them ready. You think you can extort me?" The line went dead.

William James Jefferson never came down to the Chicago Daily News Building. Within five minutes of his previous call, JJ received another from Aryn Buffet. "JJ, you will not believe what was delivered to me. A fucking tape with you blabbing about destroying Will Frazier and a video with you snorting who knows what and fucking every orifice of some woman. You are fucking grass, my friend, and I am the lawnmower. I am cutting all ties with you and your organization immediately. Find a good lawyer. You are going to need it. I would worry about what the Feds will do on this one. You are one stupid bastard." JJ did not have time to open his mouth, much less respond. His knees buckled from the weight of the conversation. He dropped like an anchor into his family room's oversized leather chair. "This can't be happening, not to me. What do I do?" He asked to no one.

On day seven, it was time to enact the instructions of the second envelope. Bill knew that the Mailman wanted his favor to be done without complications. Bill Drogemiller knew exactly where William James Jefferson silently slithered away to escape the press that was shadowing his every move and the onslaught of the judgmental eyes of his constituents. Droges had tailed JJ to his secret hideaway just north of Racine, Wisconsin, on Lake Michigan. "Far enough away to hide yet close enough to ensure you could get back and forth and not raise family suspicions. Jefferson, if nothing else, you are an industrious slime ball." Droges inspected the layout of the hideaway. It was a small home, brick, in the Cape Cod design on five acres, with trees hiding the grounds. The back opened to Lake Michigan so that JJ could take his boat out on the Lake without prying eyes knowing what he was doing. Droges would have no trouble gaining access to the house. The alarm system was ancient. The next morning, Bill Drogemiller came in by boat in the early morning darkness. He waited in the woods until around 9 o'clock, walked to the front of the house, dressed as a Wisconsin State trooper. Drogemiller knocked on the door. JJ peered out a side window and, seeing a state trooper, opened the door. "Yes".

"Sir, I am State Trooper Dick Smika." He flashed his fake credentials. "Are you the owner of this home? We have had reports of some minor break-ins and are canvassing the area. We are checking all the residents along this road to see if we can get some information on these events." Raising his clip board he gave the appearance of checking a list of home owners. This home is owned by W. J. Jefferson, correct? Are you said person? And, if you are, may I see some identification?"

"I am William James Jefferson. Here is my Illinois driver's license."

"Thank you sir. Are you alone in the house? Had any problems or noticed anything unusual while you have been here?"

"I just arrived here a couple of days ago. I am alone and, no, everything is normal. I just came up here from Chicago for a little relaxation. Things are a little wild right now. I just needed some quiet time. I plan to be here for a week or so. Thanks for checking in. Where is your car?"

"I left it up by your gate. If there were an intruder or intruders here, we did not want to prematurely alert them. There is an accompanying officer who is checking the woods around your house. Have a good day, Mr. Jefferson. Sorry for any inconvenience."

"No problem. Thanks again for checking on my property and my well being."

Drogemiller headed back up the drive toward the main road. He would double back in the woods and make sure all loose ends were taken care of. Drogemiller knew Jefferson was alone. After all, when Jefferson had gone out on the previous day to get some groceries, Drogemiller had entered the house to survey the floor plan of the house and to go through every drawer and potential hiding place looking for any weapons or drugs that were on the premises. "Jefferson, you must be really on an emotional rollercoaster right now." There in plain sight in Jefferson's bathroom were all the tools for a pick me up, the cocaine, the residue on the mirror, the razorblade. A 9mm pistol was found in the nightstand next to the bed. Drogemiller found a perfect spot in the woods to watch the house. Drogemiller had changed his clothes and looked like a giant ninja, dressed in all black with only his eyes visible. Around 10 pm, he rose from his hiding spot. Standing he could have been the shadow of some mighty oak tree. He made his way to the house. No movement had been detected for over an hour. It was too early for Jefferson to go to bed, but Drogemiller knew he need not be concerned about Jefferson's whereabouts. By now, JJ was probably comatose from snorting his powdery nerve relaxer. He again easily gained entrance into the house through the back kitchen door.

Like an armed stealth mouse, Drogemiller began his room to room search for his cheese, Jefferson. As anticipated, Drogemiller found Jefferson on the floor between the bathroom and the bedroom. "Ah Mr. Jefferson," Drogemiller's voice mocked the silhouette on the floor. "Did you like the 100 percent pure cocaine I mixed into your stash? Couldn't stay away, could we? A little too strong for your taste I bet?" Drogemiller then walked over to the night stand and pulled out the 9mm and placed it on the bed. He then walked over to the bedroom closet and extracted a white shirt, tie, suit, shoes, and neatly arranged them on the bed. He went into the adjoining room which Jefferson used as an office and brought back a sheet of Jefferson's finest stationary, one of his Mont Blanc pens, and painstakingly placed them on the nightstand next to the gun. Drogemiller then stripped Jefferson of his clothes and placed them in a clothes hamper located in the bedroom closet. Drogemiller returned to the bathroom, drew a bath and lit candles located on the neighboring sink. He did not dare move the mirror and the remaining lines of cocaine also on the sink. He retrieved a plush towel and silk robe and placed them on a chair located in the corner of the bathroom. Finally, Drogemiller looked at the landscape he had just created, made sure there would be no trace of anyone else in the room, looked at the body and left with some parting words, "For someone who makes his living being an orator, you seem to have a slight speech impediment. I think it was because you stopped breathing." Droges had completed the instructions of the second note, "Provide a delivery . . . An Accidental death."

The tabloids, television news anchors, and talk show hosts were all trying to upstage their peers regarding the escapades of one William James Jefferson. Everyone was trying to get a statement, but Mr. Jefferson seemed to have fallen off the face of the earth. Everyone was looking for him to get his side of the story. It took just two days for the media bloodhounds to find out about the Wisconsin retreat and track down William James Jefferson. When he was found, the preliminary report was that he was dead, seemingly from a drug overdose. News leaked out that Mr. Jefferson must have been overly despondent, went to a hideaway in Wisconsin, ingested a large amount of cocaine, and was possibly contemplating committing suicide. Both state and federal crime labs were called upon to investigate. All parties came back with the same conclusion. The only prints, CSI related findings, and other evidence were all tied to the victim. There was no forced entry, no sign of a struggle. There were too many open questions to really put together any story as to why Jefferson would snort so much of such a strong mix of cocaine. Finding out how he got such a mix would be like tracking a polar bear in a snowstorm. This case would fall into the chasm of indifference.

"We were only to discredit our problem. May I assume to our good fortune, the problem went completely away? I must say that one can only construe that his discrediting pushed the problem to the brink and not something else. Either way, all parties are pleased at the outcome with no backlash from any outside agencies. More to come." To Mattie's trained ear, Scott's voice revealed an uncomfortable and uncertain tone regarding the unplanned delivery. The line went dead.

Mattie smiled and silently nodded his head. *Scott, you are concerned that you may not be able to be in command of me like some puppet on a string. That was the message I wanted to send to you.* Should a mark compromise his country or his constituents to the point mankind is dramatically impacted, Mattie had determined there would be no compromises or finding some palatable middle ground. Each delivery's ending was going to be determined by Mattie, not by some committee.

The first sanctioned delivery was a success. Mattie and his team were now ready to write their legacy. Let the good times roll. Mattie continued a conversation into the disconnected phone. "We need you and I accept that all sanctioned deliveries will come from only one man, you. We accept and are well aware that should we ever be caught, all U.S. agencies would disavow any ties to our existence." Mattie knew his deliveries would initially be fairly routine, then as the team demonstrated their capabilities and discretion, more insane, some impossible, deliveries would come. He also knew that most men would not consider undertaking such deliveries. If the delivery was for the good of mankind or his country, Mattie couldn't wait for the challenge. "Well, Scott, you wanted a safe delivery and actually got one that truly addressed the issue. I bet you will wonder about "the something else" from now on. I want you to wonder if you are really in control of the situation or not. This will eat at you. I will not expose you to the answer unless it becomes absolutely necessary. I am in control from this point forward. You will be the face, I am everything else." Mattie put down the phone. He looked at his watch.

Damn, It is time to go to the next meeting on sales strategies in Central and South America. Boring!

CHAPTER 13

"WHAT IS THE key to becoming a good speaker and providing a good speech? I do not know who said it, but I heard a rule of thumb that I like. The key to being a good speaker is for me to quit speaking before you, the audience, quit listening. Ladies and gentlemen, I have reviewed our sales forecast and we have a problem. Construction Tractor has never met a problem that could not be managed. And, when managed, was solved. Through analysis, adaptable plans, and proper sponsorship, problems get solved and once solved, seem to be much simpler than originally thought. I will present the analysis summary. I would appreciate your help with finalizing the direction and posing any alternatives. Together, we will build a plan for execution and success. I need your involvement and sponsorship. Shall we begin?" Mattie was a natural at blending into any environment. This chameleon was always over prepared for the task at hand. He was no gambler who got off on uncertainty.

Mattie had become a polished businessman. It did not come without some compromise. *One thing about business dealings I must accept, quid pro quo is a big part of the deal. It is painful for me to have to compromise with such egos, but to keep moving up the corporate ladder as a franchise player in the corporate promotion game, one must do what one must do. This is a staple in the business or political arenas and is generally practiced domestically and internationally. It is sort of a twisted justice but, to those playing, an easy justification for value shifts, position changes, side stepping or just plain what is in it for me. I can use this to my advantage. But, on the other hand, one must always be on the lookout for the greedy bastard who will certainly be the one most likely to sink the metaphorical knife in your back. Often times, he is the most powerful foe who is always trying to acquire more political capital to leverage in the next round of business.* It wouldn't take long for Mattie to determine who this person was and what response Mattie felt compelled to perform.

Through his tenure with Construction Tractor, Mattie had nurtured close and intertwined relationships with a number of powerful business leaders and political leaders around the world. His network had expanded to every corner of the globe built over many years in the many countries where Construction Tractor had dealerships supported by Construction Tractor's sales force. Under the guise of in-country liaison to Construction Tractor and other US political leaders, Mattie was often provided Counter Intelligence Information from the Counterterrorism Centers of Latin America, Europe and Asia. Having the luxury of the mass of information he could utilize as a result of his brother's repository of information, Mattie was as informed as any operative of any international intelligence or private security firm around the world.

While Construction Tractor had a long-standing code of conduct that mandated all employees, officers and board members could not put themselves into compromising relationships with those who could influence business transactions. Mattie had to laugh at the liberal interpretations he had heard from his managers on what was acceptable or not. Besides, he was often told, the company had little desire to enforce such a position because the greatest offenders were officers or senior executives. If reviews were to be openly conducted, the company knew the reviews would open up too many debates of their quid pro quo dealings they had participated in under the banner of normal business conduct with many entities and individuals around the world. Construction Tractor had discussed hiring requirements including background checks and, in some cases, mandating security clearances. Good intentions which require time and money often go be the wayside. This allowed Mattie to hire and position new hires in strategic areas for activities he may need in the future.

Chapter 14

Tommie clearly couldn't wait to embark upon his newfound goal in life, a career with AndrewPolk. He truly loved the commercial shrewdness of AndrewPolk. He had researched the company from the day it was founded in 1913 to today. He had analyzed the company's strategies, their hierarchy and power structure. It did not take him long to understand the split among the company's leadership. The majority of the leadership, as well as their hand picked Board of Directors, were old school. Their hearts and culture were founded on years of good fortune which blossomed from their accounting, auditing and tax practices. Tommie felt that the culture was inhibiting anyone looking to future, new business avenues. The interview tip Mattie heard from Hofler regarding the profit opportunities which could be generated from consulting services to large corporations was spot on. *But how could I be instrumental in this venture?* It wouldn't be long for Tommie to see his opportunity. Tommie was rapidly moving up into the company's ranks.

Tommy had become a brilliant master chess player as he came up through the company's ranks. He found opportunities to align himself not only with the stodgy AndrewPolk partners but also with the next generation of hungry gifted partners. He had worked with security specialists who knew how to insert sleeper code in corporate applications which he could one day awaken to begin daily processing of information. He learned of cyber techniques which could cause mainframes to shutdown or eat up storage capacities which could require complete system reboots. He learned from programmers how leap years, new laws, or obsolete code with limited space for information like dates, names, dollars, etc would cause massive corporate software rewrites and expose mainframes to processing risks due to the coming frequency of newly introduced software. He also knew algorithms and ciphers commonly being used for government-developed software: Thomas was a master of computer code . . . he started with Assembler, FORTRAN, COBOL, and kept current ever since. The new UNIX, Linux OS and C++ were gifts because now kids in their bedrooms could code, could challenge the sanctuaries of corporate information vaults.

Tommie had managed to get himself assigned to the consulting wing of the firm within two years of joining the firm. After another three years, Tommie had worked his way up to the position of partner, faster than anyone could remember. Being on the right projects, developing the most profitable accounts, having superior intelligence and a Hollywood leading man profile, he stood out with everything he did. He was now instrumental in the direction of the arm of the company that was becoming increasingly more important, growing at a much faster rate of profitability than the more established accounting, auditing, and tax practice. Using this disproportionate growth, and working with the younger consulting division partners' belief that they were not garnering their fair share of firm profits, Tommie worked behind the scenes to create strategic and cultural friction between the two divisions. He was ready to take the next step, spearhead the change.

"We need to approach the CEO with the proposal to separate the Polk Consulting group from the AndrewPolk Accounting group. We could leverage the accounting services client list for easy access to sign up clients for our new company and services. Gentlemen, we are seeing the genesis of an information explosion. Computer processing will exponentially improve over the next 10 years. Communication networks will expand and link the global companies' computers like never thought of before. Companies will have the ability to process and analyze their captured data with only their imaginations as limits. We have been hiring the best and brightest college graduates, MBA graduates, and top notch research people. We are in the best position to consult with corporate leaders on how best to reduce inventories and improve financial positions with improved knowledge of manufacturing and sales processes. A huge factor is in our favor. Most corporate leaders do not have any understanding of their current computer processing or where the electronic age is going. They are ripe for the picking. We will be able to name our price. Just think of the mileage we will get from just simplifying manual processes, integrating sales transactions with accounting systems, or improving their knowledge of their quality problems in their manufacturing processes. We will solidify our staying power within these organizations by implying their competition is capable of doing more than they can. Infuse uncertainties that their business information requirements are not being made available to them but soon will be to their competition, and they will seek us out and pay a premium over their internal information departments."

Tommie continued his spiritual awakening. "Everyone in this room knows the value of today's gold and oil reserves. We are sitting on the next valuable commodity, information. From the vast reserve of data being generated everyday, we can extract exceptional revenues turning that data into information. Information yields knowledge. Combine knowledge with experience and you produce wisdom. Wisdom is always ahead of the business curve. But with the current organization structure and operating practices in place today within our company, we need a major shift. We need to have total control over our ability to mine this valuable commodity. Gentlemen, we need to split off the consulting company, form our own company structure of independent partnerships, and compensate accordingly. The other partners are receiving disproportionate bonuses from our hard work. I for one am tired of Polk Consulting paying our parent company 15% of our profits. We must move to split now. Rumors are that AndrewPolk is forming AndrewPolk Business Consulting to actually compete with us. What kind of strategy is this? Are we being shoved out? Bottom line is that this move will further eat away at our profits, our compensation. I believe I have a way to ensure a split. Who is for pursuing the split?"

Tommie was now in charge. He was no longer content to be a senior partner in the consulting group. He wanted to be the CEO of this new company. Thomas Anthony had worked the internal network over the years like a symphony violinist playing a prized Stradivarius. He had access to insider information from the most senior partners, board members, company lawyers and key project managers around the world. He had heard rumors that the accounting practice was in top secret meetings. After putting bits and pieces together, Tommie was in seventh heaven at his derived conclusion. If he was right, he had to move fast. He needed someone to listen to his plan, offer opinions, debate and brainstorm alternatives. There was only one person he could trust with this confession of his pursuit, his brother Mattie. He called Mattie and asked if he could come to see him over the weekend at their favorite restaurant.

It seemed like only yesterday that the two brothers were walking down Cicero Street in Chicago and came across this quaint Old World Italian restaurant called Domenica's Cucina. The restaurant was run by on elderly Italian woman who spoke 5 languages, one being broken English. At 80 years of age, Dominica was the living photograph etched in most Americans minds on what most elderly Italian women looked like. She had long gray hair rolled up in a bun, a face once so beautiful now laced with wrinkles and lines generated from World War II events and her long hours of struggle to survive in a new land. Tommie ate here at least twice a month. He loved to tease her. "My beautiful Domenica, how do you keep all of Chicago's Italian Lovers away from your doorstep?"

"I am just too good for them. I am quick for my age. With some, I just treat them like the Nazi officer who shot me in the leg when I would not bring him water. I just kicked their behinds and drive them away from the premises." She would always laugh and shuffle off to the kitchen with his order.

Domenica had seated the twins at Tommie's table, the one closest to the kitchen, furthest away from the main seating area. Tommie looked at Mattie across the table and leaned in to begin the conversation. Mattie felt as if he were in some police station about to be interrogated in a room with a big mirror on the wall. He knew someone was on the other side, but all he could see was a reflection of himself.

"Mattie, I need to tell someone about what I am about to do. I may even need some help. Some of what I am to tell you is a little hard for me to expose, especially about myself. Mattie, my ambitions may have clouded my reasoning and values. I have never wanted something so much."

Always wanting to get to the point, Mattie cut in. "Tommie, enough apologizing or second guessing. Everyone reaches a point in his or her life that may go against some of their beliefs. I have bared my soul to you about some things I did in Viet Nam. But life goes on regardless of what I did or did not do. So what is it? Let me tell you one thing, do not expect me to take your confession and absolve you like our old priests. Tell me straight so I can help or tell you to piss off."

"Here it goes. I need to convince three of our company's Board of Directors they need to do something that they may or may not want to do. I need to find out if my company is doing something shady and, if so, I want to use it for my own gain. Mattie, I want to initiate a spin-off company from our accounting practice where I work. I want to create a new company and be appointed the new CEO of that company. Brother, I have to confess that over my career with AndrewPolk, I secretly developed means which have given me access to information within my company and the many companies we have or had business contracts.

Mattie, I truly have at my disposal, information on things that one could never imagine. Techniques used to capture this information have eluded the most scrupulous, meticulous, thorough auditors employed to ensure the security of that information. I have access to information that I know is valuable, but I do not know how to go about using it to get to my end pursuit. Mattie, if I succeed with my plan to spin this company off on its own, I will head up a company that could compete with IBM one day. There is that much potential. Can you imagine me being a CEO of such a company?"

"Big Brother, if you say there is that much potential in forming a separate company, why couldn't I imagine it? You would be a terrific CEO. I could say with pride, see that guy on the cover of Time magazine? He is my brother. So, let's eat. Tell me all about your plan. Highlight where you see your challenges or have questions. Maybe I can brainstorm with you about how to proceed."

Tommie laid out the plan like a step by step instruction manual on how to build a precision time piece. Tommie's first move was to focus on AndrewPolk's existing power structure. He felt he had to neutralize the one person who would never agree to relinquish any element of AndrewPolk's revenue stream. Pressure had to be put on AndrewPolk's CEO, George O'Brien so alliances could be made. The only way to put pressure on this arrogant, egotistical man was to gain an alliance with the only group who had an influence over him, the AndrewPolk Board of Directors. Using everything he had ever learned at Northwestern's School of Business, Tommie was about to write his own Harvard Business School Case Study for future scholars to review and debate. Tommie had devised a crucial two-step plan to gain control. His first step was to orchestrate an injunction to be filed with the International Chamber of Commerce claiming breach of contract for AndrewPolk when they simultaneously established another consulting practice to compete in the same marketplace. Concurrent with this action, select Board

Members would be approached to plant the seed of doubt about breach of company business practices to ensure O'Brien would be placed under the most severe pressures to reach share holder profitability objectives. The pressure would come by writing those objectives to exclude the revenues from the Polk Consulting practice.

"Tommie, I cannot help you with the legal elements of your plan, but I may be able to help with discussions with the selected Board members. Tell me more about the kind of information you have access to and how do you get access to it. If the information is as thorough and available as you say, it is invaluable. What are their names, where do they reside, how did they become such prominent people and any other information you know about them. I have sources to information as well. If we put our information together, who knows what may be revealed." Mattie knew putting pressure on these gentlemen was right up his alley. He was about to put his covert training into action.

In August 2000, led by Thomas Anthony, Polk Consulting broke all contractual ties with AndrewPolk. Polk Consulting was required to put $1.2 billion in escrow for AndrewPolk. This move was considered a brilliant coup. Those who were the leaders of this new spin off were now viewed as Wall Street superstars. Polk Consulting was required to change its name which became Quantum Consulting. The name Quantum Consulting was derived from Thomas' mantra for "quantum leap change" from past business practices to be the industry leader. Industry analysts viewed this event as the ultimate coup by one, Thomas Anthony.

Four hours after an arbitrator made its ruling for Polk Consulting to become a separate company, AndrewPolk CEO George O'Brien resigned. Later at a Harvard Business School activity, George O'Brien provided insight regarding his resignation. Mr. O'Brien revealed that the AndrewPolk Board of Directors had passed a resolution saying he had to resign if he didn't get at least an incremental $4 billion from current core practices, excluding AndrewPolk's consulting practice. George acknowledged this was an impossible task. Once the arbitrator made his decision, George had only one option, a quick resignation. Little did George know or anyone else for that matter, a couple of the Board Members had suggested such a resolution after some personal secrets had been uncovered and were about to be revealed to the general public. These Board Members had been called on by an elderly, stately gentleman lawyer. He apologized that he was the one who had to deliver such startling revelations, but he seemed to have no feelings as he delivered ultimatums on an upcoming vote. There was not a single board member who challenged the ruling by the arbitrator. While the elderly gentlemen looked somewhat frail, fear of the consequences he implied and fear of his ability to deliver what he promised should they reject his request, ensured their compliance. Once again, the Mailman had been successful with his physical transformation and uncompromising delivery of events that were to take place.

Thomas S. Anthony was appointed CEO by a new Board of Directors. As for Tommie and his new company, the company saw a huge surge in profits over the next decade as he predicted. By 2001, Polk Consulting had achieved net revenues exceeding $9.5 billion dollars and had more than 75,000 employees in 47 countries. Tommie did not forget where he came from or where he wanted to take his new company. In his first speech to the new company's Board of Directors, he opened with, "Gentlemen, "Will it play in Peoria?" is a common phrase that resonates with the center of the US being located in Illinois. It was a measure of whether a politician or consumer product could appeal to mainstream Americans with traits associated with Midwesterners, such as stability and caution. We need to change the thinking not only of US companies, but also companies around the world. Quantum Consulting will be on the leading edge to bring technology utilization to these companies.

We need the rallying call to change to "It may not play in Peoria, but with Quantum Consulting, we can ensure it will play anywhere in the world."

Tommie's first organization move was to announce a new Quantum Consulting founding partner, Larry Barnes. With stock options, partner salary, and VP perks, Larry Barnes had received the peer recognition and compensation beyond his most desired fantasies. Larry Barnes had arrived. Tommie was true to his word and had delivered.

Chapter 15

While Thomas was busy executing his plan to separate Polk Consulting from AndrewPolk, Mattie had padded his portfolio as well.

"Do you have any travel plans to Central America in the next few weeks?" A familiar voice inquired in Mattie's ear.

It is about time I got a call. Mattie thought. "As a matter of fact, I will be traveling to Costa Rica, Monday of next week for a dealer and customer event. I will be staying at the Real Intercontinental in San Jose. The hotel is on Prospero Fernandez Highway close to the airport."

"Call when you get there. We have a pressing delivery. It will be your most challenging assignment to date." The line went dead. Mattie was eager for this meeting. He felt that his skills had been dormant for too long.

Mattie replayed the conversation. "We have a pressing delivery that will be your teams most challenging to date." *My guess is that we are finally going to get involved in this Central America mess.*

One week later, Mattie hailed a taxi. In perfect Spanish, Mattie instructed the driver to head North and take Highway 3. To ensure he was not being tailed, he asked the driver to run through Residential Los Lagos de Heredia because he was considering purchasing some property in San Jose and wanted to survey this area. Once he knew that no one was tailing him, he told the driver to head to Bernardo Benavidas. Once they reached the city limits, Mattie guided the driver to a little out of the way restaurant called Cantina Flakos. It was there Mattie was to meet Scott Johnson. Mattie knew this little town well. Scott Johnson was already there and seated in the rear of the small restaurant. Two beers had already been ordered. Scott had started without him and already downed half of his. Mattie sat down. When the waiter came over, Mattie asked for menus, then instructed the waiter that he and his guest would like two more beers and some time to talk before ordering. The waiter brought two more beers and immediately disappeared for the next 15 minutes.

As the waiter departed, Scott Johnson slid over a large leather bound dossier. "Most of the rulers in Central and South America are growing more and more insecure the last couple of years. The economy, the radicals, the drug runners, the ruling class have visible signs of growing insecurity at being alone or unprotected. They are arming themselves with weapons, doubling their body guards, reinforcing their cars with armor, and walled compounds are now the norm. The ruling power in Central America with the exception of this neutral country knows their power and anarchy is nothing more than an assassination away. We need for your team to make a permanent delivery on General Somoza in Nicaragua and bring to justice the drug dealing thug in Panama, General Noriega. The only timetable you have is to deliver as soon as you feel you can make a successful delivery. As for the financial and in country support you may need, just provide me with your requirements. We have the green light to put at your disposal whatever resources you may need for effective deliveries. I believe I mentioned you were going to receive action that would be exceedingly challenging. It goes without saying. Achieving successful deliveries of Somoza and Noriega will ignite a radical shift to the entire political structure of Central America and future relations with the United States. Do you have any questions?"

Mattie smiled like the Cheshire cat in Alice in Wonderland. "Scott, these are the precise kind of assignments my team was born and trained to do. We are more than ready to perform these deliveries. Just to let you know ahead of time; when we complete our deliveries, every member of my team will be rewarded handsomely. I will call when we are ready." The two men finished their meal in silence. With the final glass of local beer, the two raised their glasses, and Mattie gave a short toast. "God bless America and success to my team." The two got up, went to the street and caught two beat up taxis. Mattie headed back to San Jose for a business meeting. Scott disappeared.

Mattie got in his taxi and half heartedly instructed the driver to take him to the Real Intercontinental Hotel. What a let down to know he had to return to his hotel and prepare for sales meetings. The Costa Rican dealer was hosting all of Central America Construction Tractor dealers along with over 100 large customers to see demonstrations of Construction Tractor's new additions to Construction Tractor's product line.

Mattie entered the hotel bar, looked around with disinterested eyes. "Mathew, where the hell have you been? I have been trying to get in touch with you. You are late for drinks. We have been here in the bar for over an hour. You have got some catching up to do." Mattie provided his best smile, his white teeth gleaming. *What a fucking honor to be in the presence of Construction Tractor Americas Vice President, William J. Wadsworth.* He was already three full sheets to the wind and was on center stage for the Central America Dealer Principals. "Gentlemen, I am here to tell you that you can get the best blow jobs in Central America here in Costa Rica." His perverse stories began to spill like crude oil from a tanker who had run aground. Each of the dealer principals tried to hide their disgust and each wished he would just go to his hotel room so that the insults to their culture would end. Yet each did their best to patronize their distinguished lush from Peoria.

They were thankful that their customers did not have to partake in such a spectacle.

After this particular repulsive encounter with William J. Wadsworth, Mattie came to a conclusion. A non sanctioned delivery needed to be authorized. Mattie would authorize the delivery and the delivery would be made by him. *This delivery will help me get in the right frame of mine for preparation for termination of other parasites that have lived off others in Central America.* At least, that was how Mattie rationalized this most wanted exploit.

Chapter 16

The shower's warm water massaged Mattie's body and eased his mind into a tranquil state. The start of the day was always the same ritual of preparation when Mattie was to structure a delivery. Standing nude before his well lit bathroom mirror, Mattie performs a close shave with a straight razor, shaving his beard away as effectively as a cosmetic surgeon with a prized patient. Once he had dried his wet jet black hair, he would select his new color, and then finalize all the accessories needed for the new identity he would assume. Mattie needed to focus. He needed a clear vision of his intended goal, the plan to execute the goal, and especially, alternatives should his plan meet with unknown obstacles. Mattie did not fear his end. He found an inner calm in a certainty that he held. *The path of my demise will be lined with the graves of those that were destined to receive my purification deliveries.* Taking out Somoza was putting both his men and him in harms way. Reflection of a delivery he completed two months prior confirmed humanity demanded their success. He regained his perspective but also felt a sense of gratification.

A smile came over Mattie as he opened a dialogue with the man in the mirror. *"Ah, I think it is time to complete my first corporate delivery. I could not wait to make that delivery on the fat, roly-poly shit machine who constantly muses for the camera. William J. Wadsworth THE THIRD no less! Hello!* God, did Wadsworth like to hear people say his name. He really thought he was European royalty and solicited entitlements that went well beyond his station. He was a jackal who lived off the misery of those who fell. Only on the night of April 1, Wadsworth had no idea that a lion never feared any jackal and was about to act. And on that particular April night, it was going to be good for the hunter, very bad for the hunted. After all, it was a jungle out there, so Wadsworth THE THIRD should have been beware of the hunters.

This asshole has the audacity to think he can go incognito to the hottest night spots in any city and blend in as if the place was a virtual African Serengeti filled with a multitude of animals on which he can feast. Hells bells, this piece of crap smells so bad he would stand out in an overflowing latrine. I knew the old adage of the Serengeti, Wadsworth THE THIRD did not. The key to survival is to keep one step ahead of the slowest animal in the kingdom being chased by the fastest predator. Only the weak or the laggards fail to see the next day's sun. Wadsworth THE THIRD, you will always position yourself so that all notice you. Your vanity cause you to be one of the last to leave any establishment. Predictably, Wadsworth THE THIRD usually left with the drunkest gold-digger in the place.

It was now time for Wadsworth THE THIRD to see what the Mailman wanted him to see, not what he wanted. The Mailman was about to commit a mortal sin by taking this jackal's life. Mattie couldn't bring himself to think as a good Catholic and that he would go straight to hell as a result. It was time to move and make things right for all those who had been wronged. The Mailman rented a car and positioned on a side street parallel to East 54th Street. It was a perfect April night, raining. The Mailman popped open his umbrella, turned up his collar on his black trench coat and set out for his target. His rain cap wouldn't put him on the best dressed list, but the floppy hat did hide his face well. The Mailman couldn't have asked for better weather. The rain kept the streets clear of potential witnesses and the umbrella provided additional cover.

The Mailman had traveled to Chicago for this delivery and had debated the wisdom of making the delivery so close to Peoria. The possible aftermath of this delivery had to considered. The death of this man would generate questions, inquiries which undoubtedly would circle around to Mattie and others who had worked with and for this guy. One error and the Mailman, Mattie, could be caught, his family disgraced.

The Mailman never wavered with his decision to take this man's life. He was going to kill this man. There would be no hand-wringing or remorse. This delivery was sanctioned for the good of mankind. Wadsworth THE THIRD used company rules as deterrents to those which he governed. Mattie was one of his managers who had had enough of this tyrant who got extremely upset when he thought an employee acted inappropriately or broke one of "his" laws, not the company's business practices. The rules were not in this mark's vocabulary. How this mark broke every rule imaginable and still kept the position of a vice president was beyond everyone's comprehension. So many people held in their repulsions for this man. He was a cockroach low life, guilty of so many indiscretions. He had to held accountable and pay for what he had done.

It had taken time, but the Mailman followed up on the rumors, used his sources and knew why this animal had survived. What was the invisible armor that surrounded and protected him? When Wadsworth THE THIRD was moving up in the ranks, he had been stationed in the Far East. He worked for an up and comer sales manager by the name of Robert Camden. On numerous occasions, he had been the pimp for Robert or performed damage control when things got out of hand. Wadsworth made sure Robert always got home from a night of depravity and drunkenness without anyone from the company being the wiser. Through the grace of God, Robert was sent to rehab, came out clean and a reborn Christian. Time erased past ventures and community services promoted grandeur. Robert was a brilliant man. He designed new corporate organization structures and strategies which won the attention and admiration of Construction Tractor's Board of Directors. Robert Camden became CEO of Construction Tractor Co. Wadsworth THE THIRD skipped numerous rungs on his career ladder climb and became a VP. From that day forward, loyalty was cast in concrete. Wadsworth's mouth was silenced from a bountiful dining plate of position power.

The Mailman moved down the sidewalk toward the Drake Hotel where he knew his target always stayed when he had important business in Chicago. The important business usually was to meet a dealer from South America, hold a meeting for a couple of hours to talk about sales orders, product financing opportunities, local government issues, value of currency and other topics. Then the partying would begin. A dinner would be held at the company's expense. There would be an elaborate cocktail hour for the dealer and Construction Tractor hierarchy. This event allowed both parties to spread some of the spoils to their accompanying family members and support managers. Vice President William J. Wadsworth THE THIRD, loved his liquor, imported 25 year old Scotch neat. He was proud of how he could get the younger managers shit faced before the dinner was served. He would always tender the opening toast, stand before his loyal subjects, basking in their adoration which actually came from the reputable company he was representing. Dinner would then follow accompanied with an endless supply of very expensive bottles of imported wine. THE THIRD fancied himself a connoisseur of wine but in reality this equated to his ability to order the most expensive wine on the wine list. After the dinner, dessert, fine cigars and after dinner liqueurs, THE THIRD would dismiss everyone with the normal superficial "This has been a good day, job well done, kudos to everyone."

Wadsworth would then retreat to his hotel quarters which were always a different hotel from those where he had conducted business. While he stayed in a separate hotel, everyone who knew him was well aware the Drake was his hotel of choice. Often he joked to his subordinate managers in bad taste and in a smoker's gravel voice. The Drake Hotel was the proper place for him to stay; "They treat me like royalty. I deserve it, don't you think?" Then the arrogant bastard would laugh hard and cough a couple of times. This man is a piece of work who should be thrown out with the garbage.

The Mailman waited this April night in the rain across the street from the Drake. He did not worry about being noticed. He was dressed like a limo driver and stood in a doorway having a cigarette as if he was waiting for a client to ready his carriage. Limos were lying in wait in numerous spots around the hotel. Each limo was on 24/7 call for rich clients who were staying at the Drake. The Mailman's uniform was the typical black suit, white shirt, black tie, black shoes covered by a black trench coat. The rain and the wind in Chicago allowed use of an umbrella as a shield when approaching cars or as people walked by. A cab arrived. The doorman opened the rear door and William J. Wadsworth THE THIRD exited. The Mailman felt a surge of adrenaline that increased his height two inches. He had felt this feeling each time back in the jungles of Viet Nam when his group were ready to mount an attack. The Mailman knew the room number where his target would head and had a direct dial telephone number to the room. Wadsworth was required to provide this number to his secretary should an emergency arise. Mattie had gotten this number simply by seeing a copy of his itinerary that was left lying on his assistant's desk. He dialed the room. The phone rang six times before he heard a familiar voice. "Hello, who is this? The building had better be on fire and I am to evacuate or someone's ass is going to be raw from the ass chewing for interrupting me." *Oh we should all be so important and privileged.*

Mattie interrupted his tirade, "Sorry to call so late boss. This is Mathew Anthony." Wadsworth liked it when you called him boss. He relished it like some old southern plantation owner. "I got some papers that require your signature and have to be on the Chairman's desk by tomorrow. He wanted me to tell you a significant government deal just came through. The papers are for some agreements authorizing the purchase and financing with the World Bank for some mining equipment in

Chile. They need to have the Vice President of Construction Tractor Americas' signature to authorize the agreement. He said you need to act as a co-signer so the World Bank will loan the capital to the dealer to pay us for the equipment he needs for the sale to his customer. Apparently, this deal just came up out of the blue and the Chairman doesn't want anything to go wrong. I drove up because, after the corporate jet flew you to O'Hare Airport, it went on JFK for another scheduled pickup. The rain was miserable driving up. I am staying at the Palmer House. Once you sign the papers, I'll get a couple of hours sleep and head back to Peoria. If it is alright with you, I plan to grab a cab and come right over. So I could definitely be there in 30 minutes. Do you need a little more time before I come up?"

"Fuck no. I do not need anymore time to get ready to sign some papers. Get over here as soon as you can so I can get back to my nights' entertainment. You are not going to see anything that you have not already seen. Am I assuming too much? You have gotten some tail once in your life, haven't you Anthony? See you in thirty minutes or less."

Shit, he has company. There would have to be a little change in plans. Nothing was going to stand in the way of this delivery. The Mailman had a plan. It would still work with multiple people. It just required more precision on my part. The Mailman waited 30 minutes. *Showtime! No fear.*

The Mailman knew THE THIRD'S room number and knew that he would encounter a drunk who had consumed alcohol way past his capacity. He now knew that THE THIRD had a hooker in his room. This overweight unkempt man relished in the fact that he was able to "draw" beautiful women like flies to a spider web. He hired hookers every chance he could. He liked for his ladies of the night to perform kinky shit. Only large sums of money could make a lady of the night suppress the revulsion at touching his body and doing the things he demanded.

There was always potential for collateral damage on any delivery. If by the time he got to Wadsworth's room, he still had company, the company would have to die.

The Mailman made his way through the lobby. He had opened his trench coat to allow the limo driver uniform to be visible and draw attention should anyone look his way as he walked through the lobby. The brim of his hat had been pulled down in accordance with the rain outside along with his trench coat collar turned up around my neck. He used his wet umbrella, partially closed, to further shield his face as he made his way to the elevators. In his other hand, he carried a briefcase loaded with the tools he intended to use on William J. Wadsworth THE THIRD. His plan was simple. Go directly to "Bill's" room, make the delivery and head to a room four floors below that he had checked into in the wee hours of the morning as Johnson James, with a New York accent, driver's license and an untraceable credit card. False IDs and identities were always destroyed after each delivery, never to be used twice.

While Wadsworth felt he was entitled to stay in the Drake's penthouse, he never did. The company's auditors would challenge such an outlandish expenditure which would require a company officer to authorize. Wadsworth wanted to keep his activities within his expense account allowances. So Wadsworth always asked for the same room on the floor right below the Penthouse floor, room 3003. He joked with Mattie on numerous occasions the 00 in his room number were tits and he rubbed them every time he entered his room for luck with the ladies he would have during his stay. Mattie would laugh along, like all the other lemmings who were to serve the ruler.

The Mailman rang the bell to room 3003 and listened for movement. Nothing, so he rang the door bell one more time. This time he heard muffled words in a very unhappy tone. The door opened. There stood William J. Wadsworth THE THIRD, Billie, in his birthday suit with a hard on wrapped in the ugliest ribbed condom ever seen. "Christ, Anthony, you got here fast. You couldn't have waited another 10 minutes? I was ready to loose my load with the bitch in the other room. Wait here, I need to let her feel the power of this rod. Stand there by the door until I am done. Take out the papers from your briefcase and have them ready for me to sign. I want you out of here as quickly as possible. I want to play the rest of the night. Got it?" He took a quick look at the Mailman. "Jesus, Anthony, is this the way you dress after hours? You look like someone I would hire to drive me to the airport."

Billie's words were slurred. The Mailman was actually surprised he still had his wits about him to even be able to critique his wardrobe. Billie's walk back to his bed room would fail every sobriety test. His sway was at least four feet from center. The Mailman took off his hat and coat and calmly placed them by the door. He slowly walked with the briefcase to the bedroom door which was cracked open. In the bed was a young woman tied to the bed face down. Sufficient number of pillows had been placed under her stomach so that her ass was at least a couple of feet higher than her head. There was Billie on his knees hammering away. He was pulling her toward him with every bit of strength he could muster. He was holding his breath and looked like there was probably more blood going to his head than his penis. No matter, time to deliver.

The Mailman walked into the room as silently as a Siamese cat about to cause mischief. This was going to be easier than the plan he had devised. Originally, he was going to drop Billie as he opened the door with a shot to the solar plexus, then strangle him with his belt and make it look like the fat fuck had accidentally hung himself while masturbating. The Mailman walked up to the left side of the bed and sarcastically asked, "Having fun are we?"

Billie turned to the Mailman with a surprised look and his dick went soft in a big hurry. "What the hell are you doing in here? I told you to stand by the door. Are you some kind of a freak that wants to watch or did you come in here hoping I would stick my dick in your ass and fuck you like I am doing her?"

"Oh William J. Wadsworth THE THIRD, I doubt if you will ever fuck me or anyone else again." The Mailman's right hand shot out like a whip and struck directly on his left temple. His mouth opened wide like a yawn, but on this night, it wasn't about him being tired or bored. This time it was terror. His head turned just enough for the Mailman to deliver a karate chop to the back of the neck which rendered Billie unconscious. Billie fell forward on the back of his conquest for the night.

"What the hell is going on?" asked the tied-up prize breeding stock. She could not twist her head around to see me or what had done to her stallion.

The Mailman walked to the settee at the foot of the bed where Billie had discarded his pants. As he started to remove the belt from the pants, he softly responded to the question. "Be quiet my dear. I will untie you. I will pay you double to go about your business and forget what just happened. Can you live with that?"

"Yes, but hurry up. William is heavy and I cannot hold this position much longer." I could almost hear her thinking about how she envisioned she was going to further profit when I looped the belt around her neck and cinched it tight. The Mailman pulled the belt straight toward her butt hard and firm so she could not scream. She lost consciousness and died. Her eyes were wide open but saw only darkness and eternity.

Before Billie regained consciousness, the Mailman rigged up more of a hangman noose setup from the tall bedposts that surrounded the bed. He wanted to make it look like both asphyxiations were apart of a sexual ritual that had gone sadly wrong. He had brought rope in the briefcase.

He had a flash back to Viet Nam and the many snares he had rigged to catch or kill Viet Cong. The Mailman enjoyed the thought of stringing up this maggot on humanity. William J. Wadsworth THE THIRD would forever be disgraced, his position quickly filled, and he would be removed from any corporate discussions, except what would inevitably go on behind close doors and at the coffee machines. "Did you hear the bastard got so drunk that when he tried some kinky sex act with a whore, he passed out and hung himself and probably strangled the whore in the process?" Laughter would always come from some follow-up wisecrack. "He got what he deserved, and I am glad that bastard's finally gone" would be his legacy as a Vice President of Construction Tractor.

The Mailman had just finished the rigging when Billie started to regain some of his senses. "What the hell have you done, Anthony? You can't do this to me!" he asked. Billie started to pull at the rigging that was now around his neck. The Mailman pulled hard on the rope rigging and Billie started gagging while both hands were trying to loosen the rope. Denial is the first step of the grieving process when one is going to die, and make no mistake about it, Billie was going to die.

The Mailman remembered saying, "If you just listen a minute, I will ease the rope. Can you live with that?" Billie nodded yes, and Mattie released the rope tension. "Boss, I bet you are upset at not being in control over someone who works for you. You always are the Judge, Jury and Executioner on all matters. You're the classic narcissist who is pissed at the world because everyone fails to recognize your genius. Genius my ass! You are nothing more than some fat fuck that blackmailed, bribed, bullied and bought his way to the top. You see nothing wrong when you break rules or compromise the values of our company. You are so in love with yourself and your power that you can rationalize your deviant behaviors and your treatment of those who work for you. You have an elitist mentality. Your actions are always one who thinks he is entitled because of what, position, family name, what? You get a perverse thrill at making others feel inadequate or inferior. You are one SOB hypocrite. "Boss, this time things are not in your control."

The Mailman took over. "They are in mine. Tonight, I am the executioner. I am going to kill you and get away with it. People are going to see you for what you are. You are a closet drunk. It is no secret that you kill 2 bottles of vodka and 10 bottles of wine a week. Your wife left and, during divorce proceedings, spilled all your dirty habits which you managed to suppress. Tonight, all will be made right for everyone to see your true grit or should I say true girth?"

With his proclamation, the Mailman took the slack out of the rope and slowly applied pressure. It did not take much for Billie to realize his outcome, and he started to struggle, but almost instantaneously, stopped and his body went limp. The Mailman truly did not know if Billie had passed out or had a heart attack. Either way, he continued with the pressure for another 10 minutes then released the rope. He checked both Billie's and the lady's pulse to ensure the delivery was complete. He arranged the bodies with Billie lying on the back of his lady with the belt around her neck in his left hand and the end of the rope that was around his neck in his right. Once the delivery was complete, the Mailman went to his safe room, changed clothes, and James Johnson left the hotel and disappeared from the face of the universe.

The Mailman hoped for a quick assessment of William J. Wadsworth's death and closure of the case. It happened exactly as envisioned. A drunken executive who, to heighten his sexual pleasures and, fantasies, due to the alcohol levels in his bloodstream, accidentally strangled his sex partner, passed out and strangled himself. He knew Construction Tractor would do everything within its means to bring this PR nightmare to closure. There were statements to the press denouncing the man's conduct. A large settlement was paid to the ex wife from the company's dowry for executives for her silence. There were covert meetings behind the closed doors at the Peoria Country Club with the Chief of Police and a ranking Illinois senator. Many of Construction Tractor's top executives were interviewed by law enforcement including myself. The case was closed in record time and the sordid deviant behavior of William J. Wadsworth THE THIRD would be water cooler conversation for years to come.

Chapter 17

THE PLAN WAS ready to be executed. Mattie had developed close, intricate relationships with powerful business and political leaders throughout Central and South America. He had lived in Santiago, Chile for a year then Lima, Peru for a year. Under the guise as Construction Tractor's voice in Latin and South America, through business meetings, dinners and side discussions, he had become an insider to Counter Intelligence Information from the Counterterrorism Centers of Latin America and South America. Later assignments in Europe broadened his network even further. Mattie combined his portfolio of power brokers with those gathered from his brother's intelligence sources which resulted in Mattie being able to solidify contacts at a number of international intelligence firms and security firms based around the world.

As Mattie prepared to brief his team on their biggest delivery to date, he recalled a past conversation with Scott Johnson. "Scott, the revolving door is a very accepted practice between government and private industry, especially for Fortune 500 companies. But, having the ability to bring in the assets from your contacts, gives an advantage which will greatly enhance success of our deliveries." Little did Scott Johnson know how much counter intelligence Mattie had at his disposal. *We have the counter intelligence information, the technology and the team for this delivery. We will succeed.* The Mailman, looking more Latin than his Hispanic team members, was confident and direct as he addressed each member of his strike force.

"You have been hand picked for this mission. We are brothers in arms. As we discovered from the rice patties of Viet Nam and soon in the jungles and cities of Central America and South America, we fight best in the red zone. The delivery we are about to undertake will be in the very compound controlled by our enemy. The only rule to remember is to survive by whatever means and to ensure the enemies' termination. Acting in the moment will get you killed. Acting in the moment causes mistakes. Following our plan, each team member performing his assigned task and waiting for the signal to strike will be the key to our success. When the moment presents itself, turn your hatred outward and inflict a rage on others that goes beyond human expectations or capabilities. When you are the victor of any hard fought battle regardless of the pain you had to endure, nothing hurts. Whatever doesn't kill you really does make you stronger."

Mattie was specific on his orders. "When in doubt, empty your magazine. There is accuracy through volume of rounds shot. If you're not shooting at someone, then you should be loading your weapon. If you're not loading your weapon, you should be moving. And if you're not moving, someone's going to cut your head off and put it on a stick. Gentlemen, we are soldiers of war. America's soldiers of war have provided enemies of America an opportunity to die since 1775. It is God's job to forgive our enemies, it is our job to arrange the meeting. Good Luck and God Bless America."

Maybe lying in wait for the moment to strike at your enemy is how the term sleeper agent was coined. Over the next five years, Mattie and his team transformed themselves into assassins of great repute. The man who was known only as the Mailman became so feared in political and terrorist groups, the thought that this legendary ghost could appear anywhere made them reinforce their own personal security. Kidnappers, drug dealers, rapists, you name it. It got so that any death in Latin or South America was attributed to the revenge of the Mailman. The effectiveness and efficiency of the Mailman's deliveries were being viewed with awe. In coming years, the Mailman was sought after throughout Latin and South America when situations arose that required his special skills. Men who sought him revered this apparition and would pay fortunes for his services.

Chapter 18

Anastasia Somoza, nicknamed "Tahiti", had graduated from West Point. The year after his graduation, he was appointed commander of Nicaragua's National Guard by his father. As commander of the Guard, Anastasia effectively became the second most powerful man in Nicaragua. Upon the death of his father and brother, he was officially appointed to the presidency. During the 1960s and 1970s of his presidency, Nicaragua experienced economic growth largely as a result of industrialization. Nicaragua actually became one of Central America's most developed nations despite its political instability. Due to its stable and high growth economy, foreign investments grew, primarily from U.S. companies such as Citigroup, Sears, Westinghouse and Coca Cola. Construction Tractor Co was no exception. For a country to develop, it requires earthmoving equipment to prepare the land, to build roads. The Construction Tractor dealership located in Managua, and the family that owned it prospered.

In 1972, the capital city of Managua suffered a major earthquake which destroyed nearly 90% of the city creating major losses. It leveled a 600 square block area in the heart of Managua. Construction Tractor equipment was in peak demand to aid in clean up and recovery of the city. Somoza was re-elected president in the 1974 election, partially due to declaring nine opposition parties illegal, thus becoming more of a dictator than a president.

Mattie was a dealer representative for Construction Tractor in Central and South America during this time. He had built credibility in his ability to find financing for the industrialization that was taking place. Mattie had become quite the socialite with the ruling class of Nicaragua and had been to a number of functions in which Somoza attended. Mattie had heard rumors regarding the strife that seemed to be brewing in the working class ranks. At some of the building sites Mattie had visited, he had felt a change in the equipment operator's attitude about their work. They were complaining more and more about not being compensated fairly. Their view was that only the foreigners, the Nicaraguan landowners, and the government were prospering. They saw no improvement in their lives.

The '72 earthquake that devastated Managua was the final 'nail in the coffin' for Somoza. Instead of using the money that came in from all over the world to rebuild Managua, Somoza siphoned off the relief funds to pay for luxury homes for his National Guard while the homeless poor had to make do with hastily constructed wooden shacks. Even the economic elite were reluctant to support Somoza, as he had acquired monopolies in industries that were key to rebuilding the nation. Somoza had gotten too greedy and did not allow the businessmen of Nicaragua to compete for the profits that would result. Mattie knew something was up when the Managua Construction Tractor Dealer Principal moved his family to Miami and conducted all Construction Tractor business in his Miami office. Transactions were no longer done through credit lines. Cash was now king. Cash equated to the US Dollar.

In 1973, the year of reconstruction, many new buildings were built. But the corruption in the government was preventing the amount of growth that was needed to return the country to its prosperous self. Demonstrations and strikes became a common occurrence as citizens became increasingly angry and politically mobilized. Even the elite were becoming angry. Somoza was asking them to pay new emergency taxes to further his own ends. In early 1973, Mattie received long awaited instructions to contact Scott Johnson. "Mr. Johnson, this is the Mailman. You wanted me to call? What can I do for you?"

"We have been following events in Central America for the past year. There is a movement forming that could destabilize Central America. We need to better understand their leadership and the direction they may pursue. We must get close to them to understand what is going on inside their heads if we are to know their true agenda. We have to ensure they do not have ties to Cuba or any other anti-American influences. You know the drill. More and more young elite and poor Nicaraguans are joining this new counter movement. The group is called "the Sandinista Liberation Front. "More and more situations have risen which haves increased tensions and generated anti-government uprisings. We are seeing rapid deterioration in economic growth in Central America. Nicaragua epitomizes the slow growth in the last two years. This economic problem will topple the Somoza dynasty. Somoza's brazen corruption, mishandling of relief monies, and refusal to rebuild Managua has the Sandinista ranks growing rapidly with young disenchanted Nicaraguans who no longer have anything to lose. Nicaragua economic problems have propelled the Sandinistas as the only hope in the struggle against Somoza. Many middle and upper class Nicaraguans see the Sandinistas as the last opportunity to remove the brutal Somoza regime. See if you can get a private meeting with the Sandinistas leadership. We are not sure who they are, what we can do to align with them."

Mattie had already initiated such a move sensing Central America would eventually require his team's skills. He had the person who could infiltrate the group, Juan Ramirez or JR. It took JR over a year to become a trusted member of the movement. The main militant in the Sandinista group was a Daniel Ortega. JR had gained a reputation for his military skills. Most thought he was just some disgruntled Mexican looking for military action after the Viet Nam war. JR was so well thought of that he was selected to be a part of the group who, in December 1974, held some Managua Somoza backers hostage until the Somoza government met their demands for a large ransom and free transport to Cuba. Somoza granted this, then subsequently sent his National Guard out into the countryside to look for the so-called 'terrorists'. While searching, the National Guard pillaged villages, imprisoned, tortured, raped, and executed hundreds of villagers. This invariably led to the Roman Catholic Church withdrawing any and all support of the Somoza regime. The Somoza dynasty was doomed to fall.

The final straw was about to fall. A group of prominent Nicaraguan loyalists, known as Los Doce, openly denounced the Somoza regime and said that there would be no further dialogue with Somoza because he was the sole obstacle to all rational understanding through the long dark history of *Somocismo*. They urged all Nicaraguans to cut all ties with the current governing body.

The Sandinistas, supported by some of the populace of Nicaragua, elements of the Catholic Church, and neighboring regional governments including Panama, Mexico, Costa Rica, and Venezuela, took power in July 1979. The Carter administration, refusing to act unilaterally, decided to work with the new government. Being ever the humanitarian, the Carter Administration attached a provision citing that there would be a forfeiture of all aid being provided to the Sandinistas should it be found the Sandinistas were assisting insurgencies in neighboring countries.

"Mr. Johnson, Nicaragua is lost. Somoza has launched a violent campaign against the Sandinistas. The US has lost this country. Cuba and the Soviet Union are supporting the Sandinistas. They have gained supporters. The US still has supporters in the more prominent sectors of the country. When President Carter withdrew American support for Somoza citing human rights reasons plus forcing Israel to call back a ship carrying weapons vital to the survival of the Somoza regime, they became more vocal because they now knew Somoza was doomed. Somoza is getting ready to flee Nicaragua and wants to go to Miami. I would suggest that the US deny his entry if we are ever going to have any influence in Managua in the future. Wherever he finds refuge, give me the authorization to neutralize this man." The Mailman felt as if he were a jockey in the starting gate waiting for the gates to open to let him run free to the ultimate finish line.

Somoza resigned his presidency and was denied entry to the U.S. by President Carter. Somoza fled Nicaragua along with whatever he could abscond from the national treasury and was granted refuge in Paraguay. There he bought a ranch and a gated house in Paraguay's capital of Asuncion. The Sandinistas took control of Nicaragua. The Mailman received instructions to make a delivery to demonstrate the United States would never admit Somoza into their country regardless of which political party reigned. The postage for the delivery was $2 Million dollars. Mattie's return reply was to the point. "Considering time, risk, and reward, $5 Million. Await reply." The reply was returned quicker than an anxious heartbeat, "Agreed". *Let the inquisition begin.*

Mattie set out to meet with a Nicaraguan road builder contractor who was a large purchaser of Construction Tractor equipment. He was born a socialite, rebelled and started a construction company to help with the development of Managua. He was industrious, honest and rewarded his laborers with fair wages for their efforts. His business grew rapidly in Nicaragua and branched out to neighboring countries. Currently, he had various construction projects underway throughout Latin America. The two men had met on several occasions, both business situations and social gatherings. Mattie knew this man had special ties with the Sandinistas. "Jaime, I met an investor who wanted to know if I knew of any companies that could do some development work for him. If you are interested in hearing about any more opportunities in Central America, I would like to give him your name so that the two of you could meet. Interested?"

"Senor Anthony, I am always interested in opportunities that provide me a good return. Here is my private number where I can be reached. When he calls, we will set up a meeting place to go over the proposition. You do vouch for this investor to be able to produce the money should such a project be initiated?"

"Jaime, I do. I will give him your number. The name of the man who will contact you goes by the name of Juan Ramirez or JR. Good to see you again. *Saludos tu su familia.*"

The government customs agent was about twenty-five years old and hated his job, hated the U.S., and loved to irritate foreigners with his slow delivery. He loved to see if he could cause them to feel uncomfortable, to know he was in charge. When he was done with his sole source of job satisfaction, only then would come the "rubber" stamping. "Welcome to Paraguay. How many days will you be in the country, Mr. Anthony?" he asked. To cut down waiting for the same questions that he had been asked a thousand times by every customs agent in every country he had ever visited, he quickly offered a multitude of answers. He knew professional businessmen were generally passed through without incident given the information in his answers. *Did this ignoramus really think that the stare, the thumbing through the passport, the posing of such mundane questions was going to catch a criminal? Do they really think their very presence is intimidating? Please.*

"I am here on business. I plan to stay at the Camino Real/Grand Hotel/Carrera. My stay is for three days. Plans are for me to depart on Wednesday."

(Stamp, Stamp, Stamp.) "Welcome to Paraguay, Mr. Anthony. Enjoy your stay."

"Thank you. I will enjoy my time here."

On a very comfortable night in September of 1980, the Mailman rejoined JR and a group of hired mercenaries from Nicaragua on the outskirts of Asunción. Somoza met his fate four hours later when he was assassinated, allegedly by members of the Argentinean Revolutionary Workers Party. Earlier in the day, construction workers had been continuing work dozing and performing concrete and retaining wall construction in the compound where Somoza had taken asylum. The operator of the yellow Construction Tractor dozer was none other than the Mailman, memorizing the lay of the land while his crew, JR and friends, were planting explosives. Perception is everything. Control the media, you control the perception. The Mailman's surveillance information gathered over the past months revealed a pattern performed by Somoza. Each night around 9 pm, Somoza would venture out on his veranda to enjoy a Cuban cigar and a glass of his favorite liqueur after his evening meal. Only, on this fateful night, historians were about to open another chapter of *Rulers vrs Us* detailing the rise and fall of another merciless, callous, hardhearted figurehead. The only things this figurehead felt on this night were explosions of equality and redemption, not explosions from flavors of the privileged.

The press had received leads and well placed leaks on persons responsible for the assassination. Paraguayan papers printed accusations which were sent through newswires. Supposedly, evidence gathered by Paraguayan governmental sources pointed to a band of disgruntled South American revolutionaries who called themselves the Argentinean Revolutionary Workers Party as the assassins. Those in the underworld trafficking of death kept hearing a name echo through their "connected" sources and their "forever on alert" armed compounds, The Mailman. Whoever this man was, his work was inspiring to say the least.

Throughout Central and South America the word was the Mailman had a list of rogue politicians, corrupt businessmen, extortionists, kidnappers, drug dealers and terrorists. Over the next five years, the ability of the

Mailman to infiltrate and exterminate some of the most secluded and protected individuals became legendary. A well publicized "hit" contract for the Mailman's death had circulated throughout the underbelly of society, but no one of any means sought to take on such a task. It was obvious to trained professionals, the Mailman had an innate amount of resources and backing especially after the grapevine heard the Mailman had orchestrated the fall and incarceration of Panama's General Noriega and the killing of his two top aides. There was no debate. No one was safe if the Mailman had your name on his delivery list.

PART V

Chapter 1

*W*HEN I THINK *about the stories of my ancestors, the wisdom of my grandfather, and my role models over the years, I cannot identify with Americas' obsession with material things over security, love and family. Sure, I inherited money. I know I have acquired substantially more than the average American. I have money stashes around the world to hide the real me from society. The only feelings I have is the need to connect with my heritage, my mother and especially my brother. Time will tell if I can truly live in the normal world and relish its bounties as my brother has. Only the Mailman through his core team has allowed himself to feel the security of another's loyalties and trust. Mathew Anthony is a guy who has lived on survival instincts. I need to emulate my brother. He is CEO of Quantum Consulting. I should consider being the CEO of Construction Tractor. Mother would be so proud of her sons. Having two Anthony brothers as CEOs of two Fortune 500 companies would elevate the Anthony name to such prestigious heights, Grandfather would see the Anthony name almost reached to Heaven.*

During the 1980s, the world was experiencing a rare event in which all economies were headed toward recession. In the past, global companies could weather the storm because, generally, some sector of their products would do well in other world markets. While profits would diminish, company bottom lines would fall within acceptable Wall Street ranges. Hard times had fallen throughout the entire world's supply chain. At Construction Tractor, Mattie was the most experienced in world markets. He was assigned responsibility for keeping dealers and key suppliers afloat. Mattie was promoted to Construction Tractor Inc. President, second in succession only to the company CEO. The promotion was no surprise.

Mattie had earned peer, Board of Director, Dealer and employee respect throughout the Construction Tractor extended enterprise. His supporters were about to extend to Construction Tractor's largest suppliers.

In one of the most daring strategic moves since the CEO reorganized the company into global business units, Mattie proposed and convinced Construction Tractor Executives to actually build inventory in this downturn. He outlined a plan to offer dealers interest free financing for nine months for dealers willing to position with Construction Tractor that the economy would turn around in 18 months. Dealers around the world took advantage of free money. Taking delivery of this inventory at their dealerships in a sense transferred company inventory to dealers who would have stock available when the economy turned. Competition did not have this capability around the world. The gamble worked, the economy turned around and Construction Tractor product market share soared.

Mattie had also swayed other company officers that Construction Tractor should help finance suppliers who provided steel, components and parts to Construction Tractor's most profitable product lines. Never had Construction Tractor extended their financial network and resources so far into the supply chain. As with the dealer strategy, numerous suppliers competitors went under. When the economy showed signs of an upturn, preferential treatment on material availability, as well as special pricing, was given to Construction Tractor over their competition. As Construction Tractor's market share soared skyward at the expense of their competition, profitability went well above Wall Street projections. Construction Tractor, and Mattie, were the year's Wall Street darlings. Mattie was being interviewed by every money magazine, business journal, and television channel regarding Construction Tractor's supply chain strategies, dealer organizations and global goals. Mattie was a hot commodity.

Mattie's rise to officer power was actually launched by Construction Tractor Mining customers. Large mining machines generated the majority of Construction Tractor's bottom-line profits. Providing these large mining companies with quality, serviceable machines was paramount to keeping these companies as repeat buyers. The prices of commodities were at a premium. Copper, gold and silver were climbing. While living in Chile and calling on South America mining customers, Mattie provided personal attention to satisfying their product, price and performance requirements. As a result of his efforts, his regional sales more than met company sales objectives year after year. These customers open support for Mattie was known by Construction Tractor's top decision makers. While some times jealous of the praise Mattie was receiving, the powers in charge could not ignore the mining industries' clout. Mattie was assigned to a newly created position responsible for marketing and supporting Construction Tractor mining products to the top five mining companies around the world.

Mattie's destiny to attain corporate executive ranks was sealed when the CEO and president of World Mining Inc, Construction Tractor's number one purchaser of Construction Tractor equipment, was the key note speaker at an annual World Wide Dealer meeting. "In closing, those who know me know how demanding I am of Construction Tractor dealers, products and the company. Ninety two percent of our mining fleet is from Construction Tractor. We have gone through some interesting times these past five years. I believe it takes a team effort to weather the ups and downs of our business. Rarely can an individual stand out. However, tonight, I want to acknowledge a man in this room, Mathew Anthony. He is not an ordinary person who performs extraordinary things on occasion; he is an extra ordinary person who yields desired results every time. We look forward to using Construction Tractor equipment for years to come, and if Construction Tractor continues to provide people working with their dealers and customers like Mathew Anthony, Construction Tractor Co. will be around for years to come. Mattie, you can come work for me anytime."

Chapter 2

Mattie was a natural corporate chameleon. He was intelligent and thought mostly about opportunities. He never rested on past achievements. He only reflected in hindsight to improve his future plans. He was not afraid of risk. He overanalyzed his every decision as if it was part of a high stakes poker game. With everyone he met, he sized them up immediately. He trusted his eyes, his ears, his smell and his touch. He was good at stepping inside other people's persona with the goal being to understand, "Who is this person really? How can I get this person to do what I want, when I want him to do it?" Whenever he felt the slightest resistance to his will, he saw it as a sign of potential disloyalty. Immediately he would internally put up his safety defense barriers. His best defense was his sense of humor, his false smile, his charm, his quick wit which concealed his disdain and "never forget this moment" assessment and feelings. He gave the impression he could easily forgive, but inside, he never forgot. His insecurities and paranoia were masked and protected better than valuables stored in any safe.

He felt every relationship could be altered. He also had developed a network of the richest and most powerful people around the world. His assessment of the pretty people came quickly. Unless you were first generation who came from humble beginnings or you had to put your own blood, sweat and tears into the business, you were a subsequent generation of rich and famous generally vocal in intent but woefully lacking in the follow through and execution.

Mattie did respect the achievement of power. The powerful did have at least some redeeming characteristics and had inherited knowledge about most leadership scenarios and decision processes. They were generally dependent on the support of those in the chain of command or key participants in the approval sign lines. Mathew knew what he had to do. He listened to the outpouring of information trying to digest the meat of the message. He remembered his grandfather's advice when it came to business, "keep your mouth shut, your ears open, and become one of them!"

To run for power, one must look the part. Your apparel must reek of professional tailor touches, have a head of hair that is thick and razor cut, professionally styled. Apply these touches to a head of cold black wavy hair and you have a candidate. Mattie's hair caught the light and seemed to throw it back in the air around him. He always wore the whitest of white shirts. His collar and shirt were immaculately starched and pressed, so much so, they seemed like they could have stood up by themselves. As for his suits, there wasn't a man in the world who wore a suit so well. Even his worst suit looked like it had been tailored for his every body movement. But he had observed and learned, he needed a couple of power suits that were made of the finest threads. The suits were always accompanied by the finest of accessories, a gold watch that looked liked it weighed a ton, a gold ring he wore on his right hand, and the most stylish business glasses, even if he did have 20/20 eyesight and the lenses were just glass. Removing your glasses during any interaction is great gamesmanship since the action sends intangible messages. Those on the receiving end must figure it out. Mattie's cologne was not overpowering yet permeated the air with the freshest of scent. Men and women alike often asked him for the name of his cologne. He would always laugh at the inquiry and reply, "Old Spice, available at any five and dime store." Then acting as if he were somewhat embarrassed, he provided them the name of his cologne. Mattie knew women loved to see this vulnerability.

The men just wanted to be like him unless envy caused them to hate him.

If I am going to seek the CEO position of Construction Tractor, it is time to put together a strategy and plan to achieve the end goal. This is going to be one game where getting to the five yard line and not scoring means defeat. To know your target, is to defeat your target. That target is currently CEO, Robert Camden. He is not ready to retire for another five to seven years. Five years is too long to wait.

When it comes to making a delivery, you could say that I have such single mindedness until the delivery is made that I make it my obsession. When I am ready to perform, my eyes can focus on infinity. These are the situations that force me to focus and think so that the very best in me comes forward. When I make a delivery on a corporate or drug kingpin, it is often too easy. Rule one: Nourish their tastes until their bellies are overly full. Rule two: Quench their thirst until their livers are pickled. Rule three: Feed their wildest fantasy until you reach their alter ego. Follow the rules and your mark will actually reveal the plan on how to construct the delivery. Loose lips do sink ships.

While I often feel that I have an inability to feel, it does have its advantages, especially for those times I must make a decision on the punishment that must be delivered. I have never felt bad making a widow, a child parentless or leaving a community living in constant fear. I do not remember feeling any remorse, doubt or regret due to my actions. My tears have only been shed when I lost a role model. My real dilemma is the climax that comes with each delivery leaves me with a euphoric rush, a power, the sweet taste of blood in my mouth like some mythical, phantom vampire. My dilemma is why should I return to being a boring normal mortal when I take so much pleasure in this?

Chapter 3

"Gentlemen, I have learned from the Chairman that he may be traveling to Europe as part of a US delegation. This event is strictly top secret, so I cannot tell you of the details until so instructed. We have other matters to discuss regarding our sagging sales numbers." As the Vice President of Europe Marketing continued with his presentation, with eyes half closed, Mattie seemed to go into a trance like state. Upon learning of the CEO's plan to go on the trip to Europe, Mattie's mind began to fantasize about a power play the likes of which have never been imagined in this company. Replace a superficial "born again" yet flawed tyrant CEO with the next anointed one, a leader of men who walks the talk, who embodies words like integrity, honor, loyalty and team. The beating of Mattie's heart muted the voice of the presenter before him. *My next delivery will be the most innovative delivery I have ever done.*

As if watching an old black and white movie, he envisioned a desired future chain of events. The cast of players were business leaders and political figures he knew. He could see the power players enter the plane, all feeling they are the hope of the world. He could feel the player's ego predicting their presence alone could solve a war torn country's economic and humanitarian ills. Mattie envisioned shaking hands with his CEO, wishing him the safest trip only desiring the opposite. Mattie had waited years to even the score and to make things right with this so-called reformed man. This man was becoming a political power in Washington. He had gotten a country club boyhood friend from Peoria elected to Washington. That boyhood friend was now Speaker of the

House of Representatives. Behind the scenes, Mattie knew first hand he wasn't much better than William J. Wadsworth. Mattie had not forgotten or forgiven.

At 58 years of age, Robert Camden was the epitome of what one expected a chairman of a company to be. He stood out in every crowd at six foot four. He could present the perfect pose and was so photogenic that every camera shot was prime time, red carpet ready. He was stately, had white flowing hair, blemish free complexion, with a personality that swayed the strongest critic, the rich and famous, or the elected elite. He was recognized for his brilliance at leading the number one heavy equipment company in the world and one of the largest exporters of product. The company had prospered under his leadership. Behind the scenes, he was unrelenting in his positions. He was the chairman and you had better conform to his direction or else. He held dealers hostage unless they kept his order board in line with the information being fed to Wall Street analysts. The officer soldiers of Construction Tractor feared the Dr. Jekyll, Mr. Hyde who approved their stock options and pay level.

Mattie remembered how William J. Wadsworth THE THIRD had bragged to him one evening after a sales meeting. "Mathew, I am completely wasted. Could you see I get back to my hotel room without incident? You keep watching out for me and you may be as fortunate as I was for being the keeper of our illustrious, born again Chairman, Robert Camden. You know we were peers in Asia. Everyone knew he was officer material and had fast track tattooed under his tongue. I cannot count the number of jams I got him out of in the five years he spent in the Far East. I was also the one who suggested he go into rehab before returning to the states and into a Vice President role. I had become my brothers' keeper. Good old Robert never forgot and moved me up the ladder. I am sure you have learned, to keep those around you professional in their thinking, promote them as you get promoted. Promotions fog the mind of facts. Oh the stories I could tell." *And you did.*

The thought of bringing down a plane with the CEO in it pulled hard at Mattie's creative juices like a powerful electro-magnet. He swallowed hard. He could almost feel the current going through his body. Killing powerful people is as easy as killing the common man, only it is far more difficult to get away with it. Kill power and all the technology and intellectuals in the power game come after you.

Two months prior to the Construction Tractor's CEO heading for Germany, Mattie headed to Chicago for his monthly meeting with his brother. During dinner, Mattie broached the subject of Tommie's new venture. "Well, is it going the way you envisioned? Is it all it can be? How is it, sitting on the mountain top looking down at all us little people? Is this Quantum Consulting, CEO, thing what you envisioned?"

Tommie was childlike in his enthusiasm as he spoke about the work they performed. "Mattie, the stress is immense. People's livelihood, the welfare of families is now something I must consider with every decision I make. But Mattie, I get to see the impact of every decision we make, good or bad. Accountability is a bitch, but my god, when it is done right, it is so satisfying. I love the job, the company, and the people. Mattie, knowing you, I believe you would find the CEO of Construction Tractor to offer the same job satisfaction as I have found. I can only hope the Board of Directors see you as the obvious choice when Camden steps down per Construction Tractor's by-laws."

Brother, waiting for Camden to step down will take too long. Bring down would be more appropriate. "I try not to think about it Tommie. Camden may be there for another five years or so precluding any unforeseen events. Tell me more about your job and how is that lovely wife of yours doing?"

Chapter 4

The Mailman in his research through agency contacts had discovered that the plane in which Camden and his fellow travelers were to fly in a United States Air Force CT-43. Mattie acquired information on the names of all contractors who performed work or who provided parts to this particular plane. Mattie was pleased to see AndrewPolk's name on the list. During one of their monthly clan meetings, Tommie had talked about the work being performed for one branch of the US Government. Mattie acted interested and probed a little deeper. "Tommie, what kind of software does your company provide the U.S. government? If it is for the IRS, can you put some code in there to reduce my taxes?"

"Actually we do all sort of projects for all the branches of the government. We have built libraries for the Supreme Court that allows them on-line access to billions of law documents. We did write application software for the IRS, health, transportation, and most of the other departments of the government. We have written software for the Pentagon, FBI, and armed forces branches. We even have written and supported software for Air Force One and many jet fighters and support planes used by the Air force" You could see Tommie's pride inflating his chest being a part of a company who was so intimately involved. Tommie had just confirmed AndrewPolk was the company the USAF had contracted to develop the software used in USAF guidance and tracking systems. Mattie made a mental note to find out more information on an undergraduate program to train navigators for various strategic and tactical aircrafts. Bringing down a plane is very difficult if you want to make it look like an accident. *Could software bring down a plane?*

There is an Achilles heel that exists today that institutional security units have not figured out how to defend against. Technology has invaded our very fabric of life like cockroaches. It is resilient. It performs consistently as designed. It can fail. There is not debate on the dominant role technology plays in today's world. Technology controls the very decision process with sophisticated software in corporate and business computers to planes, manufacturing robots, medical processes, televisions, and other applications used by man or machine. A mandatory rule of thumb of all technology is to always backup, and duplicate where economically possible, should problems arise.

Quantum Consulting knew backup redundancy solutions were valuable. Without exception, companies and governments were willing to shell out bales of money at harvest time to minimize their operation exposures. Exposures could come from nature like a tornado wiping out a company center, a terrorist bomb or having a plane fly into the technology structure. However, the hardest exposure to minimize or prevent is the human being who wants to do mischief.

How can I bring down a plane? Do I focus on mechanical problems or software? It helps to have a brother who provided the plane's software and its backups for every situation. In a plane crash, investigators always seem to find the cause if the problem originated from mechanical problems or pilot error. This plane crash must look like pilot error as the primary cause for the accident. *How can I override a pilot's maneuver without the pilot noticing and correcting the override?* The answer is having the ability for the software to override pilot maneuvers and, at the same time, report back visuals that the maneuver was taking place as the pilot required. The plane had to react to the erroneous data being sent to it. The software would have to dismiss any actions that the pilot would take as he saw the plane taking on a life of its own.

I need to enlist expertise that would know how this plane's software could cause the pilot controls to freeze and send the tail rudder and flaps to a position in such a manner that the plane would respond and sharply dive to the ground. Who was the programmer for this software and could he alter the software to perform as The Mailman visualized?

Mattie was possessed to find a solution to get this delivery moved forward and done. If anyone knew how to come up with the information that could enable his plan, it was his brother. His brother was a man who kept secrets sacred. There wasn't a safecracker in the world who could unlock his voice to spill the secrets he held in his cerebral vault. As for Tommie, he was to be protected at all cost. *Protecting me from getting caught was to protect him. But how do I get the information without making Tommie an accessory?* The answer presented itself in the form of the flu. When Mattie called Tommie one night just to chat, he saw his opening to the solution.

"Listen Mattie, I can't talk on the phone tonight. I got something that has me vomiting and I ache all over. Sienna has been the dutiful nurse, but I told her to sleep in the other bedroom and just check on me once in a while. I called Barbara, my assistant, and left a voice mail that I was under the weather and would be out of the office for a while. Looks like my office will be my bedroom with a computer for a couple of days. Sorry we can't talk a while. Call me tomorrow. Ok?'

"Sounds like the flu. It has been going around down here in Peoria as well. Get well. I will call tomorrow. Tell Sienna hello for me."

The next day Mattie was in Chicago tracing the very steps his brother took every morning to his Quantum Consulting office. He walked into the building, was ushered to a private elevator without any words exchanged. No badges for this CEO. He exited the elevator. To his good fortune, no one was around. He looked for the nearest enclosed cubicle, picked up the phone and dialed a number.

"Barbara, it's me. Sorry for calling back. I need for you to please have the person who is the lead programmer who supports the Air Force's software technologies call this number. I got a call from the Pentagon regarding some issues. No need to get back to me, just have him call this number."

When Tommie, now Mattie, asked his secretary to find the lead programmer who supported software technologies utilized by the Air Force, there was no reason for her not to comply. "Thomas, I will get the name and have him call. Please get some sleep. It is the only thing doctors are saying is the remedy for this strain of flu."

The young programmer called the number he was given and was asked to report to a conference room on the 23rd floor. The slide on the conference room had been moved from "open" to "occupied". He knocked, poked his head in only to find one man seated at the conference table. "I spoke to someone on the phone who told me someone needed some information on the technologies we supply for the Air Force. Sorry Mr. Anthony, I thought this was the conference room where they said I was to report."

"No, you came to the right room. You must be Jim Agner. Come in. Please sit down and call me Thomas. Jim, because of the work you are doing with the Air Force for Quantum Consulting, I am about to confide in you about a secret project we have been asked to undertake by the Central Intelligence Agency. Yes, Jim, I did say CIA. I can feel your fears when I said the word CIA. You can rest at ease. Apparently, the government sold some planes to a foreign government that is no longer aligned with US policies. The CIA is asking if Quantum Consulting could modify some software that is utilized in these planes. The airplanes in question are CT-43s. I understand you support the software for these planes. Correct?"

The awestruck young man was totally clueless the gentleman asking for modifications to be completed as part of a secret project was not Tommie Anthony, CEO of Quantum Consulting, but the Mailman in his natural disguise.

"Yes sir, Mr. Anthony. I am an expert on our software. I pride myself in being knowledgeable of every line of code in our products for the Air Force."

Jim's mind was further clouded when he heard, "Jim, there are some stipulations to this assignment to which you must agree. If you cannot, then we must ask someone else to perform the requested modifications."

Before Mattie could utter one more syllable, Jim Agner almost yelled, "Mr. Anthony, I will do whatever it takes to demonstrate to you that I am good at what I do and can be trusted to meet all the requirements asked of me. Sir, please allow me to do my job."

Mattie could hardly suppress laughter. "Jim, I knew you were the right person for the job. Your enthusiasm and ability will not go unnoticed. Enclosed in the sealed folder before you are a number of scenarios the CIA wishes for you to program into the software. All I was told was the scenarios were clearly documented. When a specific air maneuver would occur, the software would respond accordingly. Upon transmission of the finished code, you will send the code to an electronic address enclosed in this sealed package. At that time you may cash the cashier's check for $100,000 as a bonus for this work. The code will be sent to the CIA in the Pentagon. Once there is confirmation the code has been received, your work is done. I do not have to tell you of the confidentiality of this project. No one, either in this company, your family or any friends must know of this project. Can you agree to those terms?" The Mailman knew there was another new element to the software included in the scenarios he did not mention, the ability to trigger the software changes when a specific remote signal was transmitted and received. The young man would find this as an opportunity and something he knew about that no one else did.

Jim had a hard time focusing on the conversation after hearing he would receive a six figure bonus for his work. "Yes sir, I understand all the conditions surrounding this project. I know this plane inside and out. I also have supported this software for four years, so I know each line of code by heart. I look forward to playing with all the software decision tables and algorithms. You did not say how soon the software was to be sent." The programmer never asked why the large bonus amount came in the form of a cashiers check versus a payroll check.

"Mr. Agner, I know the talent here. We do whatever it takes to complete our assignments through our dedication and commitment to our customers." Mattie had heard that if there was one thing Tommie's employees did, it was to work long hours seven days a week. The Mailman knew he would get the code in time.

Unfortunately for this employee named Jim, two months after meeting with the CEO of Quantum Consulting, the very day he transmitted the code electronically to an unknown destination, the programmer was killed by a drive by shooting outside a local Chicago biker bar. The shooting was investigated to no avail. The $100,000 cashier's was never cashed.

"Federal Express, may I help you?" Bill Drogemiller asked as he stared out the window of his hotel room.

"Yes you may. Could you check on a package that my daughter sent to me by air? I was to have the package delivered today. I really need to have the package today." The order for a delivery was finalized.

"Sir, I will personally check on your order to ensure we will make your delivery today. Thank you for calling." Bill was dressed in an Air Force Specialists fourth class uniform with the name tag Josh Zackman pinned above a few medals. He picked up a laptop computer bag, and headed toward O'Hare Airport to catch a transatlantic flight to Germany. There he would be met and begin to carry out a plan he knew wasn't to fail. He was to report to the Ramstein Air Base in Germany and transmit altered flight control software to a waiting CT-43 aircraft. Airman Josh Zackman left his empty hotel room never to return.

"Hello, do you have transportation for two to Ramstein Air Base in Germany? The two individuals that require right of entry into the base are Airman Josh Zackman and Airman Eric Geunther."

"Not a problem. Arrangements have been completed. We have received your arrival dates and times. We are quite familiar with the base." Urs Frey did not know what the Mailman wanted done. The only thing he knew was he was to ensure access in and out of Ramstein Air Base for a team member and himself. He was to assume the identity of Airman Eric Geunther. Urs had greased a few palms with large sums of money to look the other way and had actually moved arms from this particular airfield. He saw no problem this time. Documents had been prepared and bribes made. All was ready for their mission.

Chapter 5

On a bright, crisp day in April, 1996, an Air Force CT-43 which was a modified Boeing 737, prepared to take off. The plane was operated by the 86th Airlift Wing based at Ramstein Air Base in Germany. Unlike civilian 737s, the military CT-43 version was equipped with neither a flight data recorder nor a cockpit voice recorder. The exterior differences between the military and commercial aircrafts were that the military version had just nine windows each side of the fuselage and two less doors. The military aircraft had numerous small blade-type antennas, five overhead sextant ports and a wire antenna for HF radio. They were also fitted with an 800 gallon auxiliary aft tank as standard.

Entombed in this particular CT-43, precious cargo had been loaded. The cargo was a delegation of Commerce Department employees and some top American government officials and business leaders. The objective of the delegation was to travel to the Balkans to demonstrate US commitment to helping with economic restoration halted by the recent civil war in Bosnia-Herzegovina. The delegation included Commerce Secretary Ron Brown and 34 other people. One of the invited business dignitaries was none other than the CEO of Construction Tractor, Robert Camden. The flight plan had two European country "stop overs" before terminating in Croatia.

Mattie had found out that the delegation was first going to visit troops at the American headquarters in Tuzla, Bosnia. The delegation was then to travel to Dubrovnik, Croatia, to meet with U.S. and Croatian officials.

In a weekly staff meeting with the Vice President of Europe Marketing, Mattie offered a suggestion, "I understand the Chairman is going on a promotional visit to Europe which will terminate in Croatia. We should take advantage of the leader of Construction Tractor being in a region that needs to rebuild. Rebuild with Construction Tractor equipment of course. I believe we could get some free press that is worth huge advertising dollars. We should make arrangements to travel to meet the CEO with the regional dealer principal and use this event to show Construction Tractor's ability to assist reconstruction. We could leak plans for Construction Tractor through the local dealer to send generators and construction equipment into their region to help with reconstruction. We should not miss this opportunity to show Construction Tractor values and compassion. This move would generate future sales in Europe and, with the American contingency, US sales as well. As for visibility, we could even arrange with the local dealer for some Construction Tractor dozers, graders, and excavators to be performing some road tasks by the airport."

The idea was presented to Construction Tractor's CEO who quickly supported the idea a month prior to his departure. Mattie was provided all the confidential information regarding travel arrangements, flight and meeting itineraries. Mattie would meet the Chairman at his final destination. It was Mattie's responsibility to put personnel on the ground to ensure all accommodations would be in order upon his arrival at his hotel. Mattie, along with the local dealer, were to personally work with the local airport authorities so all paper work was properly completed for return transportation to the United States via Construction Tractor's corporate jet from the Croatian airport.

When Mattie and other ground personnel first heard reports the CT-43 airplane had reached Croatia airspace, Mattie immediately went outside the main terminal and began searching the distant sky. Mattie suddenly felt his heart beat race so strongly that the veins in his neck hurt. His senses seem to heighten at the prospect of events about to unfold. He almost laughed out loud at the thought he could possibly hyperventilate and pass out. This day the sky hung low like a bed canopy. The gray clouds looked like hundreds of pillows lying on a bed except they were moving like waves on a sea. A major storm was about to crest, but it wasn't going to be from the weather. Mattie was ready to strike on what could be his final delivery. The instant was approaching that was a test of his very being. Would he be able to get away with this one? Could they possibly implicate his brother? What would come out as the cause for the crash?

As the plane approached the Cilipi Airport, the pilot was attempting a normal instrument approach like he had done many times in this aircraft. "Dave, what the hell is going on with the instruments? The dials for altitude and speed seem to have quit working. Wait there they go. That was weird. Cilipi Tower, this is US 995. Are we cleared for Runway 12, over?"

"You are clear to land US995."

The flight continued its non-precision type of instrument approach. This approach did not incorporate vertical guidance. Suddenly, the plane that was to land on Runway 12 seemed to stray off course. The plane appeared to take evasive action, but too late, and crashed into a mountainside near the airport. Everyone aboard was killed instantly except an Air Force flight attendant, who later died while being transported to a hospital.

Oh my God! This delivery was surreal. I bet I held my breath for 10 minutes watching the plane fly overhead and circle into the mountain. I can hardly breathe. Breathe deep, Mattie. Put on your shocked disbelief mask and run to the nearest official and ask for someone to take you to the crash site so you could assist in rescue and survivor searches.

Mattie already knew what the response would be. He was told to wait and then was led to an area with others waiting for the plane. Never had Mattie felt so invigorated. As he was being led to the waiting area, he grabbed an airport security staff and asked where the nearest phone was located. He needed to contact Construction Tractor to inform them of the crash and report that the condition of the Chairman was still unknown.

"Sir, we have set up telephones in our VIP Lounge. You can call there."

"Hello, Nancy? This is Mathew Anthony. I have some terrible news. Sorry to call you at home. But since you are the first number to call in case of an emergency, I had to get you out of bed. This won't wait. You need to contact all the officers on the phone immediately and tell them that the plane carrying the Chairman just crashed here at the airport. It just happened. We do not know if there were any survivors. Nancy, I . . ." Mattie was playing his supporting actor role to perfection when Nancy interrupted.

"Mathew, Mathew, get ahold of yourself. Stop and listen for a minute. I have been trying to contact you to tell you that, on the last stop, Robert took ill and had to be taken off the plane and to a doctor. He was complaining of chest pains. So listen Mathew, Robert was not on the plane." Silence on both ends of the phone. "Mathew, are you there? Did you hear what I said? Robert was not on the plane."

Mattie paused. He actually felt like he was going to be sick. *Create the proper response. Establishing an illusion of feelings was a trait you are good at. This reality hurts because it was not an illusion but the truth.*

The ever so professional corporate chameleon responded as a priest giving absolution, "Nancy, I heard you. What great news, but I am absolutely spent from watching the plane crash thinking that Robert was on board. How can one feel so distraught, then elated, then saddened for others less fortunate? Nancy, I will sort this out and call you tomorrow. I assume I should make arrangements for the corporate jet to fly me to assist Robert and get him back to the States? I recommend Robert's personal physician catch the first flight out to Europe. Our corporate physician needs to personally examine Robert to diagnose his illness and to determine his overall condition for traveling back to the States." Mattie was spent. This delivery had taken on a whole different perspective.

Chapter 6

The official Air Force accident investigation board report would note several reasons that led to the CT-43 to crash. Chief among the findings was a *failure of command, aircrew error and an improperly designed instrument approach procedure.* Notably the inclement weather was not deemed a substantial contributing factor in the crash. The report would state that these types of approaches were essentially obsolete in the U.S. but used widely in other parts of the world. Because of their infrequent use in the U.S., many American pilots are not fully proficient in performing the manual procedures. The investigation board determined that the approach used was not approved for Department of Defense aircraft, and should not have been used by the aircraft crew. The board determined that this particular approach required two operating guidance instruments onboard the aircraft, but this aircraft only had one. One was required to track the outbound course of 119° from the Kolocep NDB (KLP). Another was required to observe when the aircraft had flown beyond the Cavtat NDB (CV) which marked the missed approach point. Further, the board noted that the approach was rushed, with the aircraft flying at 150 km/h above the proper final approach speed and had not received the proper landing clearance.

The crash site, on a 2,300 ft hill, was 1.6 miles northeast of where the aircraft should have been on the inbound course. The published approach brought the inbound aircraft down a valley, and had a minimum descent height of 2,150 feet at the missed approach point where the plane was to have climbed and turned to the right if the runway was not in view, which is below the elevation of the hills to the north. The runway was at 510 feet MSL. There were no emergency calls from the pilots, and they did not initiate a missed approach, even though they were beyond the missed approach point. The instrument approach flown by the CT-43 aircrew should not have been flown, the board concluded. Investigators said wing leaders failed to comply with directives requiring prior review of instrument approach procedures not approved by Department of Defense.

Mattie knew exactly why many of these points were missed. Just one day prior to the entourage departing, an Airman specialist, who looked very similar to Bill Drogemiller, entered their CT-43 cockpit to perform various flight checks. He uploaded new software, software that would send conflicting data to the pilot when they reached a particular altitude, location coordinates, height and speed. Standing on a mountain pass five miles away from the airport but in line with the flight landing path was another airman, Urs Frey, with electronic gear that acted as a remote trigger which awakened the Quantum Consulting sleeper code once it received the remote transmission.

Back in Peoria, Mattie read the latest Wall Street Journal article regarding the crash.

> *WASHINGTON, June 13, 1996—A combination of mistakes caused the April 3 CT-43 jet crash in Croatia that killed Commerce Secretary Ron Brown and 34 others, according to an Air Force investigation board. Calling the board "detailed and thorough," Defense Secretary William J. Perry said its report shows no single cause of the crash, but that several mistakes occurred simultaneously. The board findings, announced June 7, blamed the crash on a failure of command, aircrew error and an improperly designed instrument approach procedure.*

> President of the United States William Clinton said the Air Force was thorough, prompt and brutally honest in its investigation. "The American people should feel reassured that the top leadership of the Air Force got to the bottom of this, did it in a hurry and was completely honest in its straightforward report on this accident," Clinton said.

Chairman Robert Camden had survived his dance with the devil twice. He survived a slight heart attack and a terminal plane crash. For Mattie, he quickly dismissed the collateral damage of the lives lost in the crash. His sole focus was to ensure any and all points of light to his involvement were extinguished. There were to be no loose ends. JR was assigned the delivery of the programmer. His drive by shooting went into the unsolved files as being in the wrong place at the wrong time. Urs was assigned the delivery of the Airman whose identity Drogemiller assumed. The Airman was a casualty of a bar room fight in Germany with a bunch of local skin heads. While no one in the bar remembered the Airman in the fight, they did note he was drinking with someone in a booth prior to the fight. How he ended up on the floor with a broken sternum was a mystery. Whoever hit him had mustered lethal power. The only debate in Mattie's mind was should he personally take care of Camden at a later time. That decision could wait.

Chapter 7

Scott Johnson sat in his office going over the material compiled on his desk regarding the plane crash that took the life of Commerce Secretary Ron Brown. The CIA was getting pressure from President Clinton. Regardless of what he said to the press, he wanted assurance from the CIA that the crash was not an act of retaliation by any anti-America groups. In the material, Scott read that, prior to public release of their report, the 17th Air Force commander had relieved the three top 86th Airlift Wing officers due to the investigation.

Aircrew errors contributed to the crash, investigators reported. During mission planning the crew failed to note the Dubrovnik approach required two automatic direction finders. The CT-43 had only one. An error in planning the route added fifteen minutes to the planned flight time and may have caused the crew to rush the approach. This did not make sense. This crew had flown this aircraft for years.

According to the report, the pilots did not properly configure the aircraft for landing before starting the final approach. They came in eighty knots above final approach speed, without clearance from the tower. The rushed approach, late configuration and a radio call from a pilot on the ground distracted the crew from adequately monitoring the final approach, which proved to be nine degrees left of the correct course. "What pilot? There is no name, no detail of this conversation." Scott's gut began to hurt. "At what point could they see the runway? How could they have been so far off of the approach point? If they were unable to see the runway, why didn't they just pull up and execute a missed approach versus an evasive turn? If they had done so and not turned away, the plane would not have hit the mountain, which was more than a mile past the missed approach point. Weather was not found to be a substantial contributing factor in the crash, yet the weather conditions required the crew to do an instrument approach. This does not follow any flying manual that I have ever heard of."

Scott picked up another folder. Inside the folder were names of every foreigner who entered all the countries in which the plane stopped or was to stop within thirty days prior to the crash. All ground personnel who had access to the plane were also on the list. Scott was reviewing armed forces personnel who had left the armed forces within thirty days after the crash. Finally, he was reviewing intelligence reports to assess if any noticeable circumstances happened in a sixty day window around the crash. One name surfaced. An airman specialist had committed suicide at the home base where the flight originated. He was apart of the security surveillance team who patrolled the grounds around the base. The other name that jumped out was one Mathew S. Anthony.

Holy Christ almighty. I knew the Chairman of Construction Tractor had an angel watching over him which saved his life, but I was not aware the devil was in Dubrovnik, Croatia. Is it just a coincidence Mr. Anthony was in Croatia to conduct some business with his boss?

Scott debated with himself on whether he should contact Mathew and somewhere in the conversation see if he could uncover exactly who was in Croatia. Mathew or the Mailman? He would request the meeting under the pretense his name had come up on a list being looked at by the CIA. That should get his attention for him to attend. The telephone rang. "Johnson."

"This is Art Watson. You asked that we run through our data bases to see if anyone in our agency had been doing any inquiries on CT-43s? The only activity we retrieved were inquiries you made from your terminal."

"Thanks. I will take it from here."

Shit, it was Mattie. How the hell did he get in here and have access to my terminal? How did he bypass my security? This is too much of a coincidence. Christ, did Mattie authorize a private delivery on the Commerce Secretary of the United States? Is he free lancing and for whom?"

Scott Johnson felt like he was in the grasp of a 400 pound Sumo Wrestler, squeezing the air out of him. He had compiled more money than he could spend in a life time. He wasn't about to let Mattie run covert operations that could jeopardize his position or expose his secret bank accounts.

Mattie you bastard!. You couldn't stick to the script, you had to write your own book. Well, you went too far. Lawbreaking to you has always been in the eyes of the beholder. In your perfect world, you have never been accused of one lawbreaking act, thus you never had to think about your god like actions to right the wrongs of mankind. You went too far on this one. You wrote your own death warrant.

Scott knew he could not take a dismissal approach. How many times have well intentioned "do gooders" tried to take in a wild animal to domesticate it only to have the wild animal turn on them? Scott knew Mattie was a wild killer who showed well rehearsed sense of domestication to the general public. He would never change his stripes. He was a killing machine with the intellect, the cunning, and the capabilities to be considered the ultimate warrior. His abilities to deliver on his hunts were unquestionably ranked among the elite assassins. But this wolf now has killed a rancher's prized bull. He has put me in a dangerous position where I could be thrown to the wolves without any defense or protection.

I have to cut the cord, but how? Scott knew who he was dealing with and what he was capable of doing. The only way to get close to Mattie was for him to call a meeting, under the pretense of setting up another delivery. He knew he needed to lure Mattie to a location where he himself could cut the proverbial cord via termination.

It is time for me to retire. Why not use this to my advantage? I can use this crash for one last payday. Misinformation travels faster than the common cold, a windswept forest fire, or a political scandal. Once I let it leak out that the plane may have been sabotaged, it will be only a matter of time before they come to me to investigate and, if true, terminate those responsible. That looks like a five million dollar retirement package to me.

Chapter 8

Mattie received a call from Scott. "It's been awhile. What can I do for you?"

"We have had some interesting developments. Are there any opportunities for you to be in the Middle East? Things seem to be getting hotter there than their damn desert. I will be in your area. Meet me at the old Whirlpool factory in Canton." The conversation was terminated.

The location seemed odd, an old deserted factory near Canton, Illinois. Feeling that something was not quite right, Mattie checked his computer to see if any alerts had popped up. Using the vast network of information he had through his brother's network, Mattie had set up alerts. Should anyone conduct an inquiry or information transaction which matched his alert triggers, he would receive a notification of the transaction. His triggers were embedded in electronic technologies around the world. He had established triggers based on people names, bank transaction codes, public communications, email addresses, social security codes, medical billings, etc. On this day, he noticed significant movement of banking transactions by none other than Scott Johnson. If Scott only knew how much Mattie really knew about him. Years ago he had uncovered the names of the individuals who had selected the deliveries. Not only had the Mailman discovered the identities and their roles in the government, he was able to track the delivered monies that were wired around the world. No surprise, Scott Johnson was skimming on every delivery. Funny, Scott did not have anything going which would indicate he was working on something in the Middle East. Scott was up to something. Mattie wanted to know what.

For two weeks, Mattie monitored Scott Johnson's every movement and communication. As the Mailman, Mattie had followed him utilizing various identities. Scott seemed to be establishing false pretense for the day before, the day of and the day after their proposed upcoming meeting. It wasn't until the second week while Mattie was monitoring Scott's office phone when the clouds of uncertainty parted. "Scott, this is Dave Haney down at the Pentagon. We have been monitoring per your request to determine if the White House or CIA had any additional information come forward since the communications by President Clinton. The matter is closed as far as we can determine. Are you looking for anything specific that we could follow?

"No Dave, I just keep a file on world events that I follow for a while. Then, if nothing surfaces, I put the subject to bed. You know how it is, keep one step ahead of the politicians or else your funding could disappear. Thanks. Owe you one." The phone went dead.

Well, well, why would you still be tracking the Croatia crash, Mr. Johnson? Suddenly, you want a meeting with me on a fictional delivery? Could it be you put me at the crash scene and wondered it I had made a delivery? If I was implicated, are you worrying repercussions could get back to you? If the answer is yes, being the self preservationist that you are, you would have to distance yourself from me. Why the location for the meeting? Could it be our last? My discoveries today have given impetus to further research.

The Mailman contacted a local realtor to view the factory site. He requested the viewing be in the strictest of confidence, because should the public get wind of a major company possibly coming to their town, costs would escalate which could nix the deal. The realtor stated she had other clients who had requested the same conditions, so she had

The Corporate Chameleon

no problem with his. *Other clients, Lady, are you trying to con the conman?* Mattie carefully logged every aspect of the building in his mind. "Are the blast furnaces still operational?" Mattie probed.

"Why yes. As a matter of fact, I mentioned other clients. In two weeks, we are having another company come in for a viewing and they specifically want to see the furnaces fired up to assess their condition. I really do not know the process for turning them on. It is funny how things go. This factory has set dormant for two years with no activity and suddenly we have multiple inquiries. This must be a sign the economy is beginning to rebound. You may want to move before the other group comes in. You could put a deposit on the property with pending conditions."

"I have other sites we are looking into. Until we have visited all the sites, we are not ready to move on this one. But, I really would be interested to know how the furnace assessment turns out. Would it be a conflict of interest for you to tell me how the furnaces performed? I wouldn't think so. You say in the next two weeks there will be a test? I will give you a call after the trial and then we will be in a better position to let you know if we are still interested in this site. Thank you for your time."

So Scott, you must be the other client. After we meet here, someone wants to fire up the furnaces? Wonder what's cooking? I think you and I should meet sooner than planned."

Chapter 9

Mattie was as numb as his soul. Numb to the bone, frozen from birth with no feelings to thaw his motives. He knew there was no guarantee. How many times does everything go as planned? There were always possibilities of something going wrong. His mind was going over his plan. He did not have to wait for any numbness to subside like the cold when you swallowed a warm drink. The matter was at hand. His feeling of righteousness ensured his body was tuned to compete like a sprinter at the starting line anticipating the sound of the starter's gun.

Scott was sitting at a table having dinner with who knows who. He did not have any agency people shadowing him so his dinner companion must be a close confidant. Scott paid little attention to the tall stout man who was monitoring his every move. The Mailman could pass for some engineer. He appeared on the pale side, had bad posture, wore crepe sole shoes and was sprouting a beard so sparse that he appeared unwashed. This particular customer was dressed in a plaid shirt and a broad striped shirt. An unmade bed had more structure than this guy. This man was unassuming, but his sharp eyes were scanning the restaurant through wired rimmed glasses like some cyborg. He was finishing his after dinner drink when he saw his stalked prey shake hands with his dinner companion and prepare to leave. He placed a $100 bill on the table and walked by Scott's table. "See you at the airport tomorrow. Stay safe." *So this guy is to travel with you to Peoria. I bet he was to be at the old factory hours before our meeting.*

Mattie had followed Scott for a week and knew his routine. After any late night dinner, he always went for a two to three mile run through the quaint, well lit park a mile from his million dollar townhouse. Mattie went to an isolated spot in the park where he could sit on a park bench and wait for Scott. The sun had set. In one section of the park, trees had overgrown and had suffocated the light from two of its sources. Here, the only light that hit the floor of the park came from the beams of a three quarter moon and a street lamp by the park bench. It seemed the few stars that were out had faded. Mattie shed his disguise like a snake sheds its skin and placed it in a backpack he had brought. Mattie now resembled a jogger out for his nightly exercise. It was time for him to make his move. Mattie's entire body transformed instantly. Even though he was a big man, he now moved with a small shadow. It was like he was not there. Like a bear waking from his hibernation, Mattie's muscles were ready to move and make a kill to appease his hunger. Scott would not go easy, but he had been inactive too long. He would hesitate. The taste of blood was the only fix to curb his craving, his longing appetite. Death has a particular pungent odor which had a strong effect on the mind. Mattie could smell it on his prey. His eyes narrowed as he saw his prey running his way. Mattie rose from his park bench and stood in the runner's path.

"What the hell are you doing here?" Scott Johnson drew a pistol from behind his back.

"Put that gun away. You want to draw attention to us?" Scott momentarily glanced around, then began to assess his vulnerability. For an instance, Scott had slightly lowered his gun hand along his side. That was all Mattie needed. "You should know better than to point a gun at me!" Like a striking cobra, Mattie moved swiftly within striking distance of his soon to be delivery. Scott, having trained Mattie in the art of hand to hand combat, knew he was in trouble. There was a good chance that, at this close range, Mattie could strike and break his wrist before he got off a shot. He was right. Before Scott could level his gun and fire, Mattie hit Scott's right wrist with a blow that could break a two by four. The gun dropped to the asphalt path Scott would no longer follow. It was obvious from the constipated look on Scott's face he did not know what emotion he should be having: pain, anger, or just gut fear. It was only a split second, not long enough for an answer. Scott knew he was in a fight for his life. He immediately brought up his left arm in preparation to ward off a second blow. But it was too deliberate of a response to deter the destruction the tsunami before him was to bring. Another swift extension of Mattie's arm to Scott's throat and the confrontation was over. Scott wanted to let out a scream, only nothing could be emitted. His windpipe was crushed. Like a tall pine in the woods that had just felt the saw of the logger, Scott Johnson seemed to momentarily sway in the wind, then fell with a thud to the pavement. As he lay on the ground, Mattie stepped on his neck like a wounded rabbit and pressed down hard. "You piece of shit. You are as greedy and corrupt as the rest of the assholes in Washington." Scott Johnson lost consciousness and died.

Mattie became almost giddy from the excitement of the triumph of this delivery. What didn't matter before now did. Where some wished for riches and fame, Mattie had only wanted to reach excellence and become an influence to right wrongs. All paths to the Mailman identity were not closed. He looked down at his creator. "Scott, I expected more from you. How could you have been such an easy delivery? I know you knew I would not go easy. Scott, you forgot the law of the jungle. You cannot ever tame wild animals held in captivity. Skill will always overcome treachery. Brilliance comes with age and experience. You aged and you let your experience lag. You forgot one of your life lessons you once told me: after you put a bomb in a hole, one does not, you repeated, does not tamp the ground too much. Scott, you got powerful, you got greedy, and you forgot to keep pace with the game.

When you wallow with pigs, expect to get dirty. Here is my life lesson. In farm country we learned life is much simpler when you plow around the stump. Do not corner something that you know is meaner than you. For trying to remove this stump, your heart stopped beating. Scott, your destiny has been fulfilled. We will all experience destiny by its first name, death. No fear."

Chapter 10

I AM TRULY THE *master of my own destiny now. I do not know what lies ahead, but I do know reality asks too much of me. It is hard for me to get my mind around the "good life" when I find it too predictable. I was born to seek the thrill of being a white knight in a dark world. Nothing stays buried forever. When do I end it all and take responsibility for who I am before those I care about get hurt? How long will I ride out my true love? The ride has been a confusing rush of twisted justice, sensations, and gratification. What a thrill at having been a part of the melee. One thing I can say about my secret world and accomplishments, I will miss the circus. but I will never miss the clowns.*

I don't know if my journey has been a recurrent dream or nightmare. Was this a disfigurement of my soul or an inherent release of all my mental eccentricities which were locked up that came back with determination that I had to act upon. It was as if Pandora's Box was right in front of me challenging my courage to let my inner self loose. I knew my inner self was a most horrifying demon.

All is quiet tonight. Everyone has heard of the quiet before the storm. But few have experienced the quiet and in a situation where they knew the storm was surely coming to them. One who witnesses the storm rarely wants to explain their personal demons that surface. I have always loved the darkness. It was when I did my best work, received my source of pleasure. When I return to the light, I often feel that I have strayed too far from my safe harbor. I become more impatient and cannot wait for the time to get back to the darkness, to my playground, to further explore it, to further know it, to further use it. From the darkness, I seek out wisdom. Through my eyes, this wisdom will reach my soul. When one can see through the darkness, he will see the truth. When he knows the truth, he can obtain knowledge. Once he has the knowledge, he can gain experience. I have reached the pinnacle of having the knowledge and experience. As a result, I can claim this wisdom as my ally and part of my very soul. I have been accused of selective denial, but quite frankly, I find this a compliment. It is a wonderful buffer which has helped me survive.

Sue, Mattie's assistant, jumped from her seat and bolted around her desk and entered Mattie's wood paneled office. "Mathew are you awake? I hate to barge in on you during your quiet time, but in an hour an emergency mandatory meeting has been called for the Admin Council in the 7th floor conference room."

Mattie was back in the world of reality. "Who called this meeting?"

"I got the call from none other than the CEO of Construction Tractor, Mr. Robert Camden. This must be really important for him to call direct to ensure his Vice Presidents and Group Presidents were available for this mandatory meeting. I called around. Anyone who cannot make it to this meeting is to call in to the meeting through our corporate secure teleconference number. Complete confidentiality of conversations are taking place like I have never witnessed. Something big is about to take place."

Normally, Mattie felt like an oak tree rooted in the earth when it came to company business. He had more intel, savvy, and sponsorship through the enterprise than anyone in the corporation. There was not even the remotest rumor which could escape his web or ear. This time it was different. For Mattie to not know the purpose of this meeting was highly unusual, especially coming from the office of Robert Camden. *What's the deal Robert? Over the years, my homage, loyalty, and filtered information had you believing that I was the product of a seedling you had planted and personally mentored into executive material. So how did was purpose of this meeting kept secret?*

Chapter 11

Mattie felt he was having an old traditional dream where he was coming into a crowded room naked. Only this time he was exposed to the probing eyes of his enemies. All the other Vice Presidents and Presidents were as perplexed as he was, but always poised to best each other. These suits were lying in wait like some famished lion ready to devour their prey. Waiting like death, they were ready to pounce should their rival make a career mistake. Ever since he came into the room, Mattie had a sense of a plot. He couldn't shake the feeling as he entered the conference room and took his seat. He felt as if he had just sat down to be judged by a jury who had already found him guilty. Mattie's mind began to churn scenarios for counter attacks. Mattie was used to pressure, to political games, to egos that needed the next promotion regardless of who would be stepped on or bypassed. Mattie was never one to panic. How many times had he felt the grains of sand being washed away under his feet only to emerge victorious? His mind began to assess strategies to neutralize someone or something from being effective or harmful. Egos and pride were choking the air out of the room. Mattie had more background, more information on these pawns who wished to be king than they could ever imagine. He may not have an inkling on the moves that were about to take place, but he sure knew the strategy of chess and, for every move, there is a counter. Whatever was about to happen, Mattie was ready to think logically, carefully and deeply.

Breathe deeply, no fear. Let the games begin. Is my ingenuity to solve problems, be creative, or invent new scenarios about to be tested?

Robert Camden came into the room and took his customary seat at the head of the 7th floor executive conference room table. The room fell silent in anticipation of some emancipation proclamation. "Gentlemen, I have called this meeting to inform you that I have informed our Construction Tractor Board of Directors of my decision to retire by year end."

Brushing with death twice must have caused Robert to evaluate his life and where he wanted it to go. One month after the incidents, he announces his retirement. What irony. An unexpected change to the Construction Tractor corporate power base is about to occur without the need for the demise of one of the key players. The CEO's first move of the game was checkmate. Well played.

Everyone in the room looked like they either were having a gas attack and trying to pucker their asses or were a scavenger about to approach newfound lifeless remains. The room was buzzing as if someone had hit a bee's nest and stirred the queen. However, in this room, the king ruled. "Gentlemen, if you please. Hold the side conversations. We need to disclose my retirement decision in due time. Per Wall Street protocol, anything which alters the make up of a company, like my retirement and subsequent change of leadership of Construction Tractor, must be made known to the public. This will not be as earth shaking as our historical strike with labor or when the company disclosed that it would lay-off thousands of workers this past year." This meeting has two objectives.

"One, to ensure that nothing will be until we have a formal press conference three hours from now. Leaks prior to this news conference will cause automatic termination upon discovery. Two, there is a succession list the Board has compiled. They plan to interview candidates for my replacement from inside and outside of the company. As you all know, Construction Tractor has always hired from within. But this time the Board wants to assess all options. I personally have voiced my displeasure and have gone on record that our culture in this company has been the very key to our success. This culture has been cultivated over years of history with officers working their way up in the ranks. We know how to balance Wall Street with Main Street. Our management has always been hands-on listening to the heart beats of our customers and those of our employees on our production lines.

"Some of you may want to try to influence the Board's decision process. I know you. There are power brokers in this room who believe they are able to control everything. Good luck. This is one process in your life that cannot be influenced. You are either a candidate or not, a selection or not. One thing is now true. Only those with the innovative thought processes, the finesse to handle the press, Wall Street analysts, and our most demanding customers, plus a track record of achievements are going to be frontrunners. I can see the alliances forming as I speak. I will open up this meeting for questions. Then we need to get back to the business of the day." Standing next to the 7th floor board room windows, his silver hair shone bright. As Mattie looked over the attendees in the room, he shook his head from side to side ever so slightly.

My god, Moses has just spoken in his deepest rich voice to his flock. It is going to be interesting to see if any of the sheep will cast off their fleece and show themselves as the hungry wolf they are. Look at his faithful, already drawing the life from the air he is breathing. Son of a Bitch, I'll say this about the old boy, he goes out with style. He knows his place in Construction Tractor history will be one of glowing praise. Global leaders will show due respect for how he reorganized the company. Historians will forever talk about the longest labor strike in history and his steadfast position to not buckle as the three automotive companies did with the UAW labors. Dealers will show their affection with gifts and praise for his commitment to customers and product quality. The loving city fathers of Peoria will bestow glowing quotes in newspaper articles. For the next month, roasts and private dinners will be held at the Peoria Country Club with the powerbrokers of the city. Finally, the key to the city or the naming of a street or a day in his honor will pay homage for the money and services he channeled to every charitable organization throughout Illinois.

The meeting ended like a political convention. There was too much forced laughter, too many hand shakes, and an over abundance of back slapping. Mattie viewed the event's aftermath as one poorly disguised posturing charade. Could Mattie call any of them friends? Are we associates, yes. Are we colleagues, maybe. Are we friends, never. As the meeting participants lingered around to shake hands with the departing conqueror, Mattie kept his distance and left the room.

As Mattie began to head back to his office he heard his name being called. "Mathew, may I have a minute? Walk with me to the elevators." Mattie felt every eye follow Robert Camden and every ear stretched to sensory limits to hear what the chairman was about to say to Mattie. As the two entered the elevator, Robert closed the door manually. "Mathew, I want you to know why I kept this announcement from you. I do not want you to be like the others who will campaign for my position. You are about to witness the clashes of the gladiators in the Roman Construction Tractor Coliseum. Instead of swords, they will use tried and true strategies and politically aligned words. You have never struck me as one who sought the CEO position, yet you have all the attributes to lead this company. I want you to know that you are on the short list for my position. I want you to know this, not to be like the others and campaign, because the selection process is in the hands of the board. They will announce my replacement after the next quarterly Board of Directors meeting. So my advice to you is to keep doing what you have been doing. Establish goodwill with the dealers and customers, acknowledge the importance of manufacturing quality Construction Tractor products, and ensure this company continues to make profit. Good luck." The elevator doors opened, Mattie exited.

Did Robert just tell me that I was not the next CEO? If so, then what role will I now play? Better yet, what role do I want to play? I think I will give Thomas a call and let him in on this announcement. No fear of him leaking the announcement. It will be as much as a surprise to him as it was to me. He will instantly put on his CEO hat and want to talk about the transition of power and contenders for the throne. He will be a terrific sounding board.

Mattie wanted to give the appearance to all the executives at Construction Tractor that he was in a state of Nirvana. He wanted people to see him as someone not concerned about the selection process for the next CEO. As he entered his office, he asked Sue to hold all his calls. Mattie's mind was already pondering a strategy for a plan. Mattie was the master of the backroom. He had a wealth of information that no one else had.

Over the next two months, I could put together a plan to be heard, seen, or referenced everywhere. I can sense that everyone is talking about me. I just cannot hear them or see their lips move. My alter ego always works best in the shadows. I have never wanted the limelight. What the hell am I doing?

"Sue, get my brother on the phone. Tell his assistant it is important. If he is in a meeting, have him return the call at his earliest convenience. Thank you."

Chapter 12

"Mattie, is Mom ok, what's wrong? I have never received a call from you to my assistant where she was told your call was important. Is this an emergency?"

"Tommie, relax. There is no emergency. What I have to tell you is strictly between you and me. In three hours, a press conference is going to be held and Camden will announce his retirement. I just came out of a meeting where he made the announcement to the executive branch. The process to pick his predecessor is well underway. Believe it or not, I was totally caught off guard."

"Mattie, how do you feel about this? You will be an obvious candidate for his position. I think you would be a terrific leader for Construction Tractor."

"That is why I am calling. I believe I will be one of three candidates for consideration. One of the candidates was chosen strictly to honor his years and contributions. He has the respect of the Board and his peers. He has been openly helpful to me. I actually consider him a role model. He is 62 so, if he is selected, he would be Chairman for only 3 years. We have mandatory retirement for executives at 65. The other candidate is Owen Jameson. Owen is one man I actually respect. When it comes to financial or economic scenarios, he excels. He is well liked by his peers, as well as those he has managed. He is a sensible, no-nonsense, practical person who prefers to thoroughly research a situation before taking action. He openly solicits other opinions and alternatives. He values other opinions and lives by the values of our company's code of conduct. His laid back demeanor is deceiving. He is very aggressive in business, yet takes time for his personal life. He is more comfortable developing working relationships than me. You know me. Business takes priority over social occasions. The image people have of him is one of a gentle giant, a man who could lead Construction Tractor through its toughest challenges. He epitomizes an open door policy. He is available to whoever may want to discuss something with him. He is humble, bubbly, positive and approachable. He is unrestricted by the latest fashion trends and feels as comfortable in jeans, on a golf course or in a business suit. He would make a terrific CEO."

"Mattie, what is wrong? You should be riding the wind high in the sky with the fact that you could be the next Construction Tractor CEO. Talk to me, brother."

"Tommie, you are my most trusted friend. I love you. I do not want to let down Mom or you. I know that you are proud as I am of the accomplishments we have made. Only this time, I feel like when I received my letter from Grandfather. My destiny was not to follow you. My path took a different turn. I am not sure what path I am to follow now, but my gut says it is not at Construction Tractor. Tommie, I remember grandfather telling me never compare my life to others. He said I could not imagine the journey they were required to travel. He said take chances and, if I was wrong, time could heal almost anything. So give time, time to work its magic. I just have a feeling this is the wrong time for me, that there is something else I need to do."

A few seconds of silence seemed like eternity. Tommie's voice dropped decibels. Excitement had turned to tranquility. "Mattie, God truly made us one person. I too have been soul searching. I feel I have accomplished everything I can possibly achieve in my present capacity. I have reached the end of my road here at Quantum Consulting. I too am searching for the next quest, the next Holy Grail to re-energize me. If you are serious about wanting something so different than anything you can imagine, I have a proposal. Is it possible for you to get an extended weekend soon? I would like for you and me to go off somewhere remote and have a heart to heart talk. How about it? It would be like the old days, the Anthony boys out to make mischief. I am sure we could borrow our corporate jets to fly to Mexico, the Caribbean, or wherever? What do you say, you in?"

"What do you have up your sleeve? You have me curious. I will have Sue provide some dates. Let's do it. Tommie thanks for being there." Mattie felt better but did not know why.

Construction Tractor's Administration Building is built in the shape of a cross. The building has 7 floors. In one of the four wings of the 7th Floor reside the companies CEO and his six Presidents. The other wings house the corporate lawyers and their support staff, the corporate auditors, and a large auditorium. The Construction Tractor Board of Directors meets on the third Wednesday of the last month in a quarter. It is at this quarterly meetings that Robert Camden's successor would be selected. As was the history of the Board of Directors, the CEO of Construction Tractor was a member of the Construction Tractor Board of Directors and thus had a voice and vote as to his successor.

As was the practice, the retiring CEO would meet with the three finalists and inform them of the Board's decision. The three finalists were always a part of the Construction Tractor executives that normally attended all Board meetings. This particular meeting was held in a very plush country side hotel one hundred kilometers miles outside of London, England.

That night after the Board of Directors meeting, Mattie received a call in his hotel suite. It was Robert Camden. "Mathew, could you please come to my suite?"

"Of course. I will be right there."

"I will not keep you in suspense. Today, it will be announced that Owen Jameson will replace me as CEO. You know Owen and I am sure you feel as I, he will make a fine CEO. You also are aware you both are the same age, so you should understand the position that it puts you in. Unless Owen has some unfortunate incident which would remove him for the position, you would not have another opportunity to compete for the CEO position. If it is of any consolation, the choice was between him and you. The final decision was based on the view that the company in the future would need to focus on the strength of the US dollar, commodity trends, governmental legislations, trade regulations and the impact we see for the global economy. We viewed your strengths in the marketing, dealer relationship as important, but not the priority. We hope you understand and continue to provide Owen the support you have given Construction Tractor and me in the past. Would you like to ask any questions or have any other discussions?"

Maintain you civility. Be your grandfather. After all, you were going to kill this man. I can let it go this time.

"Robert, I want to thank you for your leadership, your support and for being upfront with me. Owen will make a great chairman and CEO. If I were on the Board of Directors and saw the challenges facing the country and this company for the next five years, Owen is the obvious selection to meet these challenges. As for my future position, I will want to talk to Owen to ascertain what role he would see me playing in his new organization. I am sure there will be changes. Once I have all the information regarding my role, I will assess and determine my options. I have loved the opportunities that Construction Tractor presented to me *and the Mailman.* Thank you and I look forward to your retirement party." Mattie rose as did Robert. Robert Camden and Mathew Anthony shook hands. Mathew left the room to ponder his future. Robert would retire not knowing he actually had skirted death not twice but three times. The Mailman had decided not to make a return delivery. He would let the aging process take its toll

Chapter 13

Thomas and Mathew decided to rendezvous in Montego Bay, Jamaica. Mattie had visited the Construction Tractor dealer in Kingston Mine and then told his assistant he was going to spend the weekend in Jamaica. No one gave a second thought that there was an ulterior motive for him being in Jamaica. Tommie had emailed him directions to the villa in which they were to stay. It was called Villa Viviana, 16,000 square feet of luxury overlooking the ocean. The villa was gated with security at every corner. As Mattie drove up, he had to laugh. *Unbelievable, brother You arrange for fun in the sun at Villa de Fort Knox. Who do you think we need isolation from anyway?*

As Mattie approached in his rented Mercedes, the gate to the villa opened. He drove through the gate up to the villa. The fountain, the landscape vegetation, the architecture of the villa was magnificent. As he stopped the car at the front of the villa, Tommie came out with arms wide open. Tommie was attired in a patterned shirt with parrots, shorts and flip flops. Tommie was a Jimmy Buffet look alike, how funny was this. The two embraced and kissed each other on the cheek. "Welcome to the sunny south, my snow bird brother. Nice huh? Come in. I will have one of the attendants of this place get your bags. Lunch is ready on the veranda. Brother, it is time to relax and enjoy the sun."

"OK Tommie, I am here. What are you up to? Why this clandestine meeting? You are cooking up something, I can just feel it. Man, you have it all. You have a beautiful wife who thinks you are the only man in the world. I personally do not see it. You have two exceptionally talented children. Thank God they took after their mother. You are rich beyond your wildest dreams and are CEO of a very influential company. So what in the world would have you running around like some secret agent man?"

"Mattie, I have a side to me that I have hidden to get to where I am today."

"You have a side? This I have to hear."

"Brother, if there is one thing we have in common that I feel we have not lost is our values. Our family came from humble beginnings. We have never lost our love for our country, our family and our faith. Mattie while I didn't serve in Viet Nam, I have witnessed war of a different nature. It is a war I am afraid we are losing and could drive America's way of life to extinction. Time is a consideration."

Words of confession spilled from Tommie's mouth. "Over the years, I have become a master at undermining the current order of things to make way for my own agenda. I did some things of which I am not proud, but I justified the means to get to the end. I know how to align the strengths of those who share my view or who have a thirst for advancement. I have accumulated intelligence on my rivals' weaknesses or insight into their private secrets. To those who are truly rising to the challenges and who have the intelligence and integrity to compete with me, I always followed the golden rule of "keep your friends close, your enemies closer". I have compartmentalized my life with absolute focus on my success, whether it is in the market place or in my market deliveries."

Tommie was now in the zone. "America as a whole is surrendering to greed. I hate to say this. I too had succumbed to one rule, look out for number one. I am here to balance the scales. I must sow a different seed if I am to harvest a different good. I have lost my feeling for the down trodden that must be rekindled. I have to display openly a loyalty to the country which has done so much for my family. I feel a void is present that I have been ordained to make right. I know what I must do, Mattie, with No Fear."

"Mattie, greed has birthed a whole new generation of men without faces or souls. I do not feel sorry for people without faces. I do detest those who steal another's face. You can see their weakness and true identities when they are revealed or discovered in a lie or wrong doing."

Especially, Tommie, when they are about to die.

Tommie continued, "Greed has bred a whole new generation of men without souls. They are not concerned about the impact on their family, their father's name or their children's future, they are only concerned about acquisitions...power, money, people, land, weapons, and so on. I am supposed to view these buffoons as counterparts, peers, team members. To me they will always be classified as adversaries to be manipulated or destroyed. Most want to give you a smile or a hand and want you to bend like a stick of licorice. I may give an appearance of unity, but my goals are as rigid as the highest mountains. In this game, I must use all the normal tools to maneuver them into checkmate. I just love the look of defeat on their faces when their king is forced to tip over. I am good at what I do. It is not too often that I throw out my net without snagging some kind of fish."

Chapter 14

M<small>ATTIE COULD SENSE</small> Tommie was about to reveal his purpose for wanting him here with him. "Mattie, America is in trouble. Depending on the next presidential election, we could be headed to the extreme left. The executive, legislative and judicial branches of our country are constitutional compasses without directional needles. Something has to be done to return our country to the intent of our forefathers. We need change to return as our founding fathers so elegantly stated, Government is for the people."

"In such political or economic crises, often the truth is guarded. Most people do not want to hear the truth because too often it isn't what they want to hear or is unpleasant, uncomfortable and causes too many questions to be asked. Politicians and the power brokers know this. They know untruths can be bent, manipulated, taken out of context to gain time or the upper hand. Look at what has happened to the world financial community. Greed prompted them to create false wealth and the illusion of economic prosperity and long term security. Look what happened when the truth surfaced. Reality hurt, and from Main Street to Wall Street, people want change. They want their voice back."

Mattie was intently studying his brother. He looked at his brother and saw his mirrored reflection. The question capturing his imagination was whether his brother had a hidden persona like his? Tommie was "normal" by mankind's definition. Had Tommie hidden secret tendencies that could not openly be viewed?

"Mattie, if there was one thing we twins share is that we are oblivious to people's religion, race, who they are or where they came from. We judge people on their behaviors, their attitudes, and their ability to share or put others in the limelight. Both of us have worked for, relied on, or had working for them whites, blacks, Latinos, Asians, Jews or Arabs."

"Mattie, those who were aligned were rewarded. Those who weren't could be put in harms way. It was nothing personal, nothing to do with gender, race, religion or nationality, just business."

"Living in Chicago, I have become very astute regarding politics. Chicago politics control all of Illinois. Make no mistake about it, downstate politicians may have won elections that sent them to Washington, but it was not without a backroom caucus to figure out where Chicago politics would play. In the next presidential election, I am convinced a newcomer can win it all. Our reigning president really screwed up. His confidant's fabricated national security intelligence has the United States engaged in costly wars. Weapons of mass destruction, my ass. The global economy is on the verge to take a dive. The financial institutions are running amuck. The market could crash. Hell, whoever becomes president is going to have challenges like never before. Given all these issues, the one thing that troubles me the most is that the American people could be the ones severely impacted. Not immediately, but from the problems that will come later. The next political regime could create Big Brother. We could have such dominant government that our children's, our children's children's way of life could be negatively impacted beyond comprehension. Big government will try to run private businesses, take over health care, structure future education. The country we love could become a welfare state caught up in a death spiral. Mattie, I have asked you here to discuss an Anthony running for the President of the United States."

Excuse me, did I hear you right? Did you say an Anthony running for the President of the United States of America?

"Brother, in this country, we must have balance of power in our government structure. While we want our power to be so strong that no other country could hurt us, it cannot be so strong that it would bring oppression to our people. The power in this state is state government. It has become so corrupt with a few powerful people dominating decisions, that something must be done. Mattie, I don't want to be an alarmist going around like Chicken Little claiming the sky is falling. I want to get involved. I want us together to get involved. Talk to me, brother. Tell me straight."

Amen, Brother Tommie. You sound like the returning prodigal son, baptized in the waters of his one true church called patriotism. We do have a common goal, the salvation, the contentment, the same feelings that we will do whatever it takes to make the world a better place. Only time would determine what chapters will be written and retained in your Bible of the saved or departed.

"For one thing, your tirade was quite an appetizer for lunch." Mattie picked up two beer bottles that were on ice and opened them. He handed one to his brother. "Salute Brother."

Where others become bogged down in the murk, not able to use reason or good judgment and finding it hard to find their way, Mattie was a figure who would always emerge confident in his capabilities and lead. Before he spoke, he never underestimated the risks before saying or doing. When in a stressful, no solutions position, he would take a deep breath. It calmed the mind. The most critical time for any operation is when the operation elements are presented and a decision is to be made.

"Thomas Anthony, you know how I have a fervent aversion to politicians. Because I have such a strong feeling of not liking politicians, the only Anthony who should be in consideration for running for President of the United States is you. Tommie, we both know that you are the velvet glove. And, yes, you are going to need an iron fist to see this thing through. There are going to be issues arise where you will need others to handle them. There is an Illinois senator's and a governor's race coming up that are ripe for someone with balls enough to take on Illinois issues. How about I run for governor or state senator? You help me with the Chicago politics and get me elected and in two years when you get elected, I could be your attorney general if you so choose. Hell we could be the re-incarnation of the Kennedy brothers. I *or the Mailman* could play the behind the scenes role and only rankle those who we feel are not in line with our country causes. We need to weld solid alliances and avoid issues that would enhance our competition's position. We form a team from lists supplied by our most trusted and respected family and friends. We need heartfelt oaths of commitment and loyalty from them which would provide supporting evidence of their honesty and integrity. Even more important is the need to uncover our competition's most telltale positions, weaknesses, and strengths. Should we start this journey, there will be no fear, no leniency. We would use whatever means we have at our disposal. We will define our strategies and the freedoms we will grant our team. We will punish bad behavior in a strong way. Should we win, we will have to form our own secret federation strategy. We will form a power structure with certain powers aimed at the central government while keeping control over local matters to ensure the people are number one priority."

"If we are to do this, we need to assemble a discovery team. We need an old school senator to reveal the inner circle processes based on a way of doing things common in the past, supported through traditional practices. Next we need a shrewd kick ass media advisor. We need someone who has the ability to understand the pulse of the people and can manipulate the media. He or she must have good, intuitive judgment, and be a master spin doctor. Finally, we need the master of the word, the person who given a spin on a topic, has the intellect to articulate the message so that both the man on Main Street as well as the man on Wall Street understands. Brother, in no way do we take part in this campaign unless we are serious. To win will take ruthless execution. We won't dabble. We will do whatever it takes to win. Your man Larry Barnes may be a droll little man with an odd sense of humor, but with the right tutelage, he could be our critical success factor. Information technology will drive our campaign across young and old venues. We will control the media. If you combine those two factors with an overflowing war chest, we both can win our respective election."

"Holy shit, Mattie. If I didn't know better, I would think you have been planning this yourself. You are amazing. Let's have another beer and eat. Think what Mom will say when you tell her you are going to run for Illinois Governor or State Senator and me for the Presidency. Whether we win or not, we are going to make some noise. We are talking about history here. Are we going to have fun or what? I have been carrying these snippets with me to keep me focused. What do you think?

Thomas Jefferson:
- The democracy will cease to exist when you take away from those who are willing to work and give to those who would not.
- I predict future happiness for Americans if they can prevent the government from wasting the labors of the people under the pretense of taking care of them.

- My reading of history convinces me that most bad government results from too much government.
- No free man shall ever be debarred the use of arms.

"Mattie, I am very concerned about the direction of our economy. The banking institutions and Wall Street are running amuck. Banking institutions are more dangerous to our liberties than standing armies. If the American people allow private banks to control the issue of currency, first by inflation, then by deflation, banks and corporations that will grow could deprive the American people of all property until one day their children wake-up homeless on the very continent their fathers conquered. I am worried that within the next couple of years, we could see an economic crash like the 1920s. Mattie, we must keep skunks and bankers at a distance.

"Tommie, you know that I am your biggest fan. I will be your biggest supporter in whatever you decide to undertake. I will do whatever you want or need me to do. My only pre-conditions come from my belief that the best sermons are lived, not preached. One of grandfather's sayings applies here. 'If you get to thinking you're a person of influence, try ordering somebody else's dog around.' Tommie, if you are ready to do whatever it takes to drive change from the school house to the courthouse, to revive this country's belief 'In God, and country, We Trust', count me in. Tommie, rule one in a gunfight is: Always win and cheat if necessary. If you find yourself in a fair fight, your tactics suck. An armed man will kill an unarmed man with monotonous regularity. We have to embark on this mission as true soldiers. We will fight endlessly, not because of what we hate, but because of what we love." *Brother, what do I feel when I shoot and kill a person? Only a little recoil. What will I feel when we take down bad politicians, dictators, terrorists or greedy tycoons? We will feel like Thomas Jefferson. Tommie, you may never kill a man yourself, but I know now, you will read their obituaries with the greatest of pleasure.*

"Brother, count me in! God Bless America."

Epilogue

There were a handful of individuals that Thomas and Mattie felt could jeopardize their political aspirations. They had compiled a list, performed the tedious task of turning over every rock on their nemesis. All but one of the individuals on the list could be handled by confronting them with a past transgression, a past political faux pas, a lack of financial backing, or family issues. The only one that seemed oblivious to temptations of the flesh or political game was Samantha Miller, Illinois Congresswoman for the 10th Chicago District.

Mattie knew she was going to be a credible political opponent the very first time their paths crossed. He saw something flicker in her eyes. Was it ego, confidence, or boredom and an eagerness for their exchange to end? His bet was on the obvious. Politicians are only interested in getting elected or re-elected. Samantha was one who felt she could persuade anyone to join her political camp. She was beyond bright. Mattie had read her dossier. She had an IQ that surpassed his. She too had a photographic memory. Magna Cum Laude graduate from Princeton. She was charming. Mattie knew that unless Samantha saw him as a threat or someone who could help her cause or causes, she had bigger fish to land in her boat. Samantha Miller was the next Chicago clown who had aspirations of being president and a thirst that could only be quenched from drinking from the cup of the oath of office. To Mattie, she did not care about what was good for the country or its citizens. Samantha Miller felt she was God's answer to everyone's issues.

Samantha, you expect everyone to accept you at face value and take every word from your lips as true and genuine. You expect acceptance without question or doubt. Lady, this dog don't hunt that way. Like I told Tommie, if you get to thinking you're a person of some influence, try ordering somebody else's dog around. I am going to engulf you like an Illinois tornado. First silent, then suffocating, and ultimately piercing, complete devastation.

The very thought of performing a covert delivery on her gave him an adrenaline rush and had Mattie's mouth watering as if the most luscious tastes were presented in front of him on a table ready for feasting. He envisioned his hands gripping her neck, his fingers applying such pressure taking its toll until he witnessed the trickle of blood like the drops of water from a cherry Popsicle coming from a tear.

Samantha was an attractive woman. Being the consummate politician, she could wear jeans and put an element of sexuality as she climbed up on some John Deere harvesting corn. Or she was just as comfortable dressed as a fashionable, professional business woman meeting with the mayor of Chicago or the CEO of Construction Tractor. This woman had stage presence. In the state of Illinois, Ms. Miller had a profile equal to any movie star. Everyone seemed to want to be seen with this woman. Mattie looked beyond the obvious elegant demeanor that was being presented to every eye in the room. The woman did have a gift when it came to the ability to influence government officials to make decisions for or against issues she designated as a priority. On a number of occasions, she had thrown her political clout on issues of importance which coincided with Construction Tractor interests. She was influential in guiding his own company to lobby for reform of United States import, export tax laws and embargos. She was seen as a messiah for her criticism of the health-care industry and her media battle against their profitability on the backs of the American people.

If Mattie was to carry out a delivery on this woman, her disappearance would bring in the best of the nation's FBI CSI experts.

How do you ensure a body is never found? How do you get a high profile person into a vulnerable location in order to make delivery? Should I think about planning an accident or consider killing, dismembering, then incinerating? What about disposal of the remains? Never make things personal because it will cloud your judgment when you need clarity most. When one is going to make a delivery, it makes my senses come alive. The anticipation is like holding your breath underwater kicking to reach the surface before you must take a breath. That gulp of air when you reach the surface knows you won. Continue to mine my brain for inspiration and direction. Remember the bottom line, Mr. Mailman, miracles are subjective, escape is definite and real.

I could strangle, dismember/incinerate, dispose of her body in a construction site or maybe spread her incinerated ashes along an interstate with a Cat scraper or motor grader. As he envisioned throwing her over a guard railing unto the rocks below, Mattie felt nothing. *What pleasure he would get when he ensured this black widow would spin no more webs of deceit. She would no longer manipulate men to do her bidding.*

Samantha, nature can be cruel but there is a raw beauty and even certain justice manifested within that cruelty. You forgot one thing about nature. It is not animals but man who is one of the oldest and ultimate predators. Delilah, you picked the wrong man to try to cut his hair. For you see, I am the ultimate predator. You really think I will fall victim to your one for the team and survival of the pack mentality. I am a pack of one.

Mattie was the eye of the hurricane, calm, deadly, surrounded by swirling rotating air of random destruction. There wasn't a shelter built that could withstand the force that was about to hit.

From the information Mattie had gathered, he knew this man was not what he seemed. Sam Brienen had grown up poor on Peoria's South Side. As a boy, he had auburn hair, not exactly red, but because he was always going around giving a great Woody Woodpecker impression, he had earned the nickname as Pecker on the playground near his neighborhood. Mattie had done his homework. The only shred of dirt Mattie had found was that Brienen, in his younger days, was a man who had a passion for women. He was a player's player. From some interviews which were conducted by various Mailman identities, many women who had dated him could not wait to talk about the sexual prowess of this man and his well endowed unit. Pecker was not a moniker, it was acknowledgement.

He was a tall man, his hands were large and the tight fitting shirt across his chest and arms suggested he was well built. This man obviously lived in a weight room. He was almost pretty for a man. He had broad lips, high cheek bones, the straightest nose and the whitest teeth. His head was perfectly shaped with hair wavy and flowing. His skin appeared to have the perfect tan, except the skin tone was natural.

"Mr. Brienen, my name is Josh. Listen, I have admired your work ethic here at Gold's Gym. Do you mind offering me a few tips? Whatever your regimen has been, your body has really responded. Your definition is fantastic." Mattie had frosted hair. His workout apparel was old and faded. He wore tinted green eye lenses under thick horned rim glasses.

"Josh, is it? Thanks for the compliment. I can see you are no stranger to working out. I would love to have a workout partner to spot and push me as well. I would be happy to show you my weekly workout routine."

The Mailman had his man. Over the next month, he would build a relationship. He would find an opportunity to get Sam Brienen to meet Samantha Miller. *Sam, meet Sam. Knowing you two like I do, there will be a private meeting at some point. Mr. Brienen will arrange for a limo. The Mailman will be the driver. Samantha's body guards will be in a trailing car or be sitting next to the limo driver. I cannot wait to see how this night will unfold.*

Edwards Brothers Malloy
Thorofare, NJ USA
November 1, 2016